WHEN HARRY HIT THE HAMPTONS

WHEN HARRY HIT THE HAMPTONS

Mara Goodman-Davies

Sourcebooks Landmark™
An Imprint of Sourcebooks, Inc.®
Naperville, Illinois

Published by Sourcebooks, Inc.
P.O. Box 4410, Naperville, Illinois 60567-4410
(630) 961-3900
FAX: (630) 961-2168
www.sourcebooks.com

Library of Congress Cataloging-in-Publication Data

Goodman-Davies, Mara.
When Harry hit the Hamptons / Mara Goodman-Davies.
p. cm.
ISBN 1-4022-0332-2 (alk. paper)
1. Triangles (Interpersonal relations)--Fiction. 2. Inheritance and succession--Fiction. 3. Hamptons (N.Y.)--Fiction. 4. Summer resorts--Fiction. I. Title.

PS3607.O59225W47 2005
813'.6--dc22

2005003183

Printed and bound in the United States of America
QW 10 9 8 7 6 5 4 3 2 1

With much love and appreciation,
this book is dedicated to Gareth Esersky...the
world's greatest friend and super agent...without
you this would not be possible.

WHEN HARRY HIT THE HAMPTONS

chapter one

The Beverly Hills gossip columns knew no mercy. "Harry Raider, son of billionaire philanthropist Sam Raider, was found in a coma during a drug bust in a $4,500 per night V.I.P suite at The Bel Aire Hotel. Harry, 38, was rushed to Cedars-Sinai Hospital where he is recovering from this life-threatening incident. No representative from the Raider family was available for comment."

Sam and Irma Raider, a stylish, aging Jewish couple in matching Fila tennis suits, walked down the corridor of the Sadie Raider Memorial Pavilion. This was the wing their contributions financed at Cedars-Sinai, Los Angeles's most prestigious medical center. Cedars-Sinai, an homage to how money can mask pain, looked more a museum of medicine than a place to go to when one needs to stay alive. The building itself was an architectural masterpiece, an imposing natural beige structure with massive floor-to-ceiling windows that afforded the visitors a breathtaking view of the Hollywood Hills. To be sick at Cedars was to suffer in style. Inside on the walls hung the finest modern art from Yaacov Agam to Raushenberg...all generous donations from the rich and famous patients who were grateful to leave there sitting upright in the back of their chauffeur-driven Rolls Royces, rather than lying down in a hearse. Today, Sam and Irma were at Cedars to see their son, their only child, who had turned their golden years into a living hell.

"I can't understand this, Irma. I can't understand this at all. How could he be such a total putz? What was he thinking? How could a son of mine be so meshugena?" Sam's mumbling to his wife in Yiddish was proof that 3.4 billion dollars later, Beverly Hills was not so far from Brooklyn. Even dressed from head to toe in five thousand dollars worth of "designer casual wear," Sam Raider couldn't shake his "shlubby-chic" appearance. In spite of some serious help from an expert personal stylist from Bijan For Men on Rodeo Drive, Sam Raider still looked like somebody's butcher.

"I don't know, Sammy. All I know, it's all my fault. He hates me. My only son hates his mother." Irma pulled out a balled-up tissue she had stuffed in her pocket. She began to wipe away the tears that were causing her mascara to drip down her newly sculpted cheekbones. To the Beverly Hills ladies who lunch, Irma's catty nickname was "The Six Million Dollar Woman." Referring, of course, to the amount of money they guessed that she had spent on plastic surgery. Not that she was alone in the "Malibu Multi-million Dollar Makeover Club." In this part of the world, once one hit puberty, cosmetic surgical enhancement was viewed as a right of passage. Even though Irma barely resembled the Coney Island girl Sam married over forty years ago, he genuinely loved this woman with the ever-evolving profile. As she wept uncontrollably in his arms, Sam tried to comfort Irma to the best of his limited ability.

"Irma, sweetheart. It's not your fault. Remember, Dr. Gerber told us it has something to do with Harry's own inner struggle."

"Struggle schmuggle. Harry hates me. Why else would he marry a nineteen-year-old girl that makes nudie movies? Why? To punish me," Irma said, wildly waving her hands over her head in frustration. It almost looked like firecrackers were going off around Irma, as her beach-ball-sized diamond rings cut through the air.

"But he divorced her in three weeks, Irma," consoled Sam.

"Only after he got Consuela pregnant," Irma said in a loud whisper, once again searching her pockets for another used tissue to wipe her eyes.

"Consuela is back in Tijuana where she belongs. I bet she has forgotten about the abortion and has sixteen kids by now," Sam mumbled, staring up at a new Calder lithograph on the hospital wall, not being able to look Irma directly in her blue contact lenses.

"Harry never liked Consuela, Sam. He never liked her. He couldn't stand the way she made his bed or his breakfast. He said she used to put too much milk in his Captain Crunch. She used to drown the Crunchberries. I should have been there for him, Sam! I should have been a better mother!" Irma was now sobbing hysterically and hyperventilating. Shaking and sweating at the same time, Irma was physically moving towards a full-blown panic attack.

Sam was at his wit's end. "Irma, darling. Dr. Gerber said you have to stop blaming yourself. It's not going to make Harry any better," Sam said, tapping his fingers nervously, while trying to recall some of the so-called brilliant psychological advice he got from Hollywood's top shrink.

"Gerber is a shmuck! Remember he sent Harry to the ten-thousand-dollar-a-week rehab in Palm Springs? The next day we found our son with a bag of cocaine driving naked across the desert in a golf car."

"I know, Irma. I'm sick and tired of these fancy-schmantzy celebrity shrinks and their crazy theories on why Harry is such a mess. It's time to cut the crap and show him what's what."

Irma looked up at her husband of forty-three years. Rarely had she seen him be so firm. As ruthless as he was in business, at home with his family Sam was always a pussycat, especially with his son.

"It's time to get tough with our boy, Irma. Enough is enough!"

As an emotionally drained, totally disheveled Sam and Irma entered Harry's hospital room, the sight of their "little boy" hooked up to all those tubes and wires was almost too much for the elderly couple to handle. Irma now fought back her tears. Her indulgence had ruined him, and now at thirty-eight years old, it was finally time to cut the cord.

Harry, still in a daze, had been out of the coma for less than twenty-four hours. He looked across the room at his father. *Man, I fucked up. Can't believe I got busted. Daddy is soooo pissed. This is really going to suck*, Harry thought to himself. Daddy had always looked at Harry with forgiveness...not this time.

"Harry, this is it." Sam's voice was strong but trembling. "Your mother and I have had it with the embarrassment you've caused our family, and the potential danger you are to yourself. We can no longer support your insane, out-of-control, life-threatening behavior. You have become a *shame and disgrace*...and have brought us nothing but sorrow. ENOUGH IS ENOUGH! GANUG!"

Harry hated when Daddy yelled in Yiddish. It confused him. Harry hadn't seen Sam so serious since he went to Vegas the morning of his Bar Mitzvah. Four hundred and fifty people were waiting in the Wilshire Boulevard Temple. Harry, with his fake ID and a load of bills stolen from Sam's secret stash, was in Caesar's Palace ringing in his thirteenth birthday with a black whore named Cherry. And that was only the beginning.

"I'm sorry, Daddy," Harry said in the exact same little boy's voice he learned to use successfully so many years ago. "I didn't mean to let you down. I love you."

It took all the strength Sam had to keep in mind the promise he'd made to himself to save his son. He absolutely would not give in, not this time. Sam straightened himself up from his usual hunched-over, "elder cocker" form and for the first time in many years, summoned what was left of his inner chutzpa.

"I love you, too, Harry. Even with all this *insanity*. That is why, as soon as you're released from the hospital, I'm getting you out of Beverly Hills, and I'm cutting you off."

"What? Sam, where is he going?" Harry's over-protective mother demanded to know, as she came back down from the other side of high anxiety. Harry was simply too scared to speak.

"I'm sending him back east...to New York."

"What, Sam, are you crazy? You can't send him back to Bensonhurst. It's all schvartzahs now—they'll kill him."

"Relax, Irma, I'm not sending him to Bensonhurst. I couldn't survive there myself these days. I'm sending Harry to stay with Jerry Ackerman's daughter Jessica and her husband Freddy in East Hampton. Jerry owes me a big favor."

"Not a bad idea," Irma said, relieved. "I hear the Hamptons are lovely. Maybe they'll introduce you to a nice Jewish girl, Harry." That thought was so comforting to Irma that she began to search around the room for a mirror, so that she could put on a little lipstick and begin to pull herself together.

"Mommy, don't make me go!" Harry pleaded.

"That's it, Harry, you're going. It's final," Sam said. "Jes and Freddy are young, clean-living people, and with them maybe you will have a chance to start over. You will have no credit cards, and no access to any bank accounts. Jerry will see that all your basic needs are met and that you are given a minimal allowance. I want you to take this summer to get your life together, Harry. Maybe a summer in Long Island, away from the Hollywood trash you surround yourself with, will show you there are decent rich people in this world who lead solid lives. Jessica and Freddy are a perfect example of that. A summer with them will teach you a new way to live. I am convinced, Harry. You need to spend time in the Hamptons with the Ackermans."

Sam had not been back to New York in almost thirty years. He was unfamiliar with the new Hampton scene. Little did he know he was sending Harry from Hollywood's Den of Iniquity into the Sodom and Gomorrah of the East Coast. Three decades ago, when Sam became the hottest children's clothing manufacturer in the business, left behind Seventh Avenue, and headed for "the hills of Beverly," the Hamptons were no more than a few clapboard houses, unevenly scattered across the untamed sand dunes. Of course, back in the old days there were elegant, Gatsby-esque mansions in Southampton, but those stately homes were strictly occupied by America's WASPy blue-blood dwellers. Brooklyn "Bagel Boys," even those on the way to becoming billionaires, were not welcome on the grass tennis courts of the "mighty white" Lawn Club or the South Hampton Beach and Swim Club, a beach club that was reserved for the pure-bred elite whose families had basically come over on the Mayflower. Even though more recently money and power had overruled anti-Semitism, and everything else for that matter, in the Hamptons, these two ancient institutions still managed to be pillars of ignorance, keeping out anyone whose last name wasn't listed in the Social Registry.

With the exception of the small pocket of seclusion in South Hampton, the rest of the Hamptons had become a free-for-all good time for anyone who was willing to fork over the bucks and play the game! Cookie-cutter type, millionaire "McMansions" sprung up practically on top of each other in what used to be the potato fields of Bridgehampton. One house was more garish and over-built than the next, each monstrous home baring witness to the joys of capitalism gone wild. The locals joked that the "summer people" had developed the world's most expensive housing project in the middle of their farmland. East Hampton, which was once the home to beatnik writers and hippy artists, now housed some of America's most famous talent. Speilberg, Sean "P. Diddy" Combs, and Jerry Seinfeld just to name a few, had private, guarded massive compounds of their own. This allowed the rich and famous to enjoy the sand and sea without sharing God's natural gifts with mere mortals.

Besides the very wealthy in the Hamptons, there were the "almost theres," who rented share houses with a group of other wannabe affluent folk, primarily in West Hampton and Quogue. This adult-fraternity setup served as a nonstop summer party for many people looking to enjoy the panache and flash of the Hamptons without parting with loads of cash.

Between the twenty-four-hour share-house shindigs, the billionaire beachfront bashes, and the roaring night clubs where drugged-up heiresses and wasted Wall Street wonder kids danced on the tables while sucking face with the waiters, the Hamptons of today was definitely *not* the innocent penny candy, ice-cream parlor, ocean-side resort of Sam Raider's yesteryear. Yet no one in Sam's family knew this truth, especially not Harry.

"Oh my God! How long do I have to stay?" Harry asked, stunned by his father's sudden pronouncement.

"As long as it takes for you to come home a man and a responsible human being. If you can stay out of trouble for the whole summer, I'll bring you back on a trial basis in the fall. One slip up, Harry, one arrest, one call from the police, one bad report from Jerry's family, and you can consider yourself cut off from your inheritance and your family. Is that clear?" Sam's voice had at last stopped shaking. He knew he was doing the right thing.

"Yes, Daddy," Harry said meekly. For once in his pathetic life, Harry knew his dad meant business.

chapter two

The news of the billionaire's son coming to the Hamptons spread like wild fire thanks to Chas Greer, Harry's childhood friend who moved to New York in his late teens. Growing up, Harry was the only one of the "Beverly Hills Billionaire Baby Brats" who defended Chas Greer and treated him like an equal. While the other privileged offspring would throw tennis balls at Chas and make him run around the court and fetch them, Harry would pick up a ball or two and slam them back at the spoiled children who taunted Chas endlessly. Even as a boy, Harry realized it must have been hard for Chas, the tennis pro's son at Beverly Hills's prestigious Pine Valley Country Club, to be pushed around like a lowly servant at such a young age. When they became teenagers and Chas started modeling, it was a ballsy sixteen-year-old Harry Raider who would call up casting directors, pretending to be Chas's agent, to get him jobs. Harry's crafty work paid off and eventually Chas was signed by a real modeling agency and moved to New York. A precocious, preppy, haute-couture homosexual, Chas became Manhattan's favorite male mannequin. When his modeling career was over, it didn't take long before he blossomed into the personal shopper to the social doyennes who graced the society papers. Chas quickly became a confidante to the rich and neurotic. Today, still considered the "Svengali of Style," Chas wore many hats. He was a dresser, decorator, an etiquette advisor, a walker, and was *always* the tattler of the hottest gossip.

Chas had carved a little niche for himself among the wealthy women in the Hamptons, Long Island's chicest summer spot. Even at thirty, Chas was still handsome, with his chiseled features, golden blond hair, ice-cold blue eyes and perennial tan. Chas's mother was Jewish, but his father was blond and Swedish. Because of his gorgeous looks and impeccable taste in clothes, rich women felt inferior to this appearance of total perfection. He made himself a necessary evil in his ladies' charmed yet complex lives. Chas knew their weaknesses and capitalized on their insecurities to find security for himself, financially and socially.

It wasn't beyond Chas to tell a certain society someone that she was too fat to fit into Chanel's summer collection, or that her hair color gave him flashbacks of Cindy Lauper. The more critical and cruel he was, the more the young rich women loved it. Perhaps they felt guilty for leading such indulgent lives, or maybe their fathers didn't love them enough. Chas didn't really care why the Hampton girls listened so intently to his advice, all he cared about was that, for whatever reason, they needed him. This was good for business. Chas got kickbacks from every "in" hairdresser, diet doctor, and plastic surgeon in town. If a new designer wanted to debut a clothing line at a happening Hampton club, Chas Greer got the first call. Even the Hamptons Rolls Royce dealership had Chas on the payroll. Anyone who wanted an entrée into the exclusive world of the Hamptons rich and famous couldn't do so without greasing Chas Greer's supple palm.

Chas lived in a small but immaculate studio walk-up in the West Village. Since being a "minimalist" was all that he could really afford, Chas decorated his space with just a large Italian glass coffee table that held one Tiffany crystal vase filled with white orchids and a Cartier china bowl full of tasteful green apples. The Tiffany and Cartier accoutrements were gifts from grateful clients, of course. Hanging on his walls was a collage of some black-and-white photos that the late legendary photographer Scavullo took of Chas at the height of his modeling career. Today, Chas was lounging on his only other piece of living room furniture, a lily-white sofa from Shabby Chic. He was sipping Chardonnay and puffing on a clove cigarette when he got the call from his mother, Barbara. Barbara had been the dining-room hostess at Pine Valley for the past thirty years. She was always one of the first to hear the latest rumblings and always kept her son filled in on the gossip from the West Coast. Barbara's juiciest pieces of news always revolved around the Raiders. She sent Chas clippings of Harry's divorce, his arrests, and now his near drug overdose. The mother-and-son team of inquiring minds had chronicled every event in the Raider family for the past ten years at least. Today Barbara was burning up the wires with the latest-breaking "Raider report."

"Chas, do you believe it, they're finally getting rid of Harry."

"Well, it's about time, Mummy. He's ruining Irma's life."

"You wouldn't believe what goes on here, Chas. Everybody's talking about her...on the tennis court, in the locker room, even in the dining room. All these yentahs are saying Irma spent too much time involved with the Women of Hadassah, the Cedars-Sinai Sisterhood, and her other charities, instead of raising Harry correctly. They're saying a nanny can't do a mother's job. Like any of them should know."

"Oh my, how dreadful. How is poor Irma taking it?"

"Not very well. Of course, the minute she walks into the room, all conversations come to a screeching halt. Irma Raider is not a stupid lady; she can see through the fake smiles behind all the bleached teeth. She knows what's being said behind her Armani-clad back, and it's devastating her. I hear she's near a nervous breakdown."

"No! Tell me more!" Chas nearly spilled his Chardonnay.

"Well, you know, it's killing their marriage. I hear Irma is so distraught by all the scandal she was absolutely bawling during her seaweed wrap. She also told Ki, her acupuncturist, that she is too upset to have sex anymore and it's really making Sam crazy."

"At seventy-two Sam Raider is still an old horny goat. God bless him," Chas giggled.

"Are you kidding? He's so horny, I hear he was seen with Nancy Millstein having drinks at Le Bistro Gardens. She's the biggest divorcée slut at Pine Valley. Nancy and about one hundred other Pine Valley piranhas are just waiting for Irma to snap so they can wrap their claws around the bulge in Sam's pants."

"You mean the bulge in Sam's wallet."

"Of course, I heard from Joe, the masseur, that it's a good thing Sam Raider has so much money. He's so small that without the cash, he'd have his hookers laughing in his face."

"Oh my, Sam Raider, you dirty dog! Do you think they'll get a divorce?"

"It's too early to tell. I know he's taking Irma to her favorite hotel, Hotel Du Cap, on the French Riviera, while Harry is in the Hamptons. This could be the make-it or break-it trip. Either Irma puts the spice back into their marriage or he'll retire her to Canyon Ranch on a permanent basis. Sam still has a lot of spunk. He needs a wife who can keep up with him. Irma's been too preoccupied to pay him the attention he needs. Boy, has this Harry thing done a number on her. She just had her face done last month, again. It's already starting to fall."

"I can't believe the situation has gotten so far out of control. Well, all I can say is that when Harry comes east, I'll do my best to see that he has a good time."

"He's not supposed to have a good time, Chas. He's supposed to get his act together."

"Oh, don't worry, Mummy. He will. I have the perfect plan to rescue Harry and the Raiders from total destruction."

"Chas, what's going on in that blond-streaked little head of yours?"

"I can't tell you until I've got it all figured out, but if it works like I think it will, Sam and Irma Raider will owe little Chassy big time! I'm going to save their son, their marriage, and, of course, their social standing. For these minor miracles, I'll bet they'll pay me enough so I can upgrade my Chardonnay addiction to Cristal."

"I don't know what you're cooking up, Chas, but I'm sure it will work. You're absolutely brilliant, honey."

"Thank you, Mummy. Ciao! Ciao!"

Chas blew kisses into his princess phone and hung up.

How fabulous... Chas thought to himself. If he could get Harry married off to one of his coterie of obedient little thirty-something social sensations, it would mean a reward for a smart Chas. Most likely he could get payment from *both* sides of the deal. Chas sensed that this was an opportunity to make some REAL MONEY for the first time in his hard life. REAL MONEY meant everything to Chas, from being able to upgrade his rental studio to owning his own Park Avenue pad to not having to beg his clients for cash advances after he overspent at Armani and was left on the brink of financial destitution. Chas was so tired of being a yes man and feeling like a second-class citizen in a wealthy woman's world. In his soul, he wanted to be just as much of a demanding diva as the lucky ladies he catered to night and day. The wrong people had all the money, Chas believed. Now, finally, the time had arrived for him to get on even footing with the "Born-Rich, Lucky-Sperm Club" kids who had kept him in a place of servitude all of his life. Then of course, there was Juan, Chas's new lover. Juan was quickly elevating himself from boy toy status to lifetime partner material by somehow penetrating the jaded walls of Chas's hardened heart. While sex fell into the same everyday category as eating, sleeping, and going to the bathroom for Chas, love was completely uncharted territory. Perhaps it was Juan's genuine innocence and real sincerity that intrigued and captivated Chas, the eternal player. It also could have been Juan's tight, tanned, and taut little ass that looked so hot every time he stepped out of the shower that had deepened Chas's interest in the young lad. Whatever Chas's reason was to be with Juan on a more permanent basis, he realized that having money could make their life together a much more enjoyable experience. Chas also was painfully aware that he wasn't getting any younger and twenty-something, gorgeous Juanita was in the prime of his homosexual life. Secretly Chas feared that an older, richer sugar daddy could come along any day and steal little-boy Juan right out of his big feathered bed. Yet Chas shared his feelings of financial inadequacy with no one. Chas knew that neediness and desperation were highly unattractive qualities to portray not only in his personal life, but professionally as well. His job was to manipulate rich people's weaknesses and go to any length to hide his own. Chas saw "desperation" as being the key word that would unlock the door to making his fortune. As "desperate" as Sam and Irma were to save their son and save face in the social circuit, there were women in the Hamptons set who actually defined the meaning of the word! Sure, these women had money, but almost everyone in the Hamptons had money, and the competition was tough. No matter how big someone's yacht was, there was always a bigger one, two slips down. Money wasn't enough to make a good marriage. The fact was that the models also poured into the Hamptons every summer. That didn't help the insecure rich girls, whose self-esteem was nonexistent. The successful Wall Street bankers or nouveau riche "Garmentos" had enough cash of their own. They did not have to put up with the demands of Fendi-flaunting, Gucci-Pucci, Jewish-American, Prada-pocketbooked Princesses or an Old Guard, WASPy, Brooks Brothers, Talbots-clad cold fish. The self-made money men were usually happy to have a drop-dead gorgeous trophy escort on an arm. They didn't care if she were a waitress in a diner as long as she could be dressed up to look the part.

It was only the boys like Harry, who needed to please their parents to stay on the payroll, who had to marry within their own tribe. Before the Raiders had time to get upset about Harry's first marriage to the porn queen, divorce proceedings had already started. This time Harry had no choice—he had to do "the right thing." Chas knew the Raiders would no longer put up with Harry's antics, and he took it upon himself to pull off the biggest social coup of the summer season! Chas knew it would be next to impossible to get Harry to behave and go along with the plan, but somehow Chas had to make him do it. This would be Chas Greer's entry into the Social Olympics and he was determined to bring home the gold, at any cost. Now it was time to get to work.

chapter three

On May 1, just three weeks before Harry's arrival on Memorial Day, people were still in the city. Chas was ultra-excited about his lunch date with Penny Marks.

Penny was the thirty-two-year-old daughter of the late discount-clothing king Bernard Marks. Just before he died prematurely, from a stroke at sixty-eight, Bernard Marks sold his national chain of discount clothing stores for $30 million. Bernard had been divorced from his wife, Penny's mother, Reba, for many years. His will split his estate between his two daughters, Penny and Bunny. With $15 million apiece, Bunny and Penny were rich, but nowhere near Raider rich.

The Marks sisters were quite visible on the Hamptons summer scene. They were famous for the Fourth of July barbeque at their white, modern Ocean Road estate, which they shared. Each sister had a separate, private wing in the sprawling, oceanfront mansion. This arrangement was not for privacy alone. Not so secretly, Penny hated Bunny, and Bunny...well, Bunny was usually too stoned or drunk to notice.

The reason for Penny's private hatred of her sister was basic to a woman's nature. While Penny was attractive enough, she was still a little too pudgy, with dark curly hair and deep brown eyes. Bunny was taller than Penny and rail thin, with bone straight blond hair and "fuck me" baby blues that no man could resist. Bunny could compete with any model for a rich gentleman's attention.

Penny had tried a string of diet doctors at Chas's suggestion. She had even gone away to exclusive spas around the world, but couldn't get her eating under control. Penny once went to the Ashram in California and survived on water, wheat grass, and yoga for over two weeks. As soon as she got back to L.A., she hit Spago, Chasen's, Ago, Mortons, and all the rest of the trendy Beverly Hills eateries. She came back to New York ten pounds heavier than when she left.

"I've had it with all that bullshit hypnosis and behavior modification crap you made me try!" Penny would scream at Chas at least once a week. "You got me a goddamn therapist or trainer for everything from raising my self-esteem to lowering my body fat. For once, Chas, can't you just find someone who can just plain talk me out of eating?"

I'd have an easier time finding a cure for cancer, Chas thought to himself, before placating her with his usual saccharine answer. "You're your own worst enemy dear. We can get you help, but nobody can shut your mouth for you."

Nothing worked with Penny. She eventually fired her "food therapist" and slept with her personal trainer.

"At least I'm getting some form of exercise I paid all that money for!" she'd tell Chas. Penny felt like she had to justify herself to Chas and to the world of stick-figured, teeny tiny New York women. She wanted so badly to look like them, but she couldn't find the discipline.

Nothing could keep Penny away from her first love—food. Like for so many people, food was a good friend and a solid comforter when what she really needed was a great big hug. When there were no arms, there were always spoons, forks, and lots and lots of napkins to clean up her guilty behavior.

Even Chas's harsh comments to Penny about her weight couldn't get her to catch some air between bites. "I've told you a million times that you'll never get the kind of man you want unless you become a social x-ray like your sister!" Chas would yell at her every time she'd call him up, frustrated after a cheesecake binge.

Penny had a secret dream and desire that one day her prince would come to her Park Avenue apartment. He would tell her he loved her and she was beautiful just the way she was. He would see she was a lonely princess buried under all those protective layers of neither gone nor forgotten "baby" fat. He would hold her and love her, and tell her she was prettier than Bunny. The two of them would get into his spaceship and fly off to a planet where the fatter you are, the more men want you. It was a big fantasy. In reality, Penny figured she would remain single, while her sister could get Prince Charles to leave Camilla, if she decided she wanted him.

The truth was, Penny wasn't really *that* heavy. She was about a size twelve or fourteen, but she lived in a world where a girl was considered a blubber-ball if she was over a size four. A size two like Bunny was considered "perfect." Penny thought that if she lived in another part of the country, like Chicago or Dallas or Boston, she'd have a better chance of finding a husband. And yet, if she wanted to "lower her standards" she could find a nice doctor, lawyer, or computer professional right there in New York. But that wasn't good enough for Penny. She had to have the best. If she didn't marry up, her whole life would be considered a failure. Penny could hear her mother Reba now. "You father worked himself to death in order to make sure his daughters had the top of the world at their feet." So how could Penny let her dear dead daddy down and make a mediocre marriage? That would be a disgrace to his memory. Penny owed Daddy everything—from her Harry Winston earrings to her Ferragamo shoes. The least she could do to pay him back for everything he gave her was to make him proud, even if he wasn't around to appreciate it.

Dad, of course, would have been proud of Bunny. When Prince Albert of Monaco came for the Annual Princess Grace Foundation Charity Ball at the Waldorf two years ago, he danced with Bunny all night. He even invited her to the Monte Carlo Grand Prix that spring. But Bunny dumped the Prince for the late Dodi Al-Fayed. It was only after Bunny left him for an even richer Kuwaiti oil baron that Dodi found solace in Princess Diana.

That year, while Bunny was all over Europe and the Middle East, Penny got to do the spring social season alone. For the first time in her life she wasn't upstaged by her gorgeous sister. She loved being in the limelight and she even dated a few Wall Street tycoons that Bunny had thrown over. But when Bunny returned to New York, it was back to the normal rejection for Penny. The Fourth of July party that summer was more like a welcome home party for Bunny. The men lined up for a chance to dance with her, as Penny sat on the beach alone with a huge plate of hot dogs, beans, and apple pie.

The most intense things about Bunny, the thing that drove Penny mad, was her unnatural means of staying so thin. Bunny was a severe anorexic-bulimic, who, when she wasn't in the bathroom throwing up, was in there snorting cocaine. Penny wondered how Bunny made it all the way to twenty-seven without dropping dead. She had been purging and snorting since she was about sixteen, and showed no real signs of having done any permanent damage to herself.

Penny hated that she didn't have Bunny's self-control and resilience. Penny tried throwing up on purpose once but it made her so sick she could never do it again. The one time Penny tried cocaine, she wound up in the emergency room at South Hampton Hospital and had to be given heavy tranquilizers for the next week and a half. Penny felt doomed to a life in her little sister's shadow. Her prince would never come. With no Mr. Wonderful on the horizon, Penny would often depend on Chas for company. Today she had come downtown to collect him in her brand-new white Bentley. As the chauffeur opened the back door for Chas to climb in, Chas saw Penny trying to furtively hide the half-eaten bag of Gummy Bears she had devoured before picking him up. Once inside his pampered client's chariot of choice, Chas knew exactly what he had to do.

"A little appetizer before the main course, honey?" Chas said, as he gently eased the bag of candy out of Penny's hand.

"I didn't eat breakfast." Penny said with a guilty look on her face as she finally released her death grip on the plastic.

"Yeah, sure," Chas replied as he tried to pass the candy bag over the seat and up to the chauffeur.

"Oh, what the hell, so I need a little sugar now and then," protested Penny, as she grabbed the sweets back from the driver who was trying to navigate his way back up Park Avenue, without getting caught in the middle of a candy war and crashing the car into an unforgiving taxi.

"Really, Penny, you don't need those," Chas continued as he forcefully took the candy away from her and threw it out the window, hitting an unsuspecting Asian-food delivery guy on a bicycle.

"Now look at that, you almost killed someone," Penny said as she ducked down below the seat, trying to escape the wrath of the man screaming at her in Chinese and banging on the window as they stopped at a red light.

"Better kill him than have you dying prematurely from a nasty bout with diabetes, my friend." Chas smiled coyly and waved at the pissed off delivery guy, as the Bentley now zoomed past him.

"Who cares when I die. It's not like I have a husband and kids to think about. I might as well enjoy myself...alone." Penny said rummaging through the bottom of her Chanel purse in hopes of finding a stray Tootsie Roll that had been long forgotten.

"My, my, aren't we the little martyr today, Penny? Shall we forget Cipriani and go straight to Riverside Memorial Chapel to plan your requiem?" Chas teased, as the Bentley passed the Empire State Building.

"Very funny, Chas. All I'm saying is that I might as well enjoy my life to the fullest, because I have no one else to live for except ME!"

"Penny, do you remember Harry Raider?" Chas asked Penny, nonchalantly while moving the air-conditioning vent to blow in his direction.

"Who?" Penny asked, not looking up from the search through the depths of her pocketbook.

"Harry Raider. You had dinner with him at Spago in L.A. with a bunch of people from Pine Valley."

"All I remember about Spago is the barbeque chicken pizza and the hot apple cake with the homemade cinnamon ice cream," Penny exclaimed with a look of delight on her face, as she finally found a mini Three Musketeers bar stuck under her sunglasses case.

"You're not going to eat that, Penn," Chas said as he quickly unstuck the chocolate and once again dropped it out the window, much to Penny's dismay. "How could you forget Harry? He paid for the whole dinner. It was his birthday party, remember?"

"I obviously know Harry and his pubescent wife. He kept interrupting dinner to take pictures with that whacked-out camera that speaks to you in Japanese or something. He really is a nutcase," Penny said, finally giving up her search for more goodies and fiddling with the CD player.

"A very rich nutcase, Penny."

"I know, I know. His father, Sam, was my father's idol. They grew up together in the same tenement house in Brooklyn. Dad did well, but Sam Raider blew him and everyone else away. The man is a fuckin' genius. Everyone in the rag business worships him," said Penny as she put on her favorite Cher CD and began to bee-bop her head back and forth to the rhythm of the music.

Chas smiled with delight. He had forgotten about the connection between Penny's late father and Sam Raider. Sam Raider was the largest women's and children's clothing manufacturer in the world. He started people like Calvin Klein, Ralph Lauren, and Oleg Cassini. Bernard Marks had been in awe of Sam, as were most people who came from humble beginnings and hit the big time.

"I can't believe your dad and Sam go so far back, and you and Harry never got together," Chas said, casting the bait, also enjoying the music and pretending to dance in place.

"Oh please, Chas," Penny said and shutting the music off with the usual tone of resignation and frustration in her voice.

"Driver, can you stop here, I want to show Penny some new baubles before lunch." Chas said pointing to an elegant-looking shop on Madison Avenue. The Bentley pulled up in front of Le Grand Bijou, one of the most expensive jewelry stores in Manhattan.

"Do you think Harry Raider would look at me? He's had every wannabe starlet bimbo in Hollywood," Penny said, turning the music back on again so that she didn't have to hear herself think out loud.

"He's not like that anymore, Penny. It was just a phase."

"A phase? Look what he married: Miss Teen Porn Queen U.S.A. The man is a sleaze-bucket."

"Okay, so he used to be a little eccentric, but he's over it. He's sick and tired of all the white-trash women out there who are just after him for his money. Harry is finally ready to meet a nice girl from his own background, with whom he can build a steady, normal life."

"What are you saying?" Penny was a little confused.

"I'm saying he's divorced. And he's coming to the Hamptons for the whole summer to meet the right kind of girl. Now come on and let me show you some fantastic stuff that Bijou is doing with jewelry this summer. There are so many exquisite pieces in there that would look amazing on the new Mrs. Harry Raider."

For a moment as she took Chas's hand and got out of the Bentley, Penny lost herself in a glimmer of hope. She'd had a crush on Harry when he was a teenager. Her father used to take the whole family to California every year and they would always have dinner with the Raiders at the Bel Aire estate. Penny remembered Harry was always nice to her. He would show her his latest cameras and computer games. Harry was always gadget crazy.

But as nice and friendly as he was to Penny, it was Bunny who wound up with him in the cabana one night after dinner. As the adults smoked cigars and reminisced about growing up poor in Bensonhurst, Bunny and Harry crept off to engage in a wild, teenage romp. Penny was so devastated she ate five plates of dim sum and twenty-two petit fours.

Remembering the incident, she snapped back to reality. "I'm sure Harry will be happy to see my sister again," Penny said, as Chas guided her inside.

"I don't think so." Chas was not giving up. "All due respect to Bunny—you know how much I love her—but Harry has really cleaned up his act. Bunny is still a wild child. Harry thinks she's a cute kid, but that's not the type of girl he wants to be around anymore. He really thinks you're fabulous and he honestly wants to spend time getting to know you again."

Penny didn't normally believe Chas's bullshit. However, the possibility of this news was too tempting not to indulge in, if only just for a minute. Besides, it was too late. Chas had already seen the glimmer of hope in Penny's eyes shining brighter than any diamond in the store. He knew he had her.

"How do you know all this, Chas?" Penny asked as she and Chas sauntered through the jewelry store salon towards a private V.I.P. viewing room in the back.

"Harry told me. He called me from L.A. to tell me he was coming to the Hamptons on Memorial Day and he really wanted to see you, Penny. Ah, Henri...wonderful to see you again," Chas gushed as he exchanged air kisses with an equally effete, suave-looking gentleman in a tailored, black suit. "Bring Miss Marks a selection of your most fantastic diamond rings. We are planning to announce her engagement to the world's most eligible suitor by the end of the summer season."

Chas loved to lie. He got such a thrill out of it, especially when he saw Penny's reaction. She was doing everything she could do to contain herself, but Chas saw right through it. He knew her all too well.

"Are you sure about this? Are you sure he hasn't got me confused with Bunny?" Penny said as she gazed hypnotically at the tray of colossal diamond rings that Henri laid out on table. She wanted to trust Chas so much, but even in this heady, marriage make-believe environment, Penny tried to keep her wits about her.

"Will you stop it with Bunny already? I think it's safe to say Harry Raider can tell the difference between you two. I mean, you look nothing alike." Chas purred as he slipped one of the mammoth rocks onto Penny's finger.

There, he said it. Chas could not even have a conversation with Penny without slipping in a backhanded insult. This time Chas was not smart to hit Penny in such a vulnerable place, just as she was beginning to believe in the fantasy he was creating. Immediately enraged, Penny took the ring off of her finger and threw it at Chas. Now losing total control of her anger, she lifted the whole tray of diamonds and dumped them over Chas's head. Poor Henri froze in complete shock. He had never seen such a violent reaction from a well-to-do shopper. At that point, Penny looked up and saw that she was being watched in an overhead security camera. Within seconds, alarms were set off, and two beefy security guards came rushing in.

"I am well aware my sister and I would never be mistaken for identical twins, Chas! That is why I'm wondering if Harry really wanted to see me. Bunny seems more his type," Penny screamed at Chas as they were both escorted out of the store.

"How many times do I have to tell you that Harry is over the Bunnys of the world? He's ready for you, Penny! He wants to get his life together. Trust me, I'm his oldest friend, I know him." Even though Penny's outburst had probably just cost Chas one of his best fine-jewelry connections, he didn't care. With the money he would make from securing a marriage between Harry and Penny, he could buy his way back into anywhere he pleased.

"You know *everybody*, Chas!" Penny said as she and Chas hurried into the Bentley.

"True...but I really know Harry. If he weren't ready to make a change, why would he leave Beverly Hills and schlep all the way to the Hamptons for the summer? If he wanted more of the same, why wouldn't he just go back to Malibu?"

"I don't know, maybe he thinks the big earthquake is coming this year. He was always into predicting stuff like that. Can we *eat* now?" Penny asked, as the car began moving past the haute couture designer stores that made Madison Avenue a famous shopping destination, known all over the globe.

"Of course, Penny. Driver, to Cipriani at once!" Chas instructed the patient man behind the wheel.

"A really good tantrum works up an appetite," Chas said, winking at Penny, with a devilish look in his eye.

The two friends shared a guilty giggle over Penny's outlandish behavior. "I'm sorry Chas, I shouldn't have lost it in there...it's just..." Penny quickly put on a pair of Versace sunglasses trying to cover up her impending water works.

"Oh, Penny, there is no need for tears, dear," Chas said feigning tenderness as he took her hand. "Harry knows that California is not going to drop off into the ocean. He is coming to the Hamptons to meet a new group of people and find a different kind of woman than what he's always had in L.A. Look, if he still wanted the party life, would he be spending the summer with Jessica and Freddy?"

"He's staying with Jerry Ackerman's daughter? Thank God, she's married," Penny said with a sign of relief as she opened the window to get a breath of air.

"Very happily married. Freddy is a great guy. He's totally at her beck and call, twenty-four seven. He's just what she needs. Besides, he looks just like Jerry—it's a little scary."

Jerry Ackerman was Sam Raider's former partner, and he was just as wealthy as Sam. For all her father's wealth, Jessica Ackerman Levitt was the salt of the earth. She was a little bit offbeat, still wearing long floral dresses and clogs. Chas had tried desperately to get her to buy a new wardrobe, but she had no interest, unlike Penny, whose Calvin Klein underwear had to match the rest of her outfit. All Jessica cared about was her painting.

She could have been a really cool, hip artist on the Soho scene, but that didn't really interest Jessica either. It was silently killing Chas that he couldn't throw big art openings in a trendy loft for Jessica, on her father's money. Jessica was content to paint in the garden of her father's East Hampton estate, then sell her work in street fairs, if she sold any at all. Jessica painted for the sheer enjoyment of it, and being a billionaire's daughter, she never had any ambition to carve a career.

Chas often thought the money was wasted on Jessica. She wore no makeup, didn't do anything to her hair, didn't drive a fancy car, and never attended any of the parties on the Hampton circuit. Jessica married Freddy Levitt, a nebbishy, balding Wall Street analyst who was the spitting image of her father, yet with none of Jerry's drive. Jessica and Freddy were happy to eat dinner on the patio all summer, then watch a movie in the screening room. Only once in a great while did Jessica and Freddy go out, and if they did it was to small, intimate dinner parties only.

Jessica was the one girl Chas wouldn't really mess with. She was too rich for him to alienate. Even though he never made a penny off her, the fact that he was "so close" to her gave him invaluable social credibility. Because Jessica wasn't interested in the Hamptons scene, the fact that she still hung around with Chas Greer made him almost seem like a real, credible person. But the truth was, she didn't hang around Chas; Chas hung around her. He would help her pick flowers in her beloved garden, go with her to walk her dog, a toy poodle named Cindy (after Cindy Brady), and sit with her for hours as she painted the sun setting over the blue Atlantic ocean. Chas was a welcome guest at the Ackerman estate—he was Jessica's number-one dogsitter. Even her husband Freddy had learned to accept Chas Greer as a permanent fixture in their lives. This friendship was the jewel in Chas's thorny crown. It defined the legitimacy of his existence.

"I can't believe Harry is staying with Freddy and Jessica. Won't he die of boredom, drowning in nebbish hell?"

"Oh, Penny, you're so mean to Jessica. That's really not very smart of you, especially since you'll be spending a lot of time with her this summer...I hope."

"What do you mean 'you hope'? I thought you said *Harry* wants to see me."

"He does want to get to know you again, Penny, but if you don't like his host and hostess...well, I wouldn't want anyone to be uncomfortable."

"I didn't say I don't like Jessica. I just think she's really, well, what's a nice way of saying it?"

"Quiet, sedate, private."

"Exactly. Are you sure this is what Harry Raider wants?"

"Well, maybe Jessica and Freddy are a little too removed for Harry. I think he's staying with them to have some peace and tranquility in his life. However, I believe he's looking to marry someone like you, Penny, who has an active social life, but also has a good head on her shoulders. Harry has had enough of extremes all his life. He needs balance now," Chas said, as the Bentley found its way past the Pierre Hotel and stopped right by The Sherry Netherland, the home to Cipriani, "where the chic meet to eat." Named after the venerable high society restaurant located in Venice, Italy, Cipriani was the height of European sophistication in New York City. With its low, swanky tables and glistening marble floors, Cipriani was packed to the gills with the "in" people and in full swing for a lavish lunchtime service. The reservation books read like a Who's Who in international society. Princess Elizabeth of Yugoslavia dined with Merv Griffin at table three. Mick Jagger was making a pasta e fagioli disappear at table two. Sarah, Duchess of York, was picking at a buffalo mozzarella and tomato salad with Barbara Walters at table four, and table one was reserved for the self-proclaimed king of New York himself, Donald Trump. All the waiters were perfectly dressed in white suits with black bow ties. The patrons were served sumptuous gourmet delicacies that complemented their exquisite sumptuous lives. Chas would soon be reveling in his element.

Before entering the restaurant, Penny stopped at the door for a moment to absorb what Chas was saying about Harry Raider. Was Chas telling the truth or was this just another one of his scams? Then again, did it really matter? For whatever reason, Chas Greer seemed intent on putting Penny together with Harry, and this was something Penny secretly wished for her whole life. Perhaps Harry Raider, the once goofy-looking teenager with wild, frizzy hair and a crater face full of popped zits, could have grown up to be her Prince Charming. Maybe, just maybe, Chas was right. Maybe Harry had had enough of the starlets reaching into his wallet. Maybe his ex-wife left such a bad taste in his mouth and such a dent in his bank account that bimbos finally turned him off. Maybe, with the grace of God, Bunny would be so busy this summer with an Arab sheik or a European prince that she wouldn't give Harry the time of day. Yes, maybe for once in her whole fat life, Penny Marks would actually stand a chance at making a marriage that would have daddy smiling at her down from heaven (or wherever he was).

"When exactly will he be here?" Penny asked, trying not to sound too excited, as she and Chas paraded past *toute le monde* of café society and were shown to a mediocre table near the back of the restaurant

"Memorial Day, I told you. Haven't you been listening?" Chas said, as he raised a disdainful eyebrow at the maitre d'. He discreetly tugged on Penny's purse, signaling for her to give the captain a fifty-dollar bill so that they would be awarded more prominent seating.

"Of course I've been listening, Chas. My, that's only three weeks away," Penny said, automatically reaching into her wallet and casually handing over a hundred bucks to the man in charge.

"That's right." Chas smiled big as they were shown to a table by the window near the front, so that they could catch a first glimpse of all who dared to enter Cipriani, Manhattan's Pasta Powerhouse. As they were served peach Bellinis and began to scan the menu, Chas knew it was time to make his moves. The games had begun.

chapter four

"I wonder how much weight I can drop in three weeks? Shit, I've been so bad lately," Penny said, as she shamelessly ordered her favorite creamy vegetable risotto and a double plate of Parma ham "for the table."

No matter what Chas told Penny about Harry wanting to meet a "nice" girl, Penny's terminal insecurities about her weight came cropping up. Deep down, she felt she wasn't thin enough or chic enough to see Harry. She could have been at her thinnest. She could have stayed on a diet for weeks, months, even a year, and in her mind it wouldn't have been enough.

Penny still remembered how hurt she was when she heard the sounds of hot passion coming from the cabana that night years ago when Harry and Bunny went off together. It may have meant nothing more to either of them than a release of teenage hormones, but it meant a lot to Penny. That night was the first of many where she would be alone while Bunny got all the action.

Even at such a young age, Penny was attracted to Harry. He wasn't a stuffy, snotty, New York brat like the boys she went to school with at Dalton. Harry was always a wild card. He was playful, comical, and totally whimsical. The most fun that Penny ever had was when the Raiders and the Marks went to Trader Vic's in the Hilton Hotel on Wilshire Boulevard. Harry put on a Hawaiian shirt and pretended he was Don Ho. Of course, he had his latest camera with him. He took pictures of everybody with these big drinks served in the carved coconuts. Penny still had a picture that Harry took of the two of them with his super camera timer. His arm was around her and he was smiling that big silly grin of his as he held a pineapple up to his ear. Harry was such an original. Penny hoped he hadn't changed. "Do you think you can get me an appointment with Dr. Jacquesteen? If I go back on those pills I bet I can lose about twenty pounds in the next few weeks," Penny begged Chas as she tried to pick out the vegetables in the risotto and mush around the rice with her fork.

"Penny, the last time Dr. Jacquesteen gave you diet pills, you were dizzy all the time and you told me you thought you were having a heart attack. You passed out at the Met Ball, remember? It was so embarrassing," Chas declared, as he pretended to shudder and hide behind his napkin.

"So I blacked out at a black tie—so what? At least I was almost thin. That Scaasi I wore was a size eight," Penny said wistfully, finally pushing her plate away.

"Yea, and everybody will always remember it as the dress Penny passed out in. It was such a scene," Chas replied, fluttering his long lashes in disgust.

Penny had had enough of Chas's catty jabs. He was constantly on her about her weight and, now when she wanted to try to get a handle on it again, he wasn't exactly cooperating.

"Look, Chas, I'm really sorry if I embarrassed you that night," Penny said sarcastically. "I know when I bought your ticket and forced you to be my date, I forgot to inform you we'd end the evening at Mount Sinai Hospital. How rude of me," Penny said, pulling her plate back in front of her and eating her now-cold lunch with full force.

"No need to get nasty, Penny. I wasn't the one who was embarrassed. I'm just simply looking out for you, dear. I don't want people to think—well, you know..."

"What? That I'm a coke whore like my sister, only she can handle it and I can't?" Penny took a big gulp of wine out of her glass and subliminally attempted to show Chas that she too, could handle her booze like her little sister.

"We are bitter, aren't we, Penny? Did someone put something in your truffles today, or perhaps someone spiked the risotto with a bad attitude pill," Chas said, daintily reaching over with his fork to taste Penny's dish before she finished it all.

Penny backed down. Her fear of not being cool, hip, pretty, or good enough for Harry was getting the best of her.

"Okay, I'm sorry. It's just that I really do want to spend some time with Harry this summer," Penny declared looking Chas straight in the eye.

Chas smiled his full-of-shit smile. *Ah, yes, I* am *the Master*, Chas thought to himself. "Well, I'm not exactly surprised! Now, if you listen to me, really listen to me this time, Penny, and don't act so stubborn, this could really work out."

"Okay, what do I have to do first?" Penny said with the fresh and willing look of an eager puppy on her face.

"Lose weight," Chas said in a matter-of-fact, deadpan demeanor, as he continued to enjoy his hefty layers of eggplant Parmesan.

There it was. The answer to everything that was wrong in Penny's life. She had heard it so much by now that sometimes it didn't even faze her. This time it did.

"No shit! I know that! That's why I wanted to see if you could make Jacquesteen squeeze me in," she said, tapping her fork on her plate impatiently.

Dr. Hervé Jacquesteen was New York's top weight-control man. His name had been Irving Jockinstein until Chas made him change it. He had all of Park Avenue popping his magic diet pills, which he said were imported from France. The pills were really made in Queens. No one knew nor cared.

But now that Jacquesteen had his clients hooked, he didn't need Chas anymore to bring them in. He made so many women so skinny, everybody who was anybody was running to Dr. Jacquesteen's Fifth Avenue Weight Control and Wellness Retreat de Paris. He no longer needed Chas, so he stopped handing him cash. This was not a smart idea. Once the ladies who lunch got off Jacquesteen's pills, the weight came back on, sometimes twice as much. This is when they turned to Chas for advice and comfort. And since being shoved aside by the good doc, Chas began making Jacquesteen the culprit. He now sent his girls to a Chinese herbalist with some kind of green tea concoction, and very deep pockets. Soon, Dr. Jacquesteen would be yesterday's news.

"Forget Jacquesteen," said Chas firmly. "I'm hearing horror stories about him. I've got a new guy, Dr. Chang. He uses an all-natural herbal mixture that the Asian royalty has been drinking for thousands of years. It's foolproof."

"Nothing's foolproof, Chas. There are no miracles that can make me shut my mouth," Penny said taking a heap of the dried, smoked pig, packing it into a freshly baked roll, drizzling on some olive oil, then enjoying a hearty bite.

"Penny, please, just try it. Have you ever seen a fat Chinaman?"

"What about Buddha?" Penny said, chewing away.

"Okay, one exception, but on the whole they are very thin people. They must be doing something right."

"Okay, I'll see Dr. Chang," Penny said, making another Parma ham sandwich

"Good. You know, Penny, I'm only looking out for your best interests. I love you like a sister," Chas cooed, letting Penny indulge herself in a fancy pork roll orgy for just the moment.

Penny looked at Chas intently. He looked right back at her and didn't bat an eyelash. *I'm a pro*, Chas told himself as he held his stare. He wasn't going to lose what could be the biggest deal of his life. Just then, Penny verbalized what had been churning around in Chas's crafty little mind since she first picked him up earlier in the day.

"Chas, what's it going to cost for you to put Harry and me together?"

Penny was her father's daughter, a no-bullshit, get-to-the-point, cut-to-the-chase kind of girl. Now faced with the ultimate question, Chas found himself at a loss for words. He knew he could ask a lot, but didn't actually think it would happen so fast. The usually "Mr. Smooth" didn't think his plan all the way through yet, and he didn't have an exact number prepared.

"Oh, Penny, don't be silly..." Chas said squirming uncomfortably in his seat.

"I'm not being silly, Chas. I want to know up front what you expect out of this, so there is no misunderstanding later. And I want this kept very quiet," Penny said lowering her voice.

"Of course it will be kept quiet. Harry is coming here to relax, not to be hustled. You don't owe me anything," Chas replied, shaking his head in avoidance.

"Nothing?" Penny said, coyly.

"Well," Chas said, "nothing up front."

"Really, Chas?" Penny pushed on.

"Yes, really. I'm going to be a true gentleman about it," Chas said, looking nervously around the crowded room.

Penny was shocked. As long as she had known Chas, he never did anything for free—ever. If it wasn't a direct cash exchange, it was tickets to a ball, bottles of Dom Perignon, sometimes even airline tickets or pre-paid vacations, depending on how big the favor.

"Are you sure? Come on, Chas, I know you better than that. There must be some catch somewhere.

"Catch? What catch?" Chas blurted out, then quickly lowered his voiced when he realized the people at the next table were starting to stare.

He was on the verge of throwing a full-blown fit. The one thing he hated more than anything was to have his own bluff called. His life of manipulation was so good at times, he even caught himself believing it.

"You know, Penny, if you are going to be so gauche as to treat me, your best friend, as some kind of a pimp, then you can just forget it."

"I don't want to forget it. I want this, Chas. I really, really want this."

By this time Penny was clutching his arm. Her perfectly manicured nails were making a huge mark in his little wrist. Chas recoiled in shock like a startled child from the sheer force of Penny's reaction. As long as Chas had known Penny, he had yet to see her get so intense about anything. Usually when Penny was upset, she'd go off to Saks, Bloomie's, or Bergdorf Goodman and shop until the stores closed. If it got really bad, she'd buy a new Mercedes. And of course, there was always food. Many a night, after escorting her to a social function, Chas would go with Penny to an all-night diner. There she would sit in Cartier jewelry, a Revillion fur, and a custom-made Valentino gown, wolfing down fries, two cheeseburgers, and a milkshake. And Chas knew better than to try to stop her during one of her pig-outs. Besides, the more out of control she was, the more she needed his diet doctors and the more money he made. Why wreck a good thing?

Yet Chas noticed something different about the intensity level in Penny's eyes this time. It almost scared him. He saw a determined fire burning in her that he had never seen before. It dawned on him at that moment just how miserable she was, and how desperately she needed someone to come along and fix her pathetic existence. At that moment her money didn't matter, food couldn't fill her, and the other trappings couldn't make a dent in the loneliness she felt in her soul.

Penny's eyes told Chas something he never realized. It wasn't just about appearances for Penny, and it wasn't really about the jealousy she felt for her sister. Chas got the idea that, for Penny, marrying Harry Raider was the difference between life and emotional death. Without Harry, she could go on living a life most people would kill for, but she'd never feel anything but empty inside. With Harry, it might not be just like Romeo and Juliet, but she'd have some of his attention part of the time.

This was even more attractive to her at the core of her soul than any hoopla surrounding a big wedding, the press coverage, or any of that bullshit. For the first time Chas felt the deep-rooted source of Penny's hunger. And he simultaneously realized there was a lot more there to manipulate and cash in on than he had ever imagined.

Chas carefully released Penny's grip on his arm by gently loosening her fingers one by one. He knew so well what he was doing.

"Penny, sweetheart, this is Chas. I know. I know it hasn't been okay since daddy's been gone. I know being around

Bunny all the time doesn't make finding a replacement any easier. Don't worry. I'm not offended."

"Good. I didn't mean to offend you, really."

A tear welled up in Penny's eye. Chas had hit a chord. The tough-talking, straight-shooting, jaded New York princess was just a wounded little girl inside. Even though she knew she was never as striking as her sister, her late father Bernie always made her feel special. He knew she was the smarter one of his two girls and he loved her for that. Penny was more like him, while Bunny was the spitting image of her skeletal-at-all-costs mother. Penny's father gave her as much special attention as he could, but because he was so busy making money, he didn't have much time for his daughter. And when he divorced her mother, Bernie was busy escorting this lady to Europe or taking that lady on his yacht.

When he did spend time with them, he lavished his girls with extravagant gifts and individual attention. Now that he was gone, so was Penny's only source of adoration.

Chas grabbed a handkerchief and gently wiped more tears from Penny's eyes.

"You don't need to cry again sweetie, really. Chas is going to fix you up with Harry and the two of you are going to live happily ever after, I promise. I'm gonna make it all right. Both you and Harry have been through a lot, and it's time the two of you found each other. Really, you guys need each other now. It's time."

He sounded so convincing. Penny hated that Chas got to see her so vulnerable.

"Look, you won't tell anyone I'm such a desperate mush ball, will you?" Penny asked, collecting herself.

"Of course not, baby. Nobody knows you like Chas. It's nobody's business. The world should only see the lovely, social, gregarious Penny Marks. Nobody needs to know any different."

"Thank you, Chas. That's kind of you," Penny said, signaling the waiter for a check.

For once Penny wasn't being sarcastic. She had almost started to believe that Chas Greer was a human being under all that schmoozing. She was wrong.

"So how and when do we start?" Penny said in a matter-of-fact tone with a new resolve in her voice.

"Well, tomorrow morning at 7:00 a.m., you'll go see Dr. Chang."

"7:00 a.m., are you kidding? I haven't gotten up before 10:00 a.m. since high school," Penny said closing her eyes and faking sleep at the table.

"Penny, you have to start drinking these herbs first thing in the morning to get your system going."

"Okay, but why so early?" Penny replied as she went into her Burberry wallet to pay the bill with cash, not even checking it to make sure it was correct.

"Because you have to kick-start your metabolism by flushing all the toxins out first thing in the morning, and honey, believe me, you've got a lot of flushing to do!"

"Fine, then what?" Penny said, waving the money and the bill at the waiter.

"Well, after you've been on the herbs and the diet that Dr. Chang gives you for about a week or two, we'll work on your summer wardrobe. I think we'll stick to solid earth tones this year. Let's go for Eileen Fisher and DKNY. The Lilly Pulitzers last summer put me on sensory overload! We don't want to run the risk of giving Harry some kind of an acid flashback!"

Because she was absolutely taken aback by Chas's nerve, Penny dropped the cash in her hand and couldn't help raising her voice. "Chas, you already bought me my summer wardrobe last week. I spent twenty-two thousand dollars. I don't think I can return twenty-two thousand dollars worth of merchandise, do you?" Penny said, trying to pick up the money from the floor, this time counting it to make sure it was all there.

"Well, the clothes I bought you last week were really cute for summer in the Hamptons, but you have to remember Harry is from L.A. He's used to something a little hipper. Too bad you can't fit into Stella McCartney yet. She cuts so small."

"I thought Harry was trying to get away from L.A."

"He is, but you can't totally shock the poor guy. I mean, everyone in the Hamptons will be dressed in the same white linen Ralph Lauren crap they wear every year."

"I have twenty-two thousand dollars of that crap in my closet thanks to you!"

"It's not crap. I didn't mean to call it that. It's just I want Harry to feel comfortable and familiar with you, that's all. I don't want him to feel like an alien in his silk Hawaiian shirts."

"So why don't you make *him* buy twenty-two thousand dollars worth of Ralph Lauren or Calvin Klein, so *he* fits in instead of the other way around?"

"You see, Penny, there you go again, being all defensive and argumentative. I mean, really, Harry Raider is a billionaire's son. He doesn't have to conform for anyone—except his father. Now if you want Harry, the way you were just crying to me about a minute ago, I'm telling you, you have to follow my directions from the hot little miniskirts right down to the Tony-and-Tina nail polish. The linen suits will be in again next year. Save everything for when Harry gets used to that look. Besides, Ralph never goes out of style."

"Oh, I get it, I'm supposed to give him a dose of Hollywood trash here in New York. Don't you think he'll just find another Soho model or off-Broadway actress to give him that?"

"For the last time, Penny, Sam and Irma Raider will not accept another model or actress. If Harry wants to keep what's coming to him, he'll bring home the right package this time. However, it can't hurt if you look a little more like what he's used to. That way he can have a girl who looks like what turns him on and is what turns his parents on. Everybody wins!"

"And what do you win, Chas?" Penny said, winning back control of the situation. Chas was definitely not expecting Penny to bounce back so fast. He was noticing a tougher side of her that he knew existed but didn't see very often. He kept forgetting that although she may have had prolonged periods of self-pity, Penny was still Bernard Marks's daughter. She was a real scrapper at heart. Wheeling and dealing with true grit was part of her natural born heritage.

"I told you, Penny, I want nothing," Chas said almost meekly.

"You said nothing up front, as I remember. What do you want if it works?" Penny said, not backing down.

Chas was getting really nervous now. He was so excited about making this deal he never actually thought about how to name his price. Good thing, maybe, because until today he never really realized the depth of Penny's desperation for this to happen. Chas also hated being put on the spot. He usually calculated everything ahead of time, so when the opportunity presented itself, the overly inflated charges could just roll right off his twisted tongue. *How can I stall her?* Chas thought to himself. *Oh damn it...maybe it's just time for jazzy Chassy to roll the dice and go for it!* Chas decided to trust his inner master manipulator and see where it would take him. "Well, Penn, if you guys start dating, that's great! I trust that you and Harry will remember Chas as the one who brought you happiness.

You know, the usual dinners, benefits, maybe even a little trip to Capri with my new sweetie, Juan, would be nice. I've always wanted to go there."

Penny wasn't buying it. She knew there had to be a bigger payoff than a trip to Capri with Juan. As social and conniving as Chas was, it still wasn't every day he had the opportunity to make a marriage of this magnitude. Penny knew Chas too well not to know that he was going to milk this one for all it was worth.

"That's it, huh? Nothing else."

Penny had regained her gumption. She felt like pushing him, and for this kind of deal, Chas let himself be pushed.

"Well, yeah, that's it ... for dating."

"And what if there's a wedding?"

Once again, Penny had asked the big question Chas had not been ready for. Chas thought it would take this lunch to enroll her in the "marry Harry" plan, then he could get her to Dr. Chang, to Barney's, Fredrick Fekkai's Hair Salon, etc. Finally, after she had sufficient time to think about it, he could ask for the big payoff. Once she got submerged in the plan, he could ask for anything. Now it was premature. She could back out if she still wanted to. Chas knew she didn't want to. Still, he wished he had gotten her going before he cut a deal. He had a split second to measure the exact degree of her desperation and translate that into a dollar figure. He couldn't buy any more time. It was now or never.

"Well then, if there is a wedding, due to all my efforts and focused attention to this project, I think it's only fair that I am properly compensated. Don't you? I mean, Penny, I love you, but you'd never be able to pull this off on your own."

"I wouldn't?" Penny asked, surprised at his words. It wasn't like him to be stupid enough to insult her when he was about to ask for money.

"Well, I mean, of course you would, but well, who is going to have to be there to keep Harry back in control? I'm going to have to really dedicate my entire summer to keeping a watch on Harry, until we know for sure he has fallen in love with you and he has totally adjusted to his new way of life," Chas said, trying to speak calmly and rationally. Chas knew he had to stay cool and make his outrageous requests sound entirely reasonable. *If I sound the least bit unsure of myself, I'll lose the bitch*, Chas thought to himself. *This has to appear to make perfect sense.* Chas continued, "I mean, I'm going to have to arrange for you guys to get together, I'm going to have to convince Jessica and Freddy to get on your side and have you over the house, and I'm going to have to keep the other girls away from Harry. Let's face it, Penny, there is a tremendous amount of work to be done here. It's all on my shoulders."

"Okay, okay, Chas. I admit it. You have to orchestrate the whole deal. That's fine. So what's one summer's work worth to you?"

Penny was relentless. Now she was the one having fun.

"Well, Penny, it may be just one summer's work to me, but it's the rest of your life, now, isn't it?"

Penny was quiet for a moment. She hadn't thought about that.

"Yeah, Chas, I guess you're right. It is."

"Right, Penny." He was back in the driver's seat. "So you can't really look at it as just some fun summer job for Chas. I mean, who really can put a price on happiness? Juan and I are happy, and we're nowhere as rich as you are."

"You seem a lot happier," Penny admitted.

"Well, we are happy, but let's face it, Juan is just a junior florist at Fleur de Fleur Party Productions in the Village. I mean, he's absolutely brilliant, but he's a long way from becoming Robert Isabel. We have a really tight budget. I make a decent living being a style consultant, but it's really just peanuts compared to how I'd like to live."

"You live pretty good, Chas," Penny said as she watched him down a second piece of Cipriani's famous lemon meringue torte, wondering why it never showed up on his body.

"Sure, it could be worse, but you know what, Penn? I'd really like to know I could provide a nice home for Juan and have the same sense of security you have."

"Fifteen million ain't what it used to be."

"Penny, you and any future children you may have, and their children, will never have to worry. I'd love to adopt a child with Juan; he'd be a great mother. But right now we can't afford it."

"Oh, puh-leeze, you've only been with him two months, Chas. He could be totally psycho, like your last two boyfriends."

"No, Penny, I have a great feeling about him. I really think Juan is life-mate material. I just hope one day we can have at least some feeling of financial security like you have now and will have even more with Harry. Even I couldn't help you spend all of a few billion dollars! That would take a team of Chas clones...and we know that there is only one!"

"That's right, Chas, you're a classic. So how much do you need to feel secure?"

She wasn't letting him get away from the real subject of the money, even after his half-assed touching story.

"Well, not anywhere *near* what you need, darling. That I can assure you."

"I can safely assume that because you are providing eternal security for me and my offspring for many generations to come, you think it's only fair that I provide some kind of security for you."

"Well, you said it. It's only fair, Penny. I mean, come on."

"Okay, Chas, so what do you want if you get me down the aisle?"

Chas had to lay his cards on the table right now or get out of the game. He was almost sweating, but forced self-control.

"A million dollars. One from you and one from Harry."

There. He said it. His offer was out. It almost brought him a welcome sense of relief.

"A million dollars?! Are you out of your mind?" She was practically screaming. "Are you out of your mind?!" Penny stood up furiously and was about to slap Chas across his face with her napkin. Lucky for Chas, he was all too familiar with Penny's temper. He grabbed her wrist and practically forced her back down into her chair before she could attack him.

"Penny, please, you'll make a scene. Think about it. A million dollars is nothing today. It's chump change to you and means even less to Harry. A million dollars would make my life. Two million would let me enjoy it."

Penny was stunned. She had dealt with Chas's outrageous prices and bogus "fees" for years. She knew he got kickbacks from everyone in town, but to ask for a million dollars for an arranged marriage just blew Penny away.

It was true, a million dollars was not much in the world they walked in, but to part with it just like that was another story. Penny knew her father would be rolling in his grave if he thought that she would pay a million dollars to get a husband, even if it was Sam Raider's son.

Penny felt like a total loser. Her sister Bunny was being wined and dined by international men of wealth and royalty, flown all over the world in private jets and spoon-fed caviar. Here Penny sat being hustled by some low-life personal shopper who held the key to her entire future in his little wimpy hand. She absolutely felt sick.

"Chas, that's insane. As much as I want to be married, as much as I want to make a 'good' marriage, and as much as I want Harry Raider, I can't justify it. I just can't. I'm sorry," Penny said, smoothing her skirt and making an attempt to collect herself again.

Chas refused to be defeated so early on. Perhaps once Harry arrived in the Hamptons, and everybody ran after him, Penny would change her mind. *I'll make sure her loneliness gets the best of her this summer. I won't return her calls, so she won't have anyone to listen to her complaints, escort her to parties or have lunch with...she won't be able to handle being overlooked and ignored. Miss Marks will have to give in sooner than later*, Chas thought to himself. Sooner came sooner than he thought.

The circular door of Cipriani swung open and Bunny Marks made a grand entrance. Bunny was wrapped tightly in a little black Versace slip dress and had on enough Bulgari jewelry to wipe out all of Italy. Penny had no idea her sister would be there today, nor did she care. Bunny was escorted to a heavy-duty power table and seated between two of Wall Street's most powerful players. The big shots acted like schoolboys trying to keep her attention. She drank Dom Perignon and, while The Donald whispered into her ear, Bunny noticed her sister sitting over at a not-so-great table in the corner with Chas. She waved at them casually, as if her own sister was a distant acquaintance. Bunny wouldn't get up from such illustrious company to say hello to her only sister, and she knew Penny would never have the nerve to come over to her power table. Bunny sipped and flirted, and Penny's heart sank to the floor. She looked at Chas.

"A million dollars?"

"The day after the wedding."

"You got a deal."

chapter five

The next day, at a gloriously sunny 7:30 a.m., Chas, dressed in Tommy Hilfiger khakis and a navy Polo blazer with a pink cardigan tied casually around his shoulders, was gleefully walking down Park Avenue, having just dropped Penny off at Dr. Chang's.

He arrived at 480 Park Avenue with a bouquet of flowers in his hand. The doorman greeted him with a familiar nod, as did almost every doorman on Park, Madison, and Fifth Avenues. Chas Greer was an institution.

"Good morning Tony, lovely day, isn't it?" Chas flirted shamelessly, batting his eyes at the hunky doorman from the Bronx.

"Yes, Mr. Greer, it is." Tony the doorman was forced to be polite, even though he hated Chas.

"I'm going up to Miss Harrington's, as usual. Lovely to see you again, dear." Chas winked at the obviously annoyed, and totally heterosexual, Tony.

"Nice to you see you, too, sir," Tony bit his tongue.

It wasn't even that Chas found Tony that attractive. The big turn-on was that neither of them could really afford to live there, but Chas was such a frequent guest that he could act as if he owned the place. Tony was hired help. Chas loved the power play. It was just enough to get the day off to a good start.

Chas took the elevator up to the twelfth floor. He didn't even bother to flirt with the elevator man—his mind was back on business.

Millicent Waterford Vanderwilde Harrington, or "Milly" to those who grew up with her in South Hampton, was in the kitchen eating white toast with jelly on a paper towel as her big yellow lab Rusty ate steak from a Minton doggy bowl. Milly's Park Avenue apartment looked like a weird mixture of Old Guard meets modern convenience. It wasn't that she was unattractive. At thirty-nine, her "jock-like" demeanor made her look a lot younger than she was. She had chic, short, straight blond hair, wore absolutely no makeup and always had a healthy tan from being outdoors so much. Milly always looked like she just got off a sailboat. Although she was no striking model, there was something about her natural sportiness that made her attractive. Milly looked like men could really enjoy themselves with her. She didn't look like they would have to resuscitate her if she broke a heel. Underneath a stuffed moose head in her hunter green library was a fax, computer, and phone with a caller I.D. box blinking away. Milly Harrington was a real Old Guard WASP, "The Real Mc-Goy" as her Jewish partners in her Wall Street firm called her. Just before her thirtieth birthday, she became the only female partner in the prestigious brokerage house of Goldstein, Bernstein, Feinstein, and Harrington. She was also the only non-Jew. Milly had the reputation on The Street as being a smart-ass you didn't fuck with, and she didn't get there overnight.

Milly's heritage was typical of those born into the American WASP Old Guard, whose wealth dwindled away generation after generation. Her father inherited the South

Hampton oceanfront estate on Gin Lane, but he didn't have the money to keep it up. Because her father hadn't worked a day in his life, and of course neither did "Mummy," they had to sell their Fifth Avenue apartment at a market low, just to have money to live on. Daddy blew most of his trust fund, going on safari with the Duke of Windsor, Lord Louis Mountbatten, and Winston Guest. Mummy worked in the garden, attended tea parties, and locked herself in her room with a bottle of vodka at night.

Milly, the only child, was often left in the care of a foul smelling, old Black Irish housekeeper with rotting teeth who let her do as she pleased. School provided Milly's only sense of gratification as a child. She was a math whiz, and won every spelling bee, even though her parents never attended.

This morning, Milly was reviewing the investment portfolio of a new multimillion-dollar client, as she sat at her kitchen table. The client decided to postpone their afternoon meeting and play golf in South Hampton instead. He had invited Milly to spend the weekend at his Gin Lane estate with his family, but she had politely declined his invitation. Even though this new client's account was of the utmost importance to her, Milly Harrington would avoid spending time in South Hampton, at all costs.

Growing up in South Hampton and going to school there in the winter was very different than the experience of the nouveau riche who just came for the summer. South Hampton High School had a mixture of rich kids, whose parents preferred the quiet country life, and the children of the local plumbers, pool men, fishermen, contractors, and even Shinnecock Indians. Milly was none of the above. She had the prestigious name—even a street was named after her family in South Hampton's estate section—but no longer any money to back it up.

The only vacation her family ever took was when a social climbing member of the nouveau riche invited them to Palm Beach around Christmas time. The Palm Beach Old Guard still were impressed with the Harrington name. It helped someone with new money to have a Harrington as a houseguest. It was enough to get someone a membership in the Everglades Club or an invitation to the Coconuts New Year's Eve Ball.

The summer jet set in South Hampton were the same social climbing fools who flocked to Palm Beach during the winter. This was lucky for the Harringtons. Perhaps the saddest, most embarrassing thing Milly could remember about her childhood was when the financial situation got so bad her family was forced to rent out their famous, but crumbling, estate for the summer season. Since it was oceanfront, they could command enough money to last them the whole year. Still, it was hard for Milly to imagine another little girl sleeping in her bed while she slept in the guesthouse of some stranger who just wanted to use the name Harrington for social gain.

Milly's mother died of liver cancer when Milly was at Harvard. Although she would never admit it, Milly mother's death had set the young girl free. For Milly, it put an official end to the *Stepford Wife*-era of suffering in silence, all for the sake of "keeping up appearances." With Mummy gone to her final tea dance at that great big country club in the sky, Milly was able to write her own ticket and live her life by her own rules.

Milly's reckless father sold the estate and ran off to play polo in Argentina. He lived down there with his new, rich wife and a stable full of world-class polo ponies. Milly didn't receive one cent from him, and graduated from Harvard Business School summa cum laude on full scholarship. After graduation, she got a job at Goldstein, Bernstein, and Feinstein, and had stayed there ever since.

At first it was amusing for the boys at the all-Jewish firm to have this WASPy wonder woman working there. But they soon learned she was worth her weight in gold. Milly always liked Jews, especially since her parents despised them. It nearly killed her mother to have to lease their family home one summer to a rich Jewish family named Cohen.

Jacob Cohen was a big player on Wall Street, and it meant nothing to him to spend one hundred fifty thousand dollars for a summer. He was originally from Boston, so he wanted to try renting in the Hamptons before he made any substantial real estate purchase.

Milly's most impassioned memory of her adolescent years was the night she lost her virginity to Jacob Cohen's eighteen-year-old son, David. As usual, Milly's family was staying at a guesthouse of a social climbing couple who lived nearby. She met David the day she stopped by the estate to pick up some bathing suits she had forgotten. Milly was a tomboyish, long, lanky, flat-chested sixteen, but that night David made her feel like a goddess.

"Don't worry, Milly, it won't hurt. How could I ever hurt you? You're so beautiful," David told her that unforgettable balmy night.

"But David...I never..."

"Ssssh. Don't worry, Milly, I love you." And with that, he took her into his arms and inducted her into womanhood on the beach in front of the estate. His skilled tongue woke her pointy nipples and her pink hooded clitoris to pleasure she had never imagined. David was so gentle, yet strong and forceful as he entered her. Milly could still remember his musky smell and the feel of his jet-black curly hair rubbing between her thighs, as he tasted her.

Since her initiation with David, Milly had a passion for Jewish men. There were two problems that white-bread-and-mayonnaise Milly encountered with the matzo-ball-movers-and-shakers of the Mosaic faith, whom she so adored. Milly was considered a "Shiksa Goddess," which meant she was a gentile girl Jewish men could enjoy "for practice," but marriage was strictly out of the question. But she was their equal intellectually and in terms of earning power. After years of hard work she was pulling down a very impressive seven-figure salary. She was considered a female force to be reckoned with on Wall Street. Yet most of the men Milly was interested in wound up with wives that spent their days at the three Bs: Bloomie's, Bergdorf's, and Bendel's. Milly was much happier riding, hunting, fishing, and working—anything but shopping. Chas bought all her outfits.

The second problem Milly faced was basic: She was not Jewish. Not even remotely close, not even Italian. Mixed marriages were no big deal, supposedly. Still, it usually turned out that once the thrill of dating the ultimate "golden goya" was over, Jewish boys found nice Jewish girls and got married. In the end, that's what happened to David Cohen.

David was Milly's classmate at Harvard, and they continued their relationship all the way through undergrad and business school. She was often his guest at the Cohen's new oceanfront estate in Bridgehampton during the summers. Unlike the decrepit Harrington estate, the Cohen home was immaculately kept. From the perfectly manicured hedgerows to the daily polished sterling silver doorknob, no detail was left uncared for.

It always bothered Milly how her family's estate was so close to the new Cohen estate, but seemed like worlds away. Mrs. Cohen was the complete opposite of Milly's mother. She was always wearing some kind of Spandex exercise outfit and was overly involved with David and his sister Rachel's activities. The house always smelled like something terrific was cooking in the oven. Not that Mrs. Cohen cooked. It smelled that way just because of the fresh food delivered every morning from The Golden Pear. Another thing that amazed Milly was that Mrs. Cohen always made a point to join her children for breakfast and lunch, every day. Not only was she overly preoccupied with their individual diet and nutrition habits, but Harriot Cohen also used this time to quiz her kids about what they were doing at day camp and who their friends were. This type of closeness and concern was absolutely foreign to Milly. Her distant, detached mother never cared about how much or what Milly ate, or had any interest in her playmates or activities.

Jacob Cohen was Milly's mentor, and even wrote her a recommendation letter that got her the first job on The Street. With the combination of Milly's fresh-looking, "Ivory Soap" natural beauty and her spunky personality, Jacob knew she would be dynamo one day. Jacob was the father she never had, and it destroyed her not to have ended up his daughter-in-law. When David graduated from Harvard Business School, the Cohens sent him to Israel for the summer. Milly desperately wanted to go with him, but at the time she couldn't afford it. She found it strange the Cohens hadn't offered to send her with David since they had generously paid for trips to Florida, California, and even Paris. But Milly sensed that something about this trip to Israel was different. It was.

When he returned, David sat down with Milly.

"Look, I'm sorry, Milly, but after spending the whole summer in Israel, I realized I just can't see you anymore."

"But why? I said I'd convert. I don't understand!" a devastated Milly cried.

"That's just it, you couldn't possibly understand what it means to be a Jew. It's not just about bagels and lox on Sunday mornings. It's about five thousand years of persecution and suffering, just to keep Judaism alive."

"Okay, so I'll study Jewish history at the Fifth Avenue Synagogue. I'll save up and go to Israel. I'll do anything for you, David. I love you."

"You can't convert for me, Milly. That wouldn't be right either. With your background, there is absolutely no way you could understand who I am and where I'm coming from. I love you, too, Milly, but I owe it to my people to continue my heritage. I need to marry a Jewish woman."

A year later, David was married to Judy Saperstein, daughter of Myron Saperstein, the real estate mogul. Milly never got over David. Over the years she dated a string of men, but nothing ever worked out. The WASPy ones reminded her of her father, which repulsed her. The Jewish boys—well, that was the same old story. Milly was left alone to concentrate on her booming Wall Street career. At thirty-nine, she put at least one Harrington back on top financially. Now she could afford a house in the Hamptons all her own—a house she would never have to rent out to strangers, not ever. She chose to buy in East Hampton on Egypt Lane. South Hampton brought back too many painful childhood memories and Bridgehampton was too reminiscent of David. Her home was simple and elegant, with fishing pictures and trophies won from horse shows. It looked more like a sportsman's lodge than it did the home of a successful single woman.

Her apartment at 480 Park Avenue was more of the same. This morning Chas found her as usual, eating her breakfast with her dog Rusty, the two of them looking at CNN on TV.

"Hey, baby, hate to come so early, but I've got something fabulous to tell you."

"Chas, please, not now," Milly said, in a matter of fact tone. She was focused on the news and wouldn't even look up at him to acknowledge his presence. "Gotta get downtown. I'm already late. Call me after two o'clock. We'll talk."

"This will only take a second. I guarantee it's more exciting than any deal you'll do today."

Milly got up and headed toward the door. Her navy blue, pinstriped Brooks Brothers suit was already wrinkled.

"Milly, I found you a husband."

Milly stopped before she could get herself out the door. Chas had said the magic word. As impatient as she was to get in her chauffeur-driven Town car and get downtown, Chas gave her a glimmer of hope on something she had almost given up.

"What are you talking about now? Let me guess. Some poor Euro-trash prince needs a rich woman to keep him in New York. I get a title and he gets a check. No thank you."

Chas laughed like a schoolgirl keeping a big secret. "Guess again, Mills. You're not even warm, honey."

Milly was quiet for a moment. This wasn't fair of Chas. Didn't he know he was baiting her? This wasn't an easy subject for her.

"Chas, I really don't have time for games today. I'm really late."

"Okay, I won't keep you. If you aren't interested in Harry Raider, then I will just find someone else."

Milly chuckled as she threw out her paper. "Harry Raider, Sam Raider's son?"

"That's right, Mills, the one and only."

Milly shook her head in disgust. "I thought I read he married some teenage porno queen in L.A."

Chas continued nonchalantly as he walked over to her couch and puffed the pillows that the dog had been lounging on. "He did, but it didn't work out and now Harry's come to his senses."

"What does that mean? He got dumped by a porno queen so now he's looking for a nun?"

Milly hated it, but she had become quite cynical from

working on Wall Street. Everyone had some kind of story. Everyone had something they were trying to hide. There was never a clean deal.

"Not a nun, Milly, but a real woman."

"A real woman? You mean one with arms, legs, hair, PMS, and everything? Wow, how big of him."

Chas realized that Milly wasn't going to be as much of a pushover as Penny, even though she was just as desperate. Milly's desperation was quieter, more reserved. She had been taught as a child to either conceal her emotions or drown them in vodka like her mother did. Milly hated booze, so she chose plan A.

Milly learned early to always stay cool. Her poker face and stone-cold countenance played a big part in her financial success. Milly never cracked under pressure in her professional life. She had been programmed not to.

"The only thing to remember is always be a lady, no matter how bad it hurts," her mother would say with an empty bottle of Absolut in one hand and a copy of *Town & Country* in the other. Milly hurt for a long time. But numbness took over, eventually.

"Mills, you really need to lighten up," Chas said. "For years I've been trying to find the right guy for you. Think of everything we've been through...the Young Presidents Club, Republican Eagles, Kips Bay Boys Club, all those parties at the Whitney Museum. I've exhausted every charity here in New York and Palm Beach. Remember the Princess Grace Fund party at the Waldorf? I got Prince Albert's attention and when he came over to talk to you, you ran away."

"He's not my type," Milly said raising an eyebrow cynically.

"Who is? Prince Charles? He's so stuffy. I bet he's a rotten lay."

"I'm sure you'd like to find out," Milly said, teasing.

"Not really. Andrew is more my type, but I'd be willing to bet Edward would be willing and able. But don't worry about me, baby, I've got Juan—I'm worried about you. You've got no one except your dog and the horses."

Milly pointed to her collection of championship blue ribbons and trophies, which were presented prominently on the mantle above her fireplace. "Well, horses are dependable. Besides, when something goes wrong, you can always shoot them."

They both laughed. Milly couldn't shoot a horse if her life depended on it. Horses were the one thing she had in common with her father. They were both excellent riders, and she cared for her horses like children. Every weekend she would drive out to Sag Pond Farms in Sagaponac and ride her horses until she couldn't move. At night she'd collapse with the dog on her bed and a good book. Milly hardly went out anymore. She really had given up, she thought.

"No need to worry, Chas. I'm fine. Really, I'm very happy the way things are. I've got no one to tell me what to do, what to say, what to wear...except you, of course. I have total freedom and I'm happy that way. Really."

"Bullshit, Milly," Chas said stamping his foot in utter frustration. "You're full of crap. There can be another David. You're not dead yet."

Milly hated when Chas brought up David. It was definitely her weak spot and, of course, Chas knew it.

"I heard he had another baby, right after his son's Bar Mitzvah. He's gone on with his life for many years now. When are you going to let go and get on with yours?"

Milly tried to hide how pissed off she was getting by picking up a brush and vigorously grooming her dog. Chas had some nerve to barge into her apartment right before she had to race downtown for a big meeting. Milly was no idiot, she knew that David was long gone. It was just that she had never felt that way for anyone again, ever. Her innocence about people was lost to David. He was the only source of love and support she had ever known, and ultimately he betrayed her. How could she ever really love again? Who was this Harry Raider, and why was Chas talking to her about him? Harry Raider was Jewish. If he got dumped by a porno queen, he had to be ready for a nice Jewish girl now. She had heard it a million times before. Milly couldn't figure out how these boys had been brainwashed into believing she was no good. She was willing to convert, she was willing to learn what it meant to be Jewish, she even could make a mean matzo ball soup. Time and time again, Milly felt the sting of rejection. Why would Harry be any different?

"C'mon, Mills. Harry's just the type you love—a short little Jew boy who, when he stands on his father's money, all of a sudden gets a lot taller."

"Chas, I'm not really up for another round of rejection. I'm not Jewish. That's it."

"That's good in this case, Mills. Harry hates Jewish American Princesses. Are you kidding? He has tribes of them at Pine Valley Country Club dying to get their long red fingernails into him. If he wanted a JAP, he certainly wouldn't need to come to the Hamptons. He has his pick of the daughters of the Beverly Hills U.J.A. or Wilshire Boulevard Temple Sisterhood—he certainly doesn't need to come east to get more of the same."

"Then why is he coming to the Hamptons, Chas?" she asked, pointing her dog's brush directly at his crotch in a crude Wall Street "you're full shit" gesture. She still didn't believe Chas about Harry not wanting a Jewish girl.

"To get his life together, Mills. Life in the Hollywood fast lane is killing him. The drugs, the bimbos, the actresses, the whole scene will be the death of him. He can't escape it there. Everyone knows who he is. Harry goes to every all-night party he's invited to, and he keeps getting involved in things he shouldn't. It's not his fault. Because he's so rich, they seek him out."

"Who's they?" Milly pressed on.

"Movie producers looking to raise cash and music people who need backing. They shower him with hookers, drugs, and parties, hoping he will write a check for their latest project. He is relentlessly bombarded by the scum of the earth, all trying to get a piece of him. He can't think straight because he has no time to think. Harry is always being pursued by somebody. He's always under attack."

"So, he's coming to the Hamptons to get away from all that?" Milly scoffed. "Why should he want to leave Beverly Hills, where he's a star getting royal treatment? In the Hamptons, he'll be just another billionaire baby brat."

"Mills, Harry doesn't want to be the center of a circus anymore. For God's sake, he's almost forty years old. He wants to settle down, have a family, live life like a normal person."

"A normal person. Right. I'm sure he wants to start a family with a nice Jewish girl."

"Mills, will you get off that already? I'm telling you, Harry isn't like the little wimpy boys who bow at Daddy's every word. He's a rebel. That's why he's had so much trouble. He has so much independence and energy, but because of his environment it's all been misdirected. The last thing Harry Raider wants to do is walk in his father's shadow."

"Yeah, but when it comes right down to it, he'll want someone who is just like his mother."

"No way, Mills, you are all wrong. Harry hates his mother. Irma never paid any attention to him when he was growing up. Harry was raised by an Irish nanny. I remember her. Her name was Agnes O'Reilly and she had a face full of freckles. If anything, he'd want a woman more like her, not Irma."

"Well, I'm not Irish either."

Chas put his arm around her. "Close enough, Mills. You know when Harry was a kid, Agnes used to take him fishing and horseback riding. She even took him skeet shooting one time, but Sam found out and had a fit. Agnes turned Harry into a little sportsman. They used to have a blast."

Milly searched Chas's face to see if he was telling her something that was even remotely true. "Really?"

"Really, Mills, I'm serious."

Chas saw a hidden glimmer of hope in Milly's eye, as she subconsciously reached for his hand. She knew what Chas said about Harry being a rebel was true. Anyone as wild as he had been certainly was not into "doing the right thing." Harry's interest in sports also got her. She knew that Jewish boys were mainly encouraged by their parents to work their minds, not their bodies. Every time she took David to shoot, fish, or ride, he was awkward, but obviously loved it. The closest David ever came to being athletic was getting season tickets to the Knicks game on the floor at Madison Square Garden.

Milly was a born athlete. As smart as she was, she was even more athletic. She'd love a guy with whom she could go on shoots in England, through the pampas on horseback in Argentina, or to Australia on a fishing expedition near the Great Barrier Reef. It wasn't that she didn't also enjoy sitting on the veranda of the Hotel de Paris in Monte Carlo sipping Veuve Cliquot. But, if she had her choice, she'd take a hiking trip through the Rockies over shopping on Rodeo Drive any day.

"So, Harry was this sportsman as a child, huh? What about now? With all his partying, when does he have time to fit a ride in? I'd be shocked if he was even sober enough to make it to a Reebok Sports Club L.A."

Chas knew he was on the right track. If she weren't starting to become interested, she would have left by now. Milly wasn't much on manners. Work was always first. She had left Chas waiting, alone, many times. Chas had already made her almost twenty minutes late, but something obviously was keeping her.

"He hasn't had any time to pursue his true loves, riding, hunting, and fishing," Chas continued his fibbing. "That's part of the problem. Today he has nobody. He was even thinking of going on a trip to India, trekking through the Himalayas, but he didn't want to do it alone. Harry is coming east to get back to nature and start a fresh, clean, wholesome life. Can you see a Jewish girl trekking through the Himalayas? Please, what would a JAP do in India, with no Bloomingdales? You are exactly what he needs, Mills. You're a strong, independent, athletic, hard-working woman who can put Harry back together. He desperately needs someone like you, Mills. You will return him to the happy, outdoorsy, rugged guy he once was. You guys can have such a wonderful life together. I'm so excited!"

Milly's famous poker face did not let on that she was getting excited about finding a Jewish man who wanted to live the sporting life. She had never met one yet, and could hardly believe such a phenomenon really existed.

"So when is he coming?"

"Memorial Day—just three weeks from now. He's staying with Jessica and Freddy. You know Jessica."

"Of course I know who she is, but I've never actually met her."

"Yes, you have. Remember a few years ago at the Hampton Classic? The year you qualified for the Olympic equestrian team? We had champagne together in the tent after you won the Grand Prix."

"Chas, I was elated that day. I don't remember anything except getting that trophy. It was one of the highlights of my life."

"I know Mills. Jessica was very impressed with you. She's a very natural girl, you know, Mills, not into the scene at all. She hates big parties. You two will get along like two peas in a pod. I bet you could even talk her into trying riding. She always did like horses, but I think Freddy's allergic. She's a very private person, but I think she'll really like you and I'm sure she'll agree you're absolutely right for Harry. Believe me, since he will be living at her house, it will help to have her blessing."

Milly caught herself emotionally slipping and knew she needed to get back in control—and fast. She quickly walked to the other side of the room and pretended to once again bury her head in her client's portfolio papers as she spoke. She said, "Chas, that really sounds terrific. I mean, I have to say it almost sounds too good to be true. There must be some catch somewhere."

"God, Mills, you're such a pessimist. Of course there's no catch. Why shouldn't it work out? Besides, you'll have me orchestrating the whole thing. I'll make sure you become Jessica's new best friend and Harry's future wife. The whole thing will just flow together naturally, dear. You'll see. I'll make sure of it."

And there's the catch, Milly thought.

Whether or not she had a chance with Harry Raider depended on Chas's efforts and, as Milly depended on no one, she hated to give up control. But, she was sharp enough to know this was definitely Chas's forté. As successful as she was in business, Milly was no social butterfly. If anything, she was a wallflower at parties. No man, in Milly's eyes, had ever lived up to David. To this point, he was her first love and her last. Secretly, she would give up anything—her career, her religion, her whole life—just to recapture that sense of total happiness again. Until today she didn't think it was possible.

"Okay, Chas, I admit it. This is definitely your area of expertise. I'm a novice in this department."

Chas didn't have to play games with Milly like he had to with Penny. Milly was a straightforward businesswoman. Milly also was unaccustomed to being babied and coddled like Penny. Chas's best bet was just to put the deal on the table.

"So, you recognize that without my intervention and orchestration, there's no deal?"

"Deal?" Even Milly was a little taken aback by Chas's brutal honesty. Milly still wanted to believe in love. Everything else in her life was a deal. She didn't want to think of finding her soul mate as another deal to be made.

"That's right Mills, we'll have a deal. An agreement between us that makes sure I am properly compensated for providing you with a good marriage."

Milly hated what she was hearing. Is this why she worked so hard all these years? Was she so impossible to be with she had to pay off a broker to get her a marriage deal? This couldn't be happening.

"What kind of deal are we talking about, Chas?"

"Cash."

"You want a cash deal to find me a husband. That's completely absurd," Milly said slamming shut her briefcase to accentuate her point.

Chas picked up the latest copy of *New York Magazine* from the coffee table and began to obviously flip through the personals section. He knew he had to appeal to Milly's sense of the rational. With Milly that was far more effective than trying to break her down emotionally. She could be too much of a WASP, a stoic ice queen at times. Milly was trained to turn her emotions off and never let them get the best of her. Or so Chas thought.

"Milly, there's a dozen dating services in here who provide you with a certain amount of dates for cash up front. You have no way of choosing who or what they give you. You are totally at their mercy. The caliber of men who join those dating services I wouldn't let touch me in a dark bathroom on a remote island. I, on the other hand, require no money up front, with the exception of the usual dinners, dances, weekends away, etc. However, if I give up my summer to successfully insure that you and Harry make it to the altar, that will require a fee for my time and energy."

"When is this fee due?" Milly said, coldly staring Chas right in the eye.

As distasteful as this was, Milly at least needed to hear the terms of the deal.

"I wouldn't take one cent until the day after the wedding. That way you are insured that your investment has paid off. Before you go off on your honeymoon, you give me a briefcase full of bills. Cash. I'd hate to have to waste my hard-earned money on Uncle Sam when I could have so much fun spending it on Juan."

Milly couldn't help but be intrigued. She had made deals to acquire everything else she enjoyed in her life. Maybe this was what she was good at. Maybe this would work in her personal life. Maybe *something* would work in her personal life. She was thirty-nine years old. Her desperation was quieter than Penny's, but it still had the same level of intensity about it. She masked it so well, though, that even Chas wasn't so sure what she would do.

"So what's the bottom line, Chas? How much is due upon completion of the deal?"

Chas looked straight in her steel blue eyes. He couldn't afford to be insecure. He had to meet her on her level.

"One million dollars."

Milly almost fell over and could barely hide her shock, reaching back to grab the counter in an effort to balance herself. She was expecting ten, maybe twenty, or even twenty-five thousand dollars at the most. He had to be insane. Who in their right mind would pay a million dollars for a husband? Chas had spent way too much time around the nouveau riche. Milly may have been self-made, but her background was still very much Old Guard blue-blood.

Not only was the amount of money Chas requested absolutely preposterous, but it was a slap in the face. How dare he treat her like some flash in the pan, glitzy, desperate-to-fit-in Hamptonite who would write a check just to get her name in the paper, or on a guest list. How dare he play her for such a fool. Who the hell did he think he was dealing with?

But as floored as she was, Milly showed no sign of emotion. Instead, she walked over to the coat closet, put on her Burberry raincoat and locked her plain leather briefcase. She said nothing.

"Mills, what are you thinking?"

Her silence was unnerving him. She still said nothing, as she searched for an umbrella.

"Mills, talk to me. Don't do this. What's going on?"

Milly didn't even look at him.

"Mills, please, a million dollars is nothing today," Chas proclaimed as he pounded on the window in frustration and gazed out at Park Avenue, America's most overpriced concrete jungle. "You know that. Besides, if you marry Harry, you'll have billions! Billions, Milly, do you hear that?" Chas turned around, ran over, and got right in her face. He was jumping up and down, shaking his fists in the air. It took all of his self-control not to grab Milly and shake her too. "You'll never have to work another minute. You could ride all day long. Think about it logically, Milly.

A million dollars won't even make a dent in your lunch money. I'm bringing you the deal of a lifetime, worth billions! The least you could do is be gracious and think about *my* life. I have to work for a living, too. Nobody ever gave me something for nothing. Why should everybody else make money while I have to live in a studio walk-up in the Village? What's fair is fair. You can't argue with that, Mills," Chas said, catching a glance of himself in the reflection in the window, and quickly regaining his composure.

"I'm not arguing, Chas," Milly said in a steady voice, having thoroughly enjoyed watching Chas become unglued. "I also won't be a sucker like everybody else in this town. Maybe a million dollars isn't considered a lot of money today, but I still respect it enough not to flush it away on some man."

"But he'll give you billions, Mills," Chas said in loud stage whisper, smoothing down his usually perfect hair that had gotten a little too tussled for his liking.

"Nobody ever gave me anything, either, Chas. There was always a price for everything. Living with the fact I had to shell out a million bucks to buy a shot at happiness is a price too high for me to pay," Milly said, coolly.

"How can you be so damn idealistic, Milly? For God's sake, you're a businesswoman aren't you? You know how the world works. So you spend a million to make over a billion. Sounds like a good deal to me."

"It's not just about the money, Chas. Once you've had what I had with David, you know you can't really think of marriage just for the money. Don't misunderstand me. Money is great. I'd never want to be without it again, but I've been fortunate—or unfortunate—to learn about love."

"So wouldn't you pay a million dollars to have a love as great a value, even greater, than you had with David? Isn't getting that feeling back worth a million dollars?"

Chas had to pull out all stops now. He had never heard Milly speak so candidly about love. Who knew WASPs were capable of such deep emotion? He was used to his JAPs crying, screaming, emoting, and sharing their feelings as their psychiatrists encouraged them to. But Chas was surprised to hear Milly, who had never been on a shrink's couch a day in her life, speak so clearly about such a touchy subject. Now he didn't know what to expect.

"You can't buy that feeling, Chas. I think something like that only comes along once in a lifetime. Sorry...all deals are off."

With that, she picked up her Hermes briefcase, headed out the door, and without paying any further attention Chas, left for work.

Chas sat alone on the big tartan couch in Milly's living room. He had to think. Chas hated when he couldn't get one of his girls to do as she was told. How dare she! Chas hated to lose, and this time he couldn't afford to.

Chas got up from the couch and stretched his arms and legs. He twirled himself around like a ballerina waiting for the music to begin. *What to do...what to do...* he thought to himself. *Come on jazzy Chazzy...get creative!* Because even a master manipulator needs a little lift at times, Chas needed to drop himself in a place of inspiration. Since fashion was his passion, Chas went to Milly's closet and began rummaging through her clothes, most of which he had picked out himself. Practically picking up her scent off of the power suits and riding clothes, Chas was like a bloodhound on a mission. He was determined to surround himself with the essence of Milly, and come up with a fail-proof plan of action. After a few minutes that seemed like forever, Chas had an idea. Was it cruel? Yes. Was it vicious? Yes. Would it work? It had to.

chapter six

Chas dialed information. To his surprise, Mr. and Mrs. David Cohen on Park Avenue were listed.

How human of them, Chas thought. Without hesitation, he dialed the number, his fingers almost sweating with excitement.

"Hello, Cohen residence," a housekeeper's voice answered.

"Yes, Judy Cohen, please." Chas spoke with the authority and familiarity that separated him from the rest of the hired help. With his cocky demeanor, he could sling the shit with the best of them. No other staff member, no butler, no chauffeur, or even personal assistant would have the nerve to act as familiar as Chas did with his rich and famous customers. He was only a personal shopper by trade, but in his mind he was a guru.

"Who may I say is calling?" the servant continued.

"Chas Greer."

"What is this in reference to, Mr. Greer?"

"Oh please, she'll know who I am. Now if you don't mind, could you put Judy on the phone?"

Chas kept his act up. He was never put off by the third degree. As a matter of fact, he got off on it.

"This is Judy Cohen," a woman's voice said.

"Hi Judy, Chas Greer, personal shopper."

"Yes, I know who you are."

Those were the four words Chas lived to hear: "I know who you are." They made his life complete.

"Great! Listen, Judy, of course everybody's talking about the fabulous baby naming you and David gave for your new daughter Raquel last Saturday. Mazel Tov!"

"Thank you," Judy said. She wasn't sure if he was congratulating her on the birth of her daughter or the success of the party, but Judy was the type of woman who was equally happy about both.

"Judy, I have the most incredible blankets for newborns—just got here from Italy. I'd love to show them to you before anyone else gets a chance to see them."

"Sure, come on over."

Oh my God, is it that simple? Chas thought to himself. Did she just open her golden doors to him? Chas even amazed himself sometimes.

"How 'bout in an hour? I just have to pick them up, then I can come right over."

"Great. 1040 Park, Penthouse One East," Judy said.

"Faaaabulous. I'll see you in an hour."

Chas hung up the phone and squealed in utter delight. This was going to be a no-brainer. So much to do, so little time. He got up from the couch and skipped out the door. Not only would he get *the* Mrs. David Cohen as a client, he also had a second chance at getting Milly to play his game.

An hour later, Chas arrived at the home of Mr. and Mrs. David Cohen at 1040 Park. A maid opened the door. Chas walked in and almost slipped on the newly polished marble floors. He had to get a grip. With its gold leopard-print walls, mirrored entrance hall, and stone fountain with a mini-pond filled with exotic fish, Chas wondered what drugs Lane Brema, Manhattan's hottest decorator had been taking when he created this Vegas-meets-Versace mess of a mansion in the sky!

Judy Saperstein-Cohen was a petite brunette with a nose job that looked like a ski jump. Must have been done by Dr. Meyer, Chas thought. Chas could spot a "Meyer Nose" a mile away. Dr. Meyer was responsible for making one-half of Park Avenue look like Bob Hope.

Still in her Fernando Sanchez robe, perched on the big, white, leather couch, Judy didn't bother to get up. With no worries, Chas made himself right at home, as usual. He proceeded to show her the different blankets, each made of the finest linen with little animals embroidered on them. Even though he hated babies, he asked to see Raquel. Thank God her nurse was giving her a bottle. Judy, of course, wouldn't attempt to breast-feed. Besides, silicone implants weren't good for babies, in case there was an unexpected leak. Naturally Judy agreed to buy the batch of blankets, one in every color, if Chas promised not to sell them to another Park Avenue matron for at least a month. Smiling victoriously he gave Mrs. David Cohen his false word that little Raquel would be the only baby at the Bridgehampton Beach Club this summer with the Milanese blankets, as he gracefully tucked the wad of cash she handed him into his Gucci bag.

Chas noticed a group of pictures lying on the glass table in front of them. They were shot from the baby naming, waiting to be put into a frame or album. They were right in front of his face. Chas picked up the photos and started to look through them.

"These are so precious! Do you mind if I have a look?"

Judy was absolutely delighted. She actually put down her Diet Coke long enough to show pictures of her baby and her party to anyone who would look at them.

"That's nothing. Would you like to see the video?"

"Of course, I'd be honored, really." Chas was only too happy to sit through a few hours of the baby naming ceremony at the Park Avenue Synagogue and the after party at the Harmonie Club. This was part of his job.

"Be right back." Judy got up from the couch and went into the other room to find the video. This gave Chas the time he needed to get what he had come for. After rummaging through the pile of pictures, he came across one that he instinctively knew would seal the deal with Milly. It was a darling picture of David and Judy holding little Raquel together, with their thirteen-year-old son Brett looking on. They looked like the perfect, happy family.

Chas quickly slipped it into his little Hérmes tote bag. Just as he was zipping it up, Judy came in and put the video in the VCR. Chas lay back on the big leather couch and began to get really comfortable. He had just sold Judy Cohen five thousand dollars worth of baby blankets, and he had the picture that could make him a millionaire. It was time to relax.

Milly walked down the long hall at Goldstein, Bernstein, Feinstein, and Harrington, making her way to her office. Everyone was talking about the Cohen baby naming. After all, the Cohens, David and Judy, represented a merger between two legendary New York family empires, one from Wall Street, the other from real estate. Anyone who was anyone from these two worlds was in the Park Avenue Synagogue last Saturday morning. The Macks, the Resnicks, the Silversteins, the Zeckendorfs, the Macklowes, the Tischs, and the Trumps were just a few giants present from the real estate side. From the Wall Street side there were the Forstmanns, Ace Greenberg, the Steinbergs, the Weils, the

Kravises, Carl Icahn, and many more who preferred to go unmentioned for security's sake. The *Post* and the *Daily News* heralded little Raquel Cohen's baby naming as the kick-off event to the summer season. "A Pre-Hampton Power Party" is how Cindy Adams put it, while Liz Smith labeled it appropriately "The Billionaire Baby Bash."

Milly finally found a safe haven in the privacy of her own office. No one at her firm could stop talking. Everybody talked in front of Milly, because nobody knew about her and David. Milly had a strict rule of keeping her personal life very private and out of the office. She wanted Wall Street to view her as a powerful woman, totally in control. Not for one second did she let anyone in business see the soft side of her. Even though she was dying deep inside because of all the commotion around David and Judy, she wore her stone face as effortlessly as her Brooks Brothers suit.

Milly locked the door behind her and took a few deep breaths. Her office was the epitome of simple elegance with a warm touch. Milly sat behind a large mahogany desk, with only one picture of her and Zara winning the Hampton Classic and another of her holding up a sailfish she caught last year in Costa Rica. There were two leather Ralph Lauren chairs for her clients to relax on while she guided their financial future. A small glass table held a Tiffany china tray with dainty cups and a selection of herbal teas. Milly liked her office to have somewhat of a homey feel to offset the overwhelming feeling one got from the monstrous, imposing Wall Street buildings visible from the floor to ceiling windows behind her.

How the hell would she ever get over David? It had been years now and the memory of his warm arms around her waist seemed like yesterday. She knew if she were ever going to have a shot at any kind of personal happiness, she had to try to love another man. Maybe Harry Raider wasn't a bad idea. He was from California; everything was more liberal out there. Perhaps his family would accept her if she converted to Judaism. Even a self-made, blue-blooded WASP like her had to be better than a nineteen-year-old porno queen. Maybe with Harry she'd have a real chance of getting the life and love she was cheated out of with David...but for a million dollars?

A million was so much money, when you've come up the hard way. All those years trying to study for exams while cleaning up tables in the Harvard Business School cafeteria. All those riding lessons she taught those whining, spoiled brats, just so she could afford a dorm room. It took her many years and many sacrifices to make her first million. Now was she just supposed to hand over that kind of money to some greedy, gold-digging, stuck-up little queer, because she was too pathetic to find her own husband? It really went against every principle she had in life. It belittled her struggle, her success, her sacrifice, and her own self-esteem to pay Chas off for something this personal.

No, she decided firmly, she wouldn't do it. She'd rather be alone a while longer than be a sucker. Milly felt her strength coming back. Maybe she would take a vacation. She had time coming to her. Instead of spending it with the horses, maybe she'd go to a travel agent and plan a trip to try and meet other singles.

Maybe there was a hunting or fishing trip somewhere with all single men. That sounded like a better idea.

Milly picked up the phone to dial the travel agent's number when her assistant Amy Feinstein knocked on the door. Amy's father was part of the Wall Street Billionaire Boy's Club, but he made her go to work every day to learn to respect the dollar. Milly knew that Amy had attended the baby naming. As much as Milly believed in her rule—no gossip, nothing personal in the office—this was even too hard for her to resist.

"I have the account numbers you asked for yesterday, Ms. Harrington."

"Great Amy, thanks. Um, Amy, could you come in a second?" Milly asked in a softer than normal tone.

"Sure, Ms. H., what can I do for you?"

Milly was always refreshed by how unspoiled and eager to work Amy was in spite of her background. Maybe Milly could trust her, just a little. Amy was a sprite, elfin-like little creature with red, naturally curly hair and a happy freckled face, which gave her an innocent childlike appearance. *Surely this jolly little thing isn't capable of causing anyone harm*, Milly thought.

"Amy, I hope you don't think this sounds unprofessional, but what was the Cohen's event like?" Milly couldn't even bring herself to say "baby naming." It was too painful. She lived through it thirteen years ago, with the arrival of David and Judy's son. Now it had all come back to hit her in the face.

"Oh, you mean the baby naming? It was awesome. The service at temple was a little long—that rabbi takes a year and a day—but the party at the Harmonie Club was kick-ass."

Milly had never heard anyone describe the Harmonie Club as "kick-ass" before. It was an old, staid Jewish-only club that had been a New York institution almost forever.

"What was so kick-ass, Amy?" Milly asked trying to hide her sadness.

"The whole deal. The music, the flowers, the food, the fact they got everybody to postpone opening their Hampton homes just to be there. I mean, that's real friendship, don't you think, Ms. H?"

Milly agreed that in New York high Jewish society, waiting an extra week to open your summerhouse to attend a party was a real show of devotion.

"Was the baby, uh, cute?"

"All babies are cute, aren't they, Ms. H? I mean, the way they had her dressed up and everything. Sure she was cute. Uh...I think," Between her giggles, Amy noticed that Milly didn't even crack a smile. This seemed strange to Amy, who was talking gleefully about what was supposed to be a happy occasion.

Although Amy was all of twenty-one years old, she could sense something was very strange about her boss's line of questioning. Milly Harrington had never shown any interest in babies, parties, or anything of that nature. Even as young and naive as she was, Amy knew that something was off with Milly. Amy didn't exactly know what was upsetting Milly, but she got the feeling it was a lot deeper than just not being invited to a baby naming. Whatever was going on, Amy wanted to protect her boss, whom she looked up to as a big sister, from whatever was bothering her.

"You know what, Ms. H, can you keep a secret?"

"Sure, Amy, what is it?"

"Well, to tell you the truth, Ms. H, the baby wasn't cute at all."

"She wasn't?" Milly sounded surprised.

"Hell, no. Matter of fact, she was butt-ugly. She looked like Judy Cohen did before her four nose jobs."

Milly laughed out loud. She couldn't help herself.

"And you know what else, Ms. H?"

"No, what?" Milly laughed.

"The whole party sucked. It was nothing but a bunch of righteous snobs trying to outdo each other. The food was rank, the music was dead, the whole club smelled like a funeral home. I was bored shitless. Even my dad couldn't wait to leave. Really, you were lucky you weren't there."

"I guess you're right, Amy." Milly was still laughing at the young girl's audacity to speak so openly. Maybe she was just trying to cheer Milly up, but Milly didn't mind. Amy was doing a damn good job of it.

"You know what also, Ms. H? I bet if you ever decide to get married and have a baby, you'll find the hottest man in New York and have the most awesome children ever."

Milly stopped laughing. She tried hard to fight the tears that were coming to her eyes. She appreciated Amy's blind belief in her, but she had hit that place deep inside her that she hated to go.

"Thank you, Amy, that's very sweet."

"No problem, Ms. H, you're the coolest boss I've ever had. You're the only boss I've ever had, but I bet they don't come any better than you."

"Thanks again, Amy. I need to make some calls now."

"Okay, Ms. H, just buzz me if you need anything."

"I will, Amy."

And then Milly did what she always did best; she buried herself deep in her work.

At the end of the day, Milly needed to escape. The market had been particularly volatile that day, and that combined with the Cohen ordeal left Milly completely drained. While her cohorts at the office went to a gym, a sauna, or a happy hour somewhere, Milly needed to get outdoors. She hopped in her Range Rover and drove to a friend's polo barn, in Old Westbury, just forty-five minutes outside of the city. She wished that she could ride her own horses, but Sag Pond Stables was too long a drive.

It was a brilliantly beautiful day and Milly didn't want to let it go to waste. Spring had just begun to soften the Long Island's Gold Coast. The air was starting to smell fresh with the scent of blooming foliage that was just waking up from a winter's sleep. Everything was looking green, healthy, and new. This was such a contrast to the harsh, gray, dirty, urban downtown Manhattan. *Maybe I should move out of the city*, Milly thought as she drove east on the Long Island Express Way. Although evening was approaching, it was still light enough for Milly to enjoy a nice long ride. Up on a polo pony she galloped across the playing field with total abandonment. Her pain wiped away as the spring wind whipped across her face. She felt timeless, ageless, free from everything she knew in this world. Riding was one of the greatest releases she ever felt.

Milly then took the tired pony on a walk through the woods to cool him off. The tall, comforting oak trees provided a leafy haven from the heat of the late afternoon. She loved to feel the horse relax beneath her. Her whole life she had heard that riding was a very sexual sport. All the years in that saddle, and she hadn't had one orgasm yet. Maybe today was the day to experiment, she thought. She encouraged her horse to pick up the pace a little. He quickly moved into a brisk trot. Milly started the posting up-down movement, letting her female parts brush lightly against the front of the saddle. As she felt her clitoris start to get hard, she quickened the up-down movement. Her vagina became wetter and wetter with every post. As her movement got quicker, so did the horse's. The next thing she knew he had broken into a canter, as she began grinding herself into the saddle. The harder she pumped, the faster the horse moved, until he was in a full-out gallop once more. She was about to climax any minute. She took the reins in one hand and pulled on her nipple with the other. That was it. As the horse galloped forward, she came harder, faster, and wetter than she had ever come with any man. Except David.

Shit, I really don't need him anymore...do I? Milly laughed to herself, feeling very sexually satisfied. *I bet my horses are a lot less hassle then David's precocious kids, and much more appreciative of the love and attention I give them. Hell, who needs a husband...I've got it all!* Milly smiled and rode tall as she headed back towards the barn.

She wanted to be ashamed or embarrassed, but she had just had too much fun. She decided at that point she really didn't need men at all.

Feeling like a new woman, Milly opened the door to her apartment. Rusty was there to greet her with a wet, sloppy lick on the face. She was in a good mood to begin with, and the company of a faithful dog was all she needed for a restful evening.

Milly put on her favorite black and red L.L. Bean flannel pajamas and flopped on her bed. Rusty jumped on the bed also and curled up at her feet. As she reached for the TV remote on the nightstand, she noticed an envelope she hadn't seen earlier. On a yellow sticky pad was a note from the maid that read "Ms. Harrington, Mr. Greer left this for you. Be in late tomorrow. Esmeralda." Milly opened the envelope carelessly, thinking it was just another shopping bill.

Milly looked in the envelope and saw no bill. What she did see mortified her—a picture of the Cohen family with their new baby. On it was taped a message that said, "Get a life, Mills...he has. If you change your mind about Harry, call me. Chas."

That fucking bastard! Milly couldn't believe he would sink so low. Emotions began to overwhelm her. She would be absolutely outraged at Chas if she didn't have such an old ache in her stomach about David. It felt like someone had taken a sledgehammer and smashed her in the chest. Her hands trembled and she started to sob uncontrollably. Her riding experience, which seemed like perfect freedom earlier, now felt dirty, desperate, and deranged, as she looked at this seemingly loving couple and their children.

Milly got up and quickly headed for the bathroom. She thought she was going to be sick. Tripping over riding boots and nearly falling on her face, Milly just about made it to the sink. She turned on the faucet and obsessively splashed cold water on her face, but nothing could soothe the burning pain Milly felt in the pit of her stomach. Emotionally she was absolutely drained, and finally stumbled back into bed. If Milly had a bullet in any one of her guns, she could have offed herself right then and there. She always kept the bullets in her car in the glove compartment. She didn't know why she did this, but she never touched them until right before a shoot. Perhaps she knew a darker side of herself that frightened her.

Her big dog just looked at his distraught mistress, with his big droopy eyes, and wagged his tail. Somehow the animal knew there was nothing he could do. This was serious human stuff.

At that moment the phone rang. Milly was in such a state, she picked it up and screamed, "Hello!" *Please God,* she thought, *don't let it be someone from the office.*

"Hey, Mills." Chas's teasing voice infuriated her even more. As out of her head with sadness as she was, she was still tough enough to let him have a piece of her mind.

"What is wrong with you, you miserable little piece of shit, you butt-fucking, cock-sucking asshole faggot?! Why did you send me this, you whore?!"

Chas was thrilled by her tirade. This was exactly the reaction he wanted. He knew Milly well enough to know that every once in a while she'd blow her top, swear like a sailor, then get over it. She could call his mother a cock-sucking whore if she liked, as long as her checks cleared. And now he knew he had really gotten her. This morning he wasn't so sure. He knew by her confession that she still loved David, but now he knew it still tormented her to the bottom of her soul.

"Mills, honey, no need to get all excited. I was just making a point."

"Point, my ass! You are trying to make me feel like a desperate old maid so you can suck money out of me by getting me married to some loser from L.A. I know you, Chas. You may fool all those stupid idiot spoiled brats, but I see the conniving, worthless piece of no-good crap you really are."

"Well, obviously, you do feel like a desperate old maid because you're taking out all your years of frustration on dear Chas. That's not fair, Mills, but I forgive you. I really care about you. I feel your pain."

Milly was too knocked out now to fight anymore. She had had enough. Chas's patronizing only annoyed her further, but she was too spent, emotionally and physically, to scream anymore.

"Look, Chas, you really have crossed my boundaries this time. Maybe you did mean well...I highly doubt it. I'm not desperate, I'm not going to pay a million dollars to you or anyone to find me a husband. Good night."

Milly hung up the phone. She was absolutely drained. She soon fell into a deep, heavy sleep. In the night she dreamed that she was in David's beach house. It was the summer of her eighteenth birthday, and they were making love as they always did, under the stars. Then all of a sudden she felt a pull, a huge whoosh that forced her away from him. Her body was flying in space above him, but she couldn't reach him. She kept screaming his name over and over again. He could not hear her. As her body circled his house, she saw his wife and kids below her. They were with David now. No matter how loud she screamed, it was like she didn't exist at all. Finally her body hit the ground with a loud thud. It was like she landed on the moon. She was sitting alone in the dark, on a cold crater-like surface with no sign of life around her. Again she screamed, "David! David!" but there was no one around to hear her crying out. She was isolated on this planet all by herself. She was alone in the cold blackness.

Milly awoke to her own screams, scaring Rusty under the bed. She was sweating, shaking, hyperventilating, and couldn't calm herself down. For a moment, she thought she was really dying. Milly felt like a prisoner, trapped in a body she couldn't control. Finally, after a few minutes of what felt like hours of utter insanity, she was able to slowly relax.

Perhaps this violent release of everything that was pent up inside her was a good catharsis, she thought. Maybe she shouldn't try so hard to pretend she was happy and everything was okay. Milly held her head between her hands and gently massaged her temples. She needed to relax and begin to "think out of the box" now. Perhaps she should just lighten up a little and go with the flow.

Milly looked at the clock on her VCR. Three a.m. As she lay back down, she had a brief moment of clarity about the grand scheme of her life. She had worked hard. She had made money, a lot of money. More money than her parents had even before her father blew it all. What good was $10 million in the bank if it brought her no happiness? She had a Park Avenue roof over her head, a house in the Hamptons, and all the horses she could ride. It wasn't enough. Her soul was empty and David was gone forever. So what was she hanging on to all that cash for? If it could be used to get her what she really needed to fulfill herself, then why was that a bad thing?

She bought everything else, why not a real chance at total fulfillment? Besides, it wasn't like she was actually buying a husband. Harry had more money than God. She would just be paying Chas for his matchmaking services, like she paid her maid, her horse trainer, and her dog walker, all of whom delivered superb results. If she thought about it in those terms, it really didn't seem so mortifying anymore. It was even beginning to make sense. Her incredible loneliness, which came through loud and clear in her achy, shaky body and her dark dreams, had made its point.

Okay, she decided. *You win, Chas.*

Milly turned on the light by her bed and put the phone on her lap. Rusty had calmed down, too, and was now sitting faithfully right beside her, licking her arm. Milly took a deep breath.

Okay, just go for it.

She dialed Chas's number. It rang what seemed like a thousand times, but no one picked up. *Come on, before I chicken out*, she thought. *Pick up, Chas, pick up. It's 3:15 a.m. and you've just won the Lotto. Now get your faggot ass out of bed and answer the goddamn phone!*

The phone rang and rang, but no one answered. *Imagine, Chas is sleeping through a million-dollar call.* Milly chuckled to herself, ironically. Slowly, and regretfully, Milly was putting down the phone, when she heard a faint voice.

"Hello?" the voice said, half asleep.

Milly snapped back. "Ah, yes, sorry to call so late..."

"Eet's all right, bay-bee, what's going on?" The voice had a very sweet, young Spanish accent. It was Chas's lover, Juan.

"Juan, I'm so sorry to bother you guys, but I have to talk to Chas. It's really important," Milly said with determination.

"I'm so sure it's important, baby. It's 3:15 a.m. Ay, can't it wait a few more hours, baby? Chas is sleeping."

"No, I'm sorry, Juan. It really can't wait another minute," Milly persisted.

"Wow, baby, you must have something really heavy going down with your sweetheart. Was the matter, niña?"

Milly was getting frustrated. She knew that Juan meant well, but it was 3:15 a.m. for God's sake! She just wanted to cut the deal with Chas and get it over with.

"I really don't want to go into it now, Juan. I'm sorry, I appreciate your concern, but I really just need to talk to Chas."

"Okay, baby, but don't blame me if he gets nasty, honey. You know how he gets when he doesn't get his beauty sleep."

Milly sighed. "He won't be nasty this time, Juan. Please just put him on the phone."

"Okay, baby, here he is."

"Hello?" a groggy, smoky, harsh voice answered the phone. It was far from the Mr. Perfect Charming Chas he showed the world every day.

"Chas? It's Mills," Milly said, forcing the words out.

"What?" was all he could mumble.

"Chas, you got a deal." There, she had said it. It was over.

"What?" Chas probably thought he was dreaming. Milly couldn't believe he was going to make her say it again.

"You got a deal, Chas. A million dollars for Harry's hand in marriage. One million dollars."

Now Chas was starting to wake up. The mention of money was louder than any bugle blowing in his ear.

"Really?" He couldn't believe it. He thought for sure she wasn't going to budge. Normally, he wouldn't act so surprised, but it was too early in the morning for even Chas to fake it.

"Really, Chas. I've been thinking about it. I'm thirty-nine years old. I want a husband and children. All the guys on Wall Street that are considered my equals are either married, fucking models, or both. Who else is available but Harry Raider? Besides, I really could use some new blood."

Chas was sitting up. His polished, affected, obnoxiously saccharine voice had returned.

"You won't be sorry, Mills. This is the best thing you could possible do for yourself at this critical turning point in your life. Chas knows you, Milly. You'd make a perfect wife, mother, and playmate for Harry. You'll be so happy in California. You can ride outdoors all the time."

Milly laughed. She felt a big sense of relief. For once she felt in her heart that she was doing the right thing.

"Thanks, Chas. I really need this to work out."

"Me, too, Mills. It definitely will, honey. We'll chat this week about Harry's arrival, etc., etc. I'll give you all the details on how to begin."

"Great, thanks."

"I love you, Mills!" Chas just had to get that in.

"Thanks, Chas. I love you, too. Good night." Milly rolled over and went into a peaceful sleep.

Neither of them meant "I love you." They loved what they had promised each other and how they thought that would change each of their lives. That was enough for both of them. Chas hung up the phone and let out a big giddy giggle of total elation. He had done it! He now had two real possibilities to make some real money that would keep him in Hugo Boss shirts for life! Chas felt like the master of his universe. Juan had a hell of a morning.

chapter seven

The next morning, Chas treated himself to a private car to get to Penny's apartment on Park Avenue from his walk-up Christopher Street studio. This brought back memories of how all the chauffeur-driven limos and Rolls Royces used to line up in the circular driveway in front of Pine Valley. *It's nice to be the pampered passenger for a change*, Chas thought, *instead of the one opening the door*. One summer Chas was reduced to working as a Pine Valley car parker, and it was the one of the most demeaning experiences of his life. The rich kids would throw change at him and make snide comments under their breath like "Don't you just wish you could go cruisin' for ass in this, BUTT BOY" while dangling the keys to their new Porches in front of his face. *Never again*, Chas had promised himself. *Never again!* His mother Barbara, a Pine Valley hostess, chose to marry the gorgeous Swedish tennis pro Sven, for love and lust. So money was always tight. It was also hard for Chas to grow up working in the pro shop at Pine Valley, surrounded by all the fancy cars, diamond tennis bracelets, and five-thousand-dollar Prince tennis racquets. One day he vowed to himself *he'd* be the one screaming at the pro, while a waiter brought *him* a Tab onto the court.

Chas had successfully parlayed his good looks and suave demeanor into a whole career. But because of his frugal roots, he hated to spend his own money. Why should he? Most of his dinners, cars, vacations, and luxuries were paid for by his devoted patrons. But today was different. Today Chas felt like he was on his way to becoming a true member of the monied set he catered to oh so well. The two million dollars he hoped to collect—one million from Harry's future wife and one million from Sam and Irma as a mere token of gratitude—was not a huge fortune by today's inflated standard. However, two million dollars was enough for Chas to finally write his own ticket. No one could call him a leech or a mooch anymore. Not that he minded so much. Money was always more important than respect. But, he was getting tired of kissing and bowing to princesses. It would be nice to finally stand in his own glass slippers.

The car dropped Chas off in front of Penny's building at Park and 63rd Street. Chas didn't play games with the doorman here because Penny's mother was on the board. Chas figured if he ever wanted to buy an apartment here himself, he didn't want to be seen as a troublemaker. Once the concierge announced his arrival, he walked through the lobby, quickly and quietly, not drawing attention to himself in any way.

Penny's apartment was a huge marbled, mirrored spread—a cross between the Sistine Chapel and Versailles. She even had a marbled waterfall, with the golden boy statue peeing into it. Of course Chas had made her buy it. He loved it.

Penny was in her gym room working out with Bobby Torento from Guy Stone Fitness. Bobby was a good-looking

Irish-Italian twenty-five-year-old stud from Jersey City. Chas got him the clients. As usual, Bobby and Chas had a deal. They split the profits. Bobby worked them out and kept them happy. Very happy. Penny was Bobby's mercy fuck. So was Chas, before Juan, but that was very hush-hush. Even though their relationship had ended, they parted amicably enough to keep their business agreement. Besides, Bobby really preferred girls. This was fine for Chas. It made them both some nice deals.

Red-faced in a black Polo sport shorts outfit, Penny looked like she was going to drop dead as she huffed and puffed on the treadmill. Chas smiled and clapped his hands limply with little genuine enthusiasm.

"That's my girl, Penn, keep up the good work. Your hubby will be here in no time."

Penny made a face and snarled at him. She was hating every minute of her grueling workout. She had a fifty-thousand-dollar custom gym from the Gym Source set up in her apartment, and she had only used it twice.

"I hate this. I think I'm going to die!"

Penny grabbed the handlebars for support and looked like she was about to quit. Bobby knew right before a client was about to give up was when he had to turn on his raw animalistic charm.

"You'll be the hottest-looking dead chick on Park Avenue. Now, keep on moving babycakes, you're almost at the finish line."

As "Guido" as he was, Bobby was irresistibly sexy in his tight Speedo shorts and tank top. Even after his lust-filled morning with Juan, Chas started to get a hard-on.

"Listen to him, Penny. Bobby really knows his stuff. I introduced him to Madonna last week. He's changing her life."

"Fuck Madonna, I can't breathe," Penny panted.

"Alright sweetie," Bobby said, "five minute cooldown then you can hit the shower."

Bobby decreased the speed on the treadmill and, after five minutes, Penny began to look like a human being again. Just as Penny was getting off the treadmill, there was a minor fracas ensuing at the front door. It sounded like someone was fumbling with keys, or even worse, about to break the door down. All of a sudden everyone heard a frustrated scream.

"Will someone open this FUCKING door. My damn key doesn't work AGAIN! Can I get some help here? PUH-LEASE!" Penny's maid Maria ran to the door and opened it immediately. Tripping over her Manolo Blahnik high heels, and just barely able to stand up, entered Penny's sister Bunny, still wearing her black Donna Karan dress from the night before. Bunny looked like she had been snorting, smoking, fucking, and boozing for at least twenty-four hours. As Bobby was wiping the sweat from Penny's brow, Bunny irreverently lit up a cigarette. "You gotta do something about that door, Penn...It's such a draaaaagggg...grrrrrrrlfriend."

"Put that out!" Penny screamed. "Can't you see I just finished working out?"

"Sorry, sis. Excuse me," Bunny said flippantly. "Just wanted to see if I could borrow your Cartier bracelet. I'm going to a luncheon at the Four Seasons and all my good jewelry is in the vault."

"Deal with it, kiddo." Penny was pissed off at Bunny, just for being Bunny. And how dare she light up while Penny was trying so hard to get in shape?

"God, sis, you're such a bummer. No wonder nobody invites you anywhere."

"Fuck you." Penny took a pitcher of ice water with lemon from the counter and poured it on Bunny. Bunny shrieked as the cold water shocked her already frazzled system.

"You're a raving lunatic. You know, you really ought to have Dr. Schwartz put you back on Klonopin!" Bunny screamed. With one lunge, she swung out and slapped Penny across the face. Penny in turn grabbed her hair. A real catfight had begun. Bobby had to restrain Penny.

"Easy, easy, babe. Relax, come on, it ain't worth it."

Bobby's strong arms around her settled Penny like a bad, angry child. Bunny was still swinging. Chas waited a long minute before he got in the middle. He actually enjoyed the action. It was so amusing.

"Alright, alright, Bun, that's enough." Chas grabbed Bunny and started to towel her off, practically holding her down.

"Maria, bring her the sweats!" Chas yelled.

Within a flash, Maria scurried in with the green Banana Republic sweatsuit Bunny always wore after she and Penny fought.

"Now, Bun, why don't you go change?" Chas could be so diplomatic when he had to. "Then back to your apartment and let your sister relax a little after her workout."

"Besides," Chas whispered in Bunny's ear, "maybe she'll be in a better mood after Bobby shtups her brains out." His knowledge of the appropriate Yiddish slang words like "shtup" always made him a big hit, and somehow made him appear as if he knew what he was talking about. Bunny laughed, threw her hands up in the air, and stormed out.

Penny calmed down and began to regain her composure. She was checking herself out in the mirrored wall to see if Bunny's outrage had left a mark on her face.

"Penny, you really shouldn't let Bunny get to you like that. It's not worth your energy. Besides, soon enough you and Harry will be the toasts of both coasts."

"Who's Harry?" Bobby asked, a little confused.

"Harry is Penny's future husband," Chas answered defiantly.

"Hey, Penn, I thought I was your main man," Bobby said, only half-joking. Secretly he wished Penny or one of his other rich, single women clients would marry him and keep him as a boy toy. Of course, Bobby knew that wasn't a real possibility. If these girls were going to get married, it had to be to someone in their own financial league or better. Who one married was the ultimate sign of success or failure for these sky-high society women. As sexy as Bobby was, he knew he would probably have to survive on perks, just like Chas. Unlike Chas, he knew he didn't have the consuming ambition it would take to be "one of them."

"Sorry, Bobby, Penny is already spoken for," Chas declared.

"Yeah, is that true, Penn? Hey, congratulations!" Bobby patted her on the back.

"It's not exactly true yet, Bobby," Penny said.

"But it will be very, very soon," Chas interrupted. He wanted Bobby to clearly understand that he was to remain in his position.

"Well, whoever he is Penn, he sure is a lucky guy." Bobby kissed her on the cheek, grabbed his gym bag, and started to make his way out.

"Leaving so soon, Bobby?" Chas cooed. "I thought maybe you and Penn were going to relax a little together. I just stopped by to say hi. I hope I didn't put a damper on your morning." Chas said, with his usual devil-may-care look in his eye.

Bobby winked seductively at Penny. "I would like to stay, but Penn said she had other plans. Maybe tomorrow."

Penny was blushing. Only Bobby made her feel alive, attractive, and wanted. She could hardly resist him, but if she was going to marry Harry, she thought she had better learn to control herself, in more ways than one.

"I'll see you out," Chas said. He loved to walk behind Bobby and watch his cute, muscular butt. Just as Bobby was almost out the door, Chas very furtively pinched Bobby's right cheek. Bobby just turned around, winked, and smiled. Like Penny, he craved attention wherever he could get it.

With Bobby gone, Chas walked back to Penny's bedroom, a gold-lamé-tented, silky paradise that resembled the Taj Mahal. Next to the bed lay a hundred-thousand-dollar blue and white Oriental rug that Bernard had brought back from one of his trips to the Far East. Hanging from the ceiling was a multi-layered crystal chandelier that swerved into a shape that resembled a dollar sign. On the walls were collages of Penny at camp, at graduation from NYU, and at various debutante parties in New York, Vienna, Washington, and Palm Beach. Displayed prominently on the space behind her bed was a giant picture of Penny shaking Prince Charles's hand when she was just fourteen. Next to it hung a framed letter from the Prince's private office. Penny and Bunny had both met Prince Charles when they accompanied their parents to a charity event for the Prince's Trust in London. It was a magical "fairy tale" time Penny would never forget. She kept this special picture of His Royal Highness hanging over her bed, in hopes that one day her very own prince would come.

Chas almost fainted when he saw a very unwanted surprise. Penny was lying face down on a massage table, and working the aches and pains out of Penny's back was Jena Prior, Chas's archrival. Jena was a naturally gorgeous, earthy Irish-Spring type, with long flowing red hair, milky white skin, and big green eyes. To Chas, she was about the only person in New York who was able to infiltrate the lives of the rich and codependent without his okay. The women were not even intimidated by her natural beauty because she was such a sweet, pure soul. Jena took her work as a massage therapist and holistic healer very seriously. She was the love child of two Woodstock hippies who taught her about auras, chakras, meditation, and the world of spirituality from an early age. Now twenty-nine, Jena had a very calming effect on her clients, and they all sooner or later spilled their guts to her. Jena knew more secrets about these women, more than anyone in New York, even Chas. Because her intention was so pure, people really trusted her and took her into their deepest confidence.

This made Chas crazy. He couldn't control Jena and sensed he couldn't get rid of her. All the nasty rumors he had started had backfired in his face. Everyone always came to Jena's defense. Chas sometime felt like he was the wicked witch of Park Avenue, and Jena was the good fairy.

Yet, it wasn't that Jena was a complete saint either. Although she had strong ethics and morals, she was very much intrigued by the lives of the women she looked after. Penny had many times given Jena her old clothing that she had gotten too chubby to wear. Once Penny found Jena waltzing around the living room in an Oscar de La Renta gown she had just given her. Jena was a modern-day Cinderella, only she had no evil stepsisters. The rich girls actually got a kick out of Jena's naiveté and often indulged her in a game of dress-up, jewels and all. Amazingly enough, no one, not even Penny, felt threatened by her. Jena loved to play pretend and never really imagined that she would be any more than a loyal, cherished servant. She hadn't yet tried to be anything more.

There was another reason, a very real reason, Jena was Chas's greatest fear. If Jena somehow got around Harry, Chas was afraid she'd put him under her spell like she had everyone else. She was young, stunningly beautiful, and had a captivating look in her eyes that enraptured people. Chas worried that Harry would find her totally irresistible, take her back to L.A., and that would be the end of the deal. Chas wished he could try and warn Penny about Jena, but that too was sure to explode in his face. Penny had to believe that Harry was now only interested in a rich, Jewish girl from his own background. If Penny thought for one minute that Harry would consider a shiksa goddess like Jena, she would lose all confidence and bow out of the game. Chas could not afford to let that happen. Somehow he had to get rid of Jena, without looking like the bad guy. This was not going to be easy.

"Jena, so lovely to see you. I didn't know that you were still working here." Chas faked his best smile.

"Of course I'm still working here. I wouldn't leave my Penny, we're soul sisters."

Jena gently gave Penny a sisterly hug, and Penny at last started to relax. Penny really needed this comforting female bonding, because of her horrific relationship with her own sister, and her empty relationship with her mother. Chas tried not to look frustrated as Penny obviously enjoyed Jena's soft attention.

"So dear, summer's finally here...bet you'll be spending lots of time soaking up the sun on Coney Island. You still live somewhere out in Brooklyn don't you?" Chas said in an attempt to make Jena feel like an unwanted outsider.

"Yes, I still live in Brooklyn," Jena said smiling sweetly, not letting Chas play her even for a second. "But I've rented out my apartment for the summer, so I'm afraid I won't be seeing much of Coney Island," Jena continued, in an unassuming, nonchalant tone.

"Oooooh, what's the matter, Jena? Strapped for cash are we? Let me guess, you have to shack up with one of your waiter boyfriends and sublease your digs, because you can't pay your monthly...poor dear!" Chas scolded, thinking he was embarrassing Jena to death in front of Penny.

Then Penny dropped the bomb. "Actually, I'm moving Jena out to South Hampton with me for the summer. She's going to be my right-hand lady. I told her she should sublease her apartment out. Indefinitely! She can stay with me as long as she likes. I enjoy the company."

The two girls giggled like two sorority sisters. Chas couldn't contain himself anymore. He was about to hit the ceiling. Chas bit his lower lip, crossed his legs, and squirmed like a two-year-old who just dirtied up his diapers.

"Oh, great. Penn, could I have a little word with you *en privé.*"

"Not now Chas. Duh. Go to the kitchen; have Maria make you something to eat. I'll be done in another hour or so."

"It can't wait, Penn! Besides, I'm late for a really important meeting downtown. Can't you just give me five minutes and finish your massage later? Jena will wait, won't you?"

Jena smiled and looked Chas directly in the eye. She was good as he was in a much subtler, more effective way.

"Go ahead, Penn," Jena said, "You know I'll be here all day."

Chas cringed. He was never allowed to stay more than a couple hours.

Penny got up from the table, still in just a towel. She walked with Chas down the long marbled corridor, being careful not to slip.

"What is so urgent, Chas?"

"Well Penny, it's just...well, I don't want to seem like the bad guy, but..."

"But what?" Penny demanded.

"Well, I know you've sort of adopted Jena as your little charity case, and I think that's very sweet, but...I don't think she's going to be so great to have around all summer."

"Why not?" Penny asked curiously.

"Well..." Chas knew he had to be really careful. One wrong move and it was all over.

"Well, Penn, Harry might think it's weird."

Penny laughed, as she playfully opened her towel, flashed her naked body in front of Chas, and did a little teasing dance. "What, like he'd think she's my girlfriend? He'd think I was a lesbian just because I had a girl around to help me out this summer? That's crazy."

"Not so, Penn. Remember, Harry's from L.A.," Chas said quickly and turned around not to subject himself to anymore of Penny's nudity. "A lot of strange shit goes on out there. He may think the reason you haven't gotten married is because you're a closet case. It's not cool, Penn," Chas said, grabbing Penny's towel and securing it back on her.

"Oh, bullshit. Besides, most hetero guys get really turned on by lesbians, Chas. I'm sure Harry could have a nice little fantasy about me and Jena."

Penny loved sarcasm. She couldn't take this seriously at all.

"He's looking for a nice wife, Penn. Not another kinky deal. If he suspects one thing, forget it."

"Well, once he gets to know me again, he'll see I'm about as interested in women sexually as you are. Besides, I'm sure he'll adore little Jena as much as I do," Penny said blowing a kiss in the direction of her bedroom.

Chas lowered his eyes to the floor. He tried not to give himself away, but it was too difficult. Penny picked up on his avoidance right away.

"Chas, are you afraid that Harry is going to like Jena better than me?" Penny said, in an accusatory tone, putting her hands on her hips.

"I didn't say that Penny, you did." Chas got defensive and once again looked her straight in the eye.

"Look Chas, if what you said is true about Harry wanting his equal, then we have no problem. I mean, Jena is a sweet girl but she's like a flower child. If Harry wants a flower child, a model, or anything else than what you promised me he wants, then I better not even go near him. I really can't handle anymore unnecessary rejection. I've had enough," she said, turning around and heading back towards her bedroom.

"I know, I know, Penn. I certainly was not insinuating that Harry would even look at a silly little creature like Jena. That's 100 percent not at all what he wants. I just want to be absolutely sure that everything goes as smoothly and as effortlessly as possible. That's all," Chas said grabbing her shoulder and stopping her in her tracks.

"Effortlessly as possible for who? You or me? You're going to be paid dearly for your efforts," Penny said, practically pouncing on top of poor Chas.

"And you're going to get a super husband, Penny, so I guess the answer applies to both of us," Chas said, slowly pulling back. "Just remember what I'm saying right now. The trick is to keep it simple. The fewer distractions, the fewer complications, the fewer diversions, the fewer obstacles in your way. Why not just make an easy, natural situation even easier by keeping out strangers?"

Penny harshly crossed her arms and stomped her feet in defiance. This is how all his girls behaved when they wanted to let you know they were going to be "right" under any circumstances. Chas referred to this action as the Yentah Stomp. He had seen it a million times. "Jena's not a stranger," Penny continued. "She's my best friend. I don't think she would do anything to hurt me. She's not that kind of a person. Some things mean more to her than money."

Penny pulled out a hundred-dollar bill from her Gucci purse on the table and pretended to rip it into pieces, which of course, she would never really do. After all, she did agree to pay Chas a million dollars upon her marriage to Harry Raider, but that didn't mean she had to like it.

Miss Penny can keep sticking it up my ass all day if she likes. I don't mind being the highest paid pimp in town. Besides, with two million dollars in my pocket, I can tell Penny or anyone else to drop dead if I want. They'll see! Chas thought to himself. But he would never do so. There was always more and more money to be made off the Pennys of the world. Chas would take their kvetching, moaning, and complaining with a smile and wink, keeping his mind on the green.

"Oh, Penn, I'm hurt, I thought I was your best friend," Chas teased. "If I didn't care about you so much I would turn Harry on to one of the Broman girls. I honestly think you and Harry are a perfect fit, so let's just stick to our plan and by the end of the summer I'll be calling Robert Isabel to do your wedding."

Penny smiled. She never let herself think seriously about actually having a wedding. But when it's going to happen, she will damn well enjoy every last little detail of it, from obsessing about the place cards to trying all the different wedding cakes. Penny's good buddy Vera Wang had promised to design a wedding gown especially for her. It would be an exclusive just for the special day. Oh, if it would ever come.

"I gotta go Penn, I'm going to be late." Chas kissed Penny on both cheeks. "I'm doing Ivanka Trump's summer wardrobe. She's such a cutie."

Chas picked up the latest issue of Vogue off of the coffee table and showed Penny a picture of the young Trumpette wearing an outfit he put together for her. Chas was always "doing" someone fabulous. This was another reason he irked Penny. She was not his biggest shining star. That would change as soon as she became Mrs. Raider. Then he'd be asking her to take him to the Paris haute couture shows. Justice would soon come, Penny thought.

"See ya later, Chas. Don't let her mommy give you any of that old fake jewelry left over from QVC. Hold out for a real tiara."

Penny had quite a biting sense of humor when she wanted to. It was often her savior. While people were looking at her sister, she could amuse them with her wit. She'd trade her wit for Bunny's body any day, but that would never happen.

Chas took a deep breath on the elevator ride down to the lobby. He knew he could only push Penny so far about Jena. He just came so close to blowing it. Somehow there had to be a way to neatly dispose of Jena without Penny getting crazy. Chas had to figure out a way to keep Jena from getting between him and the big money. How he despised that little snit for honing in on his action! He'd teach her a lesson someday, put her in her place. But for now he knew the most important thing was to keep Jena Prior far away from Harry. It was not going to be as easy as he once thought. However, with a little luck, he could somehow control everyone's destiny, including his own.

chapter eight

The Friday before Memorial Day was warmer than usual. A balmy breeze filled the ocean air as The Queen Irma II, the second of the Raiders' private Gulfstream jets, landed at East Hampton airport. Jerry Ackerman, a little old bald man in a blue LaCoste sweater and bright green golf pants, stood waiting with his daughter Jessica and his son-in-law Freddy. As a disheveled Sam and Irma Raider disembarked their aircraft, Jerry wobbled over to greet his old friend with a welcoming hug. He tried not to notice how tired and worn out the elderly couple looked.

"Sammy, bubalah! Great to see you again. It's been too long."

"It certainly has, Jerry. This is really kind of you. I'll never forget what you're willing to do for my son." Sam almost had a tear in his eye. He hated to be indebted to anyone. "This is the only hope for my kid. Meer Hashem, I hope it works," Sam said.

"I consider Harry the son I never had, Sammy. I'm thrilled to have him here," Jerry replied.

Sam chuckled ironically. "Jerry, you haven't seen Harry in a while. He's more than the handful you remember. I really hope this works out. It's his last chance."

"Now don't you worry about a thing. Jessica and Freddy will see to it that Harry has a great time here this summer."

"Not too great a time, I hope," Irma said wearily. Her meek, shaky voice sounded like she had been through supreme misery. Jerry had never seen her look so exhausted. Today, Irma's face looked more peaked and gaunt than his wife's did on her deathbed, Jerry thought. Irma stood on the tarmac, perfectly clad in an elegantly comfortable charcoal gray Donna Karan jumpsuit. Louis Lacardi's latest "do" crowned her little round head. All the Beverly Hills designer packaging, even the ten-karat Joailler diamond earrings couldn't mask her aura of personal devastation. To look in Irma's tired eyes was to see her soul sinking into hell.

"Irma, you're a doll," Jerry said, giving her a warm and gentle, but much needed hug. "You look stunning as ever. I mean it, your son is in good hands with my kids. You'll straighten him out, won't you guys?"

"Of course, Dad," Freddy chimed in. As Irma looked at Freddy's balding head, round glasses, hunched shoulders, and unfixed nose, she thought she was looking at Jerry thirty years prior. The resemblance was scary.

"Look, Mrs. Raider, I'm sure Harry just had a few wild oats to sow before he really settles down. Before I met Jessica, I had quite a reputation as a playboy on Wall Street."

Jessica turned away so she didn't have to look her nerdy husband in the face. She maybe did love Freddy, but his fantasy about being a big-time player annoyed her. Sure, Freddy was very successful as an analyst on Wall Street in his own right before he married Jessica, but socially he was always considered a big flop. His earnestness endeared him to Jessica; his self-delusion really pissed her off. She desperately hoped that Freddy wouldn't try to show off in front of Harry. Harry was there to be low-key and, she hoped, recover and maybe even start a new chapter in his life. Jessica prayed that Freddy would stick to the program of rehabilitating Harry instead of trying to show off how well he had done for himself.

"Anyway, Mrs. Raider, once I met my lovely wife, I completely changed. You couldn't meet a happier guy, and I'm sure Harry will turn out to be the same. Right, Dad?" Freddy said enthusiastically.

"You bet, Freddy, We're going to see to it. Just leave Harry to Uncle Jerry."

Jessica pulled on her curly hair and looked down at the ground trying to hide her embarrassment at her husband's behavior. Jessica also hated it when Freddy acted like such an ass-kisser around her father. For once she wished Freddy would express an opinion that wasn't also her father's. She wondered if he even had one anymore. If he did, she hadn't heard it since they got married.

"Harry is really a very sweet boy, you know," Irma said with a mother's love. "He just got involved with the wrong crowd. Underneath it all, he really is a good boy."

Just then Irma's "good boy" came walking down the stairs of the aircraft. He was dressed in a Hawaiian shirt, short nylon gym shorts, flip-flops on his feet and a bandanna tied around his head. He couldn't look more un-Hamptons if he tried. In one hand he was carrying a huge boom-box radio playing Snoop Dogg loud enough to be heard back in L.A. In the other he had his newest acquisition, a Nikon Coolpix 8800, the camera of the moment. He stopped midway down the stairs, pointed the camera at everyone, and began snapping away. He then gave the camera to a tarmac worker and quickly showed him how to use it. Harry put down his boom box and ran over to Sam, Jerry, Irma, Freddy, and Jessica. Before even saying "hello" he jumped in the middle of them. "OK, just hit the button. RIGHT NOW! Smile everyone, say SHIT!!!" Harry shouted enthusiastically with his arms around Freddy, who looked like he was about to pass out from the absolute weirdness and audacity of his new summer guest.

Jessica couldn't control her giggles, and totally enjoyed seeing her tightly wound husband getting knocked off his stride by this fascinating stranger. She gave Harry's mismatched outfit the once over and her smile grew even bigger. Harry's whole "wild and crazy" out-of-control persona was absolutely hysterical to Jessica, who was used to everybody being so serious about maintaining a too cool "Hampton" image.

Once again, Harry signaled the tarmac worker to take another group shot. "Let's see another smile, you guys!" Harry screamed. Jessica was still smiling and so was Jerry, who one could tell was immediately enjoying the idea of having a real "son" for the summer. And of course, because Jerry seemed happy, Freddy faked his biggest grin. This was Freddy's way of letting Jerry know that he was game for whatever was expected of him, even if he found "Harry the Hollywood Freak Show" to be absolutely repulsive.

After a few seconds of snapping away, Harry ran over to the car. An attendant carried his bags behind him. It was surprisingly not a large amount of baggage for a three-month stay.

"Harry, you remember Mr. Ackerman," Sam said sternly, trying to pull his son back in line. He wanted to remind Harry why he was here

"It's Uncle Jerry, please." Jerry held out his hand to Harry.

"Hi ya, Jer." Harry put down his boom box and tried to high-five Jerry. Jerry awkwardly tried to go along with it.

"And you remember Jessica and Freddy. You were at their wedding at the Pierre."

"Great fucking party, man. Jessica, you looked soooo hot that night. Definitely babe-a-licious!"

Freddy politely nodded and stammered an uncomfortable, "Mmmm Hmmm." But Jessica laughed with utter delight, entertained by this Bel Aire boy with the Valley lingo. This summer could be fun.

He has every financial reason to be a pretentious asshole, yet he's nothing like the typical stuffy wannabe Hampton crowd I've been running from all of my life. Amazing! Jessica thought to herself. *If I'm damn lucky some of Harry's carefree joie de vivre might rub off on boring Freddy. Maybe Freddy will finally stop acting like a trained seal in front of dad and learn to have fun again. Wouldn't it be great if Harry could help lighten Freddy up and help him relax? Then, please God, I could get my old husband back. Oh boy...Harry help us!* Jessica dreamed. Perhaps this would be a two-way street. They would rehabilitate Harry, and Harry would breathe life into their stale, albeit young, marriage.

Sam put his arm around Harry and took him aside, as the bags and the people were being loaded into the Rolls. "Now look, son. Remember what I told you. This is your last chance to straighten up. Your mom and I love you very much, but we aren't going to put up with any more shit. One fuck up Harry, and you're out—for good. Got it?" Sam said in a powerful voice, pointing his finger in the direction of a scruffy-looking man emptying out the large garbage pail outside the private airport. He wanted to illustrate the point to his son that without daddy's money, this is exactly what Harry could expect to be doing in the near future.

"Yes, Daddy," Harry said, hugging his father and jumping up to kiss him on both cheeks.

Sam put his arms around his son. "Good, now have a great summer. If you need anything, Jerry will take care of it. For once in your life, bring us some nachus. Behave! For gezunterate!"

Harry hugged his dad. Part of him was scared shitless. He hated letting his father down, but he just didn't know if he could ever live up to his parents' expectations. There were always so many temptations out there. It was almost impossible to behave. Until now, he had gotten away with being the renegade, the good-time party boy. Harry knew those wild times were coming to an end. Damn it, he just didn't want to grow up. But somehow, right now, he knew he had to.

"Sam," Jerry said, "are you sure I can't talk you and Irma into spending a night or two with us before you fly off to Europe? It's a long trip, you know. I've got some beautiful gefilte fish in the refrigerator."

"No thanks, Jerry. Irma and I already ate. We're going to sleep on the plane. Just had a new bedroom put in. We're anxious to get going."

Sam winked at Jerry. The old friends laughed. Jerry knew this was supposed to be Sam and Irma's "save the marriage" get-away. They had traveled extensively around the world in their private jets, the Queen Irma I and II. Every time Harry would do something crazy, Sam would whisk Irma away to avoid the public humiliation Harry caused them. This trip for Sam and Irma was more crucial than the others. They had to rekindle their lost passion, otherwise forty-three years of marriage would be over. Everything was just too much.

The plane had been refueled and was ready to jet across the Atlantic. Harry watched as his parents' plane took off to fly them to a far-away place where he couldn't screw up their lives. He felt like a kid at camp, alone for the first time. Harry had really never left L.A., except to go to the family villa in Acapulco, or to Las Vegas where everyone knew him. This was the first time he was ever without his mom and dad close to him. They even went to Hawaii with him and his now ex-wife on the honeymoon.

In the Hamptons, Harry Raider was a stranger. He stood for a second, hesitant to get into the Rolls. He looked in the car and saw Jessica's soft green eyes smiling at him. She slowly held out her hand and motioned gently for him to come sit next to her. It was very foreign to Harry, but Jessica had a soothing, big-sister-like affect on him. Harry felt somehow everything was going to be all right. He hopped into the car next to Jessica and closed the door. The chauffeur quickly pulled away from the airport.

The Rolls rambled down the leafy green Hampton lanes past the palatial beachfront estates. Harry began to feel more relaxed as he breathed in the clean, fresh, salty air. Having been raised in the L.A. smog, Harry wasn't accustomed to the pure, crisp smell of the Atlantic. He opened the window all the way and stuck his head out. Taking in a big breath of the fresh ocean air, Harry's troubled mind began to quiet. As the salty wind swept across his moistened face, he gently closed his eyes and relaxed into the simple pleasure of enjoying the cleansing sea breeze.

chapter nine

Milly drove her big, dapple-gray mare Zara over a course of jumps at Sag Pond Farms. Zara once qualified Milly for the United States Olympic Equestrian Team. The affinity between horse and rider was so intense that Chas couldn't bring himself to interrupt the ride. He sat on the mounting block dressed in a hunter green Hugo Boss shirt, white Ralph Lauren linen pants and Gucci loafers, quietly waiting for Milly to come back toward the barn. At the end of the ride, Milly dropped the reins, lay down on the horse's neck, and gave her a big hug as the mare walked slowly to cool off. *So much love wasted on an animal*, Chas thought. It was beyond his comprehension why someone would pour so much money into a facility for horses. *How come these ungodly monsters are living in spacious multimillion-dollar stalls that seem twice the size of my studio apartment? Why can these beasts graze for days in meticulously manicured green fields, when I have to work my ass off pounding the pavement of Park Ave just to make a living? Why won't one of these crazy billionaires adopt and spoil me instead of wasting a fortune on stupid animal?* Chas thought to himself.

"Life just isn't fair! So I might as well play the game and get what I can, before they put me out to pasture," Chas muttered as he ran over to greet Milly, wearing a smile as fake as his bottled tan.

Milly, wearing a pink pastel polo shirt, Miller's jodhpurs, and brown paddock boots, looked as she always looked after a ride—refreshed, relaxed, and rejuvenated. She dismounted her trusty mare and walked with the animal toward the barn. She could easily have given the horse to one of the awaiting grooms, but she enjoyed washing, brushing, cooling, and caring for the horse herself. It was her ultimate form of relaxation.

Chas walked cautiously, tiptoeing up to Milly, trying to avoid stepping in any hidden piles of manure. Much to his dismay, he wound up putting his foot in it twice. If that weren't bad enough, Chas almost slipped and fell in a wet mud slick he didn't notice. Milly was surprised to see Chas at the barn. She knew he absolutely hated horses, as much as he tried to cover up that fact when in her presence. It completely amused Milly to watch Chas suffer in silence while trying to remain elegantly clean in such a dusty and dirty environment. When Chas finally caught up with Milly, he looked like he had just walked through a minefield. Keeping his composure, he gave her an air kiss on both cheeks. Chas didn't know what grossed him out more, the sweat dripping down Milly's face or the smell of horse droppings. He was actually scared to death of horses. Galloping across a polo field, far away from a tailgate picnic, he could deal with them, but being this close to one gave him the creeps. They were so big and dirty, it almost made him sick.

"Mills, I just love this horse. I've never seen her in better form." Chas knew complimenting Milly's horse was always the way to her heart. It was like her child.

"Yeah, she's been staying in shape. I have a trainer ride her all week when I'm not here. This year will be her last Hampton Classic."

The Hampton Classic was one of the top horse shows in the country. Every year the top competitors on the show jumping circuit came to ride at the serious equestrian event. It was also one of the summer's most prestigious social events—the close of the Hamptons season. Every Labor Day weekend, Calvin Klein and his estranged wife Kelly, Joan Lunden, Paul Newman, Christie Brinkley, and a myriad of other stars and moguls could be seen mingling under the members only marquis. As a child, Milly would run around the Classic watching the little rich girls ride their fancy braided ponies. Her heart always sank to the floor as she watched child after child take home the blue ribbons she wished she had a chance to win. When she finally started to make money, she bought Zara and pounded everybody in the jumping classes.

"Her last classic! Oh, Mills, how monumental!" Chas squealed, pretending to be interested in the horrid beast. "Are you putting her out to pasture?"

Milly hated that expression—"out to pasture." It just made Zara so inhuman. Milly gave Chas a dirty look.

"No, I'm not sticking her in a pasture somewhere Chas, after she has given me the best ten years of her life. I'm going to breed her next spring. We're going to have a baby."

Milly beamed with delight. She truly loved her horse. In fact, until this matchmaking scene arose with Harry, she figured that was the closest she'd ever get to being a mother.

"How prophetic," Chas smiled. He could tell Milly was blushing, even though her face was still red from the riding workout. She had untacked Zara and had begun to wash her down with a long hose.

"When is he coming?" Milly asked as she began to scrub the horse with a soapy sponge.

"He's heeere!" Chas said teasingly.

"Oh, yeah? Really? Wow." Milly almost squirted herself in the face with the hose instead of washing down the mare. She was not emotionally prepared to hear that immediate answer. As much as she wanted this, it scared the hell out of her. What if he rejected her the way David did? What if it didn't work out? What if he just plain didn't like her? Milly picked up a pail of soap and water and began heavily scrubbing her horse with a sponge. She was channeling all of her energy into the activity at hand. She did not want to let on how insecure she really felt about this whole thing.

"What do you mean 'wow'? I told you he was coming Memorial Day weekend. I told you to get ready. Remember, we're going to take him fishing Monday," Chas said, quickly shooing the annoying horse flies away from his face.

"Of course I remember, Chas. It just seemed to come around so soon, that's all," Milly hesitated as she knelt down, picked up Zara's front hoof and rested it on her knee. With her back turned to Chas, Milly began vigorously cleaning out the mud, rocks, and stones with a metal hoof pick.

"Soon? Baby, we made our arrangement over a month ago. I thought you'd be excited, preparing for the big day," Chas continued, swatting some more relentless flies that seemed determined to nest on top of his head. The sweet, pungent smell of his Bumble and Bumble hair gel must have been a big draw to these nasty creatures.

"I am excited. I'm just..." Milly's face went blank as she finished one hoof and immediately started on another one

"Nervous? Apprehensive? Scared shitless, Milly?" Chas said, grabbing a can of Easy Off bug spray from a groom who was passing by, and frantically spritzing his space.

"Well, actually Chas...all of the above. I mean, I just don't know if this is a good idea. I really don't think I'm what he wants," Milly practically whispered, now grooming Zara's tail, and carefully braiding it.

"How do you know what he wants? You haven't even met him yet Milly," Chas replied, shaking the can of Easy Off at Milly.

"I don't know. I just get the feeling that..."

Chas cut her off. "That what? He's not going to like you because you're not a bimbo or a JAP? Knock it off, Mills, we've been through this a million times. You are exactly what he wants. For the last time—get it—Harry is not David!" Surprisingly enough, Chas slapped Zara on the ass to accentuate his point. The big horse barely moved or responded, since a slap from Chas was the equivalent of a light tickle.

Milly began to back down and this time purposely sprayed herself to cool off. She realized as much as Chas did that her fears were getting the best of her.

"You're right. Harry's not David. He sounds really terrific from what you tell me. I guess I'm just going to have to relax and trust your judgment," Milly said between gulps as she drank water right out of the hose. She loved to watch Chas cringe with disgust.

As shrewd as she was on Wall Street, Milly's loneliness and desperation clouded her senses in her personal life. She knew damn well never to trust Chas Greer to do more than pick out a dinner suit, but she figured at this point she really didn't have anything else to lose. *I can't be any more alone than I am right now*, Milly thought to herself, lovingly stroking Zara's dappled neck. *I mean, who really cares if this doesn't work; no one will know. If Harry hates me, I'll just get up, go back to work the next day, and pretend like the whole thing never happened. Then it will be back to being just me, Zara, and*

Rusty. I'll be no better, but no worse off either, Milly's rational mind told her as she fed Zara some melting sugar cubes from the pocket of her jodhpurs.

"He is terrific, Mills. You'll see what a natural fit you guys are. It will be like you two knew each other your whole lives. Do you have the boat ready and everything?" Chas said now backing away from the horse.

Milly smiled. She had a beautiful forty-foot Formula fishing boat with all the latest equipment. She bought it last summer when the market was doing wonders.

"Yes. The boat was put into the water last weekend. I took it out this morning. It was a beautiful sunrise."

"Oy, Milly. I hope you don't expect to get up at the crack of dawn to go fishing. I thought we'd go out around twelve or one o'clock. You know, bring a picnic lunch, maybe a little non-alcoholic bubbly. Harry doesn't drink," Chas said posing firmly and playing with his belt loops.

"Good, because we're there to fish, not to get loaded. Twelve or one is really too late. We should go out really just before sunrise if we want to catch anything good," Milly said, pulling off her wet Polo shirt. Standing before Chas in a bikini top-like sports bra, she revealed her toned, tanned, perfectly muscular body, as she put on something clean and dry.

"Damn, you look great, Mills. This has got to work!" Chas said, admiring Milly's athletic physique. "The only thing I'm interested in you catching, girlfriend, is Harry. You're going to have to learn to modify your schedule a little, Mills. Harry loves fishing, but remember...he is here to enjoy it and relax. You can't expect me to drag him out of bed at 4:00 a.m. and expect him to be ready to meet his future wife. Let's just take it nice, easy, and comfortable for everybody."

Milly laughed. "I thought you said he was a *real* sportsman."

"Well, he was as a kid, and he wants to be again. That doesn't mean he's ready to be in the goddamn navy!"

"Okay, Chas, I got it. Harry will have a great time, don't worry. If he doesn't catch anything, no big deal. I'll get some smoked salmon on board. I'm sure he won't know the difference."

They both chuckled. Chas was relieved she was back in the game. Chas kept up with Milly as she walked Zara up and down the graveled driveway before letting her go back into the barn.

"Now you're talking, kiddo," Chas said, putting his arm around Milly's shoulder.

"You know Chas, I was thinking. If Harry is already here, why do we have to wait until Monday? Why can't you bring him over my house for a casual barbeque Sunday night, or even cocktails?"

This was the question Chas was hoping to avoid. Sunday night was Harry's "Welcome to the Hamptons" barbeque at Jessica's. Chas managed to get Penny an invitation, so Milly was definitely not invited. Besides, Milly was still only Chas's Plan B. Penny had to have the first shot at Harry. Penny was Jewish, an old friend of Harry's family, and the most likely candidate. Milly was only to be substituted if Penny's weight started to yo-yo, or Harry just wasn't interested. First things first.

"Oh, I'm afraid Sunday night just won't work, Mills. Good idea, though. Harry will have to take a rain check."

Milly looked at Chas suspiciously. *What could Harry be doing that could be so important it would hold off my initial meeting? One would think Chas would want to get Harry to me as soon as possible. The sooner it starts to happen, the sooner Chas could start counting the money,* Milly thought.

"What's going on Sunday night that I'm missing, Chas?"

"Nothing, don't be silly. The Ackermans are making this stupid little dinner for Harry. You know, to make him feel at home. It's just the family."

"Let me guess...you are the only one who isn't 'family' that's invited, right?" Milly asked, straightforward.

"Oh, Mills, please. You know why I am going...I grew up with Harry in L.A. They only invited me so he'd have a familiar face around, that's all. You have to remember, this is all very new to him. If it's not done right, the Hamptons could be a big shock to his system. Remember, everyone knows Harry in L.A. He's as famous there as any movie star. Here, he's a total stranger."

"If Jessica Ackerman wasn't already married, I'd be damn nervous. But if that's the only rich Jewish girl that's going to be there, I guess I'm still safe."

"The only other JAP will be Joyce Ackerman, Jerry's sixty-year-old spinster sister. I don't think you have to worry about her."

"No, I just hope I don't wind up *like* her."

"You won't after this summer. Enjoy the Hamptons now, Mills. Next year Zara can deliver her foal in the Polo Lounge at the Beverly Hills Hotel. You'll be the fresh princess of Bel Aire."

"Okay, okay, see ya Monday. Now get lost. Your Guccis are drowning."

Chas looked down at his new Gucci loafers. They were sinking in the mud. At this point, he was absolutely revolted and his moment of pretending to be "Equine Friendly" had definitely run its course. "Oh my GOD. Not my Gucci cucchi coos!" Chas lamented as the $600 worth of the designer Italian leather on his feet were now just about totally ruined. "I am so *outta here*!" He blew her a kiss and tippy-toed as fast as he could back to his '86 BMW—"The Beemer." He carefully put his muddy shoes in a plastic bag, making sure not to get his hands dirty. Thank the Lord he had a spare pair of Guccis in the trunk. He had a very busy day ahead of him.

chapter ten

Chas drove down the long pebbled driveway that led to Penny and Bunny's stark white, modern beach house in Bridgehampton. He so loved the feeling of importance he got approaching his girls' estates. One day soon a driveway like this one could be his own. Maria, Penny's maid, also transplanted to the Hamptons for the summer, opened the door. She had on white linen shorts and a Juicy Couture T-shirt. Penny allowed her to dress down for the beach. Chas had advised her that was the hip thing to do.

"Hello Maria, sweetheart. Don't you look a-doooor-a-belle? I told Señorita Penny to let you be 'casz' this summer."

"Si, Señor Chas. Thank you very much. Come in please. Penny is just picking out her outfits for tomorrow tonight."

"Great, thank God I arrived just in time." The two dutiful servants exchanged giggles.

Chas then heard a familiar voice from the top of the stairs. Bunny was hanging over the railing in a skimpy Betsy Johnson shorts outfit, eating some kind of a sloppy submarine sandwich and dripping sauce on the floor. There was something very unnerving and unnatural about a sandwich looking bigger than the person eating it. Chas lived by the credo, "You can never be too rich or too thin," but in Bunny's case it was scary, not chic. "Hi BunBun!"

"Hey, jazzy Chassy! What's shakin', baby?" Bunny appeared to be a little tipsy or totally stoned. She usually was both. "Come up and give me a big huggy-wuggy."

Chas did as he was told. He bounced up the stairs and threw his arms around the skeleton called Bunny. She reeked of champagne and Italian dressing. He did his best not to make a face. Up close he could see the yellow-brown blotches between her teeth—damage from all the vomiting. Chas definitely thought Bunny looked more attractive at an arm's length, but he was one of the only men alive who thought so.

"Chas, come to my room and see what I've packed for England."

"England? I thought you weren't going to Europe till the Red Cross Ball in Monaco in August."

"Sheik Mohammed said he wouldn't take me to the Red Cross Ball unless I sat with him in the royal enclosure at Ascot. He's got five horses running. He even named his new one after me. It's a red mare named Bunny's Run. Isn't that sweet of him?"

This change was a pleasant surprise for Chas. Chas wondered how he would keep Bunny away from Harry, but that had now seemed to take care of itself.

"Very sweet, Bunny. You're a lucky girl."

"Are you kidding? He's lucky I'm still with him. Prince Albert still wants me to be his date for the ball, but last year he bored me to tears. He's gotten so serious now that he's over forty."

Chas smiled. "I hate when that happens to people, Bunny. Don't you?"

"Absolutely. I'm not schlepping all the way over there to have a drag. You know what I mean, Chassy?"

Chas went through Bunny's outfits as she finished her sandwich and washed it down with a bottle of Bollinger. He was pleased to discover all her clothes matched his suggestions. The pink Chanel suit, the Ungaro silks, the daring Versace black strapless, and of course, her green pillbox Ascot hat by Eric Javitz. As he picked up a pair of Jimmy Choo shoes and began to admire them, he noticed something stuffed in the toe. Nonchalantly he pulled out a bag of cocaine.

"Bunny, you really shouldn't travel with this shit. If you get busted, they'll throw your ass in jail, no questions asked. Can't the sheik have some waiting for you?"

Just then, Penny walked into her sister's room. All she saw was Chas holding a spiked heel in one hand and a bag of coke in the other. Her face turned red. As much as she despised her sister, she also feared for her life. Penny glared directly at Chas and instinctively knocked the drugs out of his hand. "Did you bring her that?" Penny demanded.

"No way, Penny. I swear it. Look, I may be a lot of things, but drug dealer I'm not. I won't even let Juan bring it home."

"Bullshit, Chas!" Penny screamed, as she picked the bag of coke off of the floor and shook it right under his nose.

"Calm down, Penn. I swear, you get so crazy. I didn't get it from Chas, okay. I got it from the guy at the pizza parlor. You know. The guy who deals in the back room. It's okay," Bunny said.

Penny was furious as she walked over to the window and gazed out at the deep blue sea, trying to harness her fury. She didn't know what to believe with Bunny.

"No, it's *not* okay, Bunny. It's not okay to get on a plane with some camel jockey carrying grams of blow stuffed in a shoe! When are you going to stop acting like such an irresponsible little brat and get a life?" Penny said, as she turned and looked at her pathetic mess of a sister, who was sprawled out, "spread eagle" on the big bed, now just wearing high heels and a thong.

"I have a life. You're the one who's a fat pig and stays home all the time!" Bunny screamed as she sat upright and threw a shoe in Penny's direction.

"Fuck you, bitch! You know what, I don't give a shit if you *do* get busted. I'd call the cops myself if it wouldn't kill Mom." Penny picked up another stiletto from Fredrick's of Hollywood and threw it out the window.

"You're just jealous as usual, Penny. You lard-ass!" said an infuriated Bunny, whose whole body was shaking as she hollered and hurled a Versace pillow at Penny.

"Well, I may be a lard-ass, but you are nothing but a cheap whore who services Arab cock. He probably has a million like you all over the world," Penny said in a humiliating tone, as she put the pillow between her legs and pretended to hump it.

"Girls, please! Give each other a break," Chas interjected trying not to laugh at Penny's theatrics.

"Fuck you!" Bunny screamed as she popped off of the bed ran into the bathroom and locked the door. Within seconds, the sickening sounds of Bunny throwing up came from behind the bathroom door. Chas shook in disgust. Penny seemed stoically quiet. She was used to it by now.

"Come on Chas, let's get out of here."

Chas followed Penny into her part of the sprawling estate. The long corridor that separated the two sisters and their two very different lives seemed endless. It was a large whitewashed wooden space, with gorgeous views of the Atlantic from the sliding glass doors that led out to a covered balcony they both shared. As she walked in front of him, Chas noticed that Penny had indeed lost some weight and was looking much better. The usual bloated puffiness around her face was going down.

"You look good, Penn. You got a lot to go, but it's working," Chas said, playfully pinching her butt.

"I'm down about nine pounds. Jena's been helping me."

Chas cringed. "What does Jena have to do with your weight loss? You have the best diet doctor in town," Chas snickered.

"Yes, but Jena is teaching me about mind-over-matter meditation and guided imagery. She's helping me to visualize myself thin," Penny ran her hands down her body and pulled in her waist, as she closed her eyes and took in a big breath.

"Oh, you don't really believe in any of that garbage, do you?"

Penny shot Chas a look of death. "I said it's helping me. It's very motivating." She opened the large white door at the end of the hallway that led to her private suite.

"Motivating?" Chas laughed. "You're being set up with the richest man in Bel Aire, who you adored as a child. What other motivation do you need?" Chas said, slamming the door shut behind him.

"You just don't get it, Chas, do you? Jena is helping me heal my pain, so I don't stuff it down with food," Penny replied, as she grabbed the gold railing and began to climb her private, winding staircase.

"A twenty-nine-year-old flower child is doing what a battery of psychiatrists can't. Right! If I didn't know better I'd think something was going on between you two," Chas half-teased, doing a few jazz steps and watching himself in the wall of mirrors, as he sashayed up the stairs behind her.

They finally reached Penny's bedroom, a pleasant, airy, yellow and blue, happily decorated space. Her bed was adorned by the usual monogrammed Pratesi sheets. And in front of the mirror stood Jena Prior, wearing a flowing, white silk Ungaro sundress. She looked breathtaking.

"Will this be all right for Jessica's barbeque, Chas?" Jena said, shooting daggers at Chas. Chas curled his lip and crossed his legs tightly, looking like he had just peed in his Polos. No way in hell could she show up at that barbeque looking like the angel in white. Chas was so nervous he almost started sweating, which flustered him even more. Except during sex, sweat was definitely a no-no with Chas. "What do you mean, Jessica's barbeque? You're not invited, Jena," Chas shot back, batting his eyelashes at the sweet, innocent one.

"Penny asked me to go with her. I don't have to go if Penny doesn't want me to. It's up to her," Jena said, in her usual even, unbothered tone of voice.

Jena casually shrugged her shoulders and smiled sweetly at Penny. Chas was dying a slow, torturous death.

"Penny, I don't think it's appropriate to bring another guest," Chas interjected. "Jessica has only planned this for a certain amount of people," Chas said, slowly uncrossing his legs and purposely slowing down his speech, imitating Jena's ultra-relaxed style. He knew he had to keep his cool.

"I called Jessica; she said it was fine," Penny said, rolling her eyes at Chas.

"You called Jessica? You barely know her. I'm the one who set this up. You should have called me. I would have taken care of it!" Chas screamed at Penny, holding his head in his hands and now having a complete hissy fit.

Chas hated when anyone made a social move without him. Especially when there was money involved.

"I'm sure you would have," Penny said sarcastically. "But I took the liberty of calling Jessica myself. Sorry, but don't worry, we still have a deal," Penny said crossing her arm and staring powerfully at Chas.

"This isn't about the deal, Penn. Jessica is very private. She doesn't like outsiders coming in," he said, pointing his ring finger right at Jena.

"You underestimate Jessica, Chas. She's really a lovely girl. I told her I didn't know many people, and I'd feel more comfortable if I came with a friend. She had no problem with it. Neither should you," Penny said, walking into her bathroom, and leaving the door open as she changed into a towel.

"You are there for one purpose only, let's remember Penny. That is to get reacquainted with Harry. Another person will just be in the way," Chas said, covering his eyes.

"I won't be in the way, Penny," Jena said setting up the massage table with new sheets and spraying the area around it with some kind of "aura cleansing" herbal concoction. "I promise, the minute you feel comfortable with Harry, I'll disappear."

Chas absolutely could not stand her good intentions. He didn't buy it for one minute and he couldn't understand how Penny could. *What is wrong with Penny that she needs this little girl around to hold her hand?* Chas thought to himself. Penny's depending on Jena was a big interference.

"I don't like this at all, Penny. We are supposed to keep it simple, remember?" Chas exclaimed as Penny lay down and got comfortable on to the massage table.

"Look, Chas, to be honest, I'm a little scared, okay? I admit it. Big tough Penny's a little intimidated by this whole thing. I'd feel better if I had a friend to talk to in case Harry ignores me," Penny said as she crawled between the satin sheets and hid under them.

"He won't ignore you, Penn, if you're by yourself!" Chas pleaded pulling the sheets away from her face.

"Chas, Jena's coming with me. That's it," Penny said, sitting up and grabbing the sheets out of Chas's hands

Jena smiled softly. By doing nothing, Jena always got everything done. Chas had to work so hard. It just wasn't fair.

"Suit yourself, Penny! I'll see you tomorrow night."

Chas stormed out. Even he could only take so much. Penny hopped off of the table and ran after him.

"Aren't you going to tell me what to wear?"

Chas stopped and turned half way down the winding staircase. Thank God she still needed him.

"The long black Eileen Fisher, with the white Donna Karan sweater tied around your shoulders...and the new Arche sandals, of course. I can safely assume Kevin Maple is doing your hair?"

"He is."

Penny and Chas smiled at each other. They always had an unspoken understanding.

chapter eleven

The tables in Jessica's garden were decorated patriotically with red, white, and blue tablecloths and an American flag in the middle of each centerpiece. Jessica was frantically inspecting each table. Although she didn't care so much about "the Hamptons scene," when she had a party at her home, it had to be perfect. Freddy watched with disdainful impatience as his wife busily rearranged napkin holders.

"Do you think everything looks all right?" Jessica asked, looking up at Freddy and seeking his reassuring, "Yes, dear." Tonight was just one of those nights that Freddy was having trouble biting the bullet. Every once in a while, Jessica's petty obsessions over things that he considered excessive bothered him. Freddy knew what he was getting when he became "Mr. Jessica," but sometimes the way she put so much importance on minor things got to him.

Freddy had known real struggle in his life. He came from a working-class family in New Jersey and, like Milly, bussed tables to put himself through Harvard. Although he had achieved success in Wall Street and pulled off the social coup of the century by making this marriage, he often felt at a loss on the sidelines. Is this what he had worked so hard for? Crooked napkin holders?

Freddy knew an even deeper pain. As a teenager he lost his sister Beth to anorexia. It was the early eighties and she wanted so badly to be a model. That was her way out of Newark, New Jersey. But Freddy's sister's anorexia got out of control and she died of a heart attack in her agent's office at the age of sixteen.

Freddy still hurt from the loss. So when Jessica would stress out about the color of the tablecloths, the place card settings, or the arrangement of the salads on the buffet, it drove Freddy insane. Yet he never voiced what he felt aloud. He'd usually just give her the cold shoulder and a mean glare. Tonight was different.

"Jessica, I don't know what you're worried about. You've paid a fortune to hire the best caterer in the Hamptons. You flew in that goddamn barbeque sauce from Texas. B. Smith came over an hour ago and said everything was perfect, and you're still out here playing with the silverware. What's wrong with you? Are you paranoid or something?"

Jessica had a hard time with criticism. With all her money, she was still an insecure girl who, on many levels, desperately wanted her father's and her husband's approval.

"I'm not paranoid, Freddy. I just want everything to be right." Jessica's voice was slightly trembling, as she began switching around the place cards on one of the tables.

"Everything's been right for hours! Do you really think people are going to care if the salad fork is on the wrong side? Sometimes I wish you'd just get real, Jessica," Freddy said, taking the place card out of her hand and firmly putting it back in its original spot.

"I am real, Freddy. I take great pride in my home. It's important to me that people feel comfortable when they come here," Jessica replied in a small voice, as she once again picked up the same place card and returned it to its new position. Tears were welling up in Jessica's green eyes. Why wouldn't he understand she just wanted to be a good hostess and please people?

"Being comfortable has nothing to do with table settings, Jessica. Being comfortable means being able to relax and enjoy without getting crazy over little things that don't add up to anything," Freddy said, impatiently shaking his head in disgust and storming away from the table.

"I'm doing my best, Freddy. I just want a nice evening." Jessica was crying and running after him. She wished her father would come down from his suite and make Freddy be nice. But Daddy was dressing now, and he didn't really like to interfere with Jessica and Freddy.

"Wow, this place looks outrageous!" a happy voice said from out of the blue.

Freddy turned around and Jessica managed to look up from her tears. Harry Raider stood on the balcony outside his room. His eyes lit up in utter delight as he looked down at the garden perfectly decorated with the patriotically themed tables, two stocked bars, an overloaded, gourmet barbeque buffet, and flowers in full bloom. Harry loved the pre-party excitement. He got a kick out of watching the decorators and caterers set up for the night's festivities. He had been watching them all afternoon. After showering and dressing, he now got to see the end result of the big setup. To Harry, it was like foreplay.

Harry stood on the balcony with a special zoom lens on his camera, trying to capture the whole thing from an aerial view.

"Hey Jessica, I'm going to take before, during, and after shots. They'll be awesome!"

Harry's enthusiasm made Jessica crack a smile. At least someone appreciated her efforts.

"Harry, we've hired a photographer for the evening. Don't feel like you have to do anything but have a good time," Freddy said with a smile.

Idiotic Harry is starting to bug the crap out of me. He's childish, immature, and totally out of touch with any concept of reality. Harry belongs on his own planet, and I can't wait for the day he goes back to L.A., Freddy thought to himself as he scratched his balding head. *Okay, this loser is Jerry Ackerman's charity case for the summer. Can't let that get screwed up. I better plaster that bullshit smile back onto my face.* Freddy's mind raced, as he forced his lips apart to make himself look cheerful.

"I will have a good time Freddy, my man. I love to take pop shots when people least expect it. Smile. You're on *Candid Camera*!"

Harry pointed the camera right at Freddy and began clicking away. Freddy tried to smile, even though he was boiling under his collar. Jessica was now laughing hysterically.

"That's it Freddy, work it baby! You're a natural, you're a star!" Harry loved to tease Freddy.

Freddy is such an East Coast stuffed suit. I wonder who he would have married if poor Jessica didn't have any money? I can't believe she puts up with this guy; he's dead weight, Harry thought to himself, making funny faces and fart noises as he snapped away. As crazy and reckless as Harry was most of his life, his basic nature was very perceptive. Harry was a wild man with a big heart. He sensed that Jessica needed some comic relief and he was going to make sure she got it.

Harry walked to the other end of the balcony that jutted out over the pool. Candles were floating in the water, surrounded by gardenia petals. Harry fiddled with some of the buttons on his camera and repositioned it on the balcony's ledge.

"Hey, Jes, watch this!"

Harry stripped down to his underwear, climbed up on the tall balcony and, grabbing his legs to chest, did a cannon-ball leap into the air. Freddy and Jessica both froze in total disbelief. What was really just five seconds of Harry in flight seemed like an eternity to the shell-shocked couple. *What if this nut job breaks his neck? I bet that somehow I'll get blamed for it, because I wasn't watching him close enough. That little bastard!* Freddy thought as he watched Harry in total horror.

I hope he's going to be okay. Sometimes I wish Freddy would jump off of the Empire State Building. That would make a great picture for Harry to get on film, Jessica was thinking as Harry landed safely in the pool. Automatically the camera went off, snapping two pictures. Harry bobbed up and down exuberantly, putting out half the candles and drowning the flowers.

"Pretty cool, huh? Wait till you see these shots—they'll be killer!"

Jessica and Freddy watched in utter amazement as Harry swam around the pool, ruining a five-thousand-dollar pool display to grab a few cheap snapshots. Freddy couldn't believe his audacity. Jessica couldn't believe it either. But what Jessica really couldn't believe was that Harry had just destroyed her pool setting and somehow she didn't feel upset. She was really quite amused.

"B. Smith would call the police and have him locked up," Freddy snickered quietly to his wife, who he thought was now on his side.

"Fuck B. Smith," Jessica said irreverently and walked into the house to go get dressed.

The party was in full swing when Penny, looking tan and somewhat thinner in her long black tunic, and Jena, looking like an angel, finally arrived. The latest Hamptons' gossip was passed around like hot hors d'oeuvres as Jessica's guests impatiently waited at the bar for drinks and picked at the Thai-themed goodies that the waiters passed around on red, white, and blue trays, with napkins and toothpicks to match. As she moved through the "oh-so-stunning" crowd, Penny was starting to feel an anxiety attack coming on. This was her big moment. She had spent all week preparing for it. Now that it was here, she wished she could just crawl under a rock or just become invisible. Maybe if she passed out right there they would take her away in an ambulance and she wouldn't have to deal with this right now. Just as she began to hyperventilate, Chas came rushing over to her and grabbed her hand.

"There you are! We've been waiting for you all night! What took you so long, Penn?"

"Nothing. I mean, it's very chic to arrive later, make a grand entrance."

Penny could barely speak, which was not like her at all. Chas knew he had to calm her down before making the big intro. He pretended like Jena wasn't even there.

"Did you say hello to Jessica?"

"No, not yet. We literally just got here."

"Well, come on then. She's by the bar. Besides, I think you could use a drink."

Chas pulled Penny through the small crowd of forty or so well-toned, tanned bodies in white linen. Between the silicone breasts, feline-shaped sky-high cheekbones, razor-sharp pointy noses, and unnaturally smooth foreheads, the guest list for this party looked like it was provided by the casting director from the television show *Extreme Makeover*.

Although Beverly Hills was considered the nation's capital of cosmetic enhancement, the Hamptons were definitely a close contender eagerly vying for the illustrious title. Not unlike the fabled subjects of Dr. Frankenstein's laboratory, a typical Hamptons crowd was made up of human guinea pigs who were always considered a work-in-progress.

These "Body Nazi" party patrons were also very socially sophisticated. They were not just a group of empty talking heads. Discussions of the latest fashion trends, hot spas to visit, and Wall Street quotes filled the air. In the Hamptons, the one thing that was worse than looking outdated was not keeping up with the hippest lifestyle trends and business news. Penny and Chas purposely ignored the munching and mingling mannequins and muses who were at the Ackerman house to fete the day. They went over to the bar where Jessica was drinking some kind of fruit punch and talking to Billy Joel.

Jena followed Penny. As she crossed the garden, she noticed everyone was staring at her. In the long white silk dress with her red hair flowing down her back, she looked nothing less than a goddess. Even though she had worked privately as a massage therapist to some of New York's most rich and famous, this was the first time she was actually a guest at a party. The gorgeous estate, the beautiful people, the elaborate decorations, and the smell of wonderful food almost created a sensory overload for this babe in the woods. She was truly Cinderella.

Jena was very aware of the effect she had on men. Many times some of the older men she worked for hit on her, but she turned them all down. But now there was all this talk about this Harry person, the billionaire from L.A. He was to be Penny's Prince Charming, but he could be hers too. He could give her the life she only dreamed about. He could make her a princess, like Penny. But even though he sounded totally enticing, Jena thought, she just couldn't bring herself to steal him away. She just couldn't shake her belief in karma, her "peace, love, and happiness" upbringing. Nor could she knowingly cause harm to the woman who had taken her under her wing.

"Jessica, you know Penny."

Chas had no qualms about interrupting Billy Joel. His mission had gotten off to a late start, and he needed to make up time.

"Thanks so much for coming. And this must be Jena."

"Hi, thanks for letting me come, Jessica," Jena said.

"Oh my pleasure, please make yourself at home."

Jena smiled. She wished so much that this was her home.

"Jena, why don't you ask Billy for his autograph. Penny and I have work to do," Chas said snidely.

Chas grabbed Penny again, and quickly led her away. Jena was left standing face to face with Billy Joel. She felt highly embarrassed and intimidated by Chas's comments, until she noticed the Piano Man winking at her invitingly. Perhaps her good karma was already beginning to take effect.

Penny felt her panic rise again as Chas searched for Harry. The moment of truth had come! It would be either instant attraction or immediate rejection. She had a feeling there would be no middle ground with Harry. He wasn't a let's-get-to-know-each-other type of guy. She had worked her ass off in the gym and she hadn't seen a piece of bread, a kernel of corn, a flake of potato, or a piece of pasta in four long weeks. She even paid off the waiters at Cipriani not to let her order her favorite risotto again. She had toed the mark and now it was time to see if her efforts would pay off.

Harry stood by the barbeque pits helping the chefs turn the ribs. Jerry Ackerman was practically stationed at the bar, making sure Harry didn't get near it, perhaps overcautiously. Harry really didn't like liquor too much anyway.

Cocaine and hallucinogenic drugs were his thing. He had been totally straight for the few days he was in the Hamptons. It was just a few days, but it was a start.

The other guests had tried to make polite conversation with Harry, but Harry wasn't interested in anything anyone there had to say. He knew nothing about Wall Street, real estate, or investments. His father thought that once he got straight, maybe he would start to show some interest in starting a career. But for the past thirty-eight years, Harry was allowed to remain a child, so this wasn't easy.

All the party guests wanted to hobnob with the billionaire boy, just to say they knew him. But unless they were willing to talk about cameras, Nintendo, or the latest Jim Carey flick, Harry couldn't relate to anybody there. He had the most fun wearing the big white apron, which was now full of food stains, and pretending he was the help. He loved the game.

"There he is!" Chas squealed with excitement as he waved to Harry. Harry waved back with a glazing brush in one hand that splattered barbeque sauce everywhere. Penny immediately jumped back to avoid getting totally splattered. Harry was just as Penny remembered. Frizzy hair, not too tall, not too handsome, but that devilish, childlike smile put her racked soul right at ease. There really was nothing to be so freaked out about. It was just Harry. He hadn't changed since he was sixteen years old. Penny felt a wave of relief. She could almost breathe now.

"Hey, it's Penny Marks. Oh my God, I don't believe it!" Harry came running over to Penny and gave her a big hug. He forgot to take off the cooking apron first, so he got sauce all over her black silk Eileen Fisher dress. Penny didn't even mind. She was overwhelmed with joy at Harry's warm greeting. Maybe, finally, her dream could come true.

"It's been so long, Penny, how the hell are ya? You look great!"

Penny couldn't believe the words that were coming out of Harry's mouth. Did he really mean she looked great? Had all the starvation actually been worth it? At that moment she couldn't even remember what risotto tasted like. Before she knew it, she was reaching out to give Harry a hearty bear hug.

"Oh my word. Penny!" Chas gasped, about to come in his khakis. He was the only one more excited than Penny at Harry's initial reaction to his old friend. Oh, if Harry could only stay this interested in Penny, the money would be his in no time. It just had to happen.

"I'll disappear while you guys get reacquainted. I'm sure you have a lot of catching up to do. Harry, why don't you take off that apron and have something to eat with Penny?"

Chas was always orchestrating. Before they could move he had two plates filled with ribs, chicken, and a variety of side salads. He handed Penny and Harry a plate each and pulled over two empty chairs so the two could be away from everyone else. Chas was beyond subtlety; he was going for results.

"Have fun, guys!"

In a flash Chas was gone, leaving Penny holding a plate of hot food that looked unbelievable. For the first time, her interest in a man took precedence over what was in front of her. She sat down slowly, placing the plate on her lap. Harry was already digging into his. She watched him wolf down his meal with sheer delight. He was so real and unaffected. This is exactly what she thought she wanted. "I was so excited to hear that you were coming to the Hamptons," Penny said enthusiastically.

"Really? Who told you I was coming?" Harry asked curiously, taking a healthy bite out of a big sloppy rib.

"Uh, Chas happened to mention it. Only because he knew that we were old friends, and he thought we could all have some fun together this summer," Penny said, nervously twirling her fork around some coleslaw. She had no cause for concern, but Penny was slightly paranoid that somehow Harry would find out about her mission of marriage.

"I'm not allowed to have *real* fun this summer," Harry laughed, as he offered an ear of corn to Penny. She politely replied, "No thanks, I'm getting full," even though she had not eaten a thing.

"There are different kinds of fun, Harry. Hang out with us, and I promise you, this summer won't be a total drag," Penny said, boldly winking at Harry.

"Sounds like a plan, Miss Marks," Harry answered flirtatiously. A sparkling smile seemed to take over Penny's whole being.

After Harry scarfed down everything on his plate, he and Penny began to reminisce about the fun times they shared growing up.

"I still have that radical picture of you at Trader Vic's, babe," Harry told her.

"Yeah, the one with the pineapples. I have it framed in my bedroom," Penny said.

"Cool!" Harry smiled and made some sort of acknowledging surfer-dude gesture with his hand.

Penny was done picking at her food, which was of no interest to her.

"Hey, if you're done chowing, you wanna try my new Nikon?"

"Sure," Penny said, dumping her plate on the nearest table. Like a veteran location scout, Penny began searching the area, looking to discover the most flattering place to strike a pose. *Hmmm, let's see...I don't need to worry about lighting because it's dark out and he has a flash. If I turn sideways and stand next to something long and tall like a tree, it will cut me in half, and I'll look so skinny!* Penny thought to herself, getting comfortable and doing her best *Vogue*-like stance, next to a towering oak.

Just as Penny was visualizing herself standing in a wedding dress on the cover of *Town & Country* magazine, Harry ran up to her and handed her his camera.

"Hey, Penn, what are you doing over there? Come closer to the buffet table so we can get some awesome shots of me with the boys," Harry said, as he put his arms around the caterers and posed several times by the barbeque pit. "Okay Penny, hit it!" Harry yelled with a "say cheese" grin stamped on his lips.

Not wanting to look disappointed or flustered, a bewildered Penny Marks began snapping away, dutifully.

"That's really happenin', Penn. You're getting killer shots, babe. Keep shooting. Let 'er rip!" Harry seemed impressed that Penny enjoyed the camera as much as he did.

Penny didn't know if he was genuinely intrigued with her. Possibly he was just paying so much attention to her because she was the only one he really knew besides Chas. She really didn't care either way. Penny was having the time of her life. Nothing, she thought, could ruin this sparkling time.

Harry asked a waiter to take a picture of him and Penny. He carefully set up the camera so that all the waiter would have to do was point and push a button. Harry put both arms around Penny's shoulders and held her close. She was beaming.

As the flash was going off, Penny thought she saw a stick figure coming towards them. Her sight still blurry from the flash, all of a sudden her worst nightmare came to life.

"Harry, darling, remember me, it's BunBun! How are you?"

Bunny slowly sauntered up to Harry. She playfully tickled the exposed hair on his chest before she seductively placed her arms around his neck, one after the other. In a chic European manner, she elegantly kissed him on both cheeks, as he stood there, totally mesmerized by her presence. Chas nearly fainted when he saw Bunny appear out of nowhere. He immediately ran over to Penny's rescue.

"Hey Bunny, looking like a hot mama as always, kiddo," Harry said. Penny's heart was slowly crumbling.

"Bunny, what a wonderful surprise to see you! I thought you were on a plane to England," Chas gushed, taking her hand and sending her in a slow-motion ballerina-type spin, so she'd end up facing away from Harry.

"The plane got held up. Some mechanical screwup. I'm on my way to East Hampton airport right now. Just thought I'd drop in and say hello to my old buddy Harry before I took off," Bunny purred, turning back around to Harry, and looking him up and down with an easy eye.

"Glad you did, Bunny," Harry said, practically wagging his tongue like a golden retriever and salivating at the sight of sin personified. "Penny and I were just talking about how long it's been since we've all been together." Harry couldn't help himself from staring greedily at Bunny and feeling something in his shorts starting to come alive.

Penny was so angry she was about to explode. Her face was turning a bright shade of fire-engine red. Penny dug her perfectly shaped nails into her sweaty hands that she kept behind her back, so she wouldn't subconsciously reach out and strangle Bunny. Just then a party guest walked by Penny carrying a mountain of food. It took all the self-constraint Penny had not to grab the man's dinner, pull Bunny away from Harry by the scuff of her neck, and rub her face in the pile of gravied-up mashed potatoes. As pissed off as she was, Penny knew it would be social suicide to make a scene, especially in front of Harry.

Harry hadn't even mentioned Bunny until now. *How could my selfish sister just barge in and spoil the night of my life? Bunny was supposedly on a plane—to be the guest of an Arab sheik, no less. Why does she have to rain on my parade? Why couldn't she just once think of someone besides herself?* Penny thought to herself and had seriously wonderful visions of the sheik's plane blowing up somewhere over the Atlantic ocean. Maybe they wouldn't fix the mechanical difficulty completely and the plane would crash, ridding Penny of competition with Bunny forever. Penny entertained these wild ideas while Harry continued to look at Bunny with lust in his eyes.

"What time is the plane leaving?" Chas asked, once again trying to distract Bunny by handing her a glass of champagne.

"Oh, I don't know, around midnight, I guess. Trying to get rid of me, Chas?" Bunny teased as she downed the bubbly in one gulp.

"No, I just don't want you to keep Sheik Mohammed waiting." Chas smiled transparently.

"Relax, Chassy, the plane can't leave without me, but I can take a hint," Bunny said handing the empty glass back to Chas.

Bunny threw her arms around Harry.

"Sweetie, when I get back from Europe, you and I are going to have a great time. Meanwhile, I'm sure there's plenty here to keep you occupied."

She kissed him again, this time on the lips. Penny was ready to roast her on the barbeque pit. She deserved to be tied up and burned at the stake, like they did to the witches in Old Salem so long ago. *Bunny is truly evil,*

Penny thought. *She just might have ruined my one shot at happiness.*

Bunny slinked her way across the party. After a few more hellos and good-byes, she was gone. Thank God.

"Your sister hasn't changed much. She's just like I remember her," Harry said in a cocky, I-fucked-her voice.

"Yeah, that's Bunny. You're right, she sure doesn't change." Penny did her best to hide all the feelings of rage that were boiling up inside her. But much to her surprise, Harry seemed to revert back to paying just as much attention to her as he did before Bunny showed up. As he came out of his Bunny-inspired, testosterone-fuelled, hypnotic trance, Harry noticed that Penny was still standing there holding his camera. He went back to striking funny poses by the grill and signaled for Penny to resume being his personal photographer. Happy and relieved that Bunny had vanished, Penny continued playing with the camera, like nothing ever happened. Penny thought she'd be fine as long as Bunny was gone. Thank God she'd be gone for a long while.

Chas let out a huge sigh when he looked over and saw Harry and Penny resume their interaction. For a split second, Chas caught Penny's eye. In the quick glance, they both acknowledged each other's relief. Bunny had not shattered either of their dreams.

The happiness Penny felt that night was worth a million dollars or more. For Chas, the hope for a golden future was standing right in front of him holding a camera covered in barbeque sauce.

chapter twelve

Monday was gorgeous out at Montauk Point, where Milly kept her fishing boat. The sun was shining brilliantly in the sky, and the water was a calming, crystal blue. Milly had just finished checking the bait and tackle when she saw Chas, Juan, and Harry walking down the dock. She was instantly curious about Harry. He was a lot shorter than she had imagined. She watched as he snapped pictures of all the boats in an overly excited, hyperactive manner. He was so excited, Milly wondered if he was still on cocaine. She never saw anyone get that enthused walking down a dock. It was like he had never seen a boat before.

"Milly Harrington, this is my friend Harry from L.A., and of course you know Juan," Chas casually introduced them.

"Hi, Milly, kick-ass boat. This is going to be so cool." Harry immediately jumped on the boat and started to play with the controls. Milly gently put her sun-weathered hand over his to calm him down. She was afraid he'd start the engine.

"Harry, I think it's great that you're excited about going out on the water today, but let me get us out of here. I promise I'll let you drive all you want when we get out into the ocean," Milly said, slowly putting her arm around him and moving him away from the control deck. Milly figured that letting Harry loose on the sea was the safest bet. That way, he couldn't crash into anything.

"Yeah, no sweat. I'm just checking it out," Harry said, turning and walking back towards the engines. He seemed fascinated by all the switches and buttons. Harry couldn't take his eyes off of them long enough to look at Milly. She wasn't bothered by it because he knew once she got him out on the open water, she would get his attention by showing him how everything worked. Actually, she thought it was a good sign he was so obsessed with the boat. This way they automatically had something in common. It could grow from there.

Milly noticed Chas and Juan were not as lovey-dovey as they normally were to each other. Chas was trying with Juan, but Juan seemed distant, which was strange. Juan was definitely the softer side of the relationship. He was usually emotional, flirty, and all over Chas. Today, something was different.

"What's up with you, Juan? You seem awfully quiet today," Milly said. "Still hungover from last night?"

"What do you mean last night? Last night I sat home alone while Chas was busy being the life of the party."

"What party?" Milly asked him.

"The Ackerman barbeque. Didn't you get invited either? Darling, we missed the social event of the season all because Chas still isn't comfortable taking me out in public. He can be such a bastard."

Chas sighed, but it was true. When Chas was "working" a party, the last thing he wanted was Juan around. Parties in the Hamptons were crucial to his career. He had to focus on who was there, and who was wearing what. Chas had no time to entertain Juan while he had to cater to his pampered clients.

"Oh, Juan, sweetie, you are always overreacting. Don't be so dramatic. You know I love you."

"Milly, can I drive the boat now?" Harry pleaded after snapping countless pictures of Milly at the helm, and Chas and Juan groping each other at the stern.

"Sure, Harry. We're in the ocean now, so you don't have to worry about hitting anything. Just point straight head."

"Oh, boy!" Harry shouted excitedly as he scurried up to the steering wheels and opened up the boat to full throttle. "Just sit right back and you'll hear a tale...a tale of a fateful trip..." Harry sang the opening song from *Gilligan's Island* enthusiastically. "Remember that show, Milly?" Harry asked swallowing a mouth full of wind.

"Of course I do, Harry. I love '70s TV. I watch all the reruns on *Nick at Nite*," Milly replied, smiling broadly and removing a piece of hair that was blowing in her eyes. She felt very happy that they had another subject to talk about.

"Reeeeallly? That's awesome! Hey remember this one? 'Love exciting and new, come aboard, we've been expecting you... The Love Boat...'" This time Harry kissed Milly on the cheek as he sang the *Love Boat* theme, then began doing his best imitations of Gopher, Isaac the Bartender, and Captain Stubbing. As they sprinted across the waves, Milly and Harry were having the time of their lives. Juan and Chas held each other tightly, praying that they would live to see tomorrow.

"When are we going to slow down and start fishing? Juan's getting seasick!" Chas screamed. Although he didn't want to interrupt Harry and Milly's trip down television memory lane, the bouncing boat was making his delicate stomach very queasy.

"I am not. Chas is just tired of getting his hair blown," Juan protested.

"Okay, okay," Milly laughed. "Harry, let's catch some fish."

Milly took the controls of the boat from Harry and evenly slowed the machine down until they came to a full stop. "Thank God, we're getting a break," Chas gasped with relief, when they finally stopped moving and Milly dropped anchor. She then pulled out four fishing rods and began to show Harry how to put on the bait and tackle. Of course, Harry immediately grabbed his camera and snapped a bunch of funny pictures of Chas's grossed-out face at the sight of the squirming things on the end of the line. Harry then picked up a fishing rod and threw it into the water like an old pro. Even though an hour went by and he caught nothing, Harry was having a blast. Finally he felt a tug on his line.

"Milly, Milly, it's happening, babe, it's happening!" Harry yelled, jumping up and down with sheer delight.

"Okay, let's reel it in. I feel like it's going to be a big one."

Milly put her strong, well-defined arms around Harry's shoulders and helped him reel in a flipping, writhing, wrangling fish. Chas was quick enough to pick up Harry's camera and catch the whole thing on film.

After the fish was hauled up onto the deck of the boat, Harry threw his arms around Milly and gave her a big kiss, this time smack on the lips. "We did it, kiddo," Harry said, as he grabbed Milly in a playful headlock and gave her a childlike noogie. "We certainly did," Milly said, wiggling around in Harry's arms, pretending to enjoy his playful roughhousing. Through this experience of simple pleasure, Milly and Harry bonded. She did like his inquisitiveness and his charisma. He liked her simple down-to-earthiness and he was impressed with her boating skills. Chas was right; Milly did remind him of his childhood nanny. She was attractive in a clean, wholesome, sporty way that he hadn't seen in a long time. Right now though, he treated her like a buddy because he wasn't used to a woman who could teach him so much. He didn't really know how to react, but he did know he was having a good time. Maybe the best sober time he'd had in years.

At the end of the day, as Harry helped Milly wash the boat down, Chas and Juan were all over each other again. *My God, I can barely be seen in public with this sexy spitfire. The more I look at him the hotter he gets. Juanita's pure animal magnetism just brings out the beast in me. I better keep him home in his cage, under lock and key. On Milly's little ship, we're okay, but too much PDA in more intense social situations would not be too cool,* Chas thought to himself as he pinched Juan's ass.

Because all had gone so well up until now, Milly stopped walking on eggshells around Harry. She felt so comfortable in his presence that she had totally forgotten what Chas had told her about Harry's natural pension for trouble. Milly nonchalantly turned her back for one minute to turn on the bilge pump, as Chas and Juan were making out on the deck. No one saw Harry get off the boat. While Milly was responsibly taking care of her equipment and Chas and Juan were lost in their own world of romance on the high seas, Harry became aware that all of attention was finally off of him. He was extremely relieved that he finally wasn't being watched over like an evil little mischief-maker. Instead of acting like an adult and staying put, Harry took this opportunity to sneak over to the Jet Ski rental area.

When Milly was finished doing her boat cleaning, she calmly looked around in search of her guest. She was thinking that maybe just she and Harry could go back to her house for a private swim in her pool without Chas and Juan intruding. As her eyes scanned the length and width of the boat, she slowly began to realize that Harry was nowhere in sight. "Where's Harry?" Milly asked, painfully noticing his disappearance, but trying not to sound alarmed.

Chas and Juan were so wrapped up in each other, they didn't even hear Milly's question.

"AHEM!" Milly cleared her throat loudly, as she tapped Chas on the back and practically had to pull him off of Juan.

"What did you do that for, Mills? What's going on? Are you jealous?" Chas said, utterly perturbed that Milly would have the nerve to interrupt such a passionate moment between him and his Latin lover.

"For your information, Romeo, Harry has evaporated!" Milly stammered, now getting really nervous.

"WHAT?" Chas exclaimed, not wanting to believe his ears.

"He's gone!" Milly said, her eyes turning an ice-cold blue.

"He can't be. He has to be around here somewhere. He couldn't have just vanished into thin air. I mean, Harry Raider is tricky, but he's not Harry Houdini. Besides, how could he have left? We were all right here," Chas rationalized, not wanting to fear the worse.

"Yeah, I was busy with the boat and you and Juan were pawing each other like two hormonal teen queens! None of us were on active Harry duty!" Milly said, getting angry at herself and the boys.

"Oh, relax and take a chill pill, Mill. Maybe he just went to the ladies room. *Jyou know*, for a sprinkle tinkle," Juan said in an attempt to comfort Chas and Milly.

"You know there's a bathroom down below and he's not in there. I already checked," Milly said, pointing to the cabin of her boat.

"Oh, my God, how could he disappear so quickly? Where the hell could he have gone?" Chas said getting into a panic. "Harry, Harry!" They called out for him, but he didn't answer.

"Santo dios...oh my goodness. *There he eeeessss!*" screeched Juan, pointing towards the water, then rushing into Chas's arms and burying his face in Chas's shoulder.

"Holy crap," Chas and Milly seemed to say together in slow motion, as their jaws dropped to the floor and almost hit the pavement. Their charge Harry was on a Jet Ski going full speed ahead out the inlet and into the mouth of the ocean. It was late in the day and the ocean was much rougher than it was when they went out at noon. There was no way could Harry handle the waves and swells of the blue Atlantic. It may not have been Hawaii, but the tide was strong enough to pull him under if he fell off the Jet Ski.

After the initial shock wore off, Milly quickly sprang into action and sprinted over to the Jet Ski hut, with Chas and Juan following closely on her tail.

"What the hell is wrong with you that you just give anyone a set of keys to a Jet Ski? Don't you know how dangerous they are?" Milly screamed shamelessly at a twenty-year-old summer-jobber.

"Hey, like, I'm sorry. He told me he knew what he was doing. And he gave me a hundred bucks," the scared kid replied.

"You idiot! I'll have you black-balled from any decent college on the East Coast if something happens to Harry!" Chas yelled.

"Okay, relax man, it was a mistake. I'll radio the Coast Guard and have them on the lookout. Hey, I got a Boston Whaler out back...I'll go find him myself."

He jumped into the boat with Milly to try and set out to find Harry.

"Santa Maria, please help us; little Harry is going to die," Juan said, crossing himself and crying hysterically.

"Calm down, Juan, your dramatics aren't helping," Chas said. He was also scared out of his mind that Harry could really drown out there.

Chas knew Harry had probably never even been on a Jet Ski before and could barely swim. *My God, he can't die, now there is so much money to be made*, Chas thought.

Milly and the young boy jumped the waves in the little dinghy but saw no sight of Harry. Milly was petrified. She could only blame herself for not paying total attention. Harry needed a babysitter. She knew that was part of the deal. That was okay with her, but she wasn't used to being responsible for anyone else yet. How could she mess up this early? If he drowned, she'd never forgive herself.

Much to their shock and horror, they finally saw the Jet Ski overturned, floating away from the shore. Harry was bobbing up and down next to it, hanging on for dear life.

"That's it! I see him!" Milly yelled.

They raced over towards Harry's direction but the tide seemed to pull him farther and farther away. Harry was trying desperately to stay afloat, but the strong current of the waves easily superceded his feeble strength. It would have been challenging enough for an athlete to hang on in those conditions, and Harry had never even seen the inside of a gym with the exception of the occasional trip to the sauna. Just in the nick of time the Boston Whaler finally reached poor, drowning Harry. Milly and the young man grabbed Harry out of the water and tried to pull him on board the little boat. It took all of the muscle power they had together to get Harry to safety. He had swallowed a lot of water and was barely breathing. Milly started to give Harry CPR, but at that moment the Coast Guard arrived. They had a medic on board who properly resuscitated Harry and brought him back to life.

When the Coast Guard boat brought Harry back to the dock wrapped in a blanket, he was still quite shaken from the experience. His skin was a bluish color from being in the water too long and his lips and teeth were chattering. Chas and Juan wanted to take him to the hospital, but he said he just wanted to go back to Jessica's and take a nap. The paramedics were insistent about Harry getting the proper follow-up medical attention, but he refused additional treatment. Harry knew that if his father found him in another hospital that would be the end of it all. He wasn't about to lose his family and his inheritance over a stupid boating accident. *If I have to give it up, I'm going to go out in a blaze of glory. Otherwise, I still have to play to win*, Harry thought to himself, as he thanked the paramedics for their help and drank some more Gatorade. Milly put her arms around Harry to try and warm and comfort him, but it didn't do much good. She didn't know what to do. She didn't want to lose him now after such a great day.

"Harry, I'm sorry this happened. You were a wonderful fisherman. I hope this won't stop you from coming out again real soon."

Harry smiled at her. Milly didn't know, but not much stopped Harry from having a good time, even if it almost killed him.

"No way, let's do it again next weekend. Right now I need to go home."

"Okay, sure."

Milly felt better. At least she was still in there. Chas, naturally, was relieved also. Even though she was just Plan B, she was a damn good one. He didn't want her to blow it. Chas and Juan loaded Harry into the Beemer and drove away. Milly watched, hoping that this would be the beginning of her new life with Harry. If only he could stay alive long enough to make a wedding.

Later that evening, Harry sat in bed wrapped in a terry-cloth robe over his favorite silk Kermit the Frog pajamas that Frederick's of Hollywood designed especially for him. He had a towel over his head and was still shaking. On drugs, he could handle anything. Sober, he was a terrified child. He yearned for something to make him feel good again. Quaaludes or a joint would be great right now. Harry couldn't believe he didn't have a stash of something on him. His father had searched everything, all his luggage, and even made him strip before getting on the plane. Harry was without a supply. This too freaked him out.

Downstairs, Jessica was warming up some chicken soup in a big pot in the kitchen on their professional chef-like stove. Freddy entered and watched his wife prepare soup, tea, and crackers for the stranger in the guestroom.

"It's not like he has the flu, Jes. Why don't you let the maid do that? Come up to bed."

Jessica would rather make chicken soup from scratch and watch it simmer overnight than get into bed with Freddy. As much as she wanted a baby, sex with him held no interest for her lately. He had become cold and mechanical after their marriage. Again, it was like he was performing what he was contractually obliged to do. She hated it but didn't have the courage to leave him after such a big wedding. Her father wanted grandchildren. He told her it was the only thing that would bring him happiness after Jessica's mother had died five years ago. Jessica felt it was the least she could do for him, so she made the best of it.

"I'll be there in one minute, Freddy. I just want to bring this to Harry. He didn't eat anything tonight."

"What are you, his mother, Jes? I mean, he is thirty-eight years old. If he's hungry, he can get something himself or call the friggin' butler. I mean, your father has a full staff here night and day. You don't need to baby Harry. He needs to grow up and look after himself like any other normal human being."

"Freddy, he was in a very serious accident today. He could have drowned." Jessica said, carefully sticking her pinky into the soup to make sure it was hot enough.

"That's because he's an immature idiot with a wild hair up his ass. Who rides a Jet Ski at full speed right into the middle of the ocean never having been on one before? That's nuts, and it's irresponsible, childish behavior. His father sent him here to grow up, not to remain a helpless imbecile," Freddy said, impulsively taking the bowl of soup from Jessica and emptying it out into the sink.

"Harry is not a helpless imbecile. He should be very proud of himself that he hasn't done any drugs since he's been here. That's a big accomplishment for him. So he got a little carried away on a Jet Ski, big deal. He's used to excitement. Not everybody is satisfied with the *Wall Street Journal* and a boring game of golf," Jessica replied, practically ignoring Freddy, as she ladled Harry another plate of soup.

"Oh, so now I'm boring. Hollywood Harry shows up, pulls a few crazy stunts, and Freddy is old hat. That's really great, Jessica. Maybe you are just as much a brat as he is. I'd like to see you do something with the *Wall Street Journal* besides let your goddamn poodle take a crap on it."

Jessica felt that since Harry's arrival, her husband had been nothing but a complete jerk. Every time Harry said something funny that made Jessica laugh, Freddy would roll his eyes in disgust or say something sarcastically biting about Harry's lighthearted behavior and seriously less-then-academic, wacky sense of humor. Of course Freddy *always* put on his transparent permanent fixture smile when Jerry was around, but the minute Jerry turned his back, Freddy was back to his old, bitter, "I'm above it all" self. Up until now, Jessica tried to remind herself that it must be very difficult for someone like Freddy, who had worked so hard and struggled so much, to have sympathy for a spoiled, rich, brat like Harry Raider. Yet tonight Jessica's patience with her hostile husband had come to a crashing halt. "Freddy, I'm really sick of this. You've been a total prick since Harry's arrived. Why do you have to be so jealous?"

"Why would I be jealous of a guy who can't have an afternoon out without practically getting himself killed? Just because my wife feels like it's her duty to nurture and care for a thirty-eight-year-old juvenile delinquent, why should I be upset? When I was sick, I was lucky if you got in the same bed with me. You were too afraid you'd catch my cold before the Fresh Air Fund Ball, remember?"

"Why do you always bring that up every time we have a fight? I've said I'm sorry for that about a million times now. Why can't you just get over it? For the billionth time now, I'm sorry I wouldn't sleep with you when you were sick, okay? Now get out of my way and let me take this up to Harry before it gets cold."

Freddy threw up his arms and went up to their bedroom alone. Jessica smirked; she had won this round with Freddy. He would have to learn not to push her or she'd punish him by ignoring him. She loved to frustrate him and she knew he wouldn't do a damn thing about it. It was her way of getting even with him for making her feel stupid, petty, and overly reactive. Eventually she hoped he would learn to be nice again, the way he had been when he was courting her. But she was getting tired of the games and the power struggle. Her marriage just wasn't fun anymore.

Jessica opened the guest room door to find Harry looking alone and vulnerable in the big four-poster bed. She put the tray of soup on his lap and sat down beside him.

"Thanks, Jes. This was really sweet of you."

"It's okay. Try to eat it while it's still hot."

Harry inhaled his soup. Jessica stayed a while and played some weird new computer game with him on his laptop. When Harry scored a point he would put his hands together, bow his head towards Jessica and mutter something strange in Japanese. This made Jessica crack up in a fit of giggles. She would try to copy his every move and repeat his language, but she could never make sense of his Oriental gibberish. After a few rounds, he started to doze off. Jessica removed the tray and the computer from the bed and tucked him in. Harry looked deep into her green eyes and smiled his famous innocent smile.

"Can I have a hug, Jes? I've had a really scary day."

Silently, Jessica put her arms around Harry as he nuzzled his head on her breast. *Okay, I shouldn't feel bad because this is hardly sexual*, Jessica told herself as she was getting comfortable. It was more like Harry felt the warmth and comfort with her that he never got from his mother Irma.

This is really nice and settling. Not exactly like burying my head between silicone breasts and pounding my cock into some model like there is no tomorrow, but for some reason I don't need that right now. Harry thought as he began to really relax. He just wanted to lay in her arms, feel her soothing breath on his forehead, and cuddle under her chin.

Jessica, in the same way, felt a motherly protection towards Harry. Deep down she wouldn't have minded if he would have jumped her bones, but she knew right now that's not what either of them needed. They both needed love and support they were not getting anywhere else. They both needed the time and the space to heal their lives. He needed to get over drug abuse and she needed to figure out a way to escape the emotional abuse from Freddy. For right now, all was safe and good in both their worlds. They both drifted off into the best night's sleep either one of them had in years.

chapter thirteen

As Jessica slowly woke up, she was blinded by the early morning sun reflecting off of Freddy's bald head. He stood angrily at the end of the bed, where she and Harry had slept the whole night. His puny little arms were tightly folded. The fury blazed behind his squinty eyes. As Freddy glared down at her, Jessica first noticed how much her husband resembled a Buddha on Slim Fast.

"This is unthinkable!" Freddy stammered, stomping his Bally's of Switzerland loafers on the hardwood bedroom floor.

"Sshh. You'll wake Harry," was all Jessica could say. "Nothing happened Freddy, we just fell asleep." The truth was obvious, since Jessica and Harry were both still fully clothed. No sign of foul play was evident, not even to Freddy.

"Oh, I'm supposed to be okay with this, Jessica? I'm supposed to just go in my room and mind my own business, while my wife sleeps with the guest?" Freddy shrieked. His yelling was just enough to force Harry out of deep sleep.

"Hey, man…sorry about this," Harry said, stretching like a cat and rubbing his eyes. "I know it doesn't look too cool, but I didn't touch your chick, dude. I swear. Peace, brah!" Harry then made some kind of a Malibuesque surfer peace gesture towards Freddy.

Freddy was beyond frustration. What could Jessica possibly find so damn captivating about this total piece of garbage? He could not comprehend it. After all, Freddy had an MBA from Harvard Business School. He had studied at the London School of Economics and spoke five languages. Freddy had done everything right to get himself out of Newark, New Jersey. *How could I possibly be upstaged by a thirty-eight year old who still watches* The Flintstones*?* Freddy thought to himself.

"Look, maybe nothing happened, but from now on, Jessica sleeps in *our* room, okay?" Freddy said, forcing himself to calm down after remembering that Jerry was sound asleep in a bedroom just down the hall.

"Sure, dude, like, no problem. Everything cool, man?" Harry said, genuinely wanting to apologize to Freddy.

"Yeah, let's forget it," Freddy complied, biting his tongue and grinding his fingernails into the palms of his sweaty hands.

"Killer!" Harry screamed, excited. He jumped upon the bed and gave Freddy an overwhelming bear hug that almost knocked him over.

"Okay, okay, Harry," Freddy said, untangling his body from Harry's clingy grasp. For a quick moment Freddy actually found himself being charmed by Harry's enthusiastic sincerity. "You guys behave yourselves this week. I'll be back on Thursday night," Freddy said, with a slightly helpless smile.

"You got it, dude! Don't worry...hands off!"

Harry winked mischievously at Freddy, who had no more time to linger if he was going to catch an 8:15 helicopter back to Manhattan. Freddy said nothing as he left the guestroom. He quickly made his way down the winding oak staircase towards the huge front door.

Jessica followed silently. As he was climbing into the awaiting Rolls Royce, Jessica stopped him. "Freddy, don't be upset. I'm sorry. You really don't have anything to worry about while you're at the office. You're my husband. I love you."

Freddy looked deeply into Jessica's haunting green eyes. She could really disarm him, if he let his soul be exposed. On one level Freddy wanted to give Jessica a big hug and tell her that she was right about him being jealous and intimidated by Harry. But even though he had been briefly "thawed out" by Harry's affectionate display, Freddy didn't feel secure enough in his position to let his guard down in front of his own wife. His deepest fear was to display any type of weakness. But after years of struggle, Freddy was beyond vulnerability and soft-heartedness. Those emotions were for idle rich, who could afford such human luxuries. Freddy knew only survival.

"No big deal, Jessica," Freddy said coldly as he gave her an obligatory kiss on the cheek. "See ya Thursday night."

As the powder-blue Rolls sped down the graveled driveway, Jessica's eyes welled up with huge watery tears. How could she have made such a mistake in choosing a husband? Was she doomed to spend the rest of her life with Freddy? The pain in her heart was consuming her now, as she stood in the driveway garbed only in her little La Perla robe, barefoot and alone. Thoughts of suicide ran through her mind. Maybe she should just go upstairs to her dad's medicine cabinet, swallow a bottle of his heart pills, and end it all. All the money in the world wouldn't make her feel worthy. She couldn't make her husband or her daddy happy, so what was left? Maybe the Ackerman household would be better off without her.

Jessica turned and carefully walked back towards the house, half-determined to end her sad, lonely life. *What's the use of it all? My dad's been unhappy since Mom died, I can't seem to make Freddy happy, and I am certainly not happy. So why continue on? What have I got to look forward to?* Jessica mulled over in her mind. She tiptoed through the gravel, which hurt her perfectly pedicured feet. Just as Jessica was approaching the massive front door, she looked up at the second story window. Harry was standing there, smiling that shit-eating grin, waving his camera and jumping up and down. He opened the window, stuck his head out, and began to snap shots of Jessica as she stood shivering in the cool morning air.

Jessica couldn't help but laugh at Harry. Yes, he could be silly. But this morning, she needed him more than he would ever know.

"You shouldn't stand out there without a mink, dahlink," Harry droned. "You could catch the death of you...and you wouldn't want to be caught dead without your tiara, would you, dahlink?" Harry shouted down to Jessica, doing his best imitation of Zsa Zsa Gabor.

Does Harry know what I was thinking? Is he a mind reader or is my misery that obvious? Jessica asked herself.

"I was just saying good-bye to Freddy. He has to be in the office all week. I'll really miss him," Jessica found herself saying.

"Noo Yawk is where I'd rather stay...I get allergic smelling hay..." Harry sang, switching his Gabor imitation from Zsa Zsa to Eva. Harry was ridiculously absurd...and Jessica loved it.

Harry raised his chin and stuck his nose in the air feigning his best aristocratic pose. "Dahlink, won't you join me for some smoked salmon and scrambled eggs? I hear Queen Elizabeth and her troupe of trained corgis is the opening act in the main dining room. If we hurry we can get a ringside table."

Jessica laughed. Harry's vivid imagination made a routine, everyday occurrence like eating breakfast seem like an adventure.

"You must hurry, dahling, tables are going quickly. I don't want the maitre d' to give ours away to the ghost of Princess Diana. She can be very pushy, you know." With that Harry disappeared from the window.

"Okay. I'm coming, Harry," Jessica said, her tiny hand grasping the big brass doorknob. Maybe the thoughts of eternal doom and gloom would wait until after breakfast...or maybe even until Harry went back to L.A.

Milly Harrington sat behind her huge desk plowing through seemingly endless paperwork. Nothing had gone well today. The market was way down. All her clients had called in a panic. Her horse Zara had gone lame in the front leg and the vets couldn't find the cause. If all that weren't enough, Milly was still recovering from what had happened to Harry. She couldn't believe that they were getting along so famously one minute and the next minute the coast guard was pulling him out of the water. How could it have all gone wrong so quickly?

"More proof I'll end up an old maid," Milly muttered. Harry wouldn't want any part of her now. In Milly's mind, there was not another suitable match left in New York.

"Ms. H, Chas Greer on line one," Amy's voice said over the intercom.

"What could he want?" Milly wondered. *He's probably going to charge me for some trauma therapy he had to go through after Harry's accident. After all, his million nearly sank to the bottom of the Atlantic*, Milly thought.

"Yes, Chas," Milly said, as she hesitantly picked up the phone.

"Hey Mills. How ya doing after the near-death *Titanic* episode last weekend?"

"I'm really busy today, Chas. This better be important," Milly demanded.

"The market's falling faster than a three-hundred-pound drag queen in stilettos, huh Mills?" Chas giggled.

"I didn't really think of it that way, Chas. I have a bunch of frantic clients, all calling me up screaming, and Zara isn't well, so I really don't have the time today to worry about Harry. I'm sure Jessica Ackerman is taking good care of him. What else has she got to do?"

"Now, now...don't be catty, Mills. Green is definitely not your color...in any season. Unless you're wearing money, of course."

"Yeah, well, Chas, you can forget your million. The deal is off. Harry obviously needs a woman who can watch his every move and I cannot. I'm too much of an adult. I don't make a very good nanny. Find Harry someone else." Milly always thought it was best to withdraw first. She learned on Wall Street that it is best to cut your losses quickly than to throw good money after bad. At least that way you still can walk away from a deal looking like a winner.

"Are you through with your little tirade, General Milly?" Chas said in a condescending tone. "I know you think that just because it got a little scary, that you're out of the game, but that's not true, Mills. Harry is crazy about you."

"A little scary? He almost drowned, for God's sake! I can't be responsible for something like that...I'll lose everything!"

"He's crazy about you, Mills. You could have him, if you still want him." Chas loved to taunt Milly, the powerhouse. He knew exactly what buttons to push to start a crack in her carefully applied veneer.

"He's crazy, Chas, period. Well, I mean...how do you know he likes me?"

There we go, Chas thought, *still gotcha*.

"Are you kidding, Mills, he's been calling me all week, night and day. He's bored shitless out there with Jessica, her poodle, and the old man. I mean they are nice people, but come on. If he's not watching Jessica paint flowers, or playing cards with Jerry, he's sitting in his room waiting for you to come back out to the Hamptons, so he can have some fun. He's absolutely dying to go riding this weekend."

"Riding! Harry on a horse? No way! He'll really kill himself this time. If he doesn't kill the horse first," Milly said, looking at her picture of winning her championship astride Zara.

"Now really, Mills, you underestimate Harry. He's really quite good with animals. He got Jessica's poodle to stop chewing the legs on the Louis XIV dining room chairs." Chas laughed and crossed his legs, proud of himself for knowing such intimate details from the life of such a wealthy woman.

"How'd he do that?" Milly asked curiously, chewing on the end of a pencil.

"By putting hamburger in every pair of shoes in Freddy's closet. That poodle will be chomping Bruno Maglis for weeks," Chas whispered like he was revealing a big secret straight from the *Lifestyles of The Rich and Famous*.

Milly leaned back on her chair and chuckled. Chas really was quite amusing in his own way.

"Listen Chas, I really don't think it's a good idea to put Harry on a horse. I think it's a recipe for disaster. He will definitely get hurt."

"No he won't, Mills. Hey, you just said Zara was lame, why not let him get on her? She couldn't possibly go very far." This comment about her baby infuriated Milly.

"If you think I am going to put that freak show of a man on my award-winning, multi-championship, Olympicqualifying mare, you have lost all touch with reality!" Milly screamed.

"I think you're the one losing touch with reality, Mills!" Chas was now screaming also. "If you play it right, Harry could be your future husband! Zara is only a *horse*!" *What is wrong with this woman?* Chas thought. *Has she seen* Equus *too many times?*

Milly hung up on Chas. She'd had enough trouble today, and she certainly didn't need to be subjected to his crap. As she rummaged through her paperwork, she found a gift certificate to Heavenly Hands Massage Therapy Holistic Wellness Center on Lexington and 64th Street. Some client had given it to her on a day the market was up, as a small token of appreciation. Milly *never* spent money on luxuries like massage, facials, meditations, or yoga. To Milly, that stuff was for JAPs to try when the Prozac stopped working.

Today, a little relaxation would be welcome. After all, it was already paid for by a very important client, and Milly didn't want to appear ungrateful or, even worse, wasteful. That was a definite no-no for a girl of her background. Such roundabout logic was required by Milly to allow herself some "down time." Even with all her success, Milly still harbored a scarcity in her soul.

Heavenly Hands was "the" celebrity holistic oasis in the middle of an insane city. It was a dimly lit, comfy little sanctuary hiding in a walk-up above a soup restaurant. At the spa, Milly noticed photos of Mel Gibson, Conan O'Brien, Fran Drescher, Mariah Carey, the late Gianni Versace, and a bevy of other beautiful famous people. She found the soft lights and the new age music very soothing, but the smell of the aromatherapy candles made her sick to her stomach. Milly would take the smell of a freshly oiled saddle, or even steamy hot horse manure, over a floral bouquet any day. She knew this was strange, but she couldn't help it.

As Milly felt the strong hands of the muscular, blond male therapist knead her tired body, she really began to relax. *Maybe there is something to this thing*, she thought. *A little indulgent, but not so bad.*

This was also the first time in a very long time a man had touched her body. The sensation of his strong hands all over her was more powerful than she had remembered. As if against her own will, there was moisture between her legs. Her clitoris began to rise up as he worked around her neck and breasts. Milly knew that Heavenly Hands had a strict nonsexual rule in place. They were the most reputable massage therapy company in town and one violation of their professionalism could shut their doors. Milly realized that if she acted out of line, the massage would end, and the spa director might even notify the important client who bought her the certificate to report her deviant behavior. She couldn't risk the embarrassment, but at the same time she could hardly control the rush of blood heading towards her private parts. She unconsciously started rubbing herself against the towels on the massage table, as she moaned softly under her breath.

"I think we better stop," the therapist said, wanting to avoid what was coming. Milly was caught totally off guard.

"Yes, absolutely," she said, snapping back from the moment of near-ecstasy. Milly bolted up from the table and put on her robe. She was very nervous. The therapist sensed her uneasiness. "Don't worry, we were just out of time."

"Right," Milly said, and darted out of the massage room to the privacy of the bathroom. Milly hid in the terra-cotta-tiled, made-to-look-earthy bathroom. She was too frazzled to get unnerved by Deepak Chopra's picture hanging over the toilet. As Milly showered, the hot water pounding down in hard little pellets awakened her unsatisfied sexual desire. She took a clean towel from the towel rack and placed it between her firm legs. As the water hit her nipples, Milly rubbed the towel against her, writhing on the tile of the shower stall. She fantasized about what it would have felt like to have that good-looking massage therapist climb on top and force himself inside her as he rubbed her in hot oil. She let out such a loud grunt of pleasure as she climaxed that she prayed no one heard her.

Suddenly there was a knock on the door. "Miss Harrington? Are you all right?" the Heavenly Hands attendant asked.

"Yes, I'm fine...I just, well...I just slipped. I'll be out in a minute."

Trying to get over her embarrassment, Milly got out of the shower and quickly dressed, even though she was still soaking wet. She walked out of the bathroom, poker-faced, pretending nothing had happened. She could not get out of there fast enough.

"Well, it's about time," a snotty, petite, dark-haired woman in a towel said as Milly came out of the bathroom. Milly was taken aback by this woman. She looked like a plastic surgeon had worked on her since birth. Everything from her cheek implants to her ski-jump nose to her silicone breasts had been done and redone. It wasn't just her unnaturalness that bothered Milly. It was something else, but Milly couldn't place it.

"You would think a place like this would have more bathrooms. From now on I'm only getting in-home service."

Milly stepped to get past this woman who now blocked her way.

"Hey, don't I know you?" This woman's whine was more nasal and more annoying than any Milly had heard.

"I don't think so," Milly said, now heading for the door.

"Oh, yes, I do," the woman persisted. "You're Milly. Milly Harrington. You used to go out with *my* David."

Milly stopped dead in her tracks. It was Judy Cohen, David's spoiled, obnoxious, my-father-owns-every-building-in-Queens, nerve-racking wife.

"I mean, we never met, but I saw pictures of you and David from Harvard. I never forget a face. Even if it's almost twenty years later! Isn't that fabulous? It's a real talent I have!"

Milly was truly at a loss for words. What do you say to a woman who took away the only man you had ever loved?

Milly didn't have to say a thing, though, because Judy's big mouth was nonstop. "I'm going to tell my David that I ran into you. I'm sure he'll be so thrilled. He said that he's read about you in the *Wall Street Journal* from time to time. Are you married?"

Leave it to Judy to hit the zinger. Milly felt as if all her *Wall Street Journal* write-ups may as well have been toilet paper. She was still alone.

"No, I'm not married," Milly said, unable to look Judy in the eye.

"Yeah, well, you know, you really can't have it all. A career *and* a family, I mean. See, women think they can, but they really can't. Being David's wife is a full-time job. All the entertaining I have to do, all the shopping for the right outfits, the boards of the twenty-five charities I sit on...I mean, really, who has time for anything else?"

Milly was so incensed she felt like pulling the hair extensions out of Judy's head. Was that all being David's wife meant to her? Parties, clothes, and charities? Was that it? What about the love, the bonding, the deep soul mate connection Milly had once shared with David? Didn't he want that anymore? How could he have thrown away everything they had together for this spineless, soulless, heartless, sexless, wretched little woman? Milly began to think the David she once knew and loved couldn't even exist anymore.

"Listen, Milly it was really a pleasure meeting you after all these years." Judy held out her hand to Milly. She had a twenty-carat pear-shaped diamond wedding ring, a Rock of Gibraltar. Milly couldn't make herself take Judy's hand. She forced a smile, nodded her head, and bolted out the door. As she walked down Lexington Avenue, it began to softly drizzle on her already wet head. As the summer rain got harder and harder, Milly felt sadness well up inside her. She was finally faced with the fact that David had grown up to be a stranger. He could no longer be the sweet, sensitive, passionate, caring lover she once knew. There was no sense of holding on to a memory that should have died long ago. Her David was now just a figment of her imagination, and Milly was a woman who thrived on practical reality.

Milly stood under the awning of Gino's restaurant to take shelter from the rain. She reached into her Louis Vuitton purse and took out her cell phone. She made a quick call to her vet and got his okay before she dialed Chas. She got his voice mail.

"Hey, hey...It's Chas. Wait for the beep, leave your name, number, and crisis, and I'll get back to you tout de suite. Ciao!"

"Hi Chas. It's Milly. Zara is feeling much better. The vet said she could stand a little exercise this weekend. Go to Miller's Saddlery and get Harry some boots, jodhpurs, a crop, and a hat. I'm about to take him on the ride of his life."

chapter fourteen

Thursday afternoon was particularly glorious. The temperature was a perfect seventy-five degrees and the sun shone brightly in a cloudless blue sky over East Hampton. The flowers in Jessica's English garden looked especially alive, their colors more vibrant than usual. Jessica, dressed simply in a powder blue gauze strapless dress and a big floppy sun hat, sat in a big white wicker chair, with her poodle Cindy at her side. The easel in front of her mirrored the splendor of the floral magnificence of the garden. While she recreated what she saw with watercolors, Jessica was lost in her own world of peaceful natural beauty.

Popping out of an azalea bush, wearing a bright yellow and orange Hawaiian shirt, silk shorts, flip-flops, and a bandanna around his head, Harry said "Hello, baby!" in his Austin Powers, Swinging Sixties, London-lounge voice. The Jewish Prince of Beverly Hills looked like Don Ho meets Jerry Garcia.

"Oh, my God" Jessica said, completely startled and not immediately recognizing her own houseguest.

"Relax Jes, it's only Baby Harry," Harry laughed.

"How long have you been sitting there?" Jessica said trying to hide her embarrassment.

"About an hour or two. Time stands still when a great master is at work!"

Jessica smiled as she sat. She didn't care if she was a great master or not, but it was certainly nice to hear.

"You know, Jes, I bet painting is a lot like taking pictures, except you're missing one thing," Harry said winking seductively and smiling devilishly.

Jessica's face turned bright red as she bashfully turned away from Harry and kept her eyes glued to the canvas. Harry didn't understand that when Jessica painted, she didn't miss anything. Painting made her world work.

"Here, take a look at the canvas, Harry. I've got all the roses, sunflowers, hydrangeas, and daisies. There's nothing missing. I designed this garden myself," Jessica insisted pointing to the various flowers on the painting with her brush.

"Mmmmm..." Harry put his hands on his hips and stuck his head right up against the canvas pretending to study her work like a real connoisseur of art.

"Ah, my darling, you are missing the one vital element to your work that will separate you from all the other flower painters in the universe!"

"What's that, Harry?" Jessica asked, braving to look up at him for more than a split second.

"You are missing *life*!" Harry declared in a commanding, baritone voice, as he swung his arms in the air and looked gratefully up to the sky.

"LIFE, my dear sweet lovely Jessica, *life* is art! Your work must capture the essence of life!" Harry pronounced, prancing around the garden, then jumping up on a rock like he was Moses giving Jessica God's eleventh commandment.

"Flowers are life, Harry," Jessica said, as she thoroughly enjoyed watching Harry in motion.

"So are trees and plants and all vegetation. Nature is the loveliest part of life, I think," Harry proclaimed as he hopped off of the rock and skipped around the garden picking leaves. He gathered a bunch of flowers and twisted them into a floral crown that he put majestically on his head.

"It is true, my dear creative one, that God has decorated our earth with beautiful blooms, but a few little petals are no match for the power, the glory, and the mag-ni-tude of the human spirit. It's awesome." Harry grabbed his camera from behind a rose bush and snapped a picture of her startled reaction.

"See what I mean...Madame Artiste!"

Practically sitting down right on top of Jessica and putting his face right next to hers, Harry showed her on the pictures he had taken with advanced digital technology.

"That's pretty amazing, Harry. Actually, it's incredible," Jessica said studying the picture intensely, trying to pay attention to how physically close they were to each other.

"No, you're incredible, Jessica! The camera just shows me who you are. Your painting can do the same," Harry said, softly. Their eyes met in an unnerving glance.

"What do you mean?" Jessica replied almost hypnotically, now totally enthralled. She wanted to reach right out and kiss him passionately, but she somehow managed to control her urges. Nobody had ever called her incredible before. She was so excited by Harry that the energy around him seemed electric. The charge she got from him was so strong it was almost too much to handle. The mutual sexual attraction was too intense for either of them to handle at that moment. To break the tension, Harry jumped up and once again struck a statuesque pose. Cindy was so startled by Harry's sudden movement that she jumped off the chair and ran to the bushes, but her mistress Jessica wasn't scared at all. As a matter of fact, she wanted more! More of life; more of Harry.

"Why don't you paint me?"

"What?" Jessica giggled girlishly. "I couldn't. I mean I don't think I could," she said, once again looking away from Harry and staring back into her painting

"Why not, am I that ugly? Do you think I'd burn a hole through your canvas?" Harry said, feigning a frown.

"No," Jessica said, still blushing. "It's just that I've never painted people before; only flowers, backgrounds, you know, scenery," Jessica said, not yet comfortable enough to look back at him.

"Well, now is the time to start your venture into the realm of human beings. And what better model to have than Harry the Happening. Back in L.A., Fabio is petrified of me, you know. He's afraid I'll put him out of business," Harry said, *Vogue*-ing in a myriad of model-esque poses.

This is crazy. I'm a married woman; there is no way I should be playing games with this guy, especially while he's staying in our house and Freddy is in the city. Besides I promised Freddy I'd stay away from Harry, as much as I could. But, then again, it's only art we're talking about here. And Freddy doesn't understand my art. He never did. Freddy would never work with me or take an interest in my paintings like Harry does. After Harry leaves, I may not ever find someone to stimulate me like this again. Stimulate me, artistically that is. This internal debate went on in Jessica's head, heart, and soul. She finally agreed to create the first-ever portrait of Harry Raider.

"Okay, Romeo. I'll paint you. I'll paint you! Strike a pose, Harry!" Jessica said, gaining a surge of confidence she had never experienced before.

As she was changing the canvas on her easel and refreshing her paints, Harry disappeared into the house.

Five minutes later, the French doors from the patio opened. Harry stepped out into the garden...absolutely naked. Jessica was stunned. Her jaw dropped open. She covered her mouth, but not her eyes. Even Cindy seemed to peek out from under the bushes.

"Oh my God, Harry? What are you doing?" was all Jessica could say.

"Ta da! This is 100 percent Harry live!" Harry playfully strutted his stuff, parading up and down the garden path, once again striking a series of poses. Jessica just stared in disbelief. Was he really out of his mind? Had all those years of booze and drugs killed his brain cells? Sometimes he was so in tune, so insightful, and then all of a sudden he was dancing naked in the rose bushes. Who the hell was this Harry Raider and how could little Jessica Ackerman Levitt take in all he was showing her?

"Well, what do you think, Jes?" Harry asked. "Okay, so I'm not Long Dong Silver...but for a Jewish boy who peed on a rabbi with a knife, I still have it all intact," Harry proclaimed proudly.

Actually, Jessica couldn't take her eyes off of Harry's manhood. He was the most well-endowed man she had ever seen. Jessica had not seen too many men. Before Freddy, there was Herbie Fishbein, the optometrist, and Mitchell Goldstein, the political science major, when she was up at Brown University. The real lust of Jessica's life had been Jean Valtrois, the Haitian artist Jessica had an affair with while studying in Sotheby's art history program.

Those years right before she married Freddy were filled with steamy, hot, wet sex in Jean's Soho loft. Jean awakened a passion in Jessica that died when she married Freddy. She knew Daddy would never have accepted Jean. Not really even because he was black, but more so because he wasn't interested in getting a "real" job. Jean had won his scholarship to Sotheby's but wanted desperately to return to Haiti to paint "his people." At that moment the juicy lust and true love of Jessica's life was gone for good.

So much of what Harry had said that afternoon reminded her of that blissful, exploratory time. Still, what Jessica and Jean experienced was done on the privacy of his futon, behind closed doors. Harry stood before her naked as a newborn, hung like an elephant with an erection. This sight put Jessica on sensory overload.

"Harry...you can't stand there like that. What if Daddy comes down?"

"It's cool, Jes. Jerry and his cronies are in Bridgehampton, at Atlantic Country Club playing golf. You think he'd miss eighteen holes on a kick-ass day like today? He asked me to join him, but I told him that I'd rather stay here with you. He didn't seem too upset," Harry smiled.

"Yeah, well, he left hours ago, I'm sure. He could be back any minute."

"Jessica, I'm willing to bet your entire inheritance and more that Jerry Ackerman has seen a naked butt before. I don't have anything going on here that Jerry doesn't have. I bet he still knows how to use it."

"Harry, please. That's my dad you're talking about. He doesn't have sex!" Jessica chuckled, highly embarrassed and clasping her hands around her head.

"Well, he did at some point in his life. I don't think you were found on the front porch one morning. Right?" Harry said, making the screwing motion with his two hands.

"No, not exactly." Jessica was still blushing and shaking her head in disbelief. She wondered if Harry had noticed her staring at his penis. Surely he was used to women gaga over his blessing. She tried not to be obvious, but she couldn't conceal her look of shock mixed with pure delight.

"Well, what is it, Jes? Are you going to color your canvas Harry?" Harry said nonchalantly, as he danced around in place, his manhood swinging freely in the ocean breeze.

Jessica still couldn't do anything. She sat almost paralyzed in her chair behind the safety of her easel.

"Come on, baby...it's shag-a-delic," Harry mimicked, slipping back into his best Austin Powers British accent.

Saying nothing, Jessica picked up her brush and began to paint.

Well I never thought I'd be here in the Hamptons, standing buck naked with my arms stretched out towards the sky, basking in the afternoon sun. I feel like Adam on his first day as man on earth. Here I am: God, nature, and all the elements. See what you've created? Hahaha. I also can't believe I am this comfortable being nude in front of Jessica without doing a line of blow first. That is something, Harry thought to himself.

As she began to paint, Jessica too began to relax. Yet, as lost as she could get in her work, today she was more fixated on her subject. Harry was not just some nude model. He was living under her dad's roof, with her husband.

This is a lot of fun, but I just can't let myself get crazy about Harry. I owe it to Freddy to try to make our relationship work. I mean, what kind of person would I be if I gave up on my marriage just for a few cheap thrills with a wild stranger? I'd be a total loser and failure if I did that, right? Besides, Freddy hasn't had an easy life like I've had. He deserves better. Jessica kept these thoughts in her head as she painted her seductive subject. As painful as it was to stay with Freddy, Jessica had now talked herself into giving it the old college try.

While Jessica put Harry's exuberant form onto the canvas, she concentrated and focused on the commitment she had made to Freddy. *Maybe it's my fault he has become so distant so early in the marriage. Maybe I'm not smart enough for Freddy. Here I am in the garden, painting this naked man, when he is on Wall Street analyzing the world's economy. Maybe I should put down my brush and go inside to watch CNN or read a* Crain's *business report. Wouldn't it be wonderful if Freddy came home to find me enthralled in the business section of the* New York Times? *Maybe then he'd take off his glasses, rip off my clothes, and make love to me*, Jessica thought.

The sun was slowly beginning to set as Jessica finished the final brush strokes of Harry in the buff. She was glad because she knew that Freddy would be home soon. Jessica wanted to do something special to make him feel welcome after a long week in the city. Tonight would be the start of a new time for Jessica and Freddy. She would ask him all about the market and pretend she was really interested. Then they would watch *World News Tonight* together with Daddy in the upstairs den. She would really try this time to join the debate on current events. Yes, tonight, she would win her husband back!

"Jessica, are you almost done, it's getting kind of chilly out here," Harry said shivering.

"Sure am, Harry. That does it." Jessica finished her last stroke, put her brush down, and smiled. It was her first stab at painting a person, and she had done a damn good job. *Maybe it's because I have such an exquisite, fascinating subject, or maybe I really have a natural ability as an artist*, Jessica thought.

"Great, can I see me?"

"Of course!" Jessica said, proud of her work.

Harry ran over, truly excited. He had been in millions of photos with everyone from Sylvester Stallone to Pamela Anderson and the Barbi twins, but no one had ever painted his portrait. This was a first for Harry, and he couldn't wait to see what Jessica put on the canvas.

But, he thought, it was more than that. Secretly, he wanted to know just how she saw him. Did she think he was attractive? Jessica was the one girl who Harry knew didn't need anything material or financial from him. He wanted to believe that the indulgent attention she paid him was genuine.

Harry never really cared what any woman except Irma thought of him. For some reason though, right now Jessica's impression meant everything to Harry. He wanted to be more to somebody than just a big bank account, dinner at Spago, or a shopping spree on Rodeo Drive. He didn't quite understand what he was feeling, he just knew it was extremely different than how he felt around most women.

Harry gloated with pride as he saw the image of him Jessica had created. It was stupendous. She had captured the essence of this boy/man, in all his glory. His brown hair was accentuated by the warm rays of sun she had painted. His smile was so vibrant, so alive as he looked up at the sky, it nearly jumped right off the canvas. Jessica had captured what Harry had said about painting—life. One could grasp Harry's whole magic in the soulful detail she painted in his glistening eyes.

She must really get me, Harry thought to himself. *She must get me.*

"Jessica, this is the most brilliant piece of artwork I have ever seen. I'm not saying that because you've painted me," Harry said, as modestly as a naked man could say anything at that point.

"Oh, Harry, it's not that great," Jessica said.

"Don't say that, Jessie, it's truly spectacular! If I could, I would hang it in my parent's wing at the Los Angeles County Art Museum or in the hospital we own. I don't think my dad would be too happy about that, though."

"No," Jessica said, giggling.

"Dad was always kind of jealous of Mr. Big Man," Harry joked, pointing to the massive penis dangling between his legs.

"Harry, please," Jessica said, quickly looking away from what she had been staring at for over three hours.

"Okay, I'm sorry. But seriously, Jes, you really did an excellent job. I just want to hug you."

With that, Harry threw his arms around Jessica. The musky smell of his sun-baked body was a powerful aphrodisiac. It was more alluring than the smell of fresh baked cookies wafting through a bakery. She wanted to nuzzle in his neck and take a bite out of him. He smelled so delicious.

Jessica could feel her nipples start to get hard and poke out of her dress. She wanted to push him away and capture him at the same time. Harry triggered in Jessica a desire that she hadn't felt since the days of Jean. *Oh, if he would just take me right now, I would be able to give in to my hidden passion. If he would just push me, even a little bit, then I could enjoy him, without being responsible*, Jessica thought to herself, as her lower lip began to slightly quiver with excitement.

"What's going on guys?"

Jessica looked up from Harry's embrace to find Freddy, standing at the edge of the garden. He looked rumpled and tired. His Armani suit was disheveled, and his horn-rimmed Jansen glasses were cocked to the left. The market was crazy, and the helicopter ride was unusually jolting this evening. The last thing this worn-out Wall Street-wrecker needed at the end of the week was to find his wife in the arms of a nude houseguest.

"Freddy. You're home early," Jessica said, completely caught off guard.

"I hope I didn't interrupt anything, Jessica," Freddy said defeatedly.

"No Freddy, it's not that." Jessica jumped up from her chair, almost knocking Harry over. *I can't believe I let myself slip this far. Just minutes before Harry's hug, I was planning how I'd make it right with Freddy. In a matter of seconds, my entire thought process fell apart, because of Harry and that sexy scent he exuded. How could I get thrown off track so easily? I can't believe what an idiot I am...what was I thinking?*

Jessica was panicking, crying, and hyperventilating. She could barely speak. For once, Harry was silent. Freddy calmly walked over to the easel where the naked portrait sat.

"Well, Jessica, I see you've put all your years of art study to good use," Freddy said snidely as he studied Jessica's afternoon creation.

Freddy angrily ripped the painting from the easel in one swoop. "Harry, I'm sure that your father will be relieved to hear from Mr. Ackerman that you have found a new occupation. If dad cuts you off, at least now you don't have to worry. You can always get a job with *Playgirl*. Excuse me."

Freddy took the painting and marched purposefully towards the house, his destination Jerry Ackerman's study. He was so upset that all he could do was sit on the leather couch in silence and wait for Jerry to arrive. Freddy just wanted to pounce on Jerry like a wounded animal, the minute he walked in the door. *I've taken all the crap I can handle from this Harry character and now I expect for my own father-in-law to come to my defense. I know Harry's his best friend's son, but I'm family for heaven's sake. I married his daughter; Harry didn't do that for him. That has to count for something around here*, Freddy thought to himself as he sat there stewing.

For Harry, waiting for Jerry to arrive home was like waiting on death row, as he sat there now wearing a pink robe he stole from the Beverly Hills Hotel. What was done was done. There was no turning back.

The four of them, Jerry, Jessica, Freddy, and Harry, sat on the leather couches in the dark paneled study with the big-screen TV. Jerry Ackerman, still in his Arnold Palmer golf sweater, looked carefully at the portrait of Harry naked. It was as if he was studying it, trying to figure out what was really going on under his roof.

"Jessica. Nice attention to detail...but was this really necessary?" Jerry asked his trembling little girl.

"I'm sorry, Daddy. I was just out in the garden painting, Harry joined me and well, we just got carried away."

"I think it's despicable, Mr. A., I mean, Dad," Freddy said emphatically. "Harry obviously hasn't learned anything here yet. What if the neighbors saw this? What about his parents? Maybe you should call them in Europe."

"Thank you, Freddy, for your input," Jerry said. "I can understand that you were upset to find your wife with a naked man."

"I'm not upset, sir," Freddy stammered.

"You're not? I would be," Jerry said suspiciously, putting a cigar in his mouth and lighting up.

"Well, I mean of course I'm upset, sir. I just don't think it's Jessica's fault, that's all. I think Harry has been influencing her incorrectly, while I'm away working during the week," Freddy insisted, pleading his case and throwing his hands up in the air helpless, like he finally got caught out.

"Do you think Harry took a gun to her head and forced a paint brush into her hand?" Jerry asked calmly chewing his cigar and rolling it around between his lips.

"No sir, I don't, sir. I just think that sometimes Jessica gets confused and she could easily be led astray by the wrong type of guy," Freddy said helplessly, as he stood up and pointed sharply at Harry.

"I'm not an idiot, Freddy," Jessica screamed in tears. "I painted that picture because I wanted to. Harry didn't make me. I wish you would stop treating me like a child!" Jessica cried.

Jerry put his fatherly hand on his daughter's frail, but heavily burdened shoulder. "Take it easy, Jes. Freddy is under a lot of pressure. He doesn't need to come home to this," Jerry said, trying to calm Jessica down and test her at the same time.

"Well, I'm not sorry. Neither of you understands art or what I was trying to create this afternoon. Only Harry understands."

Harry sat in a leather recliner, silently. He had never been in a situation quite like this before. In a strange way, he wanted Jessica to be with him, but what would it mean if Freddy really left her? Would *he* then have to marry Jessica? Would that mean he would have to stay here in New York forever and never go back to L.A.? Was he ready to be a responsible husband? What if she wanted kids right away?

All these questions were racing through Harry's mind as he watched the scene unfold before him. Maybe he had been too bold with Jessica. Maybe it was time to back off and not cause any more damage.

"Look, everyone, I'm real sorry about this. I just wanted to have some fun, that's all. I guess I just got out of line as usual. Freddy, once again, I'm really sorry man, and I mean it this time. Jessica, you better stick to painting flowers. Jerry, I didn't mean to disrupt your family. I'm really sorry," Harry said, bowing his head and staring at the floorboards.

If Harry wanted to, he could be a real mensch. This was one of those rare moments.

"He's not sorry, sir," Freddy snapped and paced around the room in total frustration. "He's just trying to be manipulative, so you don't call his parents. We see right through his little act, don't we, Dad?" Freddy said, almost begging for support while standing beside Jerry.

"He apologized to you, Freddy. I think that's enough," Jerry replied placidly, yet with a stern tone in his voice.

Freddy was stunned. Did he pull no weight at all in this family? Had all his ass kissing been done in vain? Once again, Freddy swallowed his pride.

Shit, I can't believe this! I must mean absolutely nothing to these people. Just because I was poor boy from the wrong side of Hudson River shouldn't mean I have to spend my entire life as a second-class citizen in my own marriage...or should it? I guess Jerry Ackerman thinks his little girl could have done better than Balding Freddy, the Nebbish From Newark, New Jersey. Jessica probably could have gotten someone of her own ilk, if I wasn't so damn persistent with her. Perhaps this is what I signed on for, a lifetime of being second best. It's my own fault really; I should have known better than to think a billionaire would ever think that I was good enough for his little girl. Oh well. I've made my bed; I guess I have no choice but to lie in it, Freddy thought to himself.

"Okay...fine. If you think that's enough, Jerry, then that's okay with me. You know what's best. You're the boss." Freddy folded, yielding completely.

Jessica felt so nauseated, she thought she'd throw up. She wanted so much for Freddy to tell her father to just fuck off. She wanted Freddy to say something like, "Mr. Ackerman, if that man isn't out of this house by tomorrow morning, I'm taking my wife and we're leaving. I love my wife and I'm not going to stand here and be humiliated. It's Harry or us."

But Jessica knew Freddy would never say that or anything even close. She hated him for it, and so much more.

"Freddy and Jessica, why don't you go change and wash for dinner. Harry, I'd like to have a word with you, son," Jerry said.

"Sure, Jerry, no sweat," Harry answered.

Freddy couldn't stand it when Jerry called Harry "son." Jerry never called Freddy "son." Freddy politely opened the study door for Jessica. "After you, Jes," Freddy said in his usual, condescending manner. Jessica said nothing as she left the room. She ran into her private dressing room and locked the door. Cindy's barking, begging, scratching, and yelping wouldn't even persuade Jessica to let her in. Freddy shook his head at the pathetic poodle.

"You'll never catch me begging, Cindy," Freddy said to the confused puppy. "Absolutely never."

Jerry continued to study the nude painting of Harry, as Harry stood in front of him, with his eyes focused on the floor.

"Harry, have you always been so…well, so…large?" Jerry asked, half-joking, half-serious. "As I remember it, with all due respect, your father was not a big man. When we were kids together growing up in Bensonhurst, the other boys used to tease him in the locker room about how small he was. It's no wonder he made so much damn money. Had to prove himself. I should know. I could be his twin."

Harry and Jerry laughed. Somehow, even in the most stressful, tenuous situations, penis jokes always broke the ice.

"Just lucky, I guess," Harry smiled.

"Listen, Harry. I know you've had your troubles, but you're basically a good kid," Jerry said, reaching into his drawer and offering a Harry a smoke, which Harry politely refused. "You've got a big heart, I can tell." Jerry shrugged his shoulders, put the cigar back in the box and put in away. "And you seem to make Jessica laugh. That's important. She hasn't been too happy lately. She doesn't think I notice, but I do. I try to stay out of the kids' business, but I hate to see her so upset. I can't help it, I'm her father. I love her and I want to see her smile again. You seem to perk her up, she really enjoys your company."

"I enjoy her company too, Jerry, she's a super girl."

"Yes, she is ... So much like her mother used to be. Don't let Freddy get to you. He means well, he just gets a little bent out of shape sometimes. You know, he's had to work very hard to get where he is, and I respect him for that."

"Yes, Jerry, I'm sure he has. I'll stay away from Jessica."

"Oh, no. I don't want you to do that."

"You don't?" Harry asked, surprised and a little relieved.

"Oh no, Harry. I want you to spend time with her, keep her laughing. But with your clothes on, of course. I want you to be the big brother she never had."

"Yes sir, I'll try my best to make Jessica happy," Harry enthusiastically agreed.

"For God's sake, Harry, don't call me 'sir.' I'm trying to break Freddy of that annoying habit. Makes me feel old. I'm just Jerry, one of the boys!"

"You got it, Jerry."

The two men embraced warmly.

"You're awesome Jerry, my man!" Harry said as he tried to show Jerry a hip hand slap by taking his hands and hitting then high in the air and twirling his fingers around.

"Not bad for an old guy, huh?" Jerry said smiling.

chapter fifteen

Penny's wind-blown hair flew into her mouth as she drove down Route 27 in her silver Mercedes convertible. She sang along loudly with the radio as it played Madonna's greatest hits. It was a great release. She didn't mind if she had a mouth full of curls for a few miles...at least it wasn't fattening.

Penny was having a hard time sticking to the "I-wanna-marry-Harry" weight loss program. It was now nearly the end of June, and he had only seen her twice since Memorial Day. Once was at a benefit for the Fresh Air Fund at Bridgehampton Beach Club, and the other time she happened to run into him at Nick and Tony's, while he was dining with Jerry, Jessica, and Freddy. It seemed to Penny that Harry was always firmly surrounded by the Ackerman crew. They rarely let him out of their sight.

Penny never seemed to be able to catch Harry alone. She had called to invite him to dinner a few times, but he always said he had to go somewhere with Jerry or Jessica and Freddy. The most time she had spent with Harry was a few lunches at Jerry Ackerman's golf club and once again at Nick and Tony's in East Hampton. These were fun, casual times, but hardly what one would call intimate dating. It was difficult for Penny because both times she ran into him, he was wonderfully attentive and always said, "Let's get together real soon." Soon was never soon enough. She felt a mixture of hope and frustration, and was beginning to feel powerless over the situation.

Even Chas found it challenging to get Harry away from the Ackermans long enough to work his plan. He had tried to steal Harry away on Penny's behalf but wasn't having much luck. Chas was way too determined to give up that easily. He figured, if you can't beat the Ackermans, which nobody could, then join them. Chas masterminded a way to enroll Jerry and Freddy into his scheme. It was easy, really. Jerry and Freddy, unbeknownst to them, would just have to become team players. In Chas's world, they had little choice.

Penny pulled her Madonna-blasting Mercedes into the driveway of the Maidstone Arms Hotel and restaurant in East Hampton. It was a big, old colonial estate with white and green awnings and beautiful tulips in the window flower boxes. The Maidstone had earned an excellent reputation for luring some of New York's best chefs out for the summer. Today Pierre Utter Van Macht from Chez Pierre was presenting a tasting of his summer fruits *de mer*, featuring the Hamptons' local fresh oysters, shrimp, and lobsters.

Penny was relieved that Pierre had agreed to cater the intimate little dinner party that Chas had finally managed to orchestrate for her. She was going to taste the food before she allowed Pierre to serve it at her party. Even though he was one of New York's top celebrity chefs, this gourmet maestro had to succumb to the taste buds of a deep-pocketed, burger-chomping chow-hound like Penny Marks. No matter how brilliant world-renowned chef Pierre was, on New York's golden beach he was only as good as his rich patrons allowed him to be. In the Hamptons, even a Cordon Bleu-educated culinary artist had to obey the golden rule: "Those who have the gold, make the rules." This applied to everyone, without exception.

Pierre's menu would open with *escargot de champions*, followed by a salmon mousse and *haricot verts turine*. The main course was to be Pierre's summer signature dish, lobster in chanterelle and white truffle sauce. Dessert, a chocolate flourless torte with creme brulée topping. Only a little Chateau d'Yquem would be served with dessert. No other alcohol would be offered. Penny didn't want to give the Ackermans an excuse to keep Harry home.

The impending dinner party was the first time that she and Harry would be together as a couple. Well, really just dinner partners, but that would be a good place to start. Penny was extremely nervous because of the other high-powered, young Jewish couples who had been invited. It was one thing to have a massive beach barbeque for a million people, but it was quite something else to impress twelve of New York's wealthiest, most-sought-after dinner guests. Would the chef from Chez Pierre and the $800 a bottle dessert wine be enough? These people ate Chez Pierre like it was McDonald's. Penny was afraid that even lobster with truffles, salmon mousse, and Chateau d'Yquem would seem like a Happy Meal. Yet, she knew it was the best that anyone could do. She prayed it would work.

Penny walked into the tasting room of the Maidstone Arms wearing a white Marina Renaldi pullover shirt, baggy J. Crew khaki shorts and Prada sandals. She looked comfortably chic.

"Where have you been, Penny? You're almost a half hour late," Chas, wearing a button down blue striped Oxford and pale yellow slacks, squeaked as he came flying through the kitchen doors. "You can't keep Pierre waiting like this.

He's doing you a very special favor tonight, and must have your sauce approval *tout de suite*!" Chas clapped his hands accentuating his use of the French language.

"I'm sorry Chas, I fell asleep by the pool after Jena's massage. I didn't realize what time it was," Penny said looking nervously at her watch.

"All right, well, I'll tell Pierre you're here now. Let's hope he's still happy to work with you. There's nothing worse than a chef who feels like he's been ignored like a limp piece of crudité…" Chas whined, flopping his wrist like a wilting piece of celery.

"Chas, I said I was sorry. I'm only twenty-five minutes late," Penny said, once again pointing to her diamond, Cartier time-telling arm piece.

"Twenty-five minutes is an eternity for a culinary master like Pierre Utter Van Macht. He has seen the rise and fall of endless soufflés during that time! When he says a dish will be at its peak at 1:33, he means it, Penny," Chas said glaring at her sternly.

"Chas, I'm freaking out about tonight enough as it is. You don't have to compound the issue with making me responsible for timing the exact moment my guests need to swallow the snails," Penny said, rolling her eyes and once again doing the Yentah Stomp.

"Okay, Penny, have it your way, as usual. But if Judy Cohen pushes her seafood fork around the plate and nothing disappears, it's not my fault," Chas said sticking his perfect nose in the air.

"Judy Cohen hasn't eaten anything since 1972. She is not exactly the greatest taste meter," Penny said, rummaging through her purse frantically searching for her ringing cell phone.

"Just because she'd rather pick at food than wear it doesn't make her a bad person, Penny," Chas said wryly.

Penny looked at her phone and saw it was her anorexic sister calling from Europe. She immediately switched it off and threw it out the window in a fit of rage. "That's it, I'm outta here, Chas. I don't need your shit today," Penny said, running outside and searching through the bushes looking for the phone that she had hastily let go of like a hot potato. Penny was in no mood for Chas's little jibes. All she wanted to do was leave Pierre a check, go home, and talk Jena into giving her another massage. Nothing was more comforting to Penny than her friend's soft, reassuring touch.

"Oh, Penny, I didn't mean anything by that. My God, you take everything so damn personally. I swear, Penny, I wish you could just come to grips with your food issue and get over it." Chas ran outside after Penny and helped her retrieve her phone.

"If I didn't have a food issue, I wouldn't be blowing all this cash to have a tight-ass, prima donna chef turn my house into a goddamn gourmet orgasm. Okay?" Penny said, brushing off her phone and putting it back into her Louis Vuitton bag.

"Ssshh, he might hear you Penny, his ears are as sensitive as his palate!" Chas said, as they walked back into the Maidstone. Practically on cue, Pierre sauntered into the room, acting like he heard their whole conversation. "Bon jour, Mademoiselle Marks. Lovely to see you looking so, so, well casz-u-al."

He was a stout iron tank of a man with greased-back black hair and a little moustache under a pug nose—like Hitler in an apron. He tried to pass himself off as being raised in San Tropez but his French didn't quite roll off his tongue as elegantly as his truffle sauce.

"Hi, Pierre. What do you have for me to eat?" Penny said. "I'm in a hurry. I want to relax a little before tonight."

"Very well, Mademoiselle Marks. I have a full tasting of tonight's menu waiting for you. If you are in that much of a hurry, I can put a sampling in a doggy bag. Perhaps you can nibble the chocolate torte in the car on the way home. Ha ha ha," Pierre laughed sarcastically at yet another of those crude Americans who he knew kept him in business. He pretended to frantically search around the room for a something that looked like a take out paper sack.

"The sampling in a doggy bag...that's sooo funny!" Chas squealed. "Oh, Pierre, it's so wonderful how you can maintain your sense of humor," Chas fawned over Pierre in order to keep him happy. He clapped his hands together as if to applaud the stuffy chef. He couldn't afford to alienate one of the best chefs in town because of Penny's lousy attitude.

Penny hated when Chas and one of his "people" ganged up on her. It made her feel so insecure, even though she was bankrolling both of them. Why couldn't they just be nice to her, like Jena was? Was that too much to ask?

"Look, Pierre, I'm sorry. This is a very stressful day for me. I'd be happy to stay and try everything. I'm sure it's all perfect."

"Beyond perfect!" Pierre proclaimed. "Follow me, Mademoiselle."

Penny followed Harry and Pierre into the kitchen. The smell of the flourless chocolate torte baking was an intoxicating aphrodisiac. After one bite, Penny was in love. For all his biting sarcasm and snippy remarks, Pierre was one master chef. His gastronomic delicacies were truly beyond perfection, and also beyond Penny's ability to control her appetite.

"This is the most incredible thing I have ever eaten," Penny said scarfing down a fourth plate of lobster. Chas grabbed her wrist and tried to stop her as she went for a fifth one, but it was no use. She was on a mission. Chas even tried to pry the lobster-filled fork out of Penny's hand, before she could stuff it in her mouth, but it was an impossible task. The two of them were engaged in a near arm wrestle when their struggling and fighting accidentally knocked over the whole lobster pot. Without even thinking about it, Penny reached down on the counter and used her bare hands to scoop up the chunks of lobster that didn't fall on the floor. She frantically shoved them into her mouth, like she was competing for a championship on "The Battle of the Vegas Buffets."

"Thank you very much, Mademoiselle Marks...Monsieur Greer thought it would meet your standards," Pierre chuckled. He loved nothing more than to see his rich and famous clients become totally unglued after eating his food. It was his own little power trip, the only one a man like Pierre could get in the "Cash Is King" Hamptons. Pierre continued to laugh triumphantly as he watched Penny devour more food than a five-hundred-pound gorilla. Chas, now feeling totally defeated in his failed attempted to stop Penny, watched in horror as she vacuumed up plate after plate of escargots. She sucked down more salmon mousse and lobster, and swallowed five miniature chocolate tortes in almost one breath. Pierre kept the feeding frenzy going with sheer delight, secretly hoping she would explode.

Chas knew he had to get her out of there tactfully and without insulting Pierre. A courtier's job was never done. *Why does a simple menu tasting have to turn into the last supper?* Chas thought. *How could she do this just a few hours before her big night with Harry? She is certifiably crazy*, Chas concluded. Still, he couldn't afford to give up. Chas needed to get Penny out of the kitchen while she could still fit into her two-seater Mercedes, let alone her Jill Sanders dinner dress.

"Penn, sweetie-pie, don't you think it's time to get going? You did say you wanted to get a massage before tonight. And oh, maybe a workout?"

"She is working out, Monsieur Greer...she's doing a hundred fork lifts a minute!" Pierre laughed. "My food has that effect on people, I'm afraid, Mademoiselle Marks."

Penny was so deep into her binge she didn't even notice what was said. She just blocked everything else out to be alone with the food, even if there were other people standing there.

"Penny, dear, really, there is so much to do before tonight," Chas said. "I think we must be going. I'm sure Pierre had a lot more preparation for this evening as well."

"None, I am all finished. Mademoiselle Marks can stay and eat as long as she likes," Pierre smiled wryly.

"Penny, it's time to go *now*!" Chas said, literally taking a fork full of lobster out of her hand, midway to her lips.

"Oh, Chas, relax, there's like no calories in fish. I'm just having one more bite," Penny said, grabbing the fork again. Just then her cell phone started to ring.

Thank the Lord, Chas thought. *She can't possibly talk and chew that much at the same time.*

"Hello," Penny said with a mouth full of truffle sauce. "Hey, Jena. Yeah, just had a little tasting of tonight's menu. Yeah, it's great. I just sampled a little bit, don't worry. I wouldn't want to get a massage on a full stomach."

Chas and Pierre looked at each other in disbelief. Did Penny actually become unconscious during her food orgy? Did she lose track of total time and space? Chas had never seen an act of such total denial. Neither had Pierre. Nonetheless, it paid their bills.

"Well, I gotta go, guys. Pierre, here's the balance. See ya tonight, and thanks for everything."

Penny wrote Pierre a check, which was stained with her sticky, sweet, fishy fingertips. She then left through the kitchen door, rubbing her stomach like she was either about to throw up or give birth to a chocolate-covered lobster.

Pierre looked at the smeary check and smiled with delight. "A client for life! She's a goner."

Chas looked like someone had just spilled black ink and prune juice over his winning lottery ticket. If Penny could pig out so heavily just a few hours before seeing her possible future husband, Chas knew he was fighting an almost impossible battle. How could she ever keep enough weight off to fit into a wedding dress?

Chas had noticed that in the past few weeks, Penny's pounds were slowly creeping back on. He had tried to talk to her about it, but she swore up and down that she was just bloated with water weight. In the summer, she said, she had a problem with swelling, and diuretics were little or no help.

Chas knew the truth. The truth was that Penny was disappointed Harry was not around as much as she hoped. Chas, too, was disappointed that it had taken so long to get them together. Yet it was better late than never. Penny's dinner party would be the beginning of a new relationship, and even if the relationship had to be with Harry and Freddy and Jessica, Chas would see to it that the four of them would become inseparable. It was time to get tough and make things happen. If Penny could put down a lobster long enough to stay in a conversation, Chas could see no further holdups.

That evening, Penny's big, shingled beach house was illuminated with absolute brilliance. The ocean view from the Coquina-stoned dining veranda just off the loggia was breathtaking. The light from a glistening full moon sparkled in the Waterford crystal. The Cartier place settings for twelve graced a marble tabletop. White orchids overflowed large urns and filled the air with a sweet, tropical fragrance.

Penny had prepared properly for her Prince Charming and her noble guests. No matter what happened that night, no one, not even Judy Cohen, could say that the house and the dining area were less than spectacular. An aura of sublime excellence was manifested. This was how the Hamptons' elite would meet and eat.

One by one, the coaches carrying six couples, Chas's twelve chosen dinner disciples, drove down Penny's long gravel driveway. A white Jaguar brought David and Judy Cohen. A huge green Porsche carrying Robert and Mayling Silverman was followed by a black Saab with Jill and Rudy Borrell. Then came Chas and Juan's flaming red BMW, and finally the baby blue "double R" rolling in Freddy, Jessica, and Harry, the Messiah of the moment.

The couples all followed Chas and Juan onto the patio. As they moved through the house, it was obvious that they were each taking their own personal survey of Penny's posh surroundings and attempting to figure out how much she was actually worth. Calculating a monetary evaluation of the hostess was the natural step one in the Hamptons' dining ritual.

Could Penny Marks be richer than we are? was the first question that ran through her guest's minds, as they cased her joint more thoroughly than a gang of professional thieves. Some noticed the Picassos hanging on the walls, while others focused on her prime real estate with the splendid ocean view. The more they tried not to be obvious, the more they caught each other "running Penny's numbers" in their heads. After completing an internal intake of

Penny's belongings that was more in depth than an IRS audit, the dinner guests gave in to the gourmet goodies that were yet another sign of Penny's prosperity and blessed fortune. The couples were served beluga on toast points and non-alcoholic Bellinis. Everyone was to wait there and converse until Penny made her grand entrance.

Upstairs, Jena was squeezing Penny into her white piqué dress. This was no easy feat, despite the holding power of every Nancy Ghantz slimming undergarment that Penny wore. Penny had consumed half the fish in the North Atlantic earlier that afternoon, along with all the chocolate in Belgium.

"You know, I'm almost tempted to do a Bunny and throw up," Penny said, gasping for air as Jena pulled at the dress, trying to force the zipper.

"I can't let you do that, honey. No matter what you did today, I can't let you punish yourself any further."

"What was I thinking today?" Penny screamed, as she angrily pinched the fat on her bloated stomach. "Why didn't Chas stop me? How could he let me eat so much? He knows I'm helpless against lobster and chocolate! He should have done something, even if he had to call the East Hampton Fire Department to come and haul my fat ass out of there!" she cried, playing with the flab under her slightly double chin making two into four.

"Penny, please. Self-abusive language is only going to make you more upset. Forgive yourself. Wear something else!" Jena said calmly, gently taking Penny's hands away from her face.

"No, damn it, Chas brought this dress in tonight and this is what I'm putting on, end of story!" Penny insisted defiantly, as she sucked herself in with all her might.

Jena gave the zipper a final heave-ho and the entire back of the dress ripped apart.

"Shit!" Penny yelled. "Shit! Shit! Shit! I've got New York's top-ten A-list couples downstairs and my only chance at marriage slurping down caviar at a hundred bucks a bite. Fat Penny can't even get out of the starting gate! I'm so fucking pathetic!" Penny said, pulling and shaking her perfectly coifed five-hundred-dollar hairdo.

Penny threw herself violently on the bed. She started bawling uncontrollably and ripping the dress to shreds. Jena lay down beside Penny and put her arms around her.

"Penny, you're beautiful just the way you are. It's not the clothes these people are here to see, it's you," Jena said, caressing Penny's throbbing head.

"Me? Bullshit! Haven't you been in New York long enough to know that you are only as good as your latest Armani? It took me months to fit into that Jill Sander and I blew it in one day. My life is over," Penny said, practically throwing Jena off of her and rolling away to the other side of the massive bed.

"It's not over, Penn, it's just beginning. Harry's downstairs waiting for you!" Jena said enthusiastically sitting up and getting herself together.

"Don't remind me. I'm too damn blimpy to face him now! I can't do it, Jena. I wish they would all just go home!" Penny cried as she looked out of her window. She could see all of her perfect guests mingling perfectly, on her perfect patio of her perfect oceanfront estate. The only thing that felt seriously less than perfect tonight was Penny herself. At that moment, the Hampton "hostess with the mostest" would have gladly traded it all for a swamp-front trailer park in the Everglades, if she could have just gotten that dress up around her waist.

"That's not what you really want, Penny. You have a closet full of beautiful things," Jena said, looking at Penny's designer-packed closet in absolute amazement. Although

Jena was used to the opulence and excessiveness of her wealthy clients, sometimes the magnitude of it all just blew her away. "Why not just put on another outfit? Go downstairs and be the flawless hostess I know you are," Jena said with encouragement.

"I can't just put *anything* on just like that! Is Chas here yet?" Penny said beginning to calm down and blowing her nose into a tissue that Jena handed her.

"I thought I saw his car pull up a while ago," Jena said reassuringly, looking out the window on the other side of the room that allowed a view of the driveway.

"Thank God, I pray he's got his cell phone with him." Penny picked up her phone and began dialing frantically. Meanwhile, Chas, head to toe in Polo for men, was floating around the party, playing queen bee until the hostess arrived. This was the first time he had brought Juan out in public. Juan had such innocent sexiness about him. If Enriqué Iglesias and J. Lo had a child, it would be the soft, sensuous Juan. Even though there was enough money in the room to end world hunger, Chas now felt comfortable introducing everyone to his new Latin love. His feelings for Juan were deepening to the extent that Chas sincerely believed that Juan could be a permanent fixture in his soon-to-be perfect life. On one level it scared him how much he was falling for Juan. On another level, it excited him tremendously. Chas had loved only money until he fell for this little Spanish boy with the big eyelashes and solid buns.

Chas was talking to Judy and David when he felt Juan come up behind him. Juan discreetly slipped the active cell phone into Chas's back pocket.

"I thought that was you, naughty," Chas teased. Shivers went up Chas's spine as he felt Juan's hand on his buttocks, thinking the vibrations he was feeling were from Juanita's sheer electric touch.

"Your phone is ringing, daaahling," Juan said.

"Oh my God, I thought it was you causing those vibrations! I must be totally losing it. Besides, who could be calling me now? Everyone who matters is here!" Chas took out his cell phone and noticed it was Penny's private number. Worried about what disaster could be ruminating upstairs, Chas excused himself and went to a private corner around the side of the house, where he was sure that no one could hear his conversation.

"Hello?" Chas whispered hesitantly.

"Chas, it's Penn. I need your help fast. There's been an emergency."

"Oh my God, everybody's here! What happened?" Chas whispered again into the phone, looking at the guests and smiling like nothing was wrong in case anyone saw him.

"The dress. It burst apart! I mean, I almost burst apart! The dress practically split in two when I tried to zip it up. What the fuck am I going to wear?" Penny said standing in her closet, as Jena was pulling out dress after dress, trying to get Penny to approve just one.

"Okay, remain calm. The fashion 911 rescue team has been dispatched. We'll be right there," Chas said, purposely turning away from the guests, who were beginning to stare at him curiously

"Hurry up, I think I'm having an anxiety attack." Penny exclaimed as she violently threw a dress that Jena handed her in the garbage pail.

"Is Jena there?" Chas asked helplessly, hating the fact that Jena might actually be necessary in this desperate situation.

"Yes," Penny said, panting heavily.

"Put her on." Chas demanded

"Hello, it's Jena."

"Jena, what are Penny's symptoms?" Chas said smiling looking down at his Gucci shoes, noticing how small and dainty his feet were. The fact that he was still gorgeous made him feel better in the worst of circumstances.

"Shaking, crying, screaming, throwing around her Manolo Blahniks," Jena said, calmly.

"Okay, try to settle her down, Jena." Chas muttered under his breath as he nonchalantly sashayed his way back into to the party. "I'm on my way," he said as he hung up the phone. "Oh Juan, Penny needs us upstairs for a moment," Chas said smoothly, as he took Juan under the arm and lead him towards the house.

"Is something wrong with Penny?" obnoxious Judy Cohen said in her signature loud voice while picking at a canapé with her long red nails.

"Of course not, Judy. She'll be down in one minute," Chas assured her. "Just give us one second, and enjoy the view and the beluga—or both!"

Chas and Juan disappeared into the house and ran up the stairs to Penny's suite. There she was, a sight to behold. Her once-coifed hair was now all tossed. The lovely makeup was smudged all over her puffy face. The dress was completely destroyed. It looked like a pile of designer confetti strewn all over her room.

"I'm a mess," Penny cried.

"Now, now, chica bonita, ees not so baad," Juan said. "Juanita and Chassy are going to make you pretty. Dunt jyou hworry about a theeng."

Even though Juan speaks like Ricky Ricardo on fairy dust, his sweetness always comes oozing through in tough times, Chas thought, as he admired his lover's ability to handle any situation with compassion. Juan immediately got a wet face cloth from the bathroom and gently washed away Penny's dripping mascara and runny lipstick. He patted her face gently, and began to apply a total fresh face of makeup. Juan could make her look even better than she had pre-tantrum.

"I jused to hwork as a makeup arteest in Caracas before I got into de flowers. I looove makeups. Jyou gonna look so beautiful..jyou see, baby!"

Meanwhile, Chas was speedily rummaging through Penny's closet trying to put together an alternative outfit.

"Penny, I think under the circumstances, we are going to have to go with another Eileen Fisher," Chas declared.

"But, he's seen me in Eileen Fisher twice already."

"Well, you should have thought of that five chocolate tortes ago!"

"Hush, Chassy, jyou'll hupset my princess," Juan chimed in as he finished blending in cheekbones where there were none.

"Juan's right. No use crying over swallowed truffles, Penny. If you can't bear another night in Eileen, Donna Karan's old black standby is your only other option. Don't even talk to me about the Donatella Versace tonight!"

"Fine, give me the Donna Karan thing. At least she comprehends real women's bodies."

Penny grabbed the black dress out of Chas's hand and went into her changing room. Two minutes later, she reappeared, looking quite nice. The dress was more understanding and forgiving than the Jill Sander. Juan had done a superior job repairing her hair and makeup. After all that, Penny really looked terrific.

"You look gorgeous," Jena said, being ever so supportive.

"Not exactly gorgeous, but it will have to do for now," Penny said.

"Dunt be so negative, chica. Jyou look juanderful." Juan waved and clapped his dainty dark hands, happy with the results he provided.

"Come on already, Penny! It's time to go downstairs. People will start to wonder what's going on!" Chas said, getting rather antsy. He could be having such a good time. How dare she almost ruin *his* party?

"Okay. Fine. Jena, are you sure you won't come?"

"I'm sure, Penn, it's your night. I'll be here when you're finished. You can tell me about it."

Chas looked at Jena and raised an eyebrow. "I'm glad to see you are finally learning your place," he said with a smirk.

Jena said nothing, but shot him a look of death.

"Chas, baby, please dunt estart! Let's just get Señorita Penny down estairs," Juan begged.

Juan and Chas each took one of Penny's arms and escorted her out the door. With their arms locked in hers, she couldn't back out now.

"Look who's here," Chas proclaimed as he and Juan practically dragged Penny onto the veranda to greet her guests. Penny tried desperately to hide a look of absolute terror. She couldn't be a relaxed hostess in her own home with all these people there.

The first thing Penny noticed was how tiny Judy Cohen looked in her Chanel midriff top and skirt. At almost forty years of age, Judy Cohen could put Kate Moss to shame, Penny thought.

Mayling Silverman, in a plain beige Armani summer suit, was a minuscule, Chinese lotus flower who married her shining Jewish American Prince, Robert. Jill Borrell looked like a Jewish version of Christie Brinkley, with her straightened blonde hair, big blue eyes and carefully maintained body displayed nicely in a sheer Max Mara slip dress.

Only Jessica Ackerman Levitt didn't appear threatening to Penny that night. Even though Jessica was on the petite side, there was a natural softness about her that the other women had lost. Jessica was dressed modestly, as usual, in a non-designer, long silk floral dress and open-toe black sandals. She looked simple and harmless. Penny was glad to have her there.

"Penny, dahlink..." Judy Cohen drawled. "Thanks so much for having us over. So good to finally catch up with you. Your house looks terrific." Penny was shocked. Judy Cohen was actually giving someone a compliment. This was a rare moment in time.

"Thanks Judy, I'm glad you and David could make it. I know how busy you are, especially with the new baby."

"Oh please. I promised myself I would never let children rob me of my social identity. I mean, I deserve to have a life too, right? I can't understand these mothers who stop everything to baby-sit their children. I don't think that's very healthy."

Penny's usually healthy apple-colored cheeks turned an ashen, ghostly white as she glared at this disgusting, puny shrew of a woman with her most evil eye. As crazy and neurotic as Penny was, she still had a big heart. Penny only dreamed of the day she would have a husband like David Cohen, and two beautiful kids to spoil rotten. It seemed like an eternity away.

"Look at Jill Borrell," Judy went on, lowering her voice to a loud whisper that she thought only Penny would hear. "Rudy spends a fortune on nannies, and Jill still sits with her kids all day. I see them at the Bridgehampton Beach Club all the time. I can't understand it. Her kids have the nanny and they are old enough for day camps. Why does Jill tie herself down like that? It's ridiculous. I'm sure Rudy isn't employing half the 'Irish Echo' so his wife can carry around pails and shovels. She should really get with it. Her kids are going to wind up resenting her for it later, anyway. You watch, in a few years, Jill's kids will be telling the shrink that mommy smothered them. Not my kids. My kids will learn to appreciate mommy when she's around. See what I mean?"

"Yeah, I guess so. I mean, I'd love to have these problems someday. Guess I should concentrate on getting married first," Penny said humbly.

"Oh, you should have no problem finding a nice husband. Look at this beautiful house, look at the ocean view, look at your exquisite Cartier china. Penny, you have everything a man could want."

As twisted as it came out, at least Judy was being complimentary. And at this point, Penny appreciated any kind of reassurance at all.

"That's nice of you to say, Judy."

"Well, it's absolutely true, dear. You're quite a nice package," Judy continued. "Where is a guy going to get a girl like you? I'm sure you'll have men lining up to have a date with you, as soon as you *lose the weight.*"

Penny's face dropped like the ball from top of the Empire State Building on New Year's Eve. She couldn't believe what Judy had just said right to her face. Judy's stage whisper was gone now and she had returned to speaking in her voice. Penny was absolutely horrified that this woman would insult her like that, in her own home, with a roomful of guests. Everybody else seemed busy talking and nibbling caviar, but what if somebody heard?

I should blast this bitch in front of everyone and then throw out on her bony ass, Penny thought to herself as she stared at Judy Cohen. *But, wait a minute. Harry Raider is here. Is it really worth it to flip out in front of him and let him see what a maniac I can be, when a scumbag like Judy runs her mouth? I think not! Why let the bitch win? For once in my life, I think I'll hold my tongue. Dad would so proud—shocked, but proud*, Penny thought, smiling up at the stars.

"People think I'm naturally thin," Judy Cohen relentlessly continued. "They think I was born this way. They should only know at my sweet sixteen party I was one-hundred-forty pounds! One-hundred-forty pounds! I know you probably can't believe it looking at me today, but I swear on my son's life, it's true," Judy declared triumphantly.

"So how do you keep it off?" Penny asked having decided to just politely play along with her and not to blow her stack.

"Discipline. Dis-ci-pline! You don't need a lot of food to survive, Penny. Just orange juice and vitamins in the morning. A little vegetable soup and salad for lunch, maybe some steamed vegetables and egg whites for dinner. It's simple. What's the big deal? If you go out for dinner, have one bite of everything and push the plate away. Who can't do that? You've got to be a complete moron not to see how easy it is. Only a dumb idiot couldn't follow my diet. If you want, I'll write it down for you before I leave."

Penny felt another panic attack coming on. She felt like that "dumb idiot" who couldn't find the willpower to survive on lettuce and egg whites. Didn't Judy Cohen have any emotions or feelings whatsoever? But looking at the other thin women in the room, Penny started to think that maybe there was something very wrong with *her*. *She* seemed to be the only one who couldn't get it under control.

Penny began to feel dizzy and light-headed, as her breathing quickened. The rest of the guests were approaching to say hello to her, but she couldn't hear them now. The room was spinning and her heart was beating so fast it felt like it was going to jump out of her chest. She felt beads of sweat gathering behind her knees and her legs began to wobble. She knew there was no wine at the bar to calm her down. Penny felt desperately marooned on an island of fat surrounded by a sea of skinny enemies. Any minute now, she thought that she would cave in and fall to the floor in utter dismay. Seconds seemed like hours as she awaited her impending blackout.

"Penny Marks! Hi ya, gorgeous! Great dress...let's get a shot. Babe-a-licious!"

All Penny could see was a flash bulb going off in her face as Harry snapped away. The next thing she knew Harry had his arms around her, and was kissing her cheek as Chas took his turn playing photographer. Slowly Penny's breathing began to slow down as she came out of her anxiety-induced daze.

"Doesn't Penny look to die for, Harry?" Chas chimed in. "When Juan and I saw how stunning she looks, we just couldn't get over it!"

"Chas is right, Penn. You're hot, baby," Harry said as he playfully danced around Penny.

"Really?" was all Penny could get out of her mouth.

"You bet, babe. Would I lie? Remember, I'm Harry of Hollywood. I see bitchin' babes strolling down Sunset Boulevard every day. Tonight, you look as awesome as any *Playboy* bunny up at Hef's place. The view from their silicone valley is the same every Sunday morning, if you know what I mean. Harry needs a real woman!"

Harry put his arms around Penny's not so tiny waist. He gave her another bear hug and planted a big kiss on her cheek. From just two minutes of Harry, Penny went from feeling like a roly-poly social pariah to the next Cindy Crawford. All of her guests gushed "Aw" and smiled with approval at the open display of affection between the Beverly Hills billionaire and his hostess, the single and available Miss Penny Marks. *Are we witnessing the beginnings of social coup? Is a merger marriage in the works?* everyone wondered, as Penny glowed brighter than a UFO in a desert sky. Harry was truly magic. No matter what would happen between them from now on, Penny would always love him for making her feel like a human again.

"Dinner is being served on the veranda," Pierre appeared from the kitchen in his chef's uniform. He waved a white napkin signaling for the couples to take their seats. The gourmet gala was about to begin.

Chas prayed that Penny had eaten enough this afternoon not to make a pig of herself again at dinner. He was watching her like the Weight Watchers police. Every time she picked up her fork, even just to play with the food on her plate, Chas held his breath and didn't exhale until she put it down again. He took some solace in the fact that Penny was so distracted she even found it difficult to eat when she was around Harry. Chas hoped Harry would keep her amused long enough for the waiters to clear away each course's plate with the food still on it.

"You must really be enjoying your summer, Harry. The weather's been great, and you seem like you've had a lot going on over the past few weeks," Penny said, trying to make conversation with Harry.

"Yeah, well, Jessica, I mean Freddy and Jessica, have been wonderful hosts. They keep me really busy."

Harry winked at Jessica, which made her blush. Freddy, of course, smiled politely.

"What have you been doing?" Penny asked.

"I've been fishing, golfing, eating, and painting."

"Painting? I didn't know you were an artist, Harry."

"Well, not exactly. Jessica's the artist, I've just been acting as her primal subject."

"Really? You mean, Jessica painted a portrait of you? I'd love to see it."

Harry burst out laughing.

"I bet you would, sweetheart. It's a revealing masterpiece to behold...and if you're lucky...I'll let you hold the masterpiece."

Jessica's face now was turning bright red. The whole table

looked at her curiously while Freddy was dying of embarrassment, dreading where this conversation was going.

"You know, I'd always thought all those nude paintings in the museums my mom used to drag me to were sooo cool. When we went to Italy and we saw that statue of that dude, you know—*David*—I thought, wow, man. Imagine what it would be like to stand there butt-naked for hours while someone tried to mold you out of clay. Would that be killer, or what? What a radical time he must have had! I loved it too. It was so freeing!"

By this time, everyone at the table was totally silent. Even Judy Cohen, with her irrepressible diarrhea of the mouth, was at a loss for words. Her husband David and the other men at the table just looked at poor Freddy Levitt with true pity. They all had just witnessed him being totally emasculated by a man who was not only much richer than he would ever be, but probably better hung. This could drive someone to suicide in the Hamptons. Nobody was quite sure how to react to the fact that Harry Raider had just divulged that his married hostess had painted him in the nude. Even for this sophisticated Hamptons crowd, who thought they had seen and heard it all, Harry was an experience! Chas knew he had to say something to break the silence.

"Harry, who knew you were such a connoisseur of fine art? How interesting."

"Oh, yes," Mayling Silverman, the forever-do-the-right-thing socialite, interjected. "You must join our table for the Parrish Art Museum Ball next Saturday," Mayling said.

"I'm not going to another museum unless Jessica's paintings are hanging on the wall. I've been to Versailles, the Pompidou, the Ufizzi, the Met, and all that crap. Why should I schlep to another museum when I can see the most kick-ass art in the world right in my new summer home?"

Freddy's face was turning every color in the rainbow, as he attempted to conceal his rage. *The Ackerman estate is* my *home, damn it. I want to take this lobster tail and ram it down Harry's throat. When will this lunatic learn his place? When will Harry just go home and stop humiliating me again and again?* he thought.

Jessica, though, was quite delighted with Harry's public approval of her art. Nobody, not even her beloved daddy, had praised her work so generously, to the point where other people had to take notice. She would have loved to gain recognition for doing something besides being Jerry Ackerman's daughter. Tonight, Harry let her be a star in her own right. That was a precious gift no one had ever given her, one that money couldn't buy.

Penny raised her glass to toast Jessica. "Jessica, I would love to see some of your work. I'm afraid to admit that I don't really know too much about art, but if Harry says it's great, I'm sure it is," Penny proclaimed, thinking she'd score points with Harry and Jessica at the same time. "To Jessica, our brilliant artist in the making," Penny said, completing the toast. "Here, Here," the other guests replied and clinked their glasses to followed suit.

"I'd like that, Penny. Come over anytime. Next week for lunch?" Jessica smiled, basking in the attention she was getting about her undiscovered art.

"Sounds fantastic!" Penny exclaimed.

Perfect, Chas thought as he squeezed Juan's thigh under the table. *A social date put into play, and I didn't even have to stop chewing my escargot to negotiate it. My life is getting easier by the second. Bring on the d'Yquem.* Chas winked knowingly at Juan. The jackpot was getting closer.

"Jessica's paintings are the greatest, Penny. Maybe she could do one of you and me together. Would you get naked with me for the sake of furthering art history?" Harry asked.

Penny didn't know what to say. She was so ashamed of her body, yet this may be her first stab at intimacy with Harry. "Well I don't know..." Penny stammered nervously, embarrassed in front of her guests who probably thought she was too robust to ever consider such a feat. Penny looked around the table to get a reaction. Mayling Silverman smiled politely, as usually. Jill Borrell pretended to stare out at the ocean, and miraculously, David Cohen seemed to nod his head in approval. Ironically, Penny could see Judy Cohen practically choking on her lobster at the thought of a naked picture of a chubby woman. This absolutely infuriated Penny. She would have to do it now, if only to piss Judy off! Penny would have to force herself to get over her fat trip and go for the gusto. *After all, Rubens made a whole career out of painting women like me*, Penny thought. *Maybe Harry has a thing for those grape-eating, harp-playing, Rubenesque beauties of yesteryear. Maybe he was even reincarnated from that period.* Penny smiled to herself. Could it be that Penny found a billionaire who likes blubber? It could be nothing less than a blessing from God.

"Okay, Harry. Let's do it," Penny said with a new surge of confidence.

"I thought we agreed, no more nude painting, Harry," Freddy said, maintaining his self-control.

"I know man, but this is different. This is like a man and woman thing, you know. Like real beauty. This would give Jessica the chance to really let her talents fly. You don't have to worry, man. You can even join us if you want to," Harry said while slapping a squirming Freddy on the back. "Two guys and a girl...great! Come on, Freddy. Let it all hang out." The whole table was giggling with delight at Harry's suggestion. "I saw you in the shower the other day, man. You're all right, dude, it's all there. You can hold your head up with pride," Freddy once again felt like the object of ridicule. Harry had gone too far.

"Excuse me, I think I've heard enough." Freddy cleared his throat, adjusted his glasses, threw his napkin down like he was whipping a bad dog and quickly got up. He almost knocked the whole table over as he violently pushed his chair out and stormed away. Jessica angrily pushed the food around on her plate with her knife, but did not go after him. "Gee, the man can't even take a joke," Harry said, totally surprised by Freddy's abrupt reaction. "Has he no sense of humor? I was just busting his balls a little, trying to get him to lighten up. I don't know why he's so serious all the time!" Harry proclaimed as he looked around the table of wide-eyed guests.

"It's not your fault, Harry, it's me," Jessica said, finally putting her knife down. "I know how super sensitive Freddy is, especially in public. I should have stopped you," Jessica said.

"It's not your fault, Jessica. I'll take care of it." Harry got up from the table and went out into the driveway, where Freddy was fumbling with the keys to the Rolls. Harry came up behind Freddy and put his hand on his shoulder.

"Look, dude, I didn't mean to piss you off again. I was just having a good time. Thought you would laugh, too."

Freddy pushed Harry's hand off of him and knocked him to the ground in one fell swoop. Harry was shocked at Freddy's hidden strength—maybe he wasn't such a wimp after all.

Freddy picked Harry up by his collar and threw him up against the car door, screaming right in Harry's face. "I am sick and tired of you having a good time at my expense. You've humiliated me in front of my friends, and made my life hell since you've been here. Sure, you can just make a clown of yourself, blow through the Hamptons and then go back to L.A. I, however, have to stay here and see these people the rest of my life. I don't appreciate the size of my dick being the topic of conversation. Do you understand that?" Freddy was screaming so loud, everyone could hear him, even though he and Harry were on the other side of the house.

"Freddy, I was just kidding around with you. Why do you take everything I say so seriously, man? I'm just a clown, you said so yourself," Harry said trying to remove Freddy's hands from his neck area.

"You may be just a sorry-ass joker, but you make my wife think you're the big man. I don't know what it is you've done to her, or what kind of bullshit you've sold her, but she is not the same sweet, naive Jessica she was before you got here." Freddy threw Harry back onto the ground. Harry didn't fight back.

"What have I done that's so wrong, Freddy? I've made her laugh and encouraged her artwork, that's it. What's the big whoop?"

"Her artwork is crap! It's just something to keep her occupied all day, while I'm at the office holding down a real job. Now, because of you, she's saying she wants to show some of her infantile paintings in a gallery. She'll make a complete ass of herself, and me, in front of the entire New York art world. It will wind up costing Jerry a lot of money, and gain her absolutely nothing. I don't talk about her art because I don't want her to get ripped to shreds by critics. She won't be able to handle the New York art scene. It's very tough and Jessica is a baby, for Christ's sake. As long as she stays in the garden with her dog, there'll be no problem. She doesn't need you giving her dangerous ideas." Freddy kicked some of the gravel from the driveway towards Harry's face while Harry quickly blocked his eyes from the flying tiny stones.

"Dangerous ideas for who, man? For you or Jessica? I think you're afraid that if she doesn't feel so helpless anymore, she'll find somebody more interesting than you. Somebody that adds a little color to her life, not somebody who pisses on her daisies," Harry said, standing up and brushing himself off.

"And who is that someone, Harry? Is it you? Why don't you just admit you're trying to steal my wife, right under my own roof?" Freddy said pointing at Harry accusingly.

"I'm not trying to steal your wife, man. I can't help it if she likes me. You think I have a chick problem? Hey, I can have any chick I want. You saw my equipment, dude. I'm one of the few rich guys who could still probably get laid without flashing the cash. I'm a babe magnet," Harry said striking a cocky pose.

"I don't care who or what you are, but you are not going to have Jessica. She's my wife, and she doesn't need your money or anything else you think you have so much of. Stay away from her. Have I made myself clear?" Freddy said, pushing up to Harry and blasting him in the face.

"That's enough, Freddy."

The two men looked up to see Jessica standing there. Neither one of them knew how much she had heard or seen.

"I think we better leave. Harry, why don't you go back to the party. I'm sure Penny would love to spend more time with you and get to know you better. Do yourself a favor and leave out the part about fucking half of Los Angeles. I'm sure it's not your most award-winning accomplishment," Jessica said with an unfamiliar tone of sarcasm.

"Yeah, uh, sure. No sweat," Harry said, trying to hide his chagrin.

"Just call the chauffeur when you're ready to come home," Jessica said, coldly.

"Yeah, uh, right. I won't be late. Goodnight," said Harry as he headed back towards the house. With shameful thoughts entering his mind for the first time, Harry hung his head as he immediately retreated back towards the party.

Jessica and Freddy stood alone in the crisp evening air. She couldn't meet his wanting glance. He took her by her delicate shoulders and tried to pull her close to him, but she resisted.

"I'm sorry about what I said about your artwork, Jes. I was just trying to look out for your own good. You know that, right?" Freddy said, hoping she would forgive him.

"I'm tired, Freddy. Let's just go *home.*" Jessica said backing away from her husband's embrace.

"Jessica, do you forgive me?" Freddy asked Jessica, with sincere remorse in his voice.

"I don't know anymore, Freddy. I just don't know," Jessica said, grabbing for the car door and not being able to look Freddy in the eye.

Without saying another word, Jessica and Freddy got into the Rolls and drove into the night.

Later that evening, the party picked up as the couples were around the pool dancing to the music of the Gypsy Kings. Chas and Juan watched like proud parents as Penny and Harry danced cheek-to-cheek. Chas was surprised and thrilled to see Harry re-enter the party and focus all of his attention on Penny. After the near disaster at dinner, the evening seemed to take on a happier shift of mood.

And Chas and Juan were not the only ones floating on air. Penny couldn't remember the last time she was this close to a man who wasn't employed by her in some capacity. Even with all her insecurities, Penny was beginning to feel as though maybe her Prince Charming had indeed arrived. As their bodies pressed together, Penny envisioned them dancing at their wedding at the Plaza or maybe at the Hotel de Paris in Monte Carlo. For such a wedding, she would pull out all the stops. It just had to happen now.

All the guests had left except Chas and Juan who continued to watch and enjoy every step of Penny and Harry's love tango. Chas whispered softly in Juan's ear while licking the outer edges of it, telling him it was time to go. The two boys slipped out the back, leaving Harry and Penny alone in a romantic embrace.

"Penny, I've had an amazing time, but I promised Freddy and Jes I wouldn't be too late," Harry said.

"Oh, I don't think they'd mind if you stayed for one more dance," Penny said, not wanting to let go of Harry just yet.

"I really should get going, babe," Harry said, loosening her grip on him.

"No, wait, how about a walk on the beach? It's such a gorgeous night. We won't be gone long," Penny said, reaching for his hand.

Harry could sense Penny's need for love and her haunting loneliness. He was a compassionate man, under any circumstances.

"Okay, just a quickie," Harry said, relenting.

Harry and Penny walked in the sand under the moonlight, while the waves tickled the soles of their bare feet.

"I love the beach at night. It's so sexy." Penny said, looking up at the moon.

"Oh yeah, what do you think is sexy about it?" Harry asked inquisitively.

"Well, for one thing, I love the feeling of sand in between my toes. You know that squishy, wet feeling. It kind of gets my juices flowing in other places, if you know what I mean." Penny laughed.

"Yeah, I sure do," Harry said, admiring Penny's bold statement. He liked the fact that unlike Jessica, she wasn't afraid to say what she was thinking, sexually. Harry liked people who were willing to take a risk and Penny seemed to fit the bill. *Maybe there's something here*, Harry thought to himself, as he wiggled his toes in the sand suggestively. Penny smiled big and shamelessly wiggled her freshly painted toes back at Harry. Her hand in his, she felt as though she could conquer the world. Penny didn't think of food, Judy Cohen's snide remarks, or even her sister Bunny far away with the Arab sheik. All she could think about was her future with the man at her side.

They came back into the kitchen and toweled the salty water from their feet and legs. Penny's $1,500 Donna Karan dress now looked like a soaking wet beach rag. She didn't care. Penny offered Harry a robe, but he declined. He liked the feeling of salt water on silk shirts. She once again reached out for his hand.

"Are you sure you have to go?" she asked, dreading the answer.

"Yeah, I'm sure, Penn. We'll do this again soon. I promise."

"Okay, Harry. I believe you." Penny smiled. She wanted so much for him to stay and make love to her, but maybe the time wasn't right yet. Perhaps she'd be better off in the long run if they waited.

The Ackerman chauffeur arrived to bring Harry home. Leaving Penny with just a kiss on the cheek and a night of glorious memories, Harry was gone. Penny stood in the doorway and watched happiness being driven away in a blue Rolls Royce.

Please let this just be the beginning, she thought to herself.

Penny glided up the stairs and went into her room, where she found Jena fast asleep in her bed. She crept under the covers next to Jena, still glowing from the events of the evening. Jena, awakened gently by Penny's presence, rolled closer to her, and whispered in her ear.

"Was it wonderful?"

"Yes, it was unbelievable."

"Great. I'm happy for you. You deserve it."

"Thanks, Jena."

Jena kissed Penny on top of her head and went back to sleep. Penny just stared out the sliding glass door, watching the waves dance upon the shorelines, dreaming of the day she would be there with Harry again.

chapter sixteen

Milly sat on the mounting block at Sag Pond Stables beside where the riders were training their horses. She could feel the beads of sweat forming under her faded gray LaCoste shirt and well worn jodhpurs as she started to boil over with anger. Chas was supposed to have Harry there an hour ago. Milly hoped that Harry hadn't changed his mind and chickened out at the last minute. Milly had only seen Harry a few times after the boating incident. There were some casual tennis and golf days, but again, nothing Milly would consider a real romantic date. Like Penny, Milly ran into the same hassle with the Ackermans. It seemed as though they had every minute of every hour of every day planned for Harry. Yet Milly let Chas keep trying. After all, she had nothing to lose.

It wasn't until last Saturday at the Bridgehampton Polo Club that Harry decided he wanted to ride a horse. Despite all his money and exotic travel, it was the first time Harry had witnessed a polo match. Apparently, Harry got so excited by the thundering of hooves across the long green grass that he wanted to learn to play polo, too. He told Chas he might even like to buy his own team. Maybe one day he would play against Prince Charles at Coudrey Park. Chas had managed to convince Harry that he'd better learn to ride a horse before he challenged the Prince, and Harry agreed.

Zara, the mare, stomped her big hoof into the soft ground. She was tired of standing there with all her tack on for so long. It wasn't like her trusty owner Milly to keep her so uncomfortable. "I know, I know, girl. This is a big pain in the butt. They're probably not going to show up anyway. I'm sorry. You don't deserve this." Milly put her arms around Zara's big gray neck and patted her lovingly. "I should know by now to always put you first," Milly said as she adoringly stroked her animal. "I hope you can forgive me. There will be an extra bag of carrots in your feed today."

Zara still looked unamused. She wanted Milly to get on, run through her paces, jump a few obstacles, then be allowed to graze leisurely in her pasture. A horse's life was quite basic.

Just as Milly was about to untack Zara and give her the afternoon off, Chas's new BMW came ripping up the barn driveway. He honked his horn loud enough to spook a few of the horses in the ring. Milly had warned him over and over again not to be so reckless around animals, but Chas never listened or learned. Chas waved enthusiastically to Milly as to announce their arrival.

Funny enough, Chas not only hated horses, he hated the fact that Milly spent more money on equestrian pursuits than she did with him on clothes. He inevitably saw the horse as competition. It made Chas crazy when Milly would spend twenty-five thousand dollars on an Hermés saddle, then bitch about the two-hundred-forty-five-dollar price of Gucci loafers. Chas thought Milly's priorities were completely screwed up. But maybe the damn beast would prove useful now, with Harry's new polo interest. The way Chas looked at it, if Zara helped Milly snag Harry, the big ole mule would eventually pay for itself.

"Hi, Mills, sorry we're late. The Ackerman's chef made an asparagus eggs benedict. Who could say no?" Chas said as he, Juan, and Harry climbed out of the Beemer.

Milly bit her tongue and smiled. She wanted to slap Chas so badly, she subconsciously smacked the riding crop against her tall boots. Zara was relieved that the boot got the brunt of Milly's anger.

"No problem. I just got here a little while ago myself," Milly lied. "Great to see you again, Harry!" Milly said, trying to sound positive and enthusiastic.

"Great to see you, too, Milly. This must be Zara. Wow. She's awesome! What a kick-ass piece of horseflesh. Hi-Ho, Silver!" Harry said, as he stroked Zara and fed her some sugar cubes from his pocket. Harry seemed to be falling for the gray mare. Zara nuzzled her nose on her new friend, licked his hand, and seemed genuinely appreciative of the treats. It was like she was telling Harry that it was worth waiting for him to show up. *It was a start,* thought Chas.

Milly had to hand it to Chas. Harry was stunningly garbed in tall riding boots, beige jodhpurs, and a blue pinstriped, rack-catcher button-down shirt. His black velvet hunt cap was also in flawless condition. He looked as if he had just stepped out of Miller's equestrian catalogue.

Milly was impressed. Obviously, when Harry Raider had an interest in something, he wasn't afraid to go all the way. Milly prayed she would be the next item on Harry's wish list.

"Doesn't he look professional?" Chas beamed, so proud of himself that he could put anyone together in anything where clothes were concerned. More important, Chas had to make sure that Mr. Raider looked the part in the "Harry

The Sportsman" fantasy that he sold Milly. "We spent nearly all day yesterday at Brennan's Bit and Bridle. I told Harry that half the trick to becoming a good horseman is looking like a pro. The horse has to learn who's the master, and learn to respect you. Who could respect anyone in old jeans and sneakers, right, Mills?"

"Sure, Chas, whatever you say," Milly said putting the reins back over Zara's head. "Anyway, Harry, you look like you're ready to ride, so let's get to it."

Harry picked up a riding crop and twirled it in the air like a wizard's magic wand. "Oh boy, am I ever ready. I'll just get on, go over some jumps, and then ride down to the beach maybe and we can hit the surf."

Milly's face turned white. There was no way she was letting Harry off a lead line his first time on a horse in over twenty years. Part of her was afraid to break it to him that he couldn't just get on and expect the horse to behave automatically, like a car. Yet she couldn't afford to have him nearly kill himself again. Certainly, Milly wasn't going to let anything happen to Zara in Harry's inexperienced hands.

"Harry, it's wonderful that you are so enthusiastic about riding, but I thought we'd start off more slowly," Milly said diplomatically. "You know, just until you get the hang of it. Then we can get you a horse of your own and you can do what you want."

"You mean I can't do what I want right now?" Harry asked. *Not many people say that to me. This chick had some balls. I like that. Maybe she's into the dominatrix thing. She doesn't look that kinky, but hey, you never know. I've heard a lot of rumors about horse chicks; they're supposedly the wildest in the sack. And she's a Wall Street girl too. Yeah, she must be into the power thing. I bet she likes to be on top. Hey that isn't so bad either. Smart and sexy. I could do worse,* Harry thought.

"Well, I just think you should get on, let me pony you around, and we'll see how it goes."

"Whatever you say, Milly, you're the horse-chick extraordinaire!" Harry chuckled.

"Great," Milly said, relieved.

After helping Harry safely mount Zara, who was tied to a fence, Milly got on her other horse, Pépé, a black gelding she was just starting to train. She untied Zara from the fence and hooked her up to a "lead line," a safety rope that connected her and Harry's horse. Milly skillfully held the lead line in her hands with the reins. There was no way she was letting go. Her future was literally riding at the end of that rope, and she knew it. Chas and Juan, in matching Tommy Hilfiger shorts and shirts, watched from the viewing bleachers. They, too, were wary, and more than a little petrified of another disaster. Juan practically jumped into Chas's arms and buried his head in Chas's neck every time Harry's horse took a step forward. Chas sat still as a stone. He knew damn well that if Harry failed as a horseman, he could count Milly out and lose his second chance at making the million-dollar marriage. Finally, the tension was too much. "Why don't we go have a Chardonnay at Bobby Van's bar around the corner and come back when it's all over," Chas said to a shaking Juan.

"Great idea, papsista. I can barley stand to watch Señor Harry ride that great big beast!" Juan proclaimed, getting up immediately and dragging Chas off of the bleachers as fast as he could. As the two were getting into Chas's Beemer, Chas noticed that Juan had a raging hard-on. Obviously being around the barnyard had stirred up some animal passion in his little friend.

Before turning the key and starting the engine, Chas put his hand over the bulge in Juan's white Tommy Hilfiger pants. "Looks like someone has a beast of his own, right there between his legs," Chas said seductively. "How 'bout we take it out and go for our own ride, before we take off," Chas continued, as he unzipped Juan's pants and went down on the hot, dark, mammoth, un-cut serpent between Juan's legs.

"Aye carumba," Juan squealed, as Chas's mouth pumped away mercilessly. After that fine oral introduction, Chas and Juan climbed into the back seat and rocked the little car parked in the middle of the big field. It was so hot between them, they almost forgot all about Harry and why they were there in the first place. After a half an hour of hard-core passion, Chas and Juan drove off to sit at a café and sip wine, like the refined Hamptons gentlemen they were.

Meanwhile, Harry and Milly were doing some horsing around of their own. Harry was a little awkward in the beginning, but sooner than later he and Milly were trotting briskly around the ring. "Wow, I can't believe it. You really are a natural horseman. I'm impressed," Milly said smiling at Harry bobbing up and down on his horse.

"Why should that shock you, Mills? We do more in California than just eat tofu and meditate you know."

"I couldn't really see you meditating either, Harry," Milly laughed. "No, it's just that Chas always exaggerates and twists everything around so much, I thought he was full of shit when he said that you loved riding," Milly continued.

"Well, this time Chas was right on, sweetheart. You know as a kid, I used to have some of my birthday parties at the Los Angeles Equestrian Center. We used to go on trails that led right up to the Hollywood sign. As a matter of a fact, I was such a good cowboy, my friends used to call me 'John Wayne Raider.'" Harry joked.

"Really?" Milly asked.

"Okay, not really. I think it was more like 'John Belushi Raider,' but hey...a ride is a ride, right?" Harry said, making a subtle a reference to his days as a famous Beverly Hills druggie.

"Yeah. Well, I'm not much into drugs or any of that scene. Horses give me enough of an enormous high," Milly said, patting her pony on the neck affectionately.

"Hey, my days as a party boy are long gone, unless I wind up as Harry the homeless. So, actually I'm open to learning more about achieving the all time natural high. Why don't you show me what this girl can do!" Harry said, squeezing his pony's girth with his legs and urging on from a trot into a faster pace. "Sounds good to me, Harry," Milly replied, making sure Pépé kept up with Harry and Zara. After a smooth, collected canter, Milly was tempted to let Harry have a go on his own, but she couldn't risk it.

"Come on, Milly, let me try it," Harry begged. "I know what I'm doing now, plus I've seen a million Western flicks. You want the horse to stop, you pull back and say 'whoa.' You want to horse to go, you loosen the reins and let her have her head. What's so difficult? Besides, we're all closed in here, where am I going?"

After thirty-five years of riding, training, and perfecting her equestrian skills, Milly had just heard her life's pursuit stripped down to nothing but push and pull. It was as if a lightbulb clicked on in her head. Maybe she had taken riding too seriously all this time. Perhaps you didn't need to be an Olympic qualifier to enjoy the pleasure of being on a horse. Maybe it was time to just let go.

"Okay, Harry, I'm dropping the line. Just be sane, alright?"

"Grrrrreat! Giddyup, Zara...let's rock, baby!"

Milly unhooked the lead rope, and in two seconds Harry was effortlessly cantering around the ring. The huge mischievous smile on his face was indication that Milly had made the right move. He took the reigns in one hand and waved the other one over his head. Harry then stood up in the stirrups and struck as many poses as he could without falling off. He was pretending to be a circus performer, as he sang "I'm a rhinestone cowboy" over and over again. Zara was a dear old friend who wasn't interested in hurting the novice on her back. Cantering around with her big head hanging low and her neck stretched out, Zara actually looked as if she was enjoying the ride. It was nice for her not to have to perform so intensely for her demanding mistress.

"I can't believe it, Harry, you're a natural," Milly said as she rode along beside him. This was the first time she could be with a man on her own turf and relax in his company. There was no "trying" to be good on the date with Harry. He was so authentic that Milly felt she could just be herself and that was enough. Harry was also enjoying being with a real woman and participating in an activity that brought him pleasure, without chemical stimulation.

"I told ya, Milly, animals love me. They think I'm a long-lost relative or something."

"Or something!" Milly laughed.

"Yeah, well. Whatever it is, they trust me." Harry smiled.

"Do you trust me, Mills?" Harry winked at her. Milly was totally caught off guard. A little embarrassed and flustered, she replied "I don't know yet Harry. I'm thinking about it!"

"Well, I got an idea," Harry said as they brought the horses back down for a walk.

"I'm afraid to hear this," Milly said, smiling. She had never ridden like that with a man before. This was a rare experience, and Milly savored every minute of it.

"I would love to take these guys to Montauk Dunes. I went on a trail ride once in Hawaii. It was outrageous!"

Milly had a death grip on her reigns and subconsciously pulled on the bit. "Harry, we can't do that. Zara and Pépé are performance horses, they're not playtoys. I can't take the chance that something would happen."

"Too bad," Harry said with a disappointed tone in his voice, reaching down to caress his horse's neck. "We could have watched the sun set, had a picnic, and gotten to know each other better. It would have been really nice. Don't you think?" Harry teased her, mischievously. Even though he was taking a stab at being clean, sober, and less of a spoiled brat, Harry would always manipulate the situation to get his way. This was something that would never change, whether he was on the beaches of Bridgehampton or deep in the hills of Beverly.

Milly was swiftly becoming undone. *He really says all the right things at just the right time. If he were a Wall Street trader, I'd throw him out of my office in two minutes. He can really swing the shit. On the other hand, he's got nothing to sell and no ax to grind, so he has to be for real. And, wouldn't you know it, just when I was about to hang up all hope, Harry finally showed some interest. How could I turn that down? I can't. No way, not when I'm having so much fun with Harry. To the dunes it is! The hell with the horse shows. What have they really bought me? I have enough trophies and ribbons to fill Madison Square Garden. Now it's time to get something in my bed besides the vibrator*, Milly thought to herself, as she prepared for the ride of her life.

One by one, Milly took the horses by the halters and loaded them into her trailer. With Harry in the passenger seat, she headed east towards Montauk Dunes, one of the farthest points on Long Island. *I can't believe I'm letting him do this*, Chas thought to himself, when he and Juan returned to pick up Harry, but he knew this was the only chance to get Harry alone with Milly. *I definitely can't tell Jessica that I left Harry unguarded; she'd kill me*, Chas's mind continued to race. He just kept his dirty little fingers crossed that Harry would survive his equestrian adventure. There was no option but to throw caution out the window of Milly's horse transporter.

Milly and Harry rode peacefully up and down the hilly, sandy dunes of Montauk. The horses enjoyed the easy time and a chance to behave more naturally. Their pace had picked up quite a bit, and at times Milly could tell that Harry was having a hard time hanging on. "Do you want to slow down and maybe stop for a while?" Milly asked Harry as the horse moved quickly forward.

"No, no, I can handle it!" Harry smiled, while hanging on to his horse's mane for dear life.

"Are you sure?" Milly asked Harry again, not wanting to embarrass him.

"I'm positive! I'm a speed freak, Mills. Haven't you figured that out by now?" Harry pushed his horse to go even faster, as Milly started to feel a little nervous, thinking the fun might be getting out of hand.

"It's not a race you know, Harry," Milly said, breathlessly making her horse keep one step ahead of his.

"Oh yes it is, kiddo! Churchill Downs, here comes Harry. YA! YA! GIDDY UP HORSE! LET'S GO!" Harry's horse was now in a full-on gallop. Instead of trying to stop him, Milly allowed her horse to go for it, letting herself join in the fun. The two riders sped across the dunes with wild abandonment. Aboard the backs of their trusty steeds, Milly and Harry were setting their souls free.

When both horses and riders were exhausted, they walked together as the sun was beginning to set. When they went back to the parked trailer, Milly produced a handsome wicker basket with a picnic of brie and smoked ham sandwiches, sparkling apple cider, and deviled eggs. The food was vastly different from the mile-high pastrami and corned beef sandwiches Harry noshed on at the Ackermans. *Milly is a unique breed of woman. She is clean and unspoiled, and definitely not like the whores, bimbos, and JAPs I know. She's a great change, but can I really live with someone who I'd be more likely to find on a bucking bronco in a rodeo, than shopping on posh Rodeo Drive back home? I mean, I've had fun on this horse, but at the end of the day, who are we kidding? I can usually be found at the bar at the Polo Lounge in the Beverly Hills Hotel, not riding across a polo field in Bridgehampton. Yet maybe this is what I need, someone totally different to keep me active. I could hang with her for a while and see where it goes*, Harry thought to himself.

"So how come you're not married?" Harry asked, as he tried to feed Zara part of his brie sandwich.

"What? Uh...don't do that. Horses don't eat brie, silly," Milly laughed, trying to cover up her embarrassment.

"Don't change the subject, Mil. How come a great girl like you is still single?" Harry persisted, taking her chin in his hands and gently pointing her face in his direction.

Milly hated being put on the spot. People of her background weren't quite so open and directly personal. Still, she knew there was no way of avoiding Harry's question. "Oh, I don't know. I've been busy working, I guess," Milly said, looking up, down, anywhere but at Harry.

"All work and no play makes Milly an unhappy camper!!" Harry said, slowly releasing his hands from her face and playfully poking around and tickling her in the stomach.

"Do I seem that unhappy, Harry? I hope I don't come across as a mean, nasty, unsatisfied person. I really don't want to be that way," Milly worried aloud and purposely let herself be tickled.

"Not at all. You're terrific to be with. You're fun, easygoing, adventurous. That's why I can't understand why a super chick like you is still single. I would think you'd have a million guys lining up to be with you. Where are these stupid dudes, man? Don't they know what's hiding on Wall Street? I mean, the finance dudes are supposed to have the brains, right? Obviously, they're a bunch of fuck-ups if they've missed you, Milly."

Despite the L.A. lingo, Milly was incredibly touched by what Harry had said. *This guy is unbelievable. Nobody, man or woman, had come right out and said anything like that to me. Who here in the shallow Hamptons would dare to care about me that much?* No one, *no one except Harry!* She fought back tears. Her steel-blue eyes couldn't handle Harry's inquisitive ones. His gaze was too penetrating. *The way he looks at me is completely unnerving*, Milly thought. *But, I* am not *going there with him, no way.* As much as she wanted to let it all out, there was no way she'd allow herself to be vulnerable.

"I guess I never met the right person," Milly managed to get out.

"I don't really believe there is one right person. I mean, I think there are lots of totally hip things about a lot of different people, but I don't think a person has to be perfect. Love is a weird trip, man. Have you ever been there, Milly?"

"Yeah, once. A long time ago," Milly said, now really hating this conversation.

"So what happened to him? Where is the lucky guy?"

"He's married, with two kids. David broke up with me after Harvard. He met Judy and that was that," Milly said, shrugging her shoulders, matter of factly, like it was no big deal.

"David Cohen?" Harry asked.

"Yes. Why, do you know him?" Milly asked, surprised. David was a big intellectual snob. How could he know Harry?

"Sat next to him at a dinner party, a while ago. His wife's a piece of work, but I thought he was an okay guy. Now I think he's a total loser, to take her over you. What was he thinking? He must have been on some pretty heavy stuff when he made that decision. Drugs can really fry your brain. Trust me. Shit happens."

Milly laughed out loud. The thought of Mr. Conservative, do-the-right-thing David on drugs was absurd. Once again Harry had lightened up the moment.

"How about scary Harry? Have you ever been in love?" Milly asked.

"Well, I've been married, so they tell me. Don't remember much of the whole experience. As I said, shit happens. I must have felt something, I mean, to stand up there at the altar in the Elvis chapel. I think heroin plays a lot of tricks on your mind, but in some ways I think it can bring out what's in your soul."

"Do you need heroin to be in love, Harry?"

"I sure hope not. If I fall in love again, I'd hate to miss it. That would be a major buzz kill."

"Yeah, I guess so," Milly smiled.

Milly didn't know if Harry would ever fall in love with her, but she adored how she felt being around him. She wanted Harry to put his arms around her and kiss her—or something romantic, anything. He never did. Harry just sat gazing off into the distance, watching the sun bow its head in the west. Something told her that underneath his party boy exterior, Harry had a lot on his frazzled mind.

"I think I should get you back, before it gets dark," Milly said.

"How about one more ride? C'mon, I'll race ya!" Harry said, untying his horse from the trailer.

"No, Harry, I think I've had enough," Milly said, taking a hold of Harry's horse by its bridle.

"Enough of riding or enough of me?" Harry asked her, pretending to be offended.

"Oh, no, I didn't mean that I was sick of you, Harry. I've had a really wonderful time, it's just it's getting late," Milly stammered, hoping she hadn't put him off.

"Late, shmate. C'mon Mills, I'm not asking you to be a midnight rider or anything. Just one more sprint! I'll have you back in no time. Promise." Harry flashed his most irresistible smile. Once again, Miss Milly Harrington couldn't get her lips to form the word "no." "Outta heeeere!" Harry shouted as he jumped on Zara and took off across the endless dunes. Milly got on her horse and caught up with him quickly. For once in her life, Milly was happy to drop the reins and follow behind.

chapter seventeen

Monday was a quiet day in East Hampton. The weekend revelers had gone back to the city. Only transplanted trophy wives and their day-camped children remained out East while their husbands worked the week in Manhattan. Chas had moved himself into a guest cottage on Egypt Lane for the summer. After all, who was an easier target than bored housewives who had nothing to do all week but buy clothes while they waited for their husbands? Chas would make a killing, shopping all week, while he awaited Juan's arrival Friday nights.

The two men were beginning to feel like an old married couple. Surprisingly, Chas didn't mind. His passion for Juan grew hotter as the long summer days deepened. The depth of emotion was truly amazing for Chas, who usually ran like shallow water. This was a first.

Chas and Harry ate lunch at their favorite place, Bobby Van's in Bridgehampton. It was extra crowded today with tanned, aging, Wall Street money-men digging into juicy steaks, while their anorexic arm-candy girlfriends picked at a variety of gourmet lettuce. Jessica was in South Hampton getting a facial at La Carezza, the spa that catered to the pampered wives who waited out the week at the beach for their workaholic husbands to come out on the Hampton Jitney. Today, the two guys had some time to kill. As Chas and Harry wandered down Bridgehampton's quaint Main Street, they stopped at several antique shops that bored the crap out of Harry. Harry liked things new and improved. He had no time for turn-of-the-century tables and chairs.

Harry did find something that interested him on Main Street, and that was an ice cream store. While Chas shopped himself into a white wicker orgasm, Harry sat on a bench with a double-mocha-mint-chip cone dripping down his hand. As Harry feverishly licked away at his melting mess, something across the street caught his eye. He slurped up the rest of the ice cream, wiped the remaining chocolate from the corner of his mouth, and headed towards the Ellen Beacon Art Gallery.

Harry walked into the main salon of the gallery to find a rail thin, tight-lipped lady curator adjusting the very modern painting on the wall.

"May I help you?" the snotty-voiced curator asked Harry, who stood there in a Hawaiian shirt covered with chocolate dribbles.

"Yes, I'd like to speak with Ellen Beacon, please," Harry said gazing at the artwork hanging on the hall.

"Ellen is in the city this week. She won't be back until Friday. Is there something I can do for you, sir?" the curator said curtly to the undesirable man who looked like he didn't belong.

"My name is Harry Raider, and I represent a very talented artist named Jessica Ackerman Levitt. Maybe you've heard of her? Her artwork is the talk of the Los Angeles art world, and she just happens to be here this summer. If you're lucky, I can maybe talk her into exhibiting her artwork here one weekend. I'd like to give Ellen Beacon the opportunity to be the first gallery on the East Coast to preview Mrs. Levitt's masterpiece," Harry said still looking at the art, pretending to really be studying it.

"Did you say you were Harry Raider, from Los Angeles?"

"Yes, that's right." Harry looked the curator straight in the eye. With just the mention of his last name, he now had total control of the situation, after playing this stuck-up broad like a fiddle.

"Do you have any connection to the Sam and Irma Raider Wing at the Los Angeles County Museum?" the pinched-nose curator asked, quickly changing her uppity tone to a smooth saccharine.

"Would it help me get in touch with Ms. Beacon if I did?" Harry asked, winking slyly at this distasteful, snobby woman.

"Ellen and I were in Los Angeles last week touring the museum, Mr. Raider. The works of modern art your parents have funded are absolutely astounding. I'm sure Ms. Beacon would be honored to speak with you," the curator replied smiling to reveal her new professionally "Zoom Whitened" smile.

"Look, just tell Ellen that I want her to hang Jessica Levitt's paintings on the walls, okay? Can you do that, sweetie?" Harry asked, disarming the art shrew.

"Of course, Mr. Raider, where can I have her reach you?" the curator said, practically genuflecting in front of Harry.

"Don't have her reach me, have her call Jessica and invite her to have a special showing. If there is any cost, a cocktail party or whatever your people do, I'll take care of it. Just tell Ellen not to let Jessica know that I had anything to do with it, okay? I want it to be a surprise. Got it honey?" Harry said as he wrote down Jessica's phone number.

"I'll call Ellen in the city tonight and have her contact Jessica right away." The curator tapped on the phone impatiently.

"That's my girl," Harry said, smiling that famous smile as he headed out the door.

"Thank you for dropping in, Mr. Raider," the curator called after him.

"See ya at the opening baby," Harry yelled as he enthusiastically ran down the cobblestone street.

A job well done, Harry thought, as he rewarded himself with a double dish of mocha fudge.

"Oh my gosh, I can't believe it! I can't believe it!" Jessica gushed as she ran into the breakfast room Saturday morning in just a babydoll nightgown. Harry and Jerry were eating their daily scrambled eggs with smoked salmon and bialys while Freddy's bald head was buried in the *Wall Street Journal*. As usual, Freddy took no notice of her, while Harry just smiled coyly. Jerry dropped his fork, as he was surprised to see his daughter look so thrilled about something obviously new.

"What's going on, Jessica? Are you pregnant?" Jerry asked only half-joking, wishing it were true.

"No, dad, don't be ridiculous," Jessica said. Freddy looked up from the paper, raising his eyebrows in disgust.

"Ellen Beacon, from the Ellen Beacon Gallery in Bridgehampton, just called me. She said she's having an exhibition of new artists next Saturday and wanted to feature all of my paintings! I can't believe it! Isn't that great?" Jessica said, barely able to contain herself. Her father had never seen her so excited about anything before. Jerry was bowled over; it was a side of Jessica he didn't know existed.

"Jessica, darling, if you wanted to show your paintings in a gallery, why didn't you tell me before? I could have called a million people; we could have arranged this ages ago," Jerry asked his bubbly daughter, picking up a new fork and taking a bite of his eggs.

"Well, Daddy, I never thought it was important. I guess I was okay with just painting for my own enjoyment...and I guess I never thought I was good enough to show my work to anyone else," Jessica admitted, taking a bite of a bagel that was on Freddy's plate.

"And how did Ellen Beacon hear of your artwork, Jessica?" Freddy inquired with a sour tone to his demeaning voice.

"She said that a friend of hers who was here for the Memorial Day barbeque told her that I was an artist. Now that she is putting this exhibition together, she remembered her friend commenting on my artwork and thought it would be a great idea for me to join the show. I can't get over it. It's unbelievable!" Jessica said, still overflowing with joy.

"Yes, it's totally unbelievable," Freddy said sarcastically, glaring at Harry. Jessica didn't even hear him.

"Well, I've got so much to do before next Saturday. Ellen says I should give her a list of people to invite. She's also having the art critic from the *New York Times* there. Oh my God, I hope this is going to be okay"

"It's going to be fabulous, Jes. You'll be the star of the show," Harry assured her, looking up from his eggs.

"You really think so, Harry?" Jessica asked, suddenly overcome by insecurity.

"I know so, Jessica. Go for it, kiddo!" Harry said, winking at her and chewing with his mouth open.

"Yeah, okay, you're right. I'm going for it!" Jessica said as she scurried out of the breakfast room in an exuberant rush.

"Let me guess, we have the Art Fairy eating among us. The truth, Harry, did you make this wild coincidence happen?" Freddy asked pointedly.

"Well, I might have suggested it, a little," Harry chuckled.

"Nice job, man. Now Jessica can be embarrassed in front of everyone. Just what I wanted to avoid. Well, we'll see who's going to have to pick up the pieces, when the critics splatter her all over the wall like cheap paint. When Jessica's sitting in the garden crying her eyes out, we'll see how you deal with that, Mr. Big Shot."

"Maybe it won't be so bad, Freddy," Jerry said, beaming with pride. "Maybe the critics will enjoy her work. You never know, people have different tastes."

"I wasn't saying that Jessica's art is less than superb, in my opinion. I was just trying to protect her from the mean-spirited attacks of New York art critics. Remember, sir, they get paid for knocking people like Jessica down. It's their job."

"I think she'll be all right, and I think it's a good idea. It's nice to see Jessica so full of spunk. Reminds me of how her mother used to be. This will be a good learning experience for Jessica, no matter what the outcome is."

"Does she really need a learning experience, Jerry? She's just going to go out to the backyard and paint the trees, when it's all over. I mean it's not like she has to make a living at it or anything," Freddy caught himself chuckling sarcastically at the thought of his spoiled wife working. Dead silence filled the room, as Jerry shot Freddy the protective-father look of death.

"Are you saying that my daughter would be incapable of earning a living, if she had to?" an insulted Jerry asked Freddy.

"*No*, I wasn't saying that at all, Jer," Freddy stammered, nervously backpedaling.

"Then what exactly were you saying, Fredrick?" Jerry only called Freddy by his full name when he was pissed off, which wasn't often.

"I was saying how lucky Jessica is to have the luxury to enjoy her artistic talents, without the pressure of having to do it for money. But if she had to do it for money, I'm sure that would work out fine too," Freddy said, lying through his teeth and trying to avoid a nasty confrontation.

"So, you think it's a good idea for Jessica, *my daughter*, to show her art at a prestigious gallery, do you Freddy?" Jerry said, having a little too much fun at his son-in-law's expense.

"If you think so, Jerry," Freddy said defeatedly, getting back to his eggs.

"What do you think, Harry?" Jerry asked his favorite houseguest.

"I think she's gonna blow them away," Harry smiled as Jerry tapped him under the table in total approval. Harry had done the right thing, and he had actually enjoyed it.

The Ellen Beacon Gallery was filled to the brim with the Hamptons' Who's Who. Calvin Klein slinked around with Christie Brinkley and Peter Cook. Billy Joel was there too, as he was a local fixture at these types of events. True to Harry's word, the most talked-about newcomer to the New York art world was Jessica Ackerman Levitt. No one could believe the simply dressed, reclusive heiress had such artistic talent. As the posh, trendy, toned-and-tanned crowd nibbled on crumbled blue cheese and endive, they wondered in audible whispers why Jessica kept her work a secret for so long. Perhaps a true artist needed time to evolve to this level. Whatever story they devised, Jessica's arrival in the modern art scene received an overflowing warm welcome. Surprisingly enough, Jessica felt totally at ease as she chatted effortlessly with the art critics from *Dan's Paper* and yes, the *New York Times*.

Somewhere deep inside of her, she knew this was meant to be. A wealthy couple visiting from Germany even bought two of her paintings. Art was in her soul...as was Harry, who, in his signature Hawaiian shirt and a tie, led a group from painting to painting explaining every detail. Even with all the buzz going on around her, Jessica marveled at how much a part of this whole thing Harry was. She had never experienced such unsolicited support. Harry was the direct opposite of Freddy, who picked at the crudités and tried to vanish into one of the corners. Jessica's first inclination was to go over and make sure Freddy was all right, but tonight, no one was going to rain on her parade. Especially not Freddy.

The weekend after Jessica's artistic debut came a glowing review in the *New York Times*. The headlines read "Art From the Heart. Meet the Hamptons' Best-Kept Secret." To celebrate her triumph, the Ackerman's cook prepared a special feast of oysters Rockefeller, Caesar salad with lime-crusted shrimp, and chocolate flambé. The dinner was set up beautifully on the table in Jessica's garden, where she normally sat creating her artwork. Even though the evening weather was as delicious as the food, Freddy could not bring himself to celebrate. It was he who looked like a fool that night, not Jessica.

Freddy was intensely uncomfortable with his wife's newfound success. It was bad enough to live in her father's financial shadow, but this publicized art star business was too much. Now people really would refer to him as "Mr. Jessica." With all this attention focused on her, Freddy's already wobbly sense of self was getting the hell kicked out of it.

"I'd like to propose a toast to the most beautiful, talented artist in the universe. Jessica, this one's for you, baby!" Harry said as he raised a glass of sparkling Perrier. "Jerry, you should be damn proud of your little girl. Her first show, and she was a huge hit...and she'll be for many more shows to follow!"

"I am proud of her, Harry."

"Oh, okay, that's enough," Jessica blushed. As much as she loved the newfound acknowledgement professionally, personally Harry rocked her world. *The more I get of Harry, the more I want him. Without his divine intervention, tonight would be just another boring dinner in Dad's backyard. Because of this wonderful, supportive, loving guy, I got to live out my secret dreams. I only wish I could live out my 'other' fantasies with Harry. He is so special,* Jessica thought.

"I bet you're really proud of Jessica tonight also, Freddy," Harry went on, gulping his designer water.

"Yes, Jes. You surprised us all. Cheers." Freddy limply raised his glass of grapefruit juice and gave Jessica a fake hug. He wanted to vomit, scream, and run away.

After the family dinner, which Freddy had to force himself to sit through, Jerry and his son-in-law went into the den to watch CNN. Freddy was so used to going on "automatic pilot, let's-follow-Jerry mode," he didn't even notice that he had left Jessica and Harry alone again.

Jessica and Harry lingered over dessert and giggled in the moonlight.

"You were so fabulous tonight, Harry. The way you got people to look at my paintings seriously. I can't thank you enough," Jessica said looking down at her chocolate flambé and pushing the spoon around in the decedent dessert.

"You don't have to thank me, Jes. It was my pleasure to show those pretentious, superficial assholes what good art really is. Soho, Schmoho; Hollywood Harry knows the good stuff when he sees it. They should thank you," Harry said, taking the spoon out of Jessica's hand and feeding her a bite of the chocolate heaven.

Jessica couldn't stop beaming. And she so loved being spoon-fed by her irreverent houseguest. Harry's say-it-like-it-is attitude was a welcome change from her ass-kissing husband. She felt so strong right now, so close to Harry.

"Harry, have you enjoyed the times you've spent with Penny Marks?" Jessica said, looking back into her dessert, only half wanting to hear Harry's answer.

"Oh, yes. Penny's great. We go way back. Always liked her as a kid. She's even better now. She really grew into herself," Harry said casually as he devoured not only his flambé, but also the ones that Jerry and Freddy didn't finish.

"Great..." Jessica said, recoiling and smiling unenthusiastically. "What about Chas's friend who plays all those sports?" Jessica continued, this time looking directly at Harry.

"Who, Milly Harrington?" Harry said, not taking his attention off of his eating. Apparently he didn't yet understand the importance of Jessica's line of questioning.

"Yes, Milly. Do you have fun with her?" Jessica said raising her voice a little bit, trying to get Harry's full attention.

"Are you kidding? Milly and I have a blast. I get to do all the things I never get to do in L.A. She's really a terrific chick...a real pisser," Harry replied, still completely oblivious to where Jessica was going with all this.

"Which one do you like better?" Jessica asked, fishing.

"I don't know, really. That's a hard question. I guess I like them both for who they are in their own unique way. They are both so entirely different, but they are both really good girls," Harry said now looking up at Jessica, finally putting the chocolate down enough to focus on the conversation.

Harry thought to himself, *Let's see, Milly is fun, adventurous, athletic, and doesn't seem afraid of anything or anyone. On one hand, I think we'd always have a good time together, but on the other hand, she's not Jewish, or spoiled for that matter, and she might really get turned off by the garish lifestyle of my friends and family in Beverly Hills. Penny would fit right in with everyone and I love her brashness. She's really funny and seems sexually open. However, she would probably be pretty controlling and is pretty used to getting her own way, just like I am. It's not really good to have two brats in a relationship—that can only cause arguments. I don't know, I like them both, but I don't know if I could live with either of them.*

"Well, if you had to be trapped on a desert island with either one of them, who would you pick?" Jessica pressed on. She wasn't giving up on this one, no way, no how.

"I don't know. I guess Milly would be a good choice. She could hunt and fish, so we wouldn't starve. Yet Chas doesn't let Penny out of his sight for more than two minutes. I'm sure he would send a rescue team to come save her before the end of the summer sales," Harry joked

Jessica laughed. "That's not what I mean, Harry. Which woman could you spend the rest of your life with, if you had to?" Jessica managed to say, looking right at him.

Harry was silent as he stared into her hypnotic green eyes.

"I don't know if I could spend the rest of my life with anyone, Jessica," Harry said looking away from her, and directing his answer to the flowers in the garden.

"Oh," Jessica said, somewhat relieved, somewhat sorry. In a way, she was thrilled that neither Penny or Milly could be considered real competition, but she definitely understood that Harry was trying to tell her that he might *never* be what a Hampton girl would call husband material.

"But I'd hate to think of the rest of my life without you in it," Harry said, returning his gaze back to Jessica. He realized that although he had spoken what he believed to be true about his inability to commit to a lifetime relationship, Harry didn't want to alienate the one person he truly adored.

"That's really sweet, Harry, but I'm not sure I understand," Jessica said, curiously.

"I'm not sure I understand either, Jessica. I know I really like you, probably more than I've ever liked anyone else in my whole life. But I don't know if I could ever give you what you want and what you deserve. I'm not very good at being a grown-up, Jes," Harry said, feeling more comfortable, like he was unloading the world from his shoulders.

"That's okay, Harry. Dad's dying for me to have children. You'd be a good start in that direction," Jessica chuckled. She was touched by his honesty and his ability to answer her tough questions without hedging or trying to change the subject.

They both laughed, relieving a bit of the tension.

"We don't have to rush into anything right away, Harry. You could still see the other girls...and I could still be with Freddy, until you could decide if this what you really want."

"Freddy! Right!" Harry howled. "Freddy, my main man. I still don't get how you got sucked into that, Jes. You're a pretty smart chick, Jessica. How could you put up with his shit?"

"Well, Mom was gone and Dad and I were very lonely. Dad said he would never remarry, but he longed to hear the scamper of little feet around the house. When we first met, Freddy was a charming gentleman who pursued me to no end. He sent cards, flowers, candy, the whole bit. He even wrote me love poems."

"Love poems? Freddy? No way!" Harry said in complete surprise.

"Yes, he did. He wrote lovely poetry. There's a very soft side to Freddy that he never lets anybody see. Lord knows I haven't seen it in a very long time. He can really be very loving, when he wants to be," Jessica said, reminiscing about days long gone. "Trouble is, Harry, he hasn't wanted to be that way in a very long time. The love is totally gone. I don't know what happened."

Jessica couldn't hold back the surge of lost emotion that had come back to her at this moment. It manifested itself in a flood of tears. *Shit, I shouldn't let Harry see me like this. He probably thinks I'm a real loose cannon. I don't want him to think I can't control myself, but it's just too painful right now not to let it all hang out*, Jessica thought to herself as she continued bawling.

Harry held Jessica in his arms and stroked her thick, auburn hair. The jasmine scent of her cologne seduced his senses. Harry traced her delicate profile with his hands. She had dainty, elegant, almost porcelain-doll-like features. Jessica was truly an ethereal creature, yet she also possessed an irresistible earthiness that made her very sexy and appealing on every level. As she lay in his arms, Harry wanted to protect her, take care of her, and ravage her intimately, all at the same time. With his emotions overtaking him, he kissed her. He could no longer hold himself back. He took her face in his hands and kissed her passionately.

Harry's hands slipped under Jessica's BCBG white cotton shirt and unhooked her Bloomingdale's bra. He began kissing her earlobes, then making his way down, sucking on her neck as he aroused her breasts. Jessica pulled off her Laura Ashley jacket, ripping off all the buttons. The next thing Harry knew, Jessica was freely wriggling and writhing on top of him. She was trying to undo his zipper with her teeth while undoing his buckle with her hands. Pretty soon, Harry's full manhood was swallowed by Jessica's welcoming throat. Her head bobbed up and down as she licked and sucked on him with utter pleasure.

Right before Harry was about to explode in ecstasy, Jessica stopped, then climbed on top of him. She rode him up and down ferociously, as Harry reached up to caress her nipples. Harry flipped her over and pulled himself out from inside her. He stuck his head where his penis had been and began to lap up all her love juices.

As Jessica stifled her orgasmic screams, Harry stuck his cock inside her for a final few strokes. Their eyes met in a passionate lock as he probed around inside Jessica's warm cavern of love. As naughty and sexy as this whole married woman "forbidden fruit" thing was for Harry, something about Jessica opened him up to a very deep level of intimacy. Before Harry could stop to think about the effect Jessica had on his heart and soul, his body was erupting beneath him. So much so that he had to quickly remove his mighty sword from inside Jessica's womanhood. Harry put himself back between her lips as he climaxed with pure pleasure. The two new lovers collapsed into each other's arms, reveling in the blissful state that only great sex can bring on.

When it was all over, Jessica and Harry cuddled together on the moist ground under the table in the garden. All they could hear was the droning of CNN on the television in the den.

As Harry held Jessica in his arms, he wondered if he could handle what he had just done. Although she was sexually skilled as any of them, Jessica was nothing like the whorish party girls he was used to.

Holy crap, what the hell did I just do? There's no going back now. What was I thinking? Once again, Harold Senior got the best of me, Harry thought to himself, looking at his large penis with great reverence. The chemistry between them was over the top, but so was the degree of responsibility that came with it. If Harry had made a mistake, this would be a big one and it was already too late.

"Are you okay with this, Jes?" was all Harry could say.

"Yes. Are you?" she asked him as she snuggled into his big, hairy chest.

"I think so, Jes," Harry said, trying to mask the tone of doubt in his voice.

"Good. You won't freak out on me, will you, Harry?"

"Like what, run away from you and shit like that?"

"Yeah," Jessica smiled. "Shit like that."

"No, I don't run," Harry said, doubting himself. This was more of a mind fuck to him than he had ever imagined.

"So we'll just carry on, then. Business as usual. We can pretend it never happened if you want. It will be our secret."

"Greaaat!" Harry said, a little relieved.

Jessica Ackerman Levitt is one cool Jewish chick! No one in Beverly Hills would ever say something like that. All the JAPs there would be calling a rabbi and booking the main dining room at Pine Valley for the wedding rehearsal dinner the minute my cock went off, Harry thought.

Harry needs time to process what just happened. If I push too much, I could lose him and I know it, Jessica thought to herself, playing with the hair on Harry's manly chest. Besides, now that the thrill of the first fuck was over, did she really want to spend her life with him? Could she ever really trust him? Was he just on semi-good behavior here in the Hamptons and would he return to drugs, booze, and whores back in L.A.? The questions clouded Jessica's mind as she lay drenched in the smell of sex. Whatever would happen, Jessica knew one thing: Harry had breathed the life back into her emotionally, spiritually, and now, even sexually. For that she would be eternally grateful.

chapter eighteen

Although they both tried at first to forget their first night of sky-rocking sex, Harry and Jessica eventually couldn't keep their hands off of each other. The passion that they felt for each other was so intense that they made love anytime and anywhere they could get away with it. Being discreet was top priority, but when backs were turned, Harry and Jessica would sneak off to be together in the maid's closet, in the garden, and in the back of her father's Rolls Royce while it was parked in the garage. During the week, while Freddy was gone, they would sleep in the same bed every night and spend romantic afternoons making love on the beach, in the garden, or in the back of the Rolls Royce. An aging "silver fox" like Jerry had a feeling about what was going on but characteristically kept his nose buried in a newspaper and feigned a blissful ignorance. Secretly, he wished that the whole situation would explode and come out into the open, so Jessica and Harry could get married and live happily ever after. It's not that Jerry didn't like Freddy, but nothing would make him happier than to have Sam Raider's offspring be the son that he never had. A marriage between Jessica and the Raider boy would be the coup de grace of a lifetime for the aging elder statesman who was losing his lust for living until Harry came into his house.

Jessica and Harry were having a great love affair privately. Publicly, nobody, not even Chas, had a clue. As a matter of fact, because of the newfound energy Jessica had gotten from the affair, even Freddy was beginning to find her more attractive. *I can't put my finger on it, but for some reason my wife seems more appealing, more open, more glowing. I actually want to be with her so much now*, Freddy thought to himself. Freddy was actually now taking more notice of Jessica and being more attentive to her.

As much as Jessica enjoyed her naughty trysts with the houseguest, she was intrigued with her husband as well. It wasn't really Freddy that amused her now. She was more impressed with her own ability to turn him on and keep him wondering. She loved her new brand of control. Little Jessica had come into power.

The one person who noticed something was wrong was Penny Marks. Jessica, Freddy, Penny, and Harry had become a regular foursome now, attending every elite social event in the Hamptons. They were photographed at the Huggy Bear Tennis Tournament, a series of charity games played on private beach-front courts that belonged to a famous Wall Street "Master of the Universe," and the after-party at his Water Mill compound; Paul Simon's Montauk outdoor concert; and the South Fork Group's Beach Bash, a black tie and ball gown gala which took place under a huge white tent on the grounds of an estate owned by a well-known New York newscaster. Just to name a few. The hot gossip on *tout le mond's* lips was that Penny and Harry were the new "it" couple. When out in public, Harry had no problem playing this role, because he thought it would help keep his affair with Jessica under wraps. The more everyone thought he was with Penny, the less suspicious they would be about his real love life.

All of the Hamptons' high-society matrons and patrons were placing their bets that Penny and Harry's official wedding announcement would happen by the end of the summer. The only one who was oblivious to the Penny and Harry wedding buzz was Milly Harrington, who wouldn't even use a Hamptons' society magazine to clean up after her dog. When Penny and Harry went out they were usually accompanied by Chas and Juan, who were already planning how to spend the millions Chas would make once Penny and Harry said "I do." Everything looked to be right on schedule, until the night Penny confronted Chas with an awful truth.

One balmy Hampton evening, Chas came early to Penny's house to arrange her outfit for their night on the town. "I don't understand it, Chas. I just don't get it!" Penny screamed, as she ran around her room clad only in a towel while Chas lounged on her bed. "We've been together every weekend and sometimes during the week and nothing happens!" Penny shrieked as she plowed through her closet looking for something to wear. Every designer that ever made anything from a scarf to a ball gown was represented in Penny's closet. She even had some of the same outfits in several sizes, being totally prepared for post-pig-out parties. At this point, Penny had tried on a Chanel dress that barely got over her chest, a Lilly Pulitzer skirt that wouldn't zipper, and an Ungaro blouse that had seen skinnier days.

"Penny, I don't think you need to be such a little slut about this. You want him to respect you. You're going to be his wife. You don't want him to treat you like some L.A. whore."

"Chas. It's not normal. I know he has a good time with me. I know he likes me. He told me how much fun he was having at the South Hampton Hospital Benefit...but no fireworks went off between us! What's wrong with me? Why won't he touch me?" Penny cried as she flopped on the bed next to Chas, who moved away from her immediately. Chas hated being physically close to anyone, except for Juan.

"Look, Penn, if you want to behave like just another gold-digging piglet, and just have him use you, then go ahead. I think it's wonderful that Harry is being such a perfect gentleman. It shows real progress."

"Progress for what, Chas? Whoever heard of two people getting married in this day and age without being intimate first? I mean, really, Chas, you can't tell me that Harry Raider, a man whose dick has been imprinted on the Hollywood Walk of Fame, has been celibate all summer. He must have something going on the side."

Frustrated, Penny threw the garments all over the room as she continued to search for something that still fit. To deal with frustration with Harry, Penny had done some serious snacking so even her fat-day sizes were tight now.

"He doesn't have anything going on, Penny, I'm telling you. When would he have time?" Chas protested. For once Chas wasn't lying. He was telling the truth as he knew it. He thought to himself, *Besides, Penny, who would he be with? Cindy, Jessica's poodle? So what if his cock once won a public service award in L.A.? In the Hamptons, Harry's been a saint.*

"I really don't believe it, Chas. Why wouldn't he come after me, then? Why?" Penny kept screaming, as Chanel skirts and Jimmy Choo shoes came flying out of the closet.

"Well, maybe he just doesn't find you all that exciting," Chas said smugly.

"What?" Penny said, scrunching her face and crinkling her eyebrows, being totally unnerved by his candid remark.

"Now don't get me wrong. That doesn't mean he won't marry you. You know, Penn, sometimes men think there are girls you marry, and girls you fuck. Maybe he thinks that you would be a good wife, but a boring lay. Who cares anyway, Penn? As long as he marries you, what difference does it make?" Chas sneered, comfortably lying back with his hands behind his head. His deal was to get one million for a marriage; for a marriage with great sex, he would have asked for at least two.

"Well, it makes a big difference to me, Chas!" Penny howled. "I don't want to marry any guy that doesn't find me sexy," Penny said, looking in the mirror, doing her best "Farrah Fawcet hair flip," and applying some fire-engine-red lipstick.

"Oh puh-leeze, girlfriend. If Harry Raider popped up here right now, gave you a diamond the size of Mount Everest, and asked you to marry him, are you telling me you would say no?" Chas laughed wryly, and ignored Penny's attempts at being the seductress.

"Well, I'd make him fuck me first!" Penny declared, squeezing her big boobs into a push-up bra that made her already heaving chest appear absolutely gargantuan.

"Excuse me, Penny, you'd make him fuck you? How, pray tell, would you do that?" Chas said, amused by Penny's assumptive audacity. *So typical of spoiled wealthy women, they think they can make anyone do anything just to please them. What rubbish!* Chas thought to himself.

"Well, I don't know, exactly," Penny said, exasperated, now trying to get into a white leather skirt.

"But I would demand to take Harry for a test drive before I bought the vehicle," Penny exclaimed, excited, as she was able to get the skirt on and up without busting the zipper.

"You're not buying this time, Penn. This time, it's Harry who'll be footing all your bills from now on. Remember, he who payeth, sayeth." This time Chas got tremendous pleasure by putting Ms. Money Bags Marks, in her place.

"So, what? I have to live a whole life with no sex? I can't even have Bobby?" Penny said, searching her closet for a top to match the white skirt.

"You can do what you want, Penn, but don't get caught. I doubt a few rounds with a sweaty exercise trainer is worth losing your title as 'Mrs. Harry Raider, Queen of Bel Aire, Beverly Hills, and Malibu.' Remember what happened to Princess Diana. Learn something from her mistakes," Chas answered, handing Penny the perfect, loose, sheer white Marina Renaldi top to go over the white leather mini.

"Okay, you're right. It's not worth risking my marriage just to have a few orgasms," Penny agreed, looking at herself in the mirror confidently, wearing Chas's ensemble. Tonight she almost liked what she saw.

"You want orgasms, Penny, marry Harry Raider and go to Harry Winston. They just redid their salon in the Beverly Hills Hotel. You'll buy jewelry there that will keep you coming in your Calvins over and over again," Chas chided, handing Penny some jewelry to accessorize her look.

"Oh Chassy, there must be some way to get Harry Raider's sexual attention. I just need to feel like I'm desirable. I need to know he wants me," Penny said, striking some sexy poses in the mirror.

"My, aren't we picky. One would think that you would be happy enough to know that Harry Raider has spent almost every weekend of his summer vacation on your arm. One would also think that you would be thrilled to know that there is a real chance now that he will marry you. But noooo...spoiled little Penny also has to feel like a sex goddess just to satisfy her own inflated ego. Maybe it's true what they say, the rich are never happy," Chas said as he lit one of his clove cigarettes in a blasé manner.

"Wouldn't you like to know, you kiss-ass faggot," Penny said as she knocked the clove cigarette out of Chas's pouty mouth. "I realize you're satisfied knowing that your payday is coming as soon as he steps on the glass. But let me tell you something right now, Mister. I am not going to spend the rest of my life wearing out the batteries on a cold vibrator while my husband screws every whore in L.A. As much as I want to get married—all right, as desperate, there, I said it—as *desperate* as I am to get married, I will not live the rest of my days as a pent-up old Stepford wife. No amount of money in the world is worth that. So, if you want to know how it feels to be rich, if you can call a million bucks rich today, then I suggest you put on your little thinking cap and come up with a way to get Harry Raider in my bed. Otherwise, you can watch your chance at the big money go just as quickly as it came."

Chas knew Penny was serious. He knew when he could play her, and he knew when he had to give in. Chas also knew that her hunger for love showed up as her hunger for food. If Harry sexually starved her, she would eventually eat herself into a fat, very un-Beverly Hills-looking, wretched matron. Mrs. Harry Raider could not be a balloon, and Chas realized this. This would not be as easy as it first seemed. Why did these petty women have to have so many hang-ups? Wasn't shopping enough?

"What are we going to do?" Penny stomped her foot at Chas, as he was not thinking quickly enough for her.

"All right, knock it off with the Yentah Stomp. We'll entice Harry into sleeping with you."

"How?" Penny wanted to know, *now*.

"Well..." Chas said hesitantly.

Just then the bedroom door opened and Jena entered. She had been lying in the sun by the pool, and her milky white skin had turned a golden tan. She still had coconut tanning oil all over her, which gave her a very sleek, wet appearance. Jena looked like she just walked out of the pages of the *Sports Illustrated Bathing Suit Edition*. This was too good to be true.

"Are you ready for your massage, Penny?" Jena asked.

"She certainly is," Chas answered seductively. He had the answer Penny needed now. His sexual mind was at work. If she would only go along with what he was thinking. That would depend on how badly she wanted to become Mrs. Harry Raider and how desperately she wanted to turn him on.

To set the stage for Penny's seduction Chas knew that there was nothing better than having them all attend the sexiest party in the Hamptons. After spending a night surrounded by sand, silicone, and sin, Harry, who had been celibate all summer, as far as Chas knew, would definitely be up for a little sexual healing. Rapper and entrepreneur Sean "P. Diddy" Combs, gave his infamous White Party every summer, and it was only attended by the youngest, hottest, most attractive people in the Hamptons. Neither Jessica nor Penny was part of the ultra-hip, up-and-coming, twenty-something clique. The two social doyennes were more Old Guard Jewish. Yet, the P. Diddy party was the rocking ticket in town, so Chas placed the appropriate call to Diddy's assistant, Ellie M.

Ellie M. was the daughter of music entertainment executive Jake Mandlebaum. Like most Manhattan born-and-bred princesses, Ellie had her "right of passage" nose job and wouldn't dream of leaving her East Village apartment without having her jet black curly hair blow-dried bone straight. Yet that is where the physical comparisons to her fellow privileged princesses stopped.

Instead of Prada pumps and Chanel skirts, Ellie went for vintage clothing from Vivian Westwood and sported several tattoos. She had a long, colored snake on her right arm, angel wings on her shoulders and a rosebud on her right ankle. She wore a stud in her pierced tongue and another in her left nostril. Ellie was always seen in her signature black and white pony-hair cowboy hat and bright red alligator boots. In case anyone missed the point, Ellie's wacky outfits would do nothing less than scream "Look, I'm a rock chick and don't you forget it!" The Mandlebaum family socialized with rock-and-roll's elite, which included Madonna, Eric Clapton, Jewel, Oasis, and several other music industry big shots. Therefore it was only natural for Jake's twenty-one-year old daughter, Ella Rebecca Mandlebaum, to grow up to be Manhattan royalty, with a special job working for a big star. Ellie M. and her new breed of "JAPs that Rap" were the young twenty-something upstarts that Chas would eventually have to win over. What better time to call and introduce himself than right now?

"Hello, Ellie?" Chas said in his most charming I'm-about-to-start-ripping-you-off voice.

"Ellie M.," the gum-snapping, hungover New York Valley Girl voice replied.

"Right, Ellie M. Of course. This is Chas Greer, personal shopper and lifestyle consultant."

"So?" Ellie M. answered curtly.

Chas was absolutely mortified at this brat's refusal to acknowledge his greatness. *How dare she?* he thought to himself, before reeling his emotions back in and regaining his ability to schmooze, even after just being insulted.

"So, I just wanted to call and introduce myself to you, dahling. I saw the piece on new nightclubs you wrote for *New York Magazine*. It was faaabulous," Chas went on.

"Have you ever heard of any of your chic friends using my services?" Chas asked, expecting that she must know at least one person whom he dressed.

"Yeah, my grandma bought some crap from you last year. Chanel and shit. Didn't really fit her. I think she had to send it back."

Chas was stunned at the audacity of this young punk. Nobody ever returned a Chas Greer purchase! Chas vaguely remembered a Sarah Mandlebaum at 1082 Park who bought Chanel, then threw a fit when the bill came. This was all too much for Chas. He actually had to sit down on the nearest chair to regroup himself.

Chas was devastated that Ellie M., a prominent member of the young, post-debutante, pre-dowager set was not impressed by him. The Ellie M.'s of New York secured Chas's personal shopping career for the future. If Ellie M. and her group discounted Chas as "grandma's shopper," Chas's days would be numbered. He was very nervous. He had to win Ellie M. over at any cost.

"Sorry Granny didn't dig the outfit. Honestly Ellie, I'm not used to buying stuff for grandmas. That's probably why I fucked up. My clientele is like totally hip, if you know what I mean?" Chas said, trying to save himself.

"Really, who do you know that's happening now?" Ellie M. wanted to know.

"Lots of celebs on the scene, can't mention any names, of course. That would be violating client-shopper confidentiality."

"Yeah, right," Ellie M. said sarcastically. She had heard enough of Chas's wannabe-in bullshit. Ellie M. was twirling the phone cord as she read the gossip on *Page Six* in the *New York Post* and only half listening to Chas.

"You know how it is, Ellie..." Chas schmoozed on.

"Ellie M.!" she screamed. "Why are you calling me?"

Ellie then demanded, when she was done with the paper and growing impatient.

"Sorry. Ellie M., I'm calling you because I wanted to see if I could snag a few invites to P. Diddy's blowout on the beach? I have a major player here from L.A. and I want to bring him and his posse," Chas said, lighting up a clove cigarette, inhaling heavily, and praying he could still get the job done.

"Who's the player?" Ellie M. inquired curiously, sticking another piece of gum into her mouth.

"I can't really tell you. He kind wants to lay low until tonight. You know, for security reasons," Chas said, smoking away. He thought that he would sound hipper if he smoked while he talked to her.

"Chas, you are so full of it, man. You're whacked. There is no way I'm letting your butt into Diddy's party. You're over, dude."

With that, Ellie M. hung up the phone on Chas immediately. Chas sat on his white wicker rocking chair. He shook with anger as well as fear. His own career mortality was staring him right in the face. Was it all coming to an end? If he didn't close this marriage deal with Harry, would he still have a way of making a living once Ellie M. and company took over social New York? This couldn't happen to Chas. He lived to shop. He lived to spend other people's money frivolously. He was good at it, damn it. He was the best.

There must be a way to crack Ellie M., Chas thought. He could offer her a free pass to the preview of Versace's show in the fall. Donatella was a personal friend. Both she and Elton John still adored Chas. He was not *over*...not by far, and he was going to let that kid know it! Chas dialed Ellie's number again, this time with a sense of purpose.

"Ellie M.," the bored, been-there-done-that voice said.

"Ellie M., Chas Greer."

"Leave me alone!" Ellie M. yelled once more, raising her middle finger, shooting a bird towards the phone.

"Ellie M., you must be having a tough day. It's okay, we all do at times. So before you hang up on me again, I just wanted to know if you wanted passes to Donatella's show this fall. It's her greatest work since Gianni died. Elton will be there. So will Mick Jagger. Hope you don't think they are *over*, also."

"Very funny. Mick is hip forever, man," Ellie M. said, settling down a little and picking her black-painted fingernails.

"Great. So it's a deal?" Chas asked, crossing his legs tightly, like he did when he was nervous.

"What's a deal?" Ellie M. asked like she missed something.

"I get you and whoever you want to bring into Donatella, and you get my L.A. guy and his entourage into Diddy's bash tonight."

There was silence. Ellie M. had grown up around stars of the music industry, but somehow the chance to meet Mick Jagger had eluded her. An introduction to the Stones' lord himself would make her daddy proud. Still, she played her game well.

"I gotta know who this guy is, Chas. Diddy has unbelievable security stalking the place. Nobody is going to get in unless their name is on the list and they show a driver's license. No shit, man. It's serious," Elle said, now biting her fingers.

Chas was stumped. If Ellie M. didn't know who Harry was, the whole thing would be off, and Chas would look like a big idiot. Yet, Chas knew that Ellie was not kidding about the security. Last year P. Diddy hired twenty-four ex-Israeli commandos to patrol his grounds. Chas had to give it up or not get in at all.

"Okay...it's Harry Raider," Chas practically whispered, trying to make Harry seem like he was somebody famous.

"Harry Raider?" Ellie M. screamed again.

"Yes, Harry Raider, don't you know who he is?" Chas asked nonchalantly, hoping Ellie wouldn't hang up on him again.

"Of course, I know who Harry Raider is. What do you think I'm a fucking moron?" Ellie M. said, excitedly.

There was a distinct change in the tone of her voice. All of a sudden the non-interested "celebutante" became Chas's new best friend. Without even knowing it or being present, Harry had just saved the future of Chas's shopping career. Even if Harry didn't marry Penny or Milly, thanks to his association, Chas could now look forward to dressing New York's next generation of rich ladies.

"Harry Raider is a party legend! I grew up on stories of Harry's wild parties in L.A. and Vegas. I was in L.A. on a trip with my dad once. Me and some friends snuck into one of Harry's all-nighters! It was the most intense scene I've ever witnessed. It was like, out-of-control. I was like sixteen then!" Ellie said.

"When was that, last year?" Chas laughed in relief and put out his cigarette.

"Yeah, almost. Definitely bring Harry, the party-meister. That's like soooooo way cool of you, Chas."

"Why, thank you, Ellie M. I really look forward to meeting you," Chas declared triumphantly.

"Likewise. You're on the list. Chas Greer, Harry, and his people. Awesome. Later, dude," Ellie M. said like Chas had just done *her* a huge favor.

"Later, Ellie M.," Chas whined as he hung up.

Oh, it was just too much, Chas thought. *That was a close call and an amazing save. Now if getting Harry married and acquiring the money are just as easy, I will never have to deal with the Ellie M.'s of the world ever again. It just has to happen.* Living in dreaded fear of surviving on the whims of temperamental brats just wouldn't do for Chas anymore. He got up from the white wicker chair and went into the Moroccan-tented bedroom. Juan lay napping on the satin sheets, his buttocks partially covered. Juan was so lovely, Chas thought. Chas ran his hand along Juan's firm buttcheek. *How could something be so firm and so soft at the same time?* Juan awakened gently to Chas's loving touch. The two men looked at each other warmly and exchanged a knowing glance. Five minutes of phone-call hell was forgotten, and the rest of Chas's afternoon was a big slice of heaven.

"That is absolutely outrageous, Chas, and out of the question!" Penny yelled as she showered off after a massage. Chas entered the pink marble bathroom, where Penny was steaming up the mirrored walls.

"Why is it so terrible, Penny? You said you would do anything to get Harry in bed with you, and when I tell you how to do it, you flip out like a child. He won't be able to resist watching you and Jena together. He'll have to jump your bones," Chas said, checking himself out in the mirror and spritzing his hair with one of Penny's bottles of hair gel.

"I would like to hear a normal idea from you, Chas. Not some kinky, perverted, gross situation you want me to get into," Penny said as she threw open the shower door and got into her red Fernando Sanchez robe.

"Penny, all heterosexual men get turned on by watching two girls get off on each other. I don't know why that is. I'm gay, I don't relate to it, but for some reason it drives them wild every time. No straight guy can resist two girls going at it. If you want to get Harry's attention and show him that you know how to party, that's the way to his dick, I'm telling you. I don't care if you've gotten him hard in the past or not, this will definitely do the trick," Chas continued, still staring at his reflection in the mirror and applying just a hint of blue mascara to his eyelashes.

Penny was so rattled from the conversation she didn't realize that she had slathered a whole bottle of Clarins moisturizer on her face.

"Besides, Chas, how can I ask Jena to do something like that? She's my best friend. She's closer to me than my own fucked-up sister. I love Jena, but not in *that* way. I'm sure she'll feel absolutely gross and completely used if I ask her to do this," Penny said as she wiped off the excess moisturizer with Clinique toner.

"I think you're making too much of a big deal out of this, Penny. You tell me Jena is such a spiritual person; I'm sure she's open about her sexuality. I bet she would see it as the ultimate expression of love. People like her are supposed to be free about all aspects of sexuality. They are not allowed to be so judgmental," Chas said, handing Penny a Hard Candy lip balm after using it himself.

"Judgmental? I don't think it's judgmental to prefer one sex to the other. Could you do it, Chas? Could you sleep with a woman?" Penny said, stopping all her primping to accentuate her point.

"For the life I'd be getting from Harry Raider, I'd sleep with one hundred women of all ages and sizes. But that's just Chas!" Chas winked and smiled, so full of himself.

"Then why haven't you?" Penny proved, going back to her makeup bag.

"What?" Chas asked, a little caught off guard.

"Come on, Chassy, I'm sure there are scads of women whom you dress that would love it if you were straight. I'm actually surprised at you, Chas, that you haven't hooked up with some rich lady by now. You'd be the perfect husband—always well dressed, socially brilliant, always up on what's hot. I would think you would marry a wealthy girl who could keep you in the style you would like to grow accustomed to, and have a little boy on the side. If you can get it up just at the thought of a multimillion-dollar lifestyle, then why haven't you?" Penny demanded as she put on some Tony and Tina sparkling eye shadow.

"Well...because I have Juan now," Chas muttered, for once totally thrown off kilter.

"Juan is a new thing. You've been around rich girls for years. Why haven't you ever tried to walk a straight line?" Penny asked, knowing she had him right where she wanted him.

"Look, Penny, my sexuality isn't the issue here. You asked me how to get Harry Raider in bed. This is *your* problem, not mine. I gave you a foolproof answer! I don't know why I haven't sold out, frankly. Maybe you're right, maybe I should have attached myself to a womanly bankbook instead of being openly gay. However, Penny, I made that choice, and came out years ago. Who would want me now? Everybody who's anybody knows Chas is a flamer. So what? I am what I am," Chas said, looking straight into the mirror and giving himself a nod of approval.

"Please, don't start doing *La Cage* now. I get your point and you should get mine. Can't you understand that I don't want to have sex with Jena?" Penny said walking out of the bathroom.

"I'm not saying you should want to do it. I'm saying you have to do it, if you feel you need to sleep with Harry. We don't always just get to do the things we want to do in life, Penny. Sometimes even princesses like you have to put themselves out to get what you want," Chas grinned. He so enjoyed making his spoiled clients face unpleasant realities every now and then.

"So what are you saying? A *ménage à trois*?" Penny cringed with disgust and ran into her voluminous closet.

"I'm saying, you bring him up to your bedroom. Tell him you have a surprise waiting for him. Then you and Jena start in and I'm sure he'll join you. It won't be so awful. Who knows, you might even enjoy it," Chas smiled, following her.

"I'll only enjoy the part when I get to be with Harry," Penny said firmly, pretending to hide behind an Emilio Pucci dress.

"Does that mean you'll do it?" Chas asked hopefully, pulling the garment away from Penny, totally exposing her.

"Do I have a choice?"

chapter ninteen

P. Diddy's party had more guards than Buckingham Palace with the queen in residence. Chas, Juan, Penny, Harry, Jessica, and Freddy were frisked at the door and practically strip-searched. The security men knew just how far they could go without offending the lucky, selected guests. Everyone who was anyone from the diverse worlds of rap music, fashion, and New York society was there to "see and be seen" by the rich and "oh-so-fabulous." Donald Trump toasted martinis with Snoop Dogg, Halle Berry talked skin care regimes with Queen Latifa, and a few Kennedy cousins were dueling over the gorgeous Beyoncé. Upon entering the party, Penny, in her biggest Versace, and Jessica, in a plain denim skirt and top, looked at each other in what could be considered as a time-warp wake-up call.

"Is this what the scene is like now?" Jessica whispered to Penny. "My gosh, everyone looks so young. Do you think we look that old?" Jessica went on.

"I don't know. I can't believe everyone is so thin," was all Penny could say as they gazed at the twenty-year-olds in leather midriffs and mini-skirts that practically exposed their crotches.

Chas carefully surveyed the wild MTV-looking crowd. He keenly noticed a group of scantily dressed girls disappearing into the bathroom, only to return ten minutes later looking chemically wired. At this point Chas began to have second thoughts about being there with Harry.

Maybe these raging party people are too much like Harry's fast times in L.A. How could Penny possibly keep Harry's attention when there are so many young ladies to behold? Why didn't I think of this before? Chas thought to himself, realizing his mistake a little too late in the game. Chas was far too intent on winning the social battle with Ellie. He prayed that his own pigheaded pride hadn't just cost him the war. Chas had to do something fast.

Ellie M. approached them, dragging a very cool-looking P. Diddy, in a white silk tunic and white Polo pants, with her. The king of rap music had come to meet his court.

"Diddy...this is Harry Raider. The party dude I told you about from L.A. He's the man," Ellie M. said as she grabbed Harry, pushing him in front of P. Diddy.

"You're the man, P. Diddy," Harry said as the two exchanged a hip handshake.

"Thank you, Harry. Ellie M. has told me a lot about you, man. I hear you're what's happening in L.A. I'd love to check out your scene. Let's hang out West, man."

"Yeah, let's hang," Harry said, enjoying what it felt like to be around this kind of action again. He thought to himself, *Wow, this party feels like home. It's been too long since I've been around this type of scene. I almost forgot what I was missing. So, the Hamptons don't have totally suck. I'm here and heavily chaperoned...let's see if Harry can have fun without losing his whole inheritance*. He smiled devilishly.

"You all have a good time. Later," P. Diddy said, and he and Ellie M. disappeared into a sea of boob-jobbed babies, leaving the three couples to fend for themselves.

The minute P. Diddy was out of sight, Harry wasted no time getting into the action. He walked right on to the dance floor and cut in between a busty blonde and a ravishing redhead, both of whom could be *Playboy* centerfolds. Within seconds, the three of them were laughing, teasing, and joking, and having sort of a dancing *ménage-a-trois*. "This is not good, not good at all. We have got to get him out of here," Chas whispered to a worried Penny who watched in horror as Harry started bumping and grinding, sandwiched happily like an Oreo cookie between the two bimbettes.

Jessica tried to hide the jealousy in her eyes as she watched Harry grab the blonde around her waist and rub himself up and down her back in rhythm with the music. This was the side to Harry she had heard about but had never seen. Perhaps their month-long affair had meant nothing to him. Maybe he would always be a party boy at heart. Jessica needed the security of her husband now. She reached down for Freddy's hand, but all she felt was empty air around her. Dear Freddy was happily chatting away with the other elder statesman at the party, Donald Trump and Ron Perelman. Once again, Jessica was alone.

Yet, so was Penny. She, too, watched in despair as Harry seemed to be having the time of his life without her. Had all her dreams just been shattered by two women young enough to be her sister's nemeses? Two women. There Harry stood nuzzled between two women, one sexier, even sluttier, than the other. Chas was so right on about what would get Harry aroused. It was time to take control, and bring Harry home.

"Do you see what I see, Penny?" Chas whispered into Penny's ear.

"How could I miss it?" Penny answered in a loud, angry voice.

"Ssssh. I told you so, Penn," Chas chided.

"So what are we going to do about it?" Penny asked in desperation.

"Are you ready, girlfriend?" Chas asked slyly, cocking up an eyebrow.

"I really did not want to do this, you know. I just couldn't believe that seeing me with another woman could be that much of a turn on, but now I see how right you are, Chassy. Let's go for it, dude," a determined, angered Penny answered.

"Why don't you leave right now and go home. Give Harry a few minutes to get really hot. Juan and I will keep a close eye on him. Just when I think he's about to go over the edge, we'll grab him and tell him you have a big surprise waiting for him back at your place. By the time I drop Harry off at your house, you and Jena should be primed and ready. Get it?" Penny already knew that Jena would be amenable to doing anything to please her patron. Having sex with a woman was no big deal to the flower child, who grew up having "love thy neighbor" exploratory group-sex sessions in the commune she grew up in just outside of Woodstock. To Jena, "doing it" with Penny was just a natural way of saying "thank you" for the extended stay at her summer retreat.

"I got it. I'm leaving. Are you sure this is going to work, Chas?"

"Answer your own question, Penn. Have a look for yourself."

Penny looked over at Harry. She could swear she saw him pinching the redhead's nipple under her halter top.

"I'm outta here. Don't be long," Penny said.

"Don't worry," Chas answered.

Besides Penny, who would fake having fun in public under any social circumstance, everyone else at the party seemed to truly be having a wonderful time. Everyone that is, except for Jessica, who didn't know how to "put on a brave face" even if her life and her marriage depended on it. The reclusive Mrs. Freddy Levitt had not been in a situation as complicated as this one ever before in her charmed little life. She didn't know how to react or how to pretend that she wasn't on the verge of tears. The whole scene itself, and the fact that Harry seemed so right at home in it, was all too much for Jessica to handle. She lost herself staring at party boy Harry in bimbo heaven. Jessica was devastated; she hadn't seen this coming. Chas noticed the usually healthy glow had gone from Jessica's fresh, rosy face. She just stood there, paralyzed with pain, looking grayish-pale, gaunt, and tired. Chas had never seen his carefree artist friend look so dismayed.

"Jessica, are you all right?" Chas asked.

"What?" she answered in a daze-like trance.

"Jessica, hello, is there anybody in there?" Chas persisted as he ran his dainty hand over her eyes.

"What, uhm...right. Yes, Chas, what is it?" Jessica mumbled.

"Honey, you don't look so good. Are you okay?"

"Uhm, yes. I'm fine. Well no, actually, uh, I don't feel good at all. I feel sick. I think it's something I ate."

"Dahling, you look white as a Pratesi sheet. Doesn't she, Juan?"

Juan, who had been watching Jessica watch Harry, had begun to get a strange inkling about what was going on. For all his youth and inexperience, Juan was highly perceptive and deeply intuitive. He also knew better than to let Chas in on what he was observing. Juan knew that Chas would freak out and probably take it out on him if he became the bearer of the bad news. Therefore, Juan thought it was better to keep his pretty mouth shut.

"Oh jyes, Jeh-see-ca, maybe jyou h-ate esomething not es-so good. Maybe jyou should go home and get esome slip, chica," Juan agreed.

"Yes, you're right, Juan. Penny left. Maybe I should go home, too."

"Juan, go over there and pry Freddy away from Mr. Trump. I'm sure the Donald is here to cavort with the hip crowd and has had enough of his royal blandness. Jessica doesn't feel well, she needs her husband to take her home *now*!" Chas said, winking at Juan.

"Oh jyes, rright away."

Juan scurried over to Freddy and got between him and the Donald. Freddy was not amused. The Donald seemed surprised to see such an openly feminine man attach himself to Freddy—Jerry Ackerman's son-in-law—so intensely. The Donald looked at Freddy quite curiously, trying to figure out if Juan was his lover. Without waiting to get his answer, Donald walked away and was relieved to greet his newly arrived fiancée who was the most beautiful woman at the whole party.

As Juan and Freddy were making their way back to Chas and Jessica, Chas's own intuition started to kick in. He didn't like what he was feeling, as he couldn't miss the fact that Jessica's eyes were glued on Harry. Chas was so set on making his million that he wouldn't even allow his mind to wander in that devastating direction.

"That Harry is quite a character, isn't he?" Chas said.

"Yes, I guess he is," Jessica said, sadly.

Chas didn't like the sound of defeat in her voice. It made him very uncomfortable. *Oh my, this can't be happening. There is no way little nebbishy Jessica Levitt could have a silly schoolgirl crush on scary Harry. No, that can't be right. What would she see in a total fuck-up like him? After all, she doesn't need his money. Holy shit, the money, just think of all of that money. If Harry and Jessica got married they could finance a small universe. It's just not fair that two people, especially these two, should have so much, while someone like me has nothing! No way will I let that happen.* Chas's mind went wild. He knew he had to kick into the master manipulator mode to save his chance at winning his millions.

"You know, Jes, even if Harry and Penny got married, Harry would always be Harry. He'd always have that wild streak in him, Jes. He'd never *really* settle down. You know what they say, you can take the boy out of Hollywood, but you can't take the Hollywood out of the boy."

Jessica didn't pay attention to a word Chas had said. All she heard was one thing.

"Oh my God. Did Harry ask Penny to marry him?" she asked, fighting back tears with all her might.

Okay, stay cool, calm, and collected, then lower the bomb. Make sure she knows she has no chance with Harry at all, Chas thought to himself. Slyly, he said to Jessica, "Well, not yet, but they've been spending so much time together. I'm hoping that by the end of the summer, he'll pop the question. Penny's just what he needs. She's fun, outgoing, from a good family. She'll fit in perfectly in Beverly Hills. The Raiders already know her. It's a perfect match. Don't you agree?"

Jessica was dumbfounded. It never occurred to her that something serious could actually evolve between Penny and Harry. She thought Penny was just his public date for the summer. Jessica felt like she was going to pass out.

"Jessica...don't you agree Harry and Penny would be an ideal couple?" Chas said again, wondering what was wrong with the zoned-out Jessica.

"Uh, yes. I guess so. I never really thought about it, to tell you the truth. Do you think I'm fun?"

"You? Of course, Jes. Nobody in the Hamptons is more fun than you, dear!"

Chas hated what he was sensing from Jessica. Her uneasiness about the subject was blowing his mind.

Jessica ignored Chas's patronizing answer. "Do you think she'll want him after tonight?" Jessica asked sarcastically, like she was asking for herself.

Chas had to really bite his tongue to hide his bitterness towards the very rich Jessica. "Oh sure, Penny's really easy-going about these things. She's ready to accept Harry for what he is. She knows he'll never change."

Freddy and Juan were now standing with Chas and Jessica.

"Thank God you got here, Freddy. Little Jes is practically dying on her sweet little tootsies. Doesn't she look pale to you? I think you should take her home at once."

"Jes, I was having this great conversation with the Donald. He said I could call him in the office on Monday. He gave me his private line," Freddy squealed, almost ejaculating in his plaid Polo pants.

"That's great, Freddy. I'm really proud of you. Can we go home now?" Jessica asked demurely of her suck-up husband.

"Sure, Jes, no need to stick around any longer. All my work is done," Freddy replied, ignoring his wife's shaky condition. "Good night, everybody. Chas, great party. Thank P. Doody for us, will ya?" Freddy said, still high on his evening's *coup de grace*.

"It's P. Diddy, Freddy. P. Diddy!" Chas said condescendingly.

"Whatever. What a night! What a night!" Freddy exclaimed as he escorted his gloomy little wife out of the festivities.

"Thank God they're gone," Chas said to Juan. "Now I have to get Harry away from those two gold-digging whores and over to Penny's," Chas said, about to bust up Harry's good time.

"Oh jyes...jyou better hhurry up, Chassy, before es too late," Juan said.

"Right! Uh, Juan, before I go rescue Harry, I want to ask you a question."

"Anythin jyou hwant, my luv," Juan answered, fluttering his long, black eyelashes.

"Did you notice anything particularly strange about the way Jessica was acting tonight?"

"No, little Jeseeca, no feel es-so good, that's all. No more," Juan lied as he knew he had to, to keep the peace.

"You think that's all? I was getting this weird feeling that there was something else. Something she's not telling me."

"Oh, Chassy, don't be es-so seely. Jyou luv to es-start trouble. Jeseeca has an es-stomach ache. She wake up tomorrow, she'll be fine, jyou'll see, no problems," Juan said convincingly.

"Yes, sweetheart, I guess you're right. I think the pressure of this situation is getting to me."

"Hwat pressure, Chassy, mi amor? Relax, es all fun. If we get de munee, que bueno, if not hwho cares, we esstill haave eeeach other," Juan said in his most seductive, disarming voice.

"Well, it would be nice if we could be together *and* have the money," Chas said, looking at the plush Hampton surroundings.

"Then, go get eet, baby," Juan said, tapping Chas on the ass.

"Right!" Chas said as he approached Harry and the bimbos.

With a renewed sense of determination, Chas cleared his throat, straightened himself up, and made a beeline for Harry and his hot babes. Moving so quickly towards the crowded dance floor, he knocked a tray of dim sum out of a waiter's hand and didn't even turn around to apologize his rudeness. He stylishly boogied through the crowd of gangsta rappers and dancing partiers until he reached Harry and his ladies. Chas was a man on a million-dollar mission. "Harry, have I got a surprise for you," Chas said, practically knocking Harry right out of the booby trap.

"It can't possibly beat this scene, Chas," Harry replied, signaling the girls to come back.

"No, really, Harry. I know you've been a good boy all summer, but this will really blow you away. Trust me, I think you deserve a nomination for sainthood after living under the strict Ackerman roof."

Yeah, if you only knew what I've been up to with my lovely hostess, sweetie pie, Harry thought to himself, knowing full well that Chas would have a cow if he even suspected that he was involved with Jessica. "It hasn't been so bad, actually. I've rather enjoyed it. It's been really quite surprising," Harry gloated.

"Right," Chas said again, feeling that unsettling "something's up" feeling he first got from Jessica. "Well, Harry. Tonight is just what you need to feel like your old self, again," Chas said, winking at Harry.

"I think I like my new self better. Besides, I haven't changed that much, really."

"Okay, whatever you say, Harry, my boy. You tell me how you feel after you see what's waiting for you."

"Whatcha got cookin', Chas?" Harry asked, filled with curiosity. He loved unexpected pleasure.

"Come with me, you won't be sorry."

chapter twenty

Chas, Juan, and Harry drove in the Beemer through the dark Hampton lanes. Finally, they reached Penny's long, gravelly driveway and made their way towards the beach house.

"What are we doing here? I thought you had some big surprise?" Harry asked, a little disappointed.

"The surprise is waiting for you upstairs, Harry. Wait till you see what's coming," Chas said, smiling seductively.

"I don't get it," Harry said. "What could possibly be happening here?"

"Just wait, my friend. You'll thank me later," Chas winked.

"Whatever," Harry said as he sat back in his seat. He was open to anything; it was after midnight.

The front door of Penny's estate was open for Chas, Juan, and Harry to let themselves in.

"Now what?" Harry asked, wandering around the living room. *Oh God, what the hell are these guys trying to do to me? More importantly, how the hell am I going to get out of whatever it is without causing a big mess?* Harry wondered to himself.

"Now, you go up to Penny's room. We'll wait down here until you're finished," Chas said, pulling Juan by his hands, across the white marbled floor.

"Penny's room? What's going on, guys?" Harry said, shrugging his shoulders, wanting desperately to head for the door and leave.

"Have a blast, Harry!" Chas said as he and Juan disappeared into the secluded den.

"Yeah, okay," Harry said defeatedly. *I guess there is no way to escape whatever they all have planned. If I try to leave, it will spoil their surprise and cause more trouble. The safest thing to do here, I think, is to just go play along and get this whole night over with as quickly as possible*, he thought to himself as he stood alone in the deserted living room.

Harry made his way up the winding staircase. He walked down the long corridor filled with Calder, Degas, and Monet. Penny certainly had good taste.

Harry softly knocked on the door to Penny's private suite.

"Come in," he heard her say in a voice that didn't sound like her own.

"AH HA!" was all Harry could say as he entered the room to find Penny sprawled out on her big bed, costumed in a bright red lace teddy, fishnet stockings, gold fuck-me pumps, and a red velvet thong.

Well I guess this was bound to happen at some point, Harry thought. At first he covered his eyes in embarrassment, but then it dawned on him that wasn't what he was expected to do.

"Hi, Harry," Penny said, sounding a little more than tipsy.

Two empty bottles of Dom Perignon were on the nightstand. There was no way she could handle this stone cold sober. When Penny got home from the party, and she was suddenly faced with the task at hand, it seemed so bizarre to her that she was shaking with nervousness. When Jena saw the crazy state of mind that Penny had worked herself into, she went right to the bar and put some champagne on ice. Jena knew that Penny's first time girl-on-girl love jitters could be easily washed away with a bit of bubbly.

"Hey, Penny. What's up?" Harry said, stuttering a little. He did not want to be in this position with her and had avoided it all summer. *Why did you have to do this Penn? Everything was going on so nicely. I can't imagine what is going to happen after this disaster*, Harry thought.

"So glad you could join us," Penny said furtively.

"US? Who's us?" Harry asked. *Now who the hell has she involved in this whole deal? It's just getting freakier by the minute*, Harry thought.

"Oh, Jena. It's time."

Jena stepped out of the bathroom in a black leather dominatrix get-up. She had pierced nipples and wore gold hoops. With the spiked dog collar, the criss-cross strap around her breasts and the light whip, little ephemeral Jena had vanished. Jena, goddess, woman of sex, had arrived.

Jena climbed into the bed and brushed Penny's ass lightly with her whip. Jena then did the same to Penny's big, round nipples. It made Penny more excited than she cared to admit.

Penny then began to suck Jena's pointy, perky right nipple, squeezing the ring between her teeth. Jena began squeezing Penny's breasts and rubbing the whip across her vagina.

After a few minutes of kissing and caressing, Jena burrowed down between Penny's legs and started nibbling. The nibbling turned to long strokes of Jena's tongue; finally Jena had her whole face pushing and sucking Penny's mound.

As the two girls enjoyed each other's pleasures, Harry watched in utter fascination. Jena couldn't take her head out of Penny's legs as she swiveled around, putting them in the 69 position. The smell of Jena's pheromones was absolutely intoxicating to Penny, as she licked away at her best friend's womanhood. In her life, Penny never felt such pleasure. But something was definitely missing—Harry.

"Aren't you going to join us?" Penny said as she glanced at Harry from between Jena's legs.

"Actually, I'm have a great time, just watching," Harry said, feeling a raging hard-on rub against his khakis.

"Come on, Harry. I want you to join us," Penny said, thinking he would joyfully give in. But he didn't.

I can't believe I'm going to walk away from this. Never in a million years would anyone back in L.A. believe that Harry Raider would leave two hot chicks in a bed by themselves. What the hell has happened to me? Why is it that all I can think about is how it would hurt Jessica if she found out that I slept with these two girls, especially Penny? Penny is a great girl, but she's like a sister to me. Instead of being able to focus on her huge tits, all I can remember is the look in Jessica's deep green eyes when I make love to her. Shit, why did I just say "make love"? Is that what is going on here? I guess, I think, no. I know, I am really in love with Jessica. Okay, well even though I know I love her, that doesn't mean I can, or I will, or I want, to marry her...or if she would really leave Freddy for me. All of a sudden, Harry needed a release.

"Really, Penny. You girls have a great one. I'll be in here."

Harry slipped away to Penny's bathroom and relieved the pressure that had been building up in his groin. As he spilled sperm all over the marble floor, he let out a sigh of pure ecstasy. Penny and Jena heard it loud and clear. It was all over. At that moment, Penny knew she had lost. She wondered if she ever really had any chance with Harry at all. Penny's whole world, the fantasy she had bought into of living happily ever after as Mrs. H. Raider had just exploded into the palm of Harry's hand.

Facing that harsh reality and fighting back tears, Penny untangled herself from Jena. She threw on an old terrycloth robe with "The Breakers Palm Beach" embroidered on it. She couldn't believe what just happened and what did not just happen. How could this have failed? She wanted to bolt through the sliding glass door and jump into the ocean. Penny felt like she would be better off dead.

Before Harry came out of the bathroom, Penny ran out of her bedroom and headed for the stairs.

"Penny, wait," Jena said, running after her.

"Leave me alone, damn it," Penny screamed back.

Penny ran into the kitchen and looked for a knife. She had every intention of slitting her Cartier-braceleted wrists. Luckily, before she found the knife she found a double-fudge chocolate layer cake the maid Maria had left out to cool. Penny dug both hands into the moist cake and began stuffing it into her mouth. Within seconds, Penny was also into leftover pizza, quiche, lobster salad, roast duck, ice cream, and pasta e fagioli. She even ate her way through open cereal boxes, spraying Lucky Charms everywhere.

Harry stumbled down the stairs, trying not to slip. It was totally dark; the only light he could see in the whole house was coming from the kitchen. Blurry-eyed, and a little post-orgasmicly out of it, he fumbled around the living room, trying to make his way towards the light without knocking into anything. Slowly Harry entered the kitchen to find Penny mid-binge. If she was ready to die of embarrassment before, now she felt like she could nail the coffin shut.

"Oh my God!" Penny said with a duck leg in one hand, a pickle in the other and chocolate all over her face. *If I didn't totally disgust him enough already, he now gets to see me stuff my fat face. Can this night get any worse?* Penny thought, not eating for a moment.

"Hey, don't sweat it, Penn, sex makes me hungry, too. Besides, I didn't eat much at the party. Mind if I get a sandwich?"

Penny could barely swallow her food. She went over the refrigerator and pulled out a bottle of no-cal Evian water and gulped it to wash down what was in her mouth. Because the shock of being discovered by Harry had frozen her throat, she didn't want to make things worse and choke in front of him. Harry purposely ignored Penny's embarrassment. He felt bad about what had happened and wanted to put her at ease. *I hope I didn't hurt her too badly; Penny is a super chick and I hope we can be friends and laugh about this one day*, Harry thought to himself.

Harry spread mustard on rye bread and filled it with roast beef that Penny had not yet devoured. At once, he started to make her feel more comfortable.

"Eating's great, isn't it? I love food," Harry said, enjoying a few bites of his roast beef.

"I wish I didn't love eating so much. Then I wouldn't be such a fat, ugly cow," Penny said, wiping some cranberry sauce from her chin.

"Penny, you're gorgeous! Don't you know big girls are in now? More is more! You're a very sexy chick."

"If I'm so sexy, then how come you won't touch me?" Penny managed to get out. She had her back to Harry and her head in the fridge. In that position, she was fearless.

Harry put down his midnight snack. He knew he would have to answer this question without hurting Penny and without telling the whole truth. He felt he still needed to keep Jessica a secret until he could figure out what exactly to do about her. *Penny, please be cool about this and don't press me too much. I'm just not ready to go public about the truth. If you can just let the whole thing ride and we can be buds, eventually everything will be fine*, Harry thought as he came up behind Penny and put his hands around her shoulders, giving her a big bear hug.

"Penn, I love you. You're my buddy and you're a very beautiful girl. I know a million, a trillion, a zillion guys in L.A. who would kill to have a hot babe like you. But Harry's a really confused guy right now. I don't know what I want. I just know I don't want to hurt you. You are too special and too wonderful for that."

Harry rocked Penny in his arms as his words penetrated Penny's stuffed body, into her hungry soul. She felt his sincerity and appreciated his honesty. Maybe he wouldn't be her husband, but he made her feel like a million bucks. For now, that was good enough. Penny let herself be soothed and comforted in Harry's arms.

"I think you're pretty special also, Harry. I hope we stay close forever. Harry, having you here this summer has been the best thing that's ever happened to me. Do you think you and I could ever be together? I mean really together?" Penny said, releasing herself from his warm grasp and looking up into his dancing eyes.

"I don't know, Penn. Right now, I just need time to figure myself out. Just know that I'll always care about you," Harry said, cleverly biding his time.

Well, at least he cares about me. That's got to mean something, especially to someone like Harry who probably never cared about anybody but himself. Maybe this is the start of something, if I take it slow and play my cards right, Penny fooled herself into thinking. They continued hugging, as Chas and Juan entered the food-filled kitchen.

"From one orgy to another. Not a hole should be left unsatisfied," Chas chuckled as Juan started to pick at the remainder of the chocolate cake.

"Juan, dahling, your figure! Your figure!" Chas squealed as he pulled Juan's finger out of the icing. "Everything satisfactory, guys?" Chas said, smiling at what looked like the loving couple.

"Just fine, Chas. Just fine," Penny said as she wallowed in Harry's all-encompassing embrace.

chapter twenty-one

On a sticky, hot, late-August afternoon, Harry and Milly were lazily hitting a tennis ball back and forth at the exclusive Lawn Club courts in South Hampton. Although Milly did not feel especially connected to her blue-blood heritage, being a Harrington still had its privileges: playing on the grass courts of the Lawn was one of them. Like all the other players, Milly wore understated, plain tennis whites: an old T-shirt and straight skirt.

Harry was well aware of the WASP-only rule at the Lawn Club. It was such a sharp contrast to the diamond-studded courts at Pine Valley Country Club back in L.A. The first difference Harry noticed was how quiet the courts were. There must have been twenty courts, all filled with players dressed in the obligatory "whites only," and no one made a sound.

Harry was used to hearing loud voices demand, "Where's my Diet Coke?" "Oh my God, watch my nose, it's new," or "Isn't my lesson over yet? I don't want to miss the lunch special," at Pine Valley. He had never seen people play tennis in such silence. Harry felt like he was in a tennis library. It was a little intimidating.

As he hit the tennis ball back and forth, his mind began to wander about what had been going on with Jessica.

Boy, it hasn't been easy lately, but I know the love is still there. It's funny, because I didn't even do anything except chat up a couple of bimbos, and Jessica sometimes acts like I committed a capital offense. I can't believe I'm not even mad at her for being a little bitchy and sarcastic about it. I think it's kind of cute actually, her possessiveness. Most girls wouldn't say anything at all. This doesn't make the whole situation any easier. Do I really want to be with a woman who won't let me get away with my usual crap? Wow. That's a lot to think about, right there! Harry said to himself as a tennis ball almost hit him in the head.

The strength of the sun did not lessen, even though it was almost four o'clock. Milly could have continued playing at least another hour, but Harry was near exhaustion. He wanted to yell across the court to Milly and tell her that he had had enough, but somehow he felt that was definitely not the thing to do. Instead, he put his racket on the court and lay down next to it, playing dead. At first Milly wasn't sure if he was faking or had passed out for real. She rushed across the court and knelt down beside him as he lay there, his mouth open and his eyes shut.

"Harry, are you okay?" she asked frantically. Milly had never seen anyone faint before. "Harry, can you hear me?"

He didn't move a muscle.

"Harry, please, say something." Milly had no idea what to do in case of emergency. She was a rugged sportswoman; a little heat never bothered her. However, this was Harry, whose underwear was probably air-conditioned. With no idea of the right thing to do, Milly checked Harry's pulse, and put her head on his chest to hear if he was still breathing.

"Oh, darling, I thought you'd never," Harry said, as he playfully pulled Milly on top of him.

"Harry! Please!" Milly squealed in a loud, shocked voice that broke the club-wide silence.

Games stopped. People turned to see what mayhem had disturbed their tranquil tennis experience. Locked jaws dropped wide open as Harry and Milly rolled around on the grass court, wrestling each other like two bad kids. No one at the Lawn had ever seen such behavior. Especially not before martini time. Ms. Harrington must have had a lapse of manners and more than a little nerve bringing this undesirable from L.A. to the last bit of green, grassy, goyishe heaven in South Hampton.

This is probably the most excitement these people have seen all summer, Milly thought to herself as she reveled in Harry's arms. The general consensus among the Lawn Club members was that Milly had been with "that Jewish firm" way too long. Today she let her acquired *chutzpah* get the best of her and indulged in making a spectacle of herself with Harry. The rest of the club could go screw itself. She was having fun.

After the wrestling was over, Milly and Harry got up and brushed each other off. Playfully, they pretended to inspect each other from head to toe, before skipping hand in hand in to the courthouse. Even the intense heat of the day could not melt the cold stares they got leaving the court. Eyebrows were raised as a few women gave Milly the "Lawn Club look of disdain," like she was letting down the entire lily-white refined race by acting out so garishly.

These people are dead, Milly thought to herself as she looked at Harry shaking the vending machine when his drink got stuck. If only he would come and shake up her life like that! She adored Harry, but she knew it was hopeless.

The wrestling was the first and only physical contact Milly had with Harry all summer. Except for a few more boat trips and horseback rides, Milly hadn't seen that much of him all summer. What she had seen was Harry on the arm of Penny Marks at the Taste of the Hamptons Party. The party was massive—there were easily over twenty-five hundred guests. It was easy for two people to be there and not run into each other. Harry was too busy slurping up oysters with Penny, Jessica, and Freddy to notice Milly hiding behind the Food Network booth.

As she stood there, alone, watching the happy couples enjoy the food-filled festivities, her worst nightmare came back to haunt her. Jewish men married Jewish girls. Sure, they could have a good game of tennis or great sex with the shiksa, but marriage was a different story. Harry hadn't even given her the great sex part. Penny must have gotten it all, Milly figured.

Now, resigned to the fact that Harry would probably end up with Penny Marks, just like David had married Judy, Milly was happy to spend whatever little time she could with Harry. The summer was slowly winding down, and Harry would be going back to L.A. right after Labor Day. And he probably would take Penny with him. Milly was going to cherish whatever time she had left with the man who had brought a little summer fun into her lonely life. One good day with Harry was worth its weight in gold. She would try to grab as many as she could before he was gone forever. If nothing else, it would make for wonderful memories as she lay alone in bed with her trusty Lab.

A refreshed Milly and a tired Harry were in her hunter green Range Rover, driving back to the Ackerman estate. *Okay, so he's not the greatest athlete, but I had more fun today than ever before at that stodgy club*, Milly thought as she sipped a Snapple iced tea.

This girl is a machine. I'm so wiped, I can barely stay awake. Better get a massive amount of caffeine or something to jump-start my engine. Otherwise, old Harry will be down for the count, Harry thought. Tonight was Penny Marks's famous clambake. Milly was not invited.

"I'm so fucking tired, Mill. You totally whipped my ass on the court. I'm like, wiped out, babe. I need to catch some serious ZZZs."

"Big night tonight?" Milly asked, trying to act nonchalant, although she already knew the answer to that question.

"Yeah, the clam bake...killer food."

"Sounds great," Milly said, trying to sound enthusiastic for him.

"You going, babe?" Harry asked, hanging his head out the window, drying the sweat on his forehead.

"No," Milly said, still trying to be cheerful.

"Why not?" Harry wanted to know.

"I wasn't invited," Milly said, trying not to sound bitter.

Surprised, Harry stuck his head back inside. "No shit? Really? Well, that's a no-brainer, Mill. I'll call Penny and tell her you're coming...that's it," Harry said.

"Oh no, Harry, you don't have to do that," Milly said, embarrassed.

"Don't worry, Milly, it's cool. There's going to be a whole crew of people there—like half the Hamptons. One person isn't going to make a difference, especially if it's you."

"Harry, that's really sweet of you, but I don't want to impose on you and your girlfriend."

"My girlfriend?" Harry asked, suddenly afraid Milly knew about Jessica. "Who's my girlfriend?" he continued.

"Oh, Harry, it's okay. You don't have to hide it from me. I know you've been with Penny Marks all summer. I've seen you at parties together. Everybody knows that you and Penny are a couple," Milly said, blinking back a few tears. It was not easy for her to have this discussion with Harry, but she had nothing to lose now. Why hold back?

"I don't know who everybody is, but Penny is *not* my girlfriend," Harry said, practically choking on his words. "I mean, she's a friend and she's a girl, but that's it." Harry continued definitively, taking off his sunglasses to accentuate his point. Milly just nodded silently, not really believing a word he was saying. Harry knew she wasn't buying it.

"I know I've been hanging out with her a lot all summer. We've had a great time, but it's been nothing serious or romantic. She's an old friend of my family's and I hope we'll be friends forever. Maybe I should marry her, but I just can't. I care about her a lot, but I just don't feel the way you're probably supposed to feel about somebody you marry. I know that may be disappointing to Penny, but it will probably be more upsetting to Chas," Harry laughed, putting his sunglasses back on and mocking the way Chas crosses his legs.

"Chas!" Milly screeched as she swerved the car, almost driving off the road. "What the hell has Chas got to do with this?" Milly demanded.

"Don't get crazy, Mill, it's no big deal. It's just that Chas and Juan have been trying to get me with Penny all summer. Jessica and Freddy didn't really know Penny very well before now, but Chas made sure the six of us were all together all the time. He even tried to tell me that the one way to secure my inheritance and patch things up with my folks was to marry Penny. I think it's hysterical," Harry continued laughing.

"The son of a bitch bastard!" Milly yelled at the top of her lungs. Milly was one sharp cookie, and she knew when she had been had. Milly realized she was nothing more than Chas's back-up plan, and this made her furious. *If he couldn't pawn Penny off on Harry, then he would try me—the second-rate gentile!* Milly thought.

"I'm going to kill him!" Milly screamed again, banging her fist on the steering wheel and practically swerving the Range Rover into an oncoming car.

"Hey take it easy!" Harry, said, totally shocked and confused by Milly's violent reaction.

How dare Chas bring me to my knees, make me agree to his insane financial request, and then treat me like last night's leftovers. He will pay for this, damn it. He will pay for degrading me, devaluating me, and making me feel like a total emotional idiot, Milly thought to herself, as she fought back tears and tried to regain her composure.

She knew better than to let her heart rule her head. Milly learned that principle years ago. "That's what I get for allowing one moment of vulnerability to hit me!" she fumed, once again pounding her fist on the steering wheel. She had built up a fortress of security around her over the years. How easily it all came crashing down, when just one brick was pulled out of place! Yes, Milly knew better. *Never again will I let my pathetic desperation get the best of me. From now on it is dogs, horses, and work, work, work! No man will ever see the soft side of Milly Harrington again. This is it! Milly Harrington's heart is now officially Out of Business*. Her mind raced as she continued to drive like a maniac down Route 27, the Hamptons' two-lane main drag.

"Take it easy, champ," Harry said, surprised by Milly's unrestrained reaction. "Penny and I are not getting married. Chas will just have to understand! No need to drive into a tree! Chill out, Milly baby. Harry's still one free dude."

"I'm sorry, Harry, I didn't mean to scare you. It's just that you never know what to expect from Chas, do you?" Milly said, forcing herself to calm down.

"Doesn't matter. Chas likes to play games. Always has. I remember the fights he used to cause when he was working for his dad in the tennis shop at Pine Valley. He used to book two women at a time with this one tennis pro everybody wanted. The lady who gave Chas the biggest tip got the lesson. The other one had to reschedule or come up with more dough. No one ever reported him. He's the classic scam artist," Harry said, with a tone of slight admiration in his voice.

"That's the understatement of the century," Milly cracked, as she continued to drive along Montauk Highway towards East Hampton. Milly started to rationally think about what had really happened. *Okay, maybe Chas has scammed me, but at least with Harry I got to see some of the lighter side of life. With Harry, I learned to laugh again, and once more be inspired by a man's company. I guess that's not too bad, even if it came from a scumbag like Chas*, Milly reasoned with herself. *Even it if was just one summer, I do value my shared moments with Harry. I feel like a carefree kid when I am around him. And that's got to be worth something*, Milly smiled to herself, as Harry whipped out his camera and began snapping pictures of Milly driving like a mad woman behind the wheel, in an attempt to make her laugh. Milly couldn't help fall prey to Harry's endless antics. This was a first for Milly—she'd never known that joy or freedom during childhood. Harry awakened in Milly a spirit of fun that had spent years stuffed into her Wall Street suits. Maybe he would leave her a little brighter, a little looser, and a lot more ready to love, not so intense all the time. What Milly learned from Harry was that every day didn't have to be a fight for life and death. She could put those kinds of days behind her now. Thanks to Harry, Milly had learned to surrender her need to be in total control of every second, and relax into the rhythm of life. He gave her all this, and it didn't cost her a cent.

chapter twenty-two

Penny had confined herself in her room all day while the caterers set up for her notorious end-of-summer clambake. She didn't dare let herself be tempted by the smells of steaming lobster and fresh clam broth. With three hundred of the Hamptons' most social arriving on her lawn in a few short hours, she could not afford a pre-party binge. She knew that if she went downstairs to taste even one crumb of cornbread, she was a goner. Tonight she wouldn't let herself make that mistake.

Jena was a real sweetheart, as usual. They never had sex again, and Jena knew better than to ever bring that night up again with Penny. The best thing was to pretend like the whole thing never happened and that's exactly what Jena did. As much as Penny wanted to hate Jena for her naturally thin, goddess-like body, she couldn't. Jena's nurturing was the only thing that Penny felt she could count on, besides money. For that, she could deal with Jena's physical perfection. Trust had a strange, calming power over Penny.

Jena brought Penny a lunch of grilled chicken breast and radicchio salad, with iced lemon water to drink. Penny gobbled up the smoky-flavored chicken and red leaves like it was the Last Supper. She hated food control more than anything on this earth, but now she felt like she had no choice.

Labor Day was right around the corner. That was when Harry was scheduled to go back to L.A. Although he had told her that he just wanted to remain good friends, she still hoped and prayed there was an opportunity for that friendship to grow into something more. After all, in a couple of years, Harry would be forty. *No one, not even Harry the wild man, wants to spend those middle-aged years alone,* Penny thought. She also assumed that Harry would want children someday, and, she hoped, sooner rather than later. *The Raiders would not put up with another* Penthouse *pinup wife,* Penny thought. *Maybe, in the long run, I still have a chance.*

Just how much of a chance she had would become clear after Labor Day. Harry would either invite Penny to come see him in L.A. or he wouldn't. It was that clear cut. Right now she had to look her absolute best. It was do or diet.

"I hate it, I hate it, I hate it!" Penny cried as she tore apart a lettuce leaf.

"Oh, Penny, it's not so bad," Jena said. "Try not to look at it as a diet, try to look at it as..."

"A different way of eating!" Penny said, cutting Jena off. "I know, I've heard all that crap a million times. I even bought those tapes from Dr. Guillo, remember? Why should a cookie control my life, he wanted to know. Well, I don't know why cookies control my life, but they do! And so do cheese dogs, truffles, Twinkies, cheese soufflés, Ho Ho's, risotto, Hershey bars, McDonald's, and friggin' crepes suzettes! It all runs me. I can't help it! I admit it, I'm totally powerless over popcorn, pretzels, and pizza. I'm a food-a-holic!" Penny was now screaming. Whenever she went on a diet, she experienced harsh withdrawal symptoms, especially instability. It made her PMS look like a day at Bergdorf's.

"Well, Penny, at least you can admit it. Acknowledging it is the first step to changing your behavior," Jena said in an encouraging tone.

"Maybe I don't want to change my behavior. Maybe I want to just live and enjoy food! But I can't do that and be Mrs. Harry Raider, can I? Not with all those Beverly Hills beauties waiting eagerly at his electric gates. I bet they all drive by his house in their little red Porsche convertibles, just waiting to get a glimpse of him. Those L.A. whores are all a bunch of piranhas waiting to attack if I put on five pounds," Penny said, crunching the ice from her glass like a maniac.

"Relax, Penny, you're not even married to him yet and already you're on the defensive. You've got to learn to release your negative energy. It's not good for you. Why don't we get some air in here," Jena said as she opened the sliding glass door.

"No! Close it quickly!" Penny screamed from her bed, burying her face in a pillow.

"Why, what's wrong?" Jena asked as she immediately shut the door.

"If you leave the door open, I can smell the lobster cooking. Steam rises!" Penny said, coming up for air.

"I'm sorry. I know how hard this must be for you. Don't worry, you'll get your prince. He'll come around eventually," Jena said enthusiastically, as she cleared Penny's plates from the bed.

"I hope so. This could be my last chance before Bunny gets home," Penny said, lying back on the pillows preparing for an afternoon nap.

"When is she coming back from Europe?" Jena asked gently, knowing this was definitely not Penny's favorite subject.

"Not till the second week in September, thank God. Harry will be gone by then, and hopefully I'll be on my way out to L.A. Bunny won't have any time to screw this up for me. If Harry and I ever really do get married, I'll pay Sheik Mohammed to keep Bunny out of the country forever, if I have to. Wouldn't it be wonderful, a terrific husband, beautiful children, all of L.A. at my feet, and no Bunny! It's almost too good to be true."

Penny let out a big yawn, and with those lovely thoughts, drifted off into a deep sleep.

The harried, hurried valet parkers retrieved and parked cars with the speed of light. So many Rolls, Jags, Porsches, Saabs, and Mercedes, so little time. Penny was not one to skimp on anything, especially parking attendants. She knew if people had to wait too long to either drop off or pick up their cars, it could ruin a party in the Hamptons. This New York East crowd expected things done yesterday—nobody would be caught dead waiting for anything.

The three hundred or so guests arrived at Penny's oceanfront estate, which had been transformed into a Caribbean paradise with fire eaters, hula dancers, real coconuts filled with piña coladas, and palm trees imported from Palm Beach. Jimmy Buffett's band serenaded the select social sensationals like Prince Albert of Monaco, Paris Hilton, Samantha Cole, Meg Ryan, and the cast from *The Apprentice* with a soft Florida beat. The weather was a perfect seventy-five and breezy, quite a change from the scorching-hot August days that preceded Penny's event. Ten food stations operated at high speed as the seafood chefs dolloped pounds of lobster, clams, chicken, corn, and potatoes onto plate after plate.

Penny glowed as she could hear from her guests' gossipy rumblings of how great she looked. Tonight she was truly the belle of her own ball in her simple, elegant white silk dress by Calvin Klein, which he personally approved. Even Judy Cohen remarked how fabulous Penny was looking these days.

Most of the time, Harry, Penny's prince, was at her side. This made her happier than ever. Although Harry and Penny had appeared together at a number of parties over the summer, having him as her escort tonight really told everyone "He's mine!" Penny only hoped to hear people gossiping about her and Harry all night long. This would be her dream come true!

This is a great party and Penny is definitely in rare form. Hopefully she'll get so involved with everyone here that I can sneak over and give Jessica a kiss, or something else, Harry chuckled to himself. At one point when Penny was deeply involved in conversation with Princess Marie Chantal of Greece, chatting about the new Diane von Furstenberg collection, Harry took the opportunity to steal a minute alone with Jessica, who had been talking to three women

As she stood there uncomfortably trapped by three white-linened, social-climbing snakettes, Jessica picked nervously at her clams. She didn't have any children in any posh private schools; she didn't wear any of the latest designer clothes; she wasn't on any charity committees; and she wasn't sleeping with anyone else's husband. Basically, she had nothing to say these ghoulish girls. She wished she could just go home.

Harry came to her rescue, bringing a new plate of food and a soft drink. Her eyes lit up like fireworks when she noticed him coming in her direction.

"Hi, Harry!" she said jubilantly, her energy level rising at the sight of him. The women smiled at Harry politely, not knowing exactly how to react to the very rich and crazy stranger in their midst.

"Hey, Jessica. I hate to take you away from these lovely creatures, but I need to have a word with you, babe."

"Uh, sure, no problem," she said, trying not to sound too excited to be relieved of her present company.

"Excuse me, girls," she said as she followed Harry to a private little table near the edge of the dance floor.

"She's such a sweetie," one of the women said as Jessica walked away. She made sure she said it loud enough for Jessica to hear.

"Are you kidding, she's lucky she's so damn rich, she's a total bore," another woman said in an accentuated whisper.

"Do you think Jessica and her houseguest are getting it on?" a third woman chimed in.

"No way," the first woman said.

"She's too dull and stupid to get involved in something that interesting," the second woman said, her whisper getting louder.

"I don't know," the third woman observed. "They look awfully close."

It was hard to conceal the fact that Jessica and Harry were lovers when they found themselves alone together. The passion was in their eyes, the way they looked at each other, in this moment. Love was written all over their faces.

Jessica and Harry sat at the little table under the stars. "Jessica I'm sorry I was a total shmuck at the White Party. Nothing happened that night I swear on my life, I was just my idiotic self," Harry said with a lump in his throat. He was absolutely blown away by how beautiful she looked under the moonlight. "It's okay, Harry, I forgive you. I know I've been giving you a hard time about it, but it's just because I'm not used to being in those types of situations. I know that you were just having fun," Jessica said, smiling at Harry. She longed to rip her party dress off and go skinny-dipping with her lover. He harbored an overwhelming desire to sneak into the house and make love to Jessica on Penny's big white bed. So intense was Harry's desire for Jessica that he slipped his hand under the tablecloth and found his way to her panties. Furtively he slipped two fingers into her moist, wet womanhood. This brought a smile to Jessica's face and a jolt through her entire body.

"What did you want to talk about, Harry?" Jessica said, trying to control her ecstasy.

"I just needed to tell you how gorgeous you look tonight. You're the most beautiful woman here. Jessica, you're just the most beautiful woman anywhere," Harry said. He was overcome by her natural earthiness—the way the moon made her hair shine, the fresh glow of her white, untanned skin. And of course, the depth of her soulful green eyes melted Harry's heart. Her innocence combined with her sexual appetite was a delicate turn on for him. She aroused feelings in him that were completely foreign, ones he had been trying to come to terms with all summer.

As he sat there with Jessica amidst the din of the party, Harry was afraid of himself and what he felt. *I'm still uncertain if I am ready to take on the responsibility of a life with Jessica. So much has happened so fast. My head feels like it is about to explode*, Harry thought. *I love Jessica so much. I've actually enjoyed my summer being sober in the Hamptons, but the L.A. parties are just a few short weeks away*, Harry smiled to himself. *I mean pretty soon, if I wanted to, I could convince my parents that I'm okay and slowly ease into the Hollywood debauchery all over again*, Harry thought.

In a way, it was very tempting. Although he had plenty of great, hot sex with Jessica, he hadn't had a cocaine high in months. Part of him missed the buzz, the ride, the trip that came with living on the edge. Part of him still wanted to party with total abandonment; his desire to "ride the white pony" had been subdued, but never really left him completely. Harry had done a remarkable job staying clean all summer, but his relationship with Mrs. Levitt was making him bottom out emotionally. The more love he felt for Jessica, the more he knew that he had to "do the right thing." As his passionate pressure increased, so did his longing to blow his mind out with drugs and destroy the whole thing with Jessica. Tonight he was so overwhelmed he found himself really jonesing for anything to distract him from the difficult demands of his heart.

When Penny noticed Harry was no longer beside her, she began to look around the party, frantically. She was relieved to find him not on the dance floor with another girl, but quietly eating his dinner alone in the corner with Jessica.

Thank God, nothing to worry about, Penny thought as she made her way over to them. Harry's hand was still in between Jessica's legs as Penny approached them. He carefully slipped his hand out of her slippery harbor, and nonchalantly sucked his fingers, like he was licking away the clam juice. No one noticed, except Jessica, who came quietly on the plastic party chair.

"Hi guys! Everything okay?" Penny asked, playing the perfect hostess.

"Just great, Penny," Harry said as he gnawed on a chicken bone.

"You really did an amazing job, Penny. It's...quite...a party," Jessica said, recovering from her quivers.

"Thanks. I'm glad you guys are enjoying yourselves. It really means a lot to me. Mind if I join you?"

"No, we'd love it," Harry said, pulling over an extra chair.

The three friends sat and ate under the moonlit sky. For the first time in years, since she had been throwing this clambake, Penny was actually enjoying her own party. *This is the shape of things to come*, Penny thought as pictures of herself presiding over parties in Harry's Bel Aire mansion danced in her head. *Yes, it was all meant to be. Pretty soon, I'll be packing up this whole place and moving west. I wonder if we should have the wedding at the Beverly Hills Hotel or the Bel Aire? The Bel Aire Hotel is so much more chic, but I absolutely love that room that overlooks the tennis court and it holds so many more people. A lot of stars get married there, so why not? Besides, Harry Winston has a salon right in the lobby. I can pick out the ring and the room in one visit, then lunch at the Polo lounge with Chas to discuss the flowers, cake, dress, and...* Penny thought.

"Hi, babies! Guess who's baaaaack!"

Penny looked up from her clamshells to see the living end to her dreams. There she stood, blonde, tan, and dressed for no good. She wore a red, strapless Versace dress and black Frederick's of Hollywood six-inch fuck-me-hard heels. Little sister Bunny was home.

"Oh my God!" was all Penny could say as Bunny descended like a vulture upon them. After giving a limp hug to a stoic Penny, Bunny flopped herself into Harry's lap, throwing her wiry arms around his neck, wafting a strong smell of liquor and marijuana smoke. The familiar old smell of booze and drugs aroused in Harry exactly what he had put to rest all summer. Bunny reeked of decadence. Every pore in her body exuded the scent that led men willingly down the road to hell. Jessica sat there completely dumbfounded. Not even she knew for sure if the love she shared with Harry would survive a visit from a seductress like Bunny Marks.

Harry was not immune to Bunny's naughty attraction. He was fighting with himself about what to do with Jessica. He had to make some big decisions and soon—in just two weeks. This self-imposed pressure was almost too much.

Now sitting in Harry's lap was the devil's angel. Wherever she went, trouble followed. There wasn't a man alive who could say "no" to Bunny Marks. And Harry Raider was no different. *I wonder if my raging boner is noticeable. Thank God I have baggy clothes on tonight. Leather pants would be a killer right now*, Harry thought, quickly his pulling his Hawaiian shirt over his pants.

"Bunny, what a surprise to see you. I thought that you weren't coming home until mid-September," Penny said, trying to keep her cool as she recovered from shock.

"Well, that was the plan, man…but Mohamed wanted to leave Monte Carlo and go back to Saudi Arabia, and he wanted to take me with him," Bunny cooed. "There was no way I was going to that flea-bitten hellhole of a country ever again. Last time I went, I had to wear a veil and shit. I couldn't find anything decent to eat and I couldn't sunbathe topless. I told him to forget it," Bunny said, lighting up a cigarette and blowing her smoke practically in Penny's face. "If he wants, he can fly me to France for the horse races in October, but for now I want to party in the Hamptons. After all, I haven't been here all summer. Have you missed me, baby?" Bunny said, using her high heel to crush out her cigarette and running her bony fingers through Harry's thick, bristled hair.

"I've had an excellent summer, but it's nice to see you, Bunny," was all Harry could say. Bunny could feel his erection rise up under her buttocks as she rocked back and forth on his legs. Bunny knew what she was doing and exactly where she wanted to go.

"Well, I hope my sister has done a good job of keeping you warmed up for me while I was gone," Bunny chuckled sarcastically while Penny gasped in horror at her sister's audacity. "Because now I'm ready to show you a side of the Hamptons I bet you haven't seen yet," Bunny teased as she felt Harry's cock grow harder.

"He said he had a great summer already, Bunny. Didn't you hear him?" Penny said, starting to lose it.

"Well, he ain't seen nothing yet," Bunny said, nibbling and blowing into Harry's ear.

"He's seen quite enough, Bunny," Penny said, just about ready to knock her sister off Harry's lap.

"I'll be the judge of that, sis," Bunny continued.

"Bunny Marks! Sweetheart, what a cool surprise!" Chas gushed as he came racing over to the table with Juan. He had caught a glimpse of what had started from across the room, and Chas was determined to put out the flame before it turned into a full-blown fire.

"Hey, Jazzy Chassy. How are you, darling?" Bunny said, getting up to give him and Juan a huggy-kissy.

Chas grabbed the skeletal Bunny and literally dragged her away from Harry's table. This was no time for discretion. This could be all-out war.

"BunBun. Come meet the faaabulous people over by the oyster bar. One of the guys there is the hottest Wall Street wizard. Everybody's saying he's going to be the new Henry Kravis. He's done three major takeovers this summer already. This could be the man for you," Chas said, physically pulling Bunny away from Harry.

"But I'd rather stay here with my sis and Harry. I haven't seen either of them all summer," Bunny whined as she tried to resist Chas's pulling.

"There will be plenty of time for catching up later BunBun. You just have to meet this guy while he's here, otherwise who knows when you'll get the chance," Chas said, not giving up, spinning her back around, and leading her away again.

Luckily, Bunny was so thin and frail she had no choice but to go wherever she was being taken. Pretty soon Bunny and Chas had disappeared into the crowd of perfect people dancing to the music and eating the fruits of the sea. Harry pulled his chair close to the table so neither Jessica nor Penny could see how aroused Bunny had left him. All three of them were extremely shaken, each for their own personal reasons. They all just looked at each other, not knowing what to say until finally, Penny broke the silence.

"Well, my sister is full of surprises. You just never know what to expect with her," Penny said, taking a big gulp of her cocktail while trying to act normal and nonchalant. It wasn't working. The tension in her voice and body was apparent. There was no returning to the previous state of grace.

"Yeah, that's Bunny," Harry said, fidgeting under the table, wishing wistfully his erection would go away.

"I think I'm ready to go," Jessica said in a no-bullshit tone. She didn't know how to handle someone like Bunny at all. Jessica Ackerman Levitt had no experience with that kind of drug-alcohol-bulimia-anorexia scene. Her instincts told her to get away, and get Harry away, fast.

"That's probably a good idea. I'll get the car. Goodnight, Penny," Harry said, kissing her on both cheeks and darting out of the party.

"Oh, no Harry, please don't leave. Bunny won't bother you anymore, I promise! Even if I have to lock her in her room," Penny said, only half joking and taking Harry's hand in a death grip.

"No, really Penn, its time for me to go," Harry insisted, freeing his hand from Penny's.

"But the party's just getting started, Harry. You don't want to miss all of the fun!" Penny pleaded with him.

"That's exactly what I'm afraid of. I really need to get out of here. I'm so sorry, Penn. It's not your fault, it's just me. I know what I have to do," Harry said softly, not wanting to insult Penny. He knew he couldn't be in the same place as Bunny anymore. She was too dangerous and he had come too far. Harry had to leave at once.

Penny's hopes were absolutely plummeted as she watched Harry, Jessica, and Freddy peel out of her driveway in the blue Rolls Royce. How dare that whacked-out sister of hers come back and ruin her life again! Penny had had it with Bunny. This was one time too many, and this time she was not going to let Bunny get away with it.

Penny managed to keep her composure until the last guest left around one in the morning. Part of Penny's getting even with Bunny was staying in control of *her* party without letting anybody see her sweat. Penny refused to let Bunny be the center of attention tonight, so she had gone around from group to group, chatting, laughing, and playing the part. But when the last Mercedes rolled out of the driveway, all hell broke loose at the Marks estate.

The Marks sisters were inside the living room that overlooked the beautiful beach. "Great party, sis," Bunny said as she swilled champagne right out of an open bottle and watched the help fold chairs. "Too bad Raider had to leave so early. He's too cute, don't you think?"

Penny glared at her sister with a look that could massacre a thousand souls. All the rage and fury she felt for her fucked-up sibling was going to come out tonight. Years of torture were bottled up inside her. Enough was enough.

Penny grabbed the champagne bottle out of Bunny's hand and smashed it on the ground at Bunny's feet, then knocked her mercilessly into the shattering glass. Bunny screamed in pain, but Penny was not done.

"What d'ya do that for?" a shell-shocked Bunny cried as she picked chipped glass off of her dress and out of her hair.

A vindicated Penny picked Bunny up off the floor and threw her against a wall. She finally felt like she was giving her sister what she deserved all of these years. Penny refused to sit back and take Bunny's crap anymore. Bunny was too frazzled to realize what was happening to her and much too weak to fight back.

"Listen to me, you drunk little whore. If you dare go near Harry Raider, I'll kill you. Do you hear me, you no-good piece of shit? I will kill you and make it look like an accident. You're so fucked-up all the time, I could definitely get away with it," Penny said, with the rage mounting inside her.

Penny repeatedly banged Bunny's head against the wall. Bunny's tears and pleas for Penny to stop didn't faze her; years of pent up hatred and frustration were making their way to the surface.

"I wish you were dead already, you whore. You're a no-good coke whore and you deserve to die." Penny threw a dazed and confused Bunny back onto the marble floor and spat on her.

"I'm serious, you touch him even once, and I promise you Harry will be the last prick you ever suck." Penny left a banged-up, bruised Bunny shivering on the cold, hard, marble living-room floor. As Bunny started to come around, she began to become aware of what had happened to her. As drunk, stoned, or otherwise as she normally was, Bunny Marks was no dope. Without yelling, screaming, or acting out like Penny, Bunny knew exactly how to get even with Penny, without ever lifting a finger.

Much to Bunny's surprise, Maria, the maid who had been hiding in the kitchen and peeping through the door from time to time, had witnessed the whole fight. She was accustomed to Penny and Bunny's screaming matches, but had never seen anything like this one before. When the coast was clear and Penny had disappeared up stairs, Maria came immediately to Bunny's aid. She was genuinely scared that Bunny had been hurt. She gave Bunny a robe and helped her into the bathroom.

"Are you okay, Miss Marks? Should we go to the hospital?" Maria asked. Bunny just looked at her, shook her head no and smiled wryly. "May I help you into a bath Miss Marks?" Maria then said sympathetically.

Bunny just stared at herself in the mirror and slowly began repairing her disheveled makeup.

"No thanks, Maria," Bunny said, smirking. "I'm going out."

chapter twenty-three

Bunny continued to swig Dom Perignon out of the bottle as she sat in the back of the white limo. The car and driver, a gift from the sheik, was almost too big to fit down the narrow Hampton lanes. But Bunny wouldn't travel any other way.

"Stop here!" Bunny slurred, banging on the divider window. The driver pulled the oversized limo up to a big iron gate. It was the Ackerman estate. Bunny got out of the car and rang the buzzer nonstop until a sleepy butler finally answered the intercom.

"Hello? Who is it?" the drowsy servant asked.

"This is Miss Bunny Marks. I must speak to Mr. Raider immediately," Bunny managed to get out.

"Mr. Raider has retired for the evening."

"Well wake his ass up, this is an emergency!" Bunny insisted.

"All right, madame. I'll see what I can do."

Within minutes, Harry's groggy voice was heard on the other end of the intercom.

"Hello," Harry said, also coming out of a deep sleep.

"Hi, sweetie. It's BunBun," Bunny gushed into the system.

"Hey, Bunny. What's up? Is everything okay?" Harry asked. *She can't be serious, it's too late for anything good to happen to now. This is a recipe for trouble*, Harry thought, even though he was half awake.

"No," Bunny pouted.

"What's wrong, honey?"

"I miss you, Harry. I didn't get to see you all summer and now you're upstairs sleeping and I'm down here all by myself."

Harry chuckled into the intercom. He couldn't resist Bunny's helpless, drunk little-bad-girl voice.

She is sooooooo bad. Who can say no to something like this? Harry thought, feeling himself becoming aroused, almost against his will.

"Harry, sweet baby, will you come out and play with Bunny tonight? Please..." Bunny whined in a fuck-me tone that woke up Harry's dick faster than his brain.

The buck stops here. There is no way I can undo what I've accomplished in the past couple of months in just one night, Harry thought to himself. "I can't, Bunny. Really. I've been good all summer. I can't blow it now," Harry said, fighting the urge to splurge. *That's right, I can do it. The "new and improved" Harry can walk away from having the time of his life, can't I?* Harry thought, as the old, out-of-control Harry was dying to make an appearance right there in the Hamptons.

"Oh, Harry, it won't be long. Just one dance, for old time's sake. Couldn't you just do me that favor? Please, Harry. BunBun needs you."

Oy vey, this is too much for any mortal member of the male race. I've been good, but I'm not God. Only a deity with a divine sense of willpower could walk away from this, Harry continued to think to himself. *I've had a handle on myself all summer. I have lived as a sober man, being privileged without paying a price, for the first time in my entire existence. I only have two weeks or so, then I could return home a different person; well, almost. At least I could hold it together long enough to get back in my father's good graces. Maybe*, Harry thought, as temptation stood strong at the front gate. *In some ways, this has been the best summer of my life. I learned what it was like to enjoy myself without being artificially stimulated. I even rediscovered sports and had a blast doing the outdoor stuff with Milly. I finally found a true friend—someone who doesn't need my money—in Penny, and Jerry Ackerman has been the father figure that Sammy was always too busy to be for me. And, if all this weren't enough, I think I might have found out about what true love is, with Jessica. And my parents, when they hear what's happened to me, will probably double my inheritance. I am one lucky son of a bitch. I'd be insane to throw it all away just for just one night with yet another wild, drunken, sex-crazed slut. I can't do it*, Harry confirmed to himself, as he was about to move away from the buzzer and go back to bed.

But just as the "Angel Harry" part of his soul was about to pack it in for the night, the "Devil Harry" inside his brain that seemed to have been on vacation all summer demanded to state his case. *You know, I've been sooooooo well-behaved this summer that I probably could go out with Bunny right now and have nothing happen. I mean, she sounds pretty out of it and if I let her go out to a club by herself, she could wind up in real trouble, and maybe even get hurt. How would I feel in the morning if I heard that something had happened to her and I could have gone along and prevented a disaster? She is Penny's sister after all. I really should accompany her, if only to protect her. I can handle myself. After all, I'm a grown man and I'm in love with Jessica*, Harry reasoned with himself, as he threw on the Hawaiian shirt he was wearing earlier that evening and a rumpled pair of shorts.

Harry was dressed and downstairs in less than five minutes. He met Bunny at the gate and climbed into the back of the limo. There she was, reeking of alcohol and pheromones.

Her tight red lycra dress exposed her heaving "enhanced" bosom—a phony that showed off her perfect, perky nipples. "Harry, it's so good of you to join me. Mind if I get comfortable?" Bunny purred as she lounged across the back seat putting her face in right in Harry's lap. Immediately his hardness began rubbing against her blonde head.

Bunny, you horny fucker, you're really asking for it, Harry thought. He was out of control.

Right before Harry could blow his load, Bunny squirmed up in the seat and reached over to the bar. She pulled out a bottle of Dom Perignon and two chilled glasses from the ice bucket. "How about a toast, Harry, to old friends," Bunny slurred, as she poured the champagne, generously.

"Uh, no thanks, I'm not drinking these days," Harry replied, doing his best to stick to his sobriety and the pact he made with himself before getting in Bunny's limo.

"Oh just one little sippy won't hurt. I promise. You're a big man Harry, you can handle it," Bunny teased, wetting her finger with the champagne, then tracing it around his lips. She raised the glass to his mouth and gently opened it up, as he sat there becoming a slave to her seductive prowess.

"Okay, that's enough, Bunny," Harry said, moving the champagne away before he could swallow too much of it.

"Aw, c'mon Harry, you know you want it," Bunny continued, as she lifted the glass up to his lips with one hand and began slowly rubbing the outside of his pants around his cock area with the other. At this point, Harry was a goner.

"Oh, all right, what the hell, one little drink of champagne couldn't hurt anything," Harry replied. He tilted his head back and finished the glass. The bubbles seemed to go straight to his head. Harry had stayed away from booze for so long now he almost forgot just how good a beginning buzz could feel. As the limo sat stuck in typical Saturday night Hampton traffic, Bunny and Harry emptied the bottle. And that was just the beginning. Bunny reached under the seat with one hand and pulled out a bag of cocaine. It was filled practically to the brim with the white, snowy powder. Harry, who had been around drugs all his life, was surprised to see such a large quantity.

"Damn, Bunny. What did you have to pay for that? I hope you didn't sell your Porsche," Harry said.

"Don't be silly; it was a gift," Bunny chuckled.

"I really shouldn't be doing this," Harry slurred, now totally drunk from the champagne.

"Oh, please, Harry, we're just having some real fun. That's all," Bunny said, winking at him.

Still lying on Harry's lap, Bunny pulled down the top of her dress and put a few lumps of cocaine on her chest. Reaching under the seat again, she handed Harry a credit card and a hundred-dollar bill. Harry was now faced with the biggest decision of the summer. He knew that once he started there was no turning back. Even though he had gained so much, the addict in him now took over his entire being. Jessica Ackerman Levitt's reformed Harry Raider had totally checked out. With a dizzy head and blurry eyes, he knew exactly what to do from there.

Harry chopped and divided the cocaine delicately, trying not to dig into Bunny's flesh. He then rolled up the hundred-dollar bill and snorted the lines right off of Bunny's plastic bosom. What he didn't snort, he licked up feverishly, feeling the numbness take over his tongue.

Harry had almost forgotten the feeling that was now rushing through his body. His legs began shaking, and he had to move. His hands were sweating.

"I gotta get out of here, Bunny," Harry said, rolling her off his lap onto the floor of the limo.

"Relax, Harry, we're almost at The Coup." Bunny reached up into the bar and popped open another bottle of Dom Perignon. She took a big gulp, then handed it to Harry. Harry guzzled the entire bottle of champagne, while Bunny, still topless, snorted lines of coke off of the window ledge.

His mind was spinning out of control as his whole body seemed to be tingling and floating faster and faster away from himself. He didn't feel like he could put the brakes on anytime soon. When Harry looked up from the bottle, Bunny was totally naked, lying on the seat opposite him. She had her dress in one hand and the bag of coke in the other. The only thing still left on her skinny body was her black Prada sandals. She lay spread-eagled as she let go of her dress to play with her clitoris. All of a sudden, Bunny threw the big bag of coke almost violently at Harry.

"Dust my cunt, then fuck me," she demanded.

"What?" Harry said, dazed and confused.

"Dust my cunt with coke, and fuck me. It prolongs the buzz, dude. What part of that don't you understand?"

Harry spread Bunny's legs even farther apart and scattered the inside of her clitoris with cocaine.

"Deeper," Bunny commanded. Harry, getting off on this drug-induced fantasy, dipped his third finger in the white crystal and shoved it way up into Bunny's vagina.

"More," Bunny went on until Harry had practically stuffed Bunny full of the white stuff. For one minute, part of him almost thought about not having sex with Bunny, but he had gone too far, too fast. It was humanly impossible to walk away now, with his dick intact. He pulled out his cock and rammed it into her coke-filled crevice, pounding away until he could barely feel himself come. This was one of the strangest sensations of his life. Inside he felt his release, but outside all he felt was this weird rubbing sensation.

Sweat was rolling down his forehead, dropping onto his numb lips, as he pulled out of Bunny and rolled down the window. The heat inside his body was so intense he felt he might explode.

"Bunny, I mean it, I gotta get the fuck out of here, *now*," Harry said, nervously playing with the door as the limo slowed down.

"Relax, we're here," Bunny said as she slipped her dress over her head, twitching sporadically with the cocaine shakes. Harry looked out the window of the limo hoping to find a sign of escape, somewhere in this distorted night.

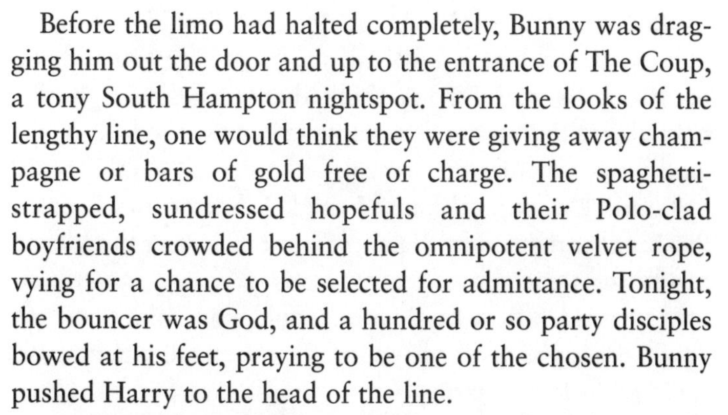

Before the limo had halted completely, Bunny was dragging him out the door and up to the entrance of The Coup, a tony South Hampton nightspot. From the looks of the lengthy line, one would think they were giving away champagne or bars of gold free of charge. The spaghetti-strapped, sundressed hopefuls and their Polo-clad boyfriends crowded behind the omnipotent velvet rope, vying for a chance to be selected for admittance. Tonight, the bouncer was God, and a hundred or so party disciples bowed at his feet, praying to be one of the chosen. Bunny pushed Harry to the head of the line.

"Hey, Freddie, remember me?" Bunny said, winking at the overgrown, Neanderthal-looking guy who guarded the door.

"Who could forget you, Ms. Marks?" the Missing Link man said, as he slipped Bunny and Harry past the desperate crowd, who looked on with longing in their color contact lenses. The inside of the overpriced celebrity nightspot was surprisingly simple and had a college hangout feel to it. It almost looked like someone had done over an old barn. The party people were anything but simple, as they wore less and less of their tiny designer outfits, exposing various plastic surgery enhancements, tattoos, and body piercings. This was the Hamptons at its most extreme. Bunny and Harry were granted the gift of exclusivity, and they were escorted not only into the nightclub, but to a private table in the VIP section. Another velvet rope crossed, showing that Bunny and Harry were as "in" as one could be.

Harry was still sweating like a pig, and his left foot was tapping the wooden floor uncontrollably. *Shit, I've been clean all summer and my body doesn't have the tolerance for drugs it once had. I used to love a cocaine trip more than anything. Right now, I'm nothing but nauseous, dizzy, and like everybody's watching my every move. This sucks,* Harry thought, trying to steady himself.

"Bunny, I don't feel so great. Maybe I should go home."

"Oh, please, Harry. I wait all summer to see you and you poop out on me? I don't think that's very nice," Bunny pouted, rocking in her seat, moving against the beat of the loud retro-seventies disco music.

"Look, I'm sorry, Bunny. I think I did too much blow. I've been straight for the last few months. I don't think I can handle it anymore."

"Oh for God's sake, Harry, would you calm the fuck down already? I just ordered dinner," she said, pinching his cheeks a little too hard.

Within what seemed like a cocaine nanosecond, a huge meal of chateaubriand, grilled portobello mushrooms, garlic mashed potatoes, and Caesar salad filled the table. Bunny attacked the food like a hungry vulture diving down on its prey. Harry didn't touch a thing.

"Why ain't you eating, baby?" Bunny said, shoving salad, steak, and potatoes in her mouth all at once.

"I can't eat on blow; it totally kills my appetite," Harry said, not feeling any better. The throbbing music, the gyrating crowds, the smell of over-seasoned food, and the flashing disco lights were making him crazy. If he couldn't leave, he had to do something to take the edge off, very quickly.

"Got any pills, Bun?" Harry asked, his face turning a grayish shade.

"Like what, Valium?"

"Valium, 'ludes, Xanax...anything to bring me down a little bit. I'm jonesing way too fast," he said, shaking, twitching, and chewing in place, like he had a mouth full of bubble gum.

"Okay bummer boy, I'll see what I can do."

Bunny slowly got up from the table. She slinked across the dance floor and disappeared into the ladies room. The attendant, a generation X-er with black fingernail polish and striped magenta hair, recognized her right away.

"Hey, Bun, long time no see."

"Yeah, I've been partying on the continent. Got any Valium or Xanax? My buddy's being a real baby, a major pain in the ass. He was like the most happening dude in L.A. All of a sudden, he can't handle the shit. He sucks now."

"Sorry, Bun, don't have anything. My supplier got busted last week," the attendant said, rearranging the mints and the hairbrushes on the sink.

"There's got to be something in here. There always is," Bunny said, opening up the paper towel holder, frantically searching her old hiding place for pills.

"Well, I do have this," the attendant said, hesitantly handing Bunny an open medicine bottle.

"Klonopin?" Bunny said, reading the label on the prescription.

"I think it's some kind of antipsychotic tranquilizer. Some girl left it in here last night. You can have it, if you want."

"Cool," Bunny said, air-kissing the attendant on both cheeks, almost knocking the poor girl over with her garlic-champagne breath.

Bunny got back to the table to find Harry already heading for the exit.

"Wait a minute," she said as she grabbed his wrist and started pulling him back toward her unfinished dinner.

"Bunny, it's enough," Harry said as she tried to push him back in his chair. He was too weak, sick, and strung out to fight her.

"Here, take these. They'll make you relax," Bunny said, now sitting in Harry's lap. She opened his mouth and put two Klonopin on his tongue.

"Swallow!" she commanded, handing him a glass of champagne to wash them down.

Harry took the medicine. He had no idea what he had just ingested. All he hoped was that the buzzing in his head and the electricity running through his body would slow down. He felt intense jitters and shakes take him over, like he was no longer master of his own being.

"Good boy. Now wait right here and try to chill out, while I go freshen up, okay? I'll be right back."

Bunny got up from Harry's lap and headed back towards the ladies' room. Harry finished off the champagne, hoping it would help the pills work quicker. *I can't deal with this shit anymore. I've gotta come down man and like right now*, Harry thought. Within seconds, he got his wish. With his head facedown in a half-eaten bowl of mashed potatoes, Harry was out cold.

Bunny slipped the bathroom attendant a hundred-dollar bill she had picked from Harry's pocket. The attendant knew what this meant. She left the bathroom immediately, locked the door, and stood out front like a watchdog so Bunny could have her privacy.

Bunny then went into a stall, not bothering to close the door. Sticking two fingers down her red, ravaged throat, Bunny began to rid herself of the meal she had just devoured. It all came up with ease, since Bunny's system was used to working in reverse. But this time something happened that Bunny didn't count on. After the last drop of the dinner was in the toilet, Bunny kept on fiercely dry-heaving. She tried to stop, but once she realized that she couldn't she went into a full-fledged panic. Bunny could not control herself as her body seemed to jolt, contract, and contort in the purging motion. Her heart was racing so fast it felt like it was going to burst right through her silicone breasts. Struggling to take care of herself, she tried to get over to the door to bang for help, but it was too late. She fell, lying slumped over the toilet with vomit dripping out of her red-painted lips.

Back at the table, the bouncers found a passed out Harry and did their best to try to revive him. A famous plastic surgeon, who was partying with a group of his latest Botox filled friends, even tried administering CPR. Having little luck, an ambulance was called and an ailing Harry was whisked away at once.

chapter twenty-four

The morning sun poured in the window of a private room at South Hampton Hospital. He had stayed in the hospital for almost a week for observation. Apparently, Harry had suffered a mild heart attack. This morning Harry opened his eyes and looked up to see an IV tube hanging out of his arm. In that very second, he knew this was not what he wanted anymore. For the first time in almost forty years, Harry's head and his heart were about to work together. He knew what he had to do.

Jerry Ackerman, clad in Ralph Lauren sweatpants and a white and blue LaCoste sweater, paced slowly in front of Harry's bed. The worried elder statesman looked like he had aged twenty years in the week that he spent pacing and praying in Harry's hospital room. This morning, a balding Freddy Levitt sat in a reclining chair in the corner, his head buried in the *Sunday Times*. Jessica, in a white silk sundress with little yellow daisies on the straps, stood with her back towards Harry, just staring out the window. She was painfully aware of what must have happened between him and Bunny. There was no way she could face him.

When the emergency room called the Ackerman house at 4:30 a.m. exactly a week ago, Jessica's hopes and dreams sank. This was the first time she could bring herself to come see Harry in the hospital. Originally, she was ready to believe that the old destructive Harry was a thing of the past. Jessica thought the self-discovery and passionate love they shared all summer had awakened Harry to a new sense of true contentment that didn't have to come from drugs or booze. Deep in her heart, she felt that by the end of the summer Harry would come to realize that she was his soulmate. She had wanted so much for them to end up together. Now she was confronted with the ugly reality surrounding Harry. Jessica feared the rest of her life would be painted with Freddy-centered gloom, doom, and disappointment. The last thing that she wanted was to go back to her life of pre-Harry, pent-up misery.

As she continued to fixate on the leaves of the majestic oak trees outside of the hospital window, Jessica's inner voice cried out to the heavens for a change of fate. That morning, somebody heard her.

"Jerry, I know you may not believe me, but I am truly sorry," Harry said, in a voice that was exceptionally clear for a man who had narrowly escaped another drug overdose.

"I'm sorry for you, my son. I was hoping we were past this," Jerry said, burying his silver-haired head in his hands.

Tears began to well up in Harry's glassy eyes. In the past, he said what he had to in order to manipulate his own father, but this was different. Harry had grown to love Jerry, and hurting him felt worse than hurting himself.

"We are past this. I know I've let you down. I'm ready to face any consequences my actions may have caused. I know you haven't called my dad yet, but if you have to do it now, go ahead," Harry said, swallowing his pride and handing Jerry the hospital phone. "I'm ready to be responsible for myself. I just hope that I haven't caused you too much inconvenience, and I'm sorry the hospital got you out of bed so early on Sunday. I hope I didn't totally fuck up your golf game." Tinted with his own brand of irrevocable humor, Harry spoke like a man. He was no longer a little boy trying to get out of trouble.

"Do you think I care about a lousy game of golf? You're like the son I never had," Jerry said, putting the phone down, not being able to bring himself to call Sam and Irma overseas. In a way, he felt like he failed them too. "All I wanted was for you to be happy here with us. Look, I wasn't a saint all my life, but when I married Jessica's mom, had a family, made some money, I began to find enjoyment in things that wouldn't kill me," Jerry said sitting on Harry's bed.

"I've known Sam and Irma a long time, and I know they tried their best for you. I guess I thought if you felt like you were missing something in life, I could give it to you. Maybe I was jealous that my old buddy Sam had a son and I didn't," Jerry said, looking at Harry with love in his aging eyes. "Maybe in some ways, the reason I wanted this to work out so badly was to prove I could be a better father than Sammy. As much as your father and I love each other, we are and always will be fierce competitors. We really get a kick out of outdoing each other. Whatever my reasons were for having you here, Harry, you have to know that I love you just for being you. Nude paintings and all! Please, son, I don't want to see you end up dead. What can I do to help you?"

The two men hugged and wept. Even with all the high emotion in the room, Jessica did not move from the window.

"I'm going to help myself now, Jerry. When I get out of here, I'm going to call my dad and tell him what happened. I'm also going to tell him that if he'll have me back, I want to go to work for him and get a real life. Then once I get my shit together and start living like a normal human being, I'm going to marry Jessica."

Neither Jessica nor Jerry could believe their ears. A gorgeous golden silence fell upon the hospital room. Not even the beeping and buzzing of the hospital machinery could be heard above the quiet.

A smile wider than the Grand Canyon covered Jerry Ackerman's whole face. His secret hope had just materialized. Harry would now be his real son, forever. Jerry hadn't felt this much joy since his own marriage day, over forty years ago.

Jessica turned around from the window and looked at her future husband sitting up proud and strong in his hospital bed. The angels had heard her plea and had delivered Harry safely from evil. Something told her that this time she could believe what Harry was saying, even though he had hurt her earlier this summer. It was a feeling she couldn't express with words, but every inch of her knew that their time had come. "Dad, what do you think? He's not so perfect you know," Jessica said, searching her father's eyes for his approval.

"I think you should give the Raider boy a chance. Nobody's perfect, Jessica," Jerry said confidently, beaming at Harry.

"Well then, I guess I'll have to do my best to keep him in line," Jessica replied. "I won't fight you on that Jes," Harry said, as Jessica slowly moved towards Harry. He opened up his arms and pulled her onto the bed with him. He held her tightly to his chest, kissing and cuddling her like a dearly loved child. Freddy finally put down his paper.

Meeting his surprised and shocked glare, Harry was ready to fully take on Freddy.

"Ten million dollars," Harry said firmly.

"Excuse me?" Freddy muttered in total confusion.

"Ten million dollars is what I will pay you to give Jessica a no-contest divorce and to go away quickly and quietly. If my dad doesn't disinherit me after this incident, I'll have my bank in L.A. wire the money directly into your account as soon as you sign the divorce papers. No problems, no questions asked," Harry said, speaking with his newfound confidence and self-assurance.

"It's a deal, Raider," Freddy said, rising up from the chair, putting the newspaper under his arm.

Freddy walked over to Harry's bedside and shook his hand.

"Goodbye, Jessica. I hope you'll be happy now," Freddy said in an unusually gentlemanly way. On some level, he was as relived as she was to be out of this loveless marriage and was well paid for it. Freddy then stretched out his hand to Jerry who watched in amazement as the two young turks settled the score in a most civilized manner.

"Mr. A., Jerry, it's been a pleasure knowing you, sir. Thank you for your time," Freddy said in a very businesslike tone.

"Freddy, you're a good man. If you ever need any help or advice, or if there is anything I can do for you, please don't hesitate to call," Jerry said, admiring Freddy's graceful acquiescence.

"Thank you, sir, I'll remember that. I'm going back to the house to pack my things. I'll be at the Maidstone Arms until after Labor Day, then I'll look for an apartment."

"Freddy, feel free to stay at the house until we get this all sorted out," Jessica said.

"No, thank you. I think this will be better for all of us."

"Good luck, Freddy." Freddy and Jerry shook hands, and with that he was gone.

chapter twenty-five

The baby blue Rolls Royce was waiting in front of the hospital, ready to take Harry, his fiancée Jessica, and Jerry, his father-in-law-to-be, back to the Ackerman's East Hampton estate. As the happy family rode together in the car, Harry had to deal with another awful truth.

"I want our engagement party to be the biggest blowout the Hamptons has ever seen," Harry said, grinning from ear to ear. "I want to fly in Wolfgang Puck from L.A. to do the food, maybe even get Billy Joel to do a mini-concert. I don't see why he wouldn't, I mean, he had fun at your last party," Harry said excitedly.

Jessica and Jerry both shared Harry's enthusiasm about the upcoming engagement, but with so much going on, they neglected to tell Harry about Bunny. Even in the midst of all the delightful planning for the future, Jerry thought that the sooner Harry knew the truth, the faster he could come to grips with it.

"Harry, there is something we have to talk about," Jerry said, his voice growing gravely low as the Rolls Royce rambled on.

"What's that, Dad?" Harry said, tickling Jessica as she

sat on his lap.

"We have to talk about Bunny Marks. She was found dead in the nightclub's bathroom. She died of a bulimia-induced heart attack. She wasn't as lucky as you were, Harry. I'm sorry, but please don't blame yourself. I know Bunny's mother. She's had big trouble with her for a long time. No one could save her. It's not your fault."

Harry was dead quiet. His face turned white and he felt as if the blood were draining out of his body. *I know this isn't my fault, because she was already too far gone. What a waste of what could have been such a beautiful girl. It's a tragedy, something that could have easily happened to me,* Harry thought.

Bunny's death was her own doing, yet somehow Harry felt incredible pain and loss. As he held Jessica warmly in his arms, Harry knew that a part of himself had died along with Bunny that night. Harry, the billionaire bachelor, king of crack, coke, whores, and porno parties, had lived ten of the nine wild lives everyone believed he had. Today he was ready for his new role as Jessica's life partner and maybe even one day, a father. Too hip Hollywood Harry had metamorphosed into a happy, homey husband-to-be.

The mirrors in Penny's beach house were covered with long sheets—to mourn the dead during the weeklong Shiva, the Jewish wake. As hordes of Hamptonites came by to pay their respects, Reba, Penny and Bunny's mother, sat Prozac-ed out on a blue lounge chair surrounded by two nurses. The death of her youngest daughter had turned the once luminous social Manhattan doyenne into a withered gray old woman. The mourners tried to offer Reba words of comfort, but all she could do was stare blankly at the sea. Reba was in a near coma of her own. On her wrist, underneath the Cartier watch, were the slash marks, evidence of how she had tried to deal with Bunny's death. It would be a long way back for Reba, who wished that both her daughters had lived to one day bury her.

Upstairs, Penny sat in bed with the lights off. She had not come out of her room since Bunny's death. Jena had to take care of all the funeral arrangements, since both mother and sister were too destroyed to act. Penny hadn't eaten or drank much lately either. Food was of no interest to her now; her stomach was ice cold.

The last thing that Penny could remember saying to Bunny was, "I wish you were dead." *I didn't really want my sister dead, I didn't mean that, but the green-eyed jealousy monster got the best of me. I was so damn afraid of losing Harry to my younger sister. I destroyed the poor thing. I should have tried to save her and not been so selfish. What the hell was wrong with me? And what about our pathetic mother? Why didn't she get that stupid lawyer she pays so much money to, to fix Bunny's trust papers and stop her cash flow? We both should have seen to it that Bunny got the help she needed. If Bunny had a better mother and sister, and Daddy were still alive, she would still be here today*, Penny thought as she cried tears of sadness and guilt.

Now Bunny was with her dad, and Penny and Reba were left to torture themselves with blame and shame. Penny was filled with such remorse she wished that she were dead too.

As she lay in bed, with the covers pulled up over her unwashed head, there was a knock on the door. She refused to answer. Penny knew that Jena was downstairs tending to the guests. If she came up to be with Penny, Jena wouldn't have to knock. Penny was in no mood to meet or greet anyone. She thought if she just lay there in silence, whoever it was would get the hint and go away.

The gentle knocking persisted. Finally it was so aggravating that Penny had to come to the door. She opened it just a crack to see who was there. Freddy Levitt, Jessica Ackerman's soon-to-be ex-husband, was standing on the other side.

The nerve of him, Penny thought to herself. *What the fuck could he possibly want?*

"Penny, I'm really sorry to disturb you. May I come in?" Freddy said, poking two fingers in the doorway.

"Freddy, I really don't want to see anybody right now," Penny answered, closing the door, hoping he would remove his fingers.

"Please, it will only take a minute. There is something I have to talk to you about. It's really important."

There was a long pause of silence from Penny. Although she hadn't washed or showered in days, she didn't care that this little nebbish saw her in her far less than perfect condition.

"Whatever, Freddy. Nothing is important now," Penny said.

"Just give me five minutes, Penny, please," Freddy said, pushing the door open a little further.

"Okay," Penny relented, figuring it would be easier to give in than to fight with him. She had no energy left anyway. The poor girl was drained.

Penny was not used to having a man in her bedroom, yet she felt surprisingly at ease with Freddy there, as she crawled back under her covers. Freddy politely stood at the end of her bed. *As crazy as this feels, there is something very non-threatening about him. His presence is almost comfortable and reassuring, like a big, nerdy brother. Maybe talking to him is not such a bad idea*, Penny thought to herself as Freddy came into her private space.

"Penny, the reason that I insisted on coming in here was to talk to you about what I went through with my sister fifteen years ago," Freddy said, beginning to speak anxiously like he was unloading the world from his shoulders, pacing back and forth. "I don't mean to dump this on you. I just feel like it would do us both a world of good to talk about what you just went through, and what I've stuffed away for so long," Freddy said, sitting himself down on the end of Penny's bed and fighting back tears.

Penny sat up, touched. "I didn't even know you had a sister, Freddy," she said sitting up next to him.

"She was sixteen years old when she decided to become a model," Freddy said, looking down at the floor. Penny's eyes followed his as she listened intently.

"Even though we were living in the slums of Newark, New Jersey, Beth had great big ideas," Freddy said, smiling fondly at the memory of his lost sister. "She used to sneak off and take the bus into the city on Saturdays and go into all the fancy stores on Madison Avenue. Of course, she couldn't afford to buy anything, but she'd just try everything on, thinking one day she'd have a closet full." Almost simultaneously, Freddy and Penny glanced in the direction of Penny's over-stuffed closet. Penny shot him a look of guilty pleasure, as Freddy smiled and nodded as to signal to her that it was okay to enjoy her good fashion fortune.

"Lucky for Beth, she took after my grandfather, who was a very elegant, regal-looking Russian Jew. You wouldn't know it by looking at me, but we actually have a very tall side to our family. Beth inherited all Grandpa's good looks and grace. She was one of the most beautiful kids you'd want to see. Beth was so poised for her age, also. We all thought she had great maturity beyond her years, but really she was a little girl in a blossoming young lady's body. My mom would forget that sometimes and expect her to act and think like an adult. It was awful. One day, when Beth came back from New York, she said she had been on a 'go-see' for a modeling agency. They told her that they would take her on if she lost fifteen pounds. Well, that was all Beth had to hear. The life of glamour that she dreamed about was just fifteen pounds away!"

"I can sure understand that," Penny said, playing with the flesh around her stomach.

"At first, she went on a sensible diet, but then came the pills," Freddy continued, patting Penny's stomach in a sweet way that told her it was cute and cuddly, like baby fat. "Eventually Beth stopped eating altogether. She lost over forty pounds and when she died, she weighed just seventy-three pounds. Like Bunny, nobody could help Beth either. Her desire to get out of Newark and create an exciting life for herself was overwhelming. It drove her right over the edge. I tried many times to straighten Beth out, but I was on my own fast track—Harvard on a full scholarship. It was like only one of us could survive."

"Wow, that's really something," Penny said genuinely impressed with Freddy's accomplishments, while being stunned by his terrible story.

"When Beth died, I blamed myself for not being there to help her more. I thought if I hadn't gone away to school, everything would have been all right. Dad had left us, and I was the man of the house. I was supposed to take care of my little sister and I couldn't save her. For a long time, I punished myself with feelings of guilt. It used to consume me to the point where I would just have to throw myself into my work," Freddy admitted to a shell-shocked Penny.

"When I married Jessica, I felt it was my reward for getting out of Newark. Yet whenever Jessica would act like a spoiled brat, it would make me crazy because I knew Beth died trying to get into the life Jes had been born into. I realize now that I may have been too hard on Jessica. My anger and guilt made me push her away, and ultimately ruined my marriage. Now I know Jessica was never right for me. I married her for the wrong reasons, and I never really gave her a chance. My resentment ate me up inside, and I made some stupid mistakes," Freddy said making a fist and pounding the bed.

"We all make mistakes," Penny said in a comforting voice. "Believe me, we all make mistakes," she said coming to grips with her own sense of guilt.

"The reason I am sitting here spewing like an emotional idiot is because I would hate to see you let Bunny's death screw up the rest of your life. Jessica and I are getting a divorce, and I am going to try to start over, without carrying around this plague from the past. I need to let Beth rest in peace and get on with it. I hope you can do the same, Penny. I really do."

Freddy was bawling uncontrollably—thirty-seven years of bottled-up feelings flowing free. Penny had never seen a man cry like that. Certainly her father never shed a tear. Penny didn't know that men could be as vulnerable like Freddy was now. His show of raw emotion was something that moved her in a way she had not known before. To see a man this tender, this delicate, this exposed, was inviting.

Penny very slowly and gently put her arms around Freddy. She cradled him in her arms and stroked the top of his bald head. It was softer than she had imagined, decorated with fine baby hair. As Freddy lay in Penny's embrace, he subconsciously began to reach for her breast under her night T-shirt. He lovingly fumbled around until he found her nipples, and taking comfort in her generous womanhood, lifted up the shirt and gently began to suck. She held him softly to her breast and encouraged him.

His vulnerability totally and completely turned her on. Penny was experiencing a passion that she didn't even know she had. Without saying a word, Freddy went deep inside her now, thrusting his hard, taut prick into her meaty vagina. Penny's extra rolls and love handles were like diving into a big feather bed for Freddy. He loved the feeling of her soft, warm, enveloping flesh around him. As he sucked and fucked her, releasing all of his emotion that he had hidden away for years, he felt more alive than he ever had in his life. Penny also felt more connected to Freddy than she did with any other man, as far as she could remember. As he ravaged and relished her Rubenesque form, she felt as if somebody had finally welcomed her full-bodied being. Penny had been sexually fucked before. Today with Freddy, she was making love. Penny wanted and needed this type of closeness and intimacy to last forever. This time, it would.

chapter twenty-six

On Labor Day evening, the Ackerman mansion was transformed into a floral-filled fantasy for Harry and Jessica's engagement party. Chas, with Jena's help, had flown in orchids from Hawaii, tulips from Holland, and roses from the English countryside. Big yellow sunflowers lined the path to the house, and guests were given bountiful bouquets to carry or wear. The whole house bloomed with love and joy as every corner was overflowing with decorative foliage. This night was the mark of new beginnings, and not just for Jessica and Harry.

The end of summer weather was just right. A blanket of stars in the sky made for a magnificent canopy over the outside grounds. The poolside dinner tables were lavishly adorned with gold and silver sparkles daintily sitting on the Herringbone china and Lalique crystal glasses. A bottle of 1967 Chateau d'Yquem, worth around a thousand dollars, was placed in the middle of each table for the after-dinner toast. Tonight was a night of many celebrations and personal victories. No expense was spared.

The glittering guests began to arrive around eight o'clock. There were so many celebrities, an *Entertainment*

Tonight crew was interviewing people like crazy. Kim Basinger, Steven Spielberg, Arnold Schwarzenegger and Maria Shriver, John Bon Jovi, Jay Leno, Robin Williams, Mick Jagger, Rod Stewart, Elton John, and several more of Harry's Hollywood show biz buddies had flown in for the special occasion. As promised, Billy Joel, a regular at the Ackerman parties, was dabbling around on a white piano, surprising everyone as they came into the festivities.

Famed chef Wolfgang Puck had also flown in, bringing his gourmet Beverly Hills goodies like barbequed duck pizza, ginger-seared salmon, and tuna tarragon tartare. The sit-down dinner consisted of scallops napoleon, beef chinois with baby artichokes, salad de la mer, and baked Alaska for dessert accompanied by Gavi di Gavi La Scolca Black Label 1993, Red Bordeux from Chateau Lefite Rothchild, and Dom Perignon with the Chateau d'Yquem. When Billy Joel sat down to eat, Justin Timberlake took over, rocking the Ackerman house with lively dance music.

Even with all the fabulous food, expensive wine, massive caviar-laden ice sculptures, and famous faces at the party that evening, the real star was Jessica. Having found the love of her life, she shone brighter than any star in the heavens or on Hollywood Boulevard. Harry, too, radiated a genuine glow of happiness that came from a hidden place inside himself he discovered that summer.

As they danced together cheek-to-cheek, body-to-body, and soul-to-soul, their love overpowered their prestige, wealth, notoriety, and anything else that wasn't from the heart.

Jena alone sat at a table with Penny and Freddy, who could not keep their hands off of each other. Freddy had his hand in between Penny's thighs all night. As soon as he was done eating an appetizer, his hand slipped right back to his favorite place.

"Jena," Penny said. "I want you to take note of anything you see here tonight that could be interesting for our engagement party next month at the Plaza. Not that I would dare copy Jessica, but she was nice enough to give me her ex-husband, maybe she has some good ideas," Penny chuckled. Even Freddy was able to laugh at himself now. Somehow Penny's smart-ass remarks didn't upset him. He understood that was her protective device. In time, when he could make her feel safe, Freddy knew Penny would feel more comfortable with her softer side.

Although Jena was laughing with Penny, she was bowled over by the star power at the party. With Penny and Freddy planning to get married, Jena wondered if there would be a place for her in Penny's glamorous life anymore. Jena knew they would always be friends, but now Freddy was there to take care of Penny in a much more intricate way. As Freddy and Penny kissed, flirted, and played footsie under the table, Jena pondered her plans for the future. She wanted so much to be a part of what she saw there tonight, but she didn't have the faintest idea how to begin.

"Is this seat taken?" a young, good-looking, red-haired man in his thirties asked Jena.

"No, go ahead," she said as she noticed the sparkle in his blue-gray eyes.

"Great. I'm Cleve Wischer, from the Renegade Agency. Who are you, gorgeous?" he asked, winking at Jena playfully.

"My name's Jena Prior. I'm here with Penny Marks," Jena said, still feeling like she had to justify herself.

"You ever think about modeling or acting, Jena?" he asked, taking a big bite out of his scallops.

"Not really. Well, I'd like to think about it. I just never had a chance," Jena said, blushing.

"Well, I'll tell you what, Jena. Harry Raider and I go way back. We went to high school together. He helped me start my first business. Today I run the largest talent agency on both coasts. If you're a friend of Harry's then the least I could do is give you the break he gave me. Here's my card; give me a jingle. You've got a great face, kid, let's see what we can do."

Cleve finished his scallops, put his card in Jena's hand, and headed off to schmooze at Barbara Streisand's table. Jena was absolutely stunned by what just happened.

"Do you think he's serious?" Jena asked Penny.

"Of course he is. You heard him, he owes Harry a favor. Go for it, Jena. You're beautiful, you're a sweetheart, and you've got a real presence about you. You could put Kate Moss out of business. It's about time she retired and ate something already!"

Jena smiled. She had star power. Tonight someone saw that, someone who, thanks to Harry, could make it happen for her. Magic was everywhere.

Just after Harry announced his engagement to Jessica, Chas ran into Milly at the Starbucks in Bridgehampton. He was waiting in line just as she was leaving holding a large frappucino with extra whipped cream. Milly asked Chas to meet her outside and then proceeded to pour her ice-cream-sundae-like coffee drink all over him, right in the parking lot, with everyone watching. Instead of flying off the handle into a tizzy, Chas took his punishment like a man, and the two old friends genuinely made up. As much as Milly wanted to hate Chas forever for what he had done, she got her satisfaction knowing his plan had backfired in his fine-toned face.

Tonight, at a table close to the dance floor sat Chas and Juan, who both escorted Milly to the party.

"This is the most incredibly party I have ever been to. Look at Joan Rivers, she just had another face lift," Chas gushed as he squeezed Juan's hand. The two men were wearing wedding bands on their ring fingers. The next weekend they were off to Hawaii to celebrate their union.

"You know something, Mills, it's almost worth losing the money. There are so many stars here, I feel like I'm at the Oscars. Oh, there's Goldie Hawn. I swear she doesn't look a day over thirty-five."

"You didn't lose the money, Chas. You never had it to begin with. Besides, there'll be another chance to make your millions. I hear there's an heiress in Palm Beach flying in next week in desperate search of a husband. She's only seventy-three, you gotta know someone."

"Hmm, I'll put on my thinking cap," Chas said, winking at her.

"You don't change, Chas. That's what I love about you," Milly said sarcastically as she sipped her champagne out of a crystal flute.

"Actually, Mills, I have changed," Chas said, getting serious for once. "Since Juan and I decided to exchange vows, I realize how lucky I am to have such a wonderful man in my life. No amount of money could equal what we have together. I can only wish the same for you, dear," Chas said as he sweetly kissed her on the cheek.

"Thanks, Chas, but I don't think that will happen any time in the twenty-first century," Milly said, getting a little choked up. "Excuse me, I think it's time for some more beluga," Milly said as she got up from the table.

She quietly headed over to the ice sculpture that held enough fish eggs to populate every ocean on the planet. As Milly stood piling the black driblets on the toast points, she felt a tap on her left shoulder. She was wearing a strapless Ungaro evening dress, so she could feel the familiarity of the hand patting her sun-kissed skin. It was a touch she could never forget.

Milly turned around to find David Cohen standing behind her, older and more distinguished than she remembered. He still had the thick, black, wavy curls she used to run her fingers through, but now he was graying at the temples. His dark eyes were still as warm and inviting as they were when they were kids. His caress still sent shock waves up and down her spine. As she stood in front of him, her hand with the caviar quivered. There she was for the first time in many years, face to face with the only love of her life. Milly was absolutely speechless.

"Milly Harrington, my, the years have been good to you," David said, removing the shaking plate of caviar from her trembling hands.

"David, I can't believe it. How are you?" Milly said, regaining her composure.

"I'm okay. I've been better, and I guess I've been worse. I saw you enter earlier with those two gentlemen. I wanted to come up and say hello, but I lost my nerve." David smiled that irresistible smile.

How is it possible that after all this time, he still had the same effect on her? It wasn't right. Here she was at this romantic extravaganza, all alone, with two gay walkers. If David was there, Judy could not be far behind. Milly tried to keep her grip on reality as she lost herself in his gaze.

"It's been a long time, Milly," David said. "I thought you'd be married with five kids by now."

"Well, I guess it just never worked out that way," Milly said, trying to hold it together. "I've read quite a bit in the papers about your family over the past few years. Seems like you were able to create the life you've always wanted. Congratulations," Milly said, forcing a smile.

"Yeah, well, don't believe everything you read," David said, his dark eyes cast downward.

"Oh?" Milly said, trying to catch his focus.

"I don't want to think about it tonight. Would you like to dance with me?" David spoke as earnestly as he had so many years ago. It was as if they were teenagers all over again.

I must be dreaming, Milly thought to herself. "Is it okay? Wouldn't Judy mind?" Milly asked hesitantly.

"It doesn't really matter anymore. Are you ready?" David held out his arm and led Milly onto the dance floor.

He held his old love close to his chest, and they connected with each other all over again. Milly and David were in a world all of their own, as the soft ocean breezes acted as a wonderful aphrodisiac. The electric chemistry they had years ago had grown stronger with age. They were enthralled with each other.

Milly and David swayed together to the lovely music. They were so lost in each other that on the dance floor they bumped into Jessica and Harry, who hadn't been out of each other's arms for one second. Harry looked at Milly and smiled knowingly. He had developed a real fondness for his sporty, best-gal buddy and he was glad to see her have a taste of happiness. Harry only wished that he could do something to get Milly and David together forever.

Jessica excused herself from the dance floor to greet some guests who had flown all the way from Australia. Harry loved his fiancée dearly, but needed very badly to relieve himself of all the club soda he had been drinking that night. Harry knew if he tried to get to the bathroom in the house, he would be barraged by people and would probably end up wetting his new Armani slacks. Very furtively, he disappeared behind the cabana and found an unassuming bush that looked like it could use a good watering.

Harry was spraying the bush gleefully when he heard loud grunting sounds from the cabana. It reminded Harry of the sound of two horses mating, like he'd heard one time at Del Mar racetrack.

Harry put his masterpiece back in his pants, pulled up his zipper, and went to investigate what was rocking the little pool house. As he peeped through the door, Harry couldn't believe what he saw. Judy, Mrs. David Cohen, was getting serviced by Bobby the workout trainer.

Harry quietly pulled out his newest digital camera and began to snap away. Judy was so involved in her sexy session with the hunky hulk that she didn't even realize that she was being photographed. Having captured the very horny Mrs. Cohen on film, Harry ran back to the party. *Oh boy, this is just what Milly needs. David's ugly wife caught red-handed. There is no way David's pride will let him stay married to that pig. This is excellent!* Harry thought.

David escorted Milly off the dance floor as the band took a break. It was time for dessert to be served.

"Mind if I sit with you for a while, Milly? My wife seems to be M.I.A.," David said as he pulled out her chair at the table.

"That would be wonderful," Milly answered. *Better enjoy this while it lasts*, Milly thought to herself, cherishing every moment she thought would be fleeting. *After all of these years, David is still the love of my life. He is truly magic. But, I better not let myself fall in love all over again, because any minute Judy Cohen will probably appear out of nowhere and demand David's full attention. Who could blame her? He's the best*, Milly sadly thought to herself. She wished she could freeze time so that every minute she was sharing with David would expand into a lifetime. This was the one incidence when Milly could not put on her ice-queen demeanor. The market could crash right now and Milly wouldn't have noticed. All she could see, hear, and feel was her darling David in front of her. No one nor anything else existed.

On the dance floor, Chas and Juan made their way over to the loving couple. "Aren't you going to introduce us to your friend, Mills? My gosh, how rude," Chas whined as Milly ignored him in David's divine presence.

"Sorry Chas, Juan, this is an old friend of mine, David Cohen."

"Es sooo nice to meet jyu, hunneee," Juan said, extending his hand to David.

"Nice to meet you too, Juan," David said politely.

"David Cohen, of course, you're Judy's husband," Chas gushed.

Milly looked down at her napkin, trying to hide her hurt and disappointment. Why did Chas have to chime in with his unwelcome reality check? But just as well, Milly thought. No use living in a fantasy bubble that was about to burst anyway.

At that moment, Harry came rushing over to the table with a look of urgency on his otherwise happy-go-lucky face.

"David, man, I, uh, need to talk to you for a minute. Dude, like now."

"Is something wrong, Harry?" David asked, very surprised to see his host in such a state.

"I gotta show you something, that's all," Harry said, increasing the amount of anxiety in his voice.

"Okay, whatever you say," David said, not wanting to be rude to his host. "If you'll excuse me," David said, getting up to follow Harry.

"Sure, no problem," Milly said, trying to regain her cool.

"What was that all about?" Chas asked curiously.

"I have no idea, Chas, but I'm sure you'll find out at the first opportunity," Milly said, taking a sip of hot, sobering coffee. It must be time to come back to earth, she felt.

Harry took David into the house, and then led him up to Jerry's den. David couldn't understand what could be so important to make Harry leave his own party.

"David, man, it really is none of my business what goes on with you and your chick, Judy, but like she is your wife, dude...and like, I think you're a really cool guy, so I think you should check these out. I hope you're not pissed at me. I just thought you should know." Harry showed David the picture of Judy and Bobby on the camera's screen.

David took a quick look and instantly hit the delete button.

"It doesn't surprise me at all. I'd like to blame our whole divorce on that Jersey City Guido jock-head, but I can't. Judy and I have been growing apart for years. We just filed last week, but we agreed to live under one roof until everything is final. You know, for the kids' sake. Listen, Harry, I'm trying to keep my personal life quiet, so it doesn't get messy. The gossip columns would have a field day with us. I'm trying to protect my children from that, so I would appreciate your silence," David said, offering Harry a gesture of friendship.

"You got it, man," Harry said, shaking David's hand.

"Now, if you don't mind, I'd like to get back to Milly Harrington. We have a lot of catching up to do," David said, winking at Harry.

"Gotcha! Milly's the best," Harry said with a big smile.

"I know, Harry. I know," David said as he walked out of the den. Harry grinned his mischievous grin from ear to ear.

David returned to Milly's table to find her picking listlessly at the Baked Alaska.

"What's wrong, Mills? You used to love that," David said, sitting back down beside her.

"I still do. I guess I'm not very hungry tonight, that's all. Have you found Judy yet? I'm sure she must be looking for you," Milly asked, trying not to go back to her previous state of David-induced euphoria.

"Let's just say I know where Judy is, and no, she is definitely not trying to find me right now."

"Wow, what a permissive wife you have, David," Chas said, smirking and raising an eyebrow.

"Soon to be ex-wife, Chas."

Milly almost choked on a piece of chocolate. Did she hear him correctly? Did he say the wonderful word "ex-wife"?

"Ex-wife?" Milly said, looking deeply into her soulmate's dark eyes.

"Yes, Milly, Judy and I are finished," David said firmly. "We both want out of it, as soon as possible. Judy can be a very difficult lady, but she's actually being very cooperative about the whole process. I think we both knew it was never really right between us," David said, justifying his whole sham marriage to himself, as he stared down at the dessert.

"We got married for the wrong reasons, and the next thing you know we had a family. Lord knows we both tried to make it work for a really long time, but finally we both realized there was nothing worth saving. It's time to move on," David declared looking back up at Milly and softly smiling.

"Wow. That is unbelievable," Milly said, still astonished from David's revelation. "The papers have made you look like the happiest couple in the world."

"Most of those reporters are on Judy's father's payroll," David laughed. "He slipped them big time payola to keep his little girl looking good. It's pretty sick, but even with all he greases them, they would still blow up our divorce into the World War Three if they had the chance. We're trying to keep it low-key, for our children's benefit," David said, purposely lowering his voice and looking around to see if anyone was listening to his conversation.

"I didn't hear a thing, David, don't you worry," Chas said, putting his fingers in his ears. As much as he lived to gossip, he knew when to keep his mouth shut. Chas wouldn't dare leak this news and jeopardize losing his new client Judy Cohen. With or without David, she was still a reigning rich-bitch diva of New York society.

"Thanks Chas. I'm sure Judy will thank you appropriately for keeping a tight lip. Milly, could I talk to you a minute in private?"

"Of course."

David took Milly's hand. Together they got up from the table and walked around, until they found a quiet, secluded spot in Jessica's garden. They sat together on the little bench, under a birch tree, where they could have some privacy. The full moon above shone brightly, illuminating Milly's ageless face. An angelic glow surrounded her, as she beamed with love from the inside out.

"Milly, I'm so sorry about what happened to us. I was just a confused kid, that's all. I thought I was doing what I had to, but the truth is I never fell out of love with you," David said putting his arms around her shoulder. Milly was shivering with excitement, so David put his jacket around her, thinking she had caught a chill in the crisp night air.

"Really?" Milly said, tears welling up in her crystal blue eyes, pulling David's jacket warmly around her, loving his smell on the chic garment.

David caressed her face gently, outlining her pointy nose and high cheek bones. "I'd think about you so often, I had to be very strict with myself not to call you. So many times I've wished I had done things differently. Milly, I still love you very much. I always have. I just need some time to work out the details with Judy. After that, I'd really like to see if you and I can rebuild what we once had. I know that's a lot to ask of you, but you know I'm used to being married. The next time I want to be married to the only woman I ever really loved. That's you, Milly. Please give me a second chance."

Milly could not speak. All she could do was throw her arms around him and hold on tightly to her dear David. The one and only love of *her* life. True soul mates together at last.

From the upstairs veranda, overlooking the crowds, Jerry Ackerman observed his daughter's fairy-tale engagement party like the proud papa he was. On his left stood Sam and Irma Raider, arm in arm, once again madly in love. Irma looked happier, healthier, younger, and more radiant than she ever looked after any of her face-lifts. The peace of knowing that her little boy had grown up into a solid young man had made a new woman out of her. No plastic surgeon in all of Beverly Hills could do for her what Harry did for his mom that night. Irma kvelled. This was not just a night to celebrate an engagement; this was a victory party!

Sam, too, couldn't get over how his best friend Jerry helped Harry turn around. Part of Sam wanted to hate Jerry—the old devils of competition and jealousy still pricked him—but he was too overwhelmed with joy and gratitude to be petty. The two men, once business partners, were now partners for life.

On Jerry's right was a stunning, elegant Countess from Monaco, who accompanied Sam and Irma home from their trip to the south of France. The regal blond, sixty-five years old, an Eva Gabor look-alike, had lost her husband eight years prior. She had been alone ever since and left to ramble around her villa overlooking the Mediterranean. Sam and Irma thought the elegant European beauty was just what Jerry needed to get a life of his own. They couldn't have been more on target. One look, and Jerry and the Countess fell in love. After only two weeks in East Hampton, Jerry persuaded her to put her villa up for sale. She just flipped her royal wig for the dashing Mr. Ackerman. The Countess ordered her servants to pack up her wardrobes and put them on a private plane to New York. With Jessica moving to Beverly Hills, the Ackerman estate would have a new mistress.

"Well, we've done it, Sammy," Jerry said, putting his arms around his old buddy.

"No, you've done it, Jerry. You saved my son's life. Without you, I'd hate to think where he'd be. I don't know what to say." The old man's voice was shaken and a stream of tears rolled down his San-Tropez-tanned cheeks.

"He's our son, now, Sammy. And look at our daughter. Harry has made her the happiest little girl in the world."

The two couples looked down to see Harry and Jessica kissing by the cake. With so much to be thankful for, it was time to toast the match made in heaven.

"Ladies and gentlemen, may I have your attention for just one minute, please," Jerry said, raising his glass to his guests like Jay Gatsby. Looking up at Jerry, a slow silence fell upon the crowd, after a lot of hushing and shushing.

"First of all, I would like to thank you for coming here tonight to share this terrific occasion that has brought me so much nachus...that means happiness, for the few people here tonight who don't like to admit they're Jewish."

A roar of laughter swept through the party people.

"Three months ago, my best friend and now my machatunim, Sammy Raider, called me and asked if his son could spend the summer here.

"When Harry got here, I didn't know what to do with him. I thought we'd play a little golf, and if I were lucky, Harry wouldn't run out of things to keep him occupied. Thanks to my daughter Jessica, I'm happy to report, Harry was kept very active all summer. How active he was certainly surprised me!

"And it was the best surprise I could ask for. Sam and Irma have always been like my lost relatives. Now thanks to my daughter and their son, we are family forever. After my wife died six years ago, I never thought I would experience such a sense of complete bliss, ever again.

"It's a wonderful thing to be so alive again. My whole world changed the day Harry Raider stepped onto the runway at the East Hampton airport, schlepping that crazy camera. I will always look back with great memories recalling that miraculous, magic moment when Harry hit the Hamptons. Cheers!"

As Harry and Jessica shared a passionate smooch for the first the time in front of an adoring public, a surprise round of brilliant, sparkling, multicolored fireworks crackled through the sky behind them. This was Harry's way of letting the whole world that he finally found true love. Was it schmaltzy? Sure. Was it over-the-top, even for the Hamptons? Of course! Yet there seemed like no better way to celebrate a summer that was coming to an end, just as Harry and Jessica's life together was about to begin.

acknowledgments

To my husband Justin and daughter Halle, for giving me so much love and support and for giving me a reason to write books.

To Peter Lynch, the best editor in the universe, who gave me a chance to tell my stories.

To Dominique Raccah, a brilliant and fearless female entrepreneur.

To my mother Roni and late dad Howie, who first brought me to the Hamptons.

To Andy Sachs, my little brother, who helped me "break the ice."

To Angie Cimarolli and the whole Sourcebooks PR team, who helped me "make it happen."

To Michelle Schoob and her team of fantastic technicians.

To my best friends Katelyn O'Connell, Joan O'Connell and family, Lisa Applebaum Haddad, Maria Cassidy, Stacey Bereda, Lori Peters, Uncle Michael Orland, Mary Paula Cabulong, Cheryl Kramer, Susan Zeitlan, Thomas Jackowski, and Thomas Cook, for always being there and telling me, "You can do it."

And finally to all the truly "fabulous" people of the Hamptons...who make "billionare's beach" the greatest place on earth to spend the summer...

about the author

Mara Goodman-Davies is a former stand-up comedienne turned international public relations/media placement consultant in the areas of health, beauty, and lifestyle. Mara was also the guest romance expert for the WABC *Weekend News New York*, GMTV-London, and is often quoted in magazines such as *Redbook*, *Cosmopolitan*, and *Complete Woman*. After spending almost every summer of her life in the Hamptons, Mara and her family now split their time between New York, the Berkshires, and her hometown of Palm Beach, Florida.